THE CRYSTALLINE HEART

ANAM CARA
BOOK 3

SILK AUBREY

ISBN \

Amazon: 9798339657484

Ingrams: 978-1-953100-65-8

Cover design by dreams2media

First Trade Paperback Printing by Scarsdale Publishing September 2024

10 9 8 7 6 5 4 3 2

Editor: Ezra O'Neil

www.scarsdalepublishing.com

1

KINNIA

Dark blues, greens, and purples whipped past me so quickly I couldn't identify the foliage, but my feet—my four paws—pounded across the ground with practiced ease. A flash of sunlight mixed with shadow, and another wolf yipped excitedly. I turned my head from the path to see the gold and white wolf darting through the forest alongside me. My heart filled with warmth. He dove for me and sank his teeth into my shoulder. I slowed and squirmed to bite at his back leg.

We tumbled out of the tree line together, and blue-black haze overtook my view as a wild song rose in my ears. Heat seared across my skin, then aching cold with the strength of gale force winds. Finally, I dissolved into itchiness.

I blinked and stared at the lakeshore where we'd landed. A terrible homesickness overtook me. We could never go back. A hand lightly gripped my shoulder, and I looked up into the young face I knew so well. Laughing black and white eyes that mirrored my own, and a head topped with curling golden hair, underlined by a brilliant smile. My brother. The very center of my universe.

"We no longer have a home, Light." My voice cracked on the final word, a recent development.

He laughed. "We don't need to stay somewhere we're not wanted. Plus, you were out of things to reanimate there anyway."

I slowly closed my hand into a fist, and the world around me turned gray. The ground lit with a network of corpses as a haunting melody I recognized as the song of Thrae hummed in my ears.

He sat down next to me, swaying with the rhythm. "We'll build our own home here. We'll keep each other safe, beat the odds." He shook his head and met my gaze. "I won't let the magic burn you out."

I grinned. "I won't let the magic burn *you* out."

The ground beneath me rocked, and my brother—Shade's brother— exploded into nothingness in front of me.

There you go, Bash said in my mind. *You're not Shade. Separate your thoughts.*

I sucked in a breath. Pain blossomed across my abdomen. Before I could scream, I floated away from the agony.

Whatever I sat on fell away. I forced my eyes open to the darkness around me as Zelimir roared. He clung to a large, white spike, a jut of bone on the top of the ancient skull of the dragon we rode. His copper twists streamed through in the night air as I fought to contextualize the flying dragon skeleton in my memory. I jostled back onto the bone in our steep descent, and someone wrapped an arm around my ribs. Another spike of pain burst through my body, so sharp I almost blacked out. Droplets of moisture whipped through the air, stinging my skin like bees. Where was I?

I remembered Shade's trial, the agony of banging helplessly against what felt increasingly like a death trap. I remembered my mates turning to me as one when my head slipped beneath the water. I remembered the pressure of the water, my lungs screaming for air. I remembered a single moment of peace before I inhaled what I thought would be my last breath.

Teyr clutched my waist, the long side of his fiery hair flapping in the wind. Bash clasped a lilac hand around him. My stomach churned. I wanted to be done running, done fighting, but I never wanted to be done with my mates.

After that, my memory fell to flashes of pain, bright lights, and screaming. A kiss. Bash's hand in mine. Or Teyr's? My Cara with Shade had widened into a bridge, so clearly, I had done something to create that.

Our steep descent suddenly evened out. I bit back a scream. More pieces of memory fell into place. Somewhere deep within myself, I knew I'd forgotten on purpose. But now, I couldn't stop the memories. Zelimir's panicked voice, his dark hand on mine. I'd shaken out of a trance. He'd pressed my hand to the searing pain in my side. Then, sparks. Coming out of me.

The bone dragon hit the ground with a *boom*. The sounds of insects and frogs rushed in as the wind died down. I fought Teyr's grip, clawing and scratching. I might have remembered wrong. My memories were fragmented. Chunks had disappeared. Some of them could be wrong.

"Please," Teyr whispered in my ear. "Please relax."

I sank my teeth into his arm. He swore and released me. I slid down the cold bone of the skeletal dragon. Bash caught me with his telekinesis and lowered me onto the grass of a small clearing. Teyr lit two fireballs behind me. The world took on a soft, orange glow. My body screamed in agony as I struggled against Bash's hold, but I had to know. My dragon landed in front of me, Shade cradled in his arms.

"Let me go," I spat. "You promised."

Don't do this, Bash said across our bridge. But, true to his word, he did not disobey my wishes. His telekinetic hold loosened.

I'd been injured before, even seriously. I'd stood on death's door more than once during my five years on Earth. Nothing should have changed. I took a deep breath and looked down. On my left side, along the seam of my cuirass, a deep, angry wound oozed a trickle of blood. I touched the edge experimentally. Charred leather crumbled, but I couldn't see anything with the armor in the way. My mates stood in a half-circle around me. I pulled off my cuirass, ignoring the blazing pain the action triggered in my side. I had to know.

I tugged the blood-soaked, burnt edges of my trainee greens away from the gash and stared. Angry red and black curls of skin peeled away from the wound, blistered and bleeding. Beneath that, I saw flesh and bone. Beneath that—

I retched.

"Kinnia," Teyr murmured.

He had clearly seen what I had. Metal gleaming under my own flesh.

It could be a trick, an illusion, a hallucination. I wiped my mouth with the back of my hand and straightened. I had to be sure. I pressed a finger into the wound, swallowing down a scream and another round of vomiting as agony darkened my vision. Wet flesh. The jagged scrape of bone. And smooth, warm metal. A frayed cable that ached dully when I tugged at it.

The wound ran deep enough that it should have hit my heart. I should be dead. If I were human. If I were ever alive in the first place. Zelimir took a step forward with his hands up. I looked up into his purple eyes. His Cara stuttered open. Worry, confusion, fear, and underneath it all, hate.

I had to get the Tech out. I plunged more of my hand into the wound, grabbing for the cable, intent to yank it out of my body. With a scream, I blacked out before I hit the ground.

2

ZELIMIR

TEYR'S FIRE FLICKERED ON KINNIA'S UNCONSCIOUS FACE, glinted off the blood and metal inside her. My instincts warred with my heart. Force magic coated my fingers, and I itched to shape a weapon. What *thing* had tethered itself to my Cara—to my mates' very souls?

"Inside." Shade clambered out of Bash's arms. "Before my own defense spells attack us."

I didn't know when the necromancer had woken, if he even knew about the Tech, but he met my gaze resolutely with his black-and-white eyes and tottered toward me.

Bash rushed to Kinnia. Shame joined the revulsion in my stomach. I should be at her side. I should convince my mates to leave her and let the defenses work. Before she'd fallen unconscious, I'd lost control of my Cara. Everyone knew I held as much hate and disgust for the metal in her side as she did. A perverse desire to laugh climbed up my throat. I'd demanded she accept her true self.

"Teyr, your tunic, now," Bash called.

Teyr stripped, and my second bound her injury. She became our Kinnia again, crumpled on the dirt, her dark curls splayed around her face. She wheezed but gave no sign of waking.

Shade tugged on my arm, *pulsing* his urgency. When I remained in place, he took a step away and crumpled. I caught him around the waist and pulled him back to my side. Instead of concern for his mind or body, anger flooded me. Shade had pushed beyond his limits, used up every scrap of magic he could reach. He'd forced me to choose between him and my chain of command. For what?

"You tried to kill the Council," I hissed.

"They tried to kill my Kitty," Shade growled. "They tried to break us. She needs help, now. I will crawl inside my tower and let my spells suck the life out of you if you don't begin walking."

I flinched. Whatever he knew, he still claimed her as his own, and he was willing to let me burn for that. Teyr's firelight tangled in Shade's loose, black braid, highlighting the pale skin under his shaved sides, and I remembered how he cackled in the colosseum. The shame and revulsion in my gut intensified.

Bash stood with Kinnia in his arms. Teyr hovered nearby, fluttering his hands uselessly. The Councils had tried to kill Kinnia, but the Lower Council couldn't have known about the Tech inside her. Their response would have been swift and punitive. The Upper Council, however….

Teyr stroked a lock of hair back from her face, and I winced. He knew the truth about her. How could he touch her? How could I turn my back on her? I swallowed hard and opened my Cara to Shade carefully. Discomfort, worry, no more. The necromancer opened his, all frantic anger and fear. He didn't know anything more than me, except that we would be killed if we stayed out here.

"Where are we?" I took most of Shade's weight and let him guide me forward.

"Bittermist Thicket." Shade nodded at a tall, crooked tower I hadn't noticed in the clearing ahead of us. "My home, before the Cara called." He swallowed. "Light and I built it together."

Teyr caught up with us quickly and fell into step beside Shade, his fireball turning his slit-pupiled eyes molten gold. "And you picked the creepiest, most unstable part of the wilds because…?"

"There are lots of toys to entertain me here." Shade shrugged.

The ember frowned. "Did Light like it here?"

I forced myself not to check if Bash was following. I didn't even listen for his footsteps. He would bring her, or he wouldn't. Both options made my heart pound unevenly.

I cast through my memories for any sign I missed, any clue I ignored. Her eyes sparkled with pleasure, deepened with rage, shifted with all her wild emotions just like Tech eyes did not. She moved fluidly, but she lacked their inhuman grace. Some of her mannerisms might have been awkward or uncouth, but I chalked that up to her years as a mercenary.

"I never thought to ask if he liked it here," Shade said. "My twin chose this spot. That was enough for me."

Teyr just nodded.

We reached a wooden double-door at the base of the deep-blue stone tower. The necromancer wobbled forward, traced a finger over the door, and murmured something. His blue-black power inked the wood. Something clicked behind the door, and it swung open with a whine.

Shade wobbled, and I caught him to my side as we entered a large, empty, dirt-floored room. A round, stone well sat in the center next to a fire pit. A bucket hung on by a single thread above the well. I held him close as we walked past the well and climbed a spiral staircase to the second floor. Shade murmured at another door, which burned light blue and left glowing lines in its wake. This door opened into a space the same size but divided into three rooms with open doorways between each. A large fireplace and a rotting couch lay ahead of me. Faded tapestries and paintings hung askew on the walls.

I walked Shade to a desk and pulled out the high-backed chair. He collapsed onto the hard wood, sending up a puff of dust. When I turned, Bash and Teyr stood behind me. Kinnia still lay in Bash's lilac arms. I breathed a sigh of relief and choked down the feeling I was a traitor to all I'd ever stood for.

"This place needs to be secured." Scales swirled over Bash's face, collecting and breaking apart again. "But Dee needs my help, and I...I don't...." He hugged her tighter to his chest.

Shade stood and stumbled to Bash's side. "Go do what you're good at." He squeezed his eyes shut. "My defense runes are on the lower floor."

I stared at my mates, all clustered around something that shouldn't be. Bash's helpless confusion made more sense than anything else that had happened in the last few minutes.

Shade turned to me. "Zelimir?"

He wanted me to take her—it—her. My stomach squirmed. Like this, she just looked like Kinnia, the woman I'd spent the last couple months with, had maybe even come to love. But I knew. I had seen. A few curls tumbled off her forehead, and my stomach churned. Even her hair gave her away. She'd only been growing it out for a month, and already, the curls brushed her chin.

Shade crossed his arms. "She's ours. She always has been."

Bash nodded.

Teyr scowled. "Like I would think anything else."

I leveled a stare back at him, and he dropped his gaze. We'd spent most of our lives fighting Tech, and what time we hadn't been fighting, we'd heard stories about their horrors. This woman, whatever else she was, had Tech inside her. Not tech like Jalan, with their strangeness displayed for all to see like a poisonous creature's colors. She hid whatever machinery she had inside, like a secret, to blend into our world. We couldn't ignore that because just we loved her.

Shade stared at me. His strength seemed to be returning. Drops of his power spilled down his cheeks. "I just brought a dragon back from the dead. With my Kitty now a part of me, I hesitate to think what I am capable of."

I had felt Shade's wrath. I didn't want to face him in a place like this.

"She's our mate." I held up my hands, searched Teyr's gaze, then Bash's. "But we have to be smart. We can't allow emotion to blind us."

Teyr kicked a clump of dust. Bash frowned but nodded sharply. Shade let out a pitiful howl and leaned against the wall as though he hadn't just threatened my life.

My second held her out, and I swallowed. Despite everything, I was the leader. I had to lead. I took her into my arms, struggling to repress a shiver.

She hung limply, and I remembered the moment in the arena when I had been certain she was dead. I missed Light every day. When he died, a piece of me died with him. But nothing in my life had broken my heart like the moment I thought I lost her. I cradled her gently against my chest.

"My Kitty can curl up in my old bedroom, through the left door," Shade said.

Bash began to head downstairs, and Teyr drifted toward the window.

"Wait," I said. "Secure the location, destroy the trainee greens because the Councils can track them and then"—I swallowed—"and then we'll talk through everything when she wakes up. Together."

Shade grinned. Teyr hesitated, then offered a soft smile. Bash patted me on the shoulder as he passed.

I knew you could be the leader we needed, he thought to me.

I almost smiled.

3

KINNIA

Sunlight woke me slowly. I fought to stay asleep, where my mind lay quiet. Dust tickled my nose. A thin quilt and what felt like bandages scratched my naked skin. The warmth of other bodies blanketed me on each side, but I kept my limbs still enough not to draw their attention. Bash on my right and Teyr on my left, I realized as enough sleep cleared my brain to feel them through the bond.

I can tell you're awake, Teyr murmured in my head.

The last of my rest fled me, and the agony of last night returned with soft, throbbing pain across my ribs. Teyr moved closer in the large bed we shared but didn't touch me, thankfully. Fresh pine and cardamom filled my nose. Above the blanket, he ran his hand down my arm and across my hip, then rested his palm at the juncture of my legs. Love and need poured across our bond. Memory of the slick feeling of warm metal under my skin churned my empty stomach, and I twitched away from Teyr. Bash's warmth behind me on the mattress startled me forward again.

Kinnia. Teyr cupped my face, forcing me to look into his cat-pupiled eyes. *Relax, please. You shouldn't be moving.*

I'd felt sparking cables under my skin. Like Tech energy ran through me. My *energy*....

"I shouldn't be alive," I said. "If I ever was alive."

"You breathe, you cry, you feel." Bash pushed Teyr away and leaned over me on both his arms. "There's Tech inside you. That means nothing unless you let it. We aren't defined by what is done to us."

I met his gaze, my thoughts spinning like a tornado. The time after my family's death on Earth came to me in shards when I remembered at all. The cables the Tech that was plugged into me over my years on Earth haunted my dreams, but I had no idea what the Tech really did. My stomach squirmed. I fingered the edge of the bandage on my chest. I wanted to open everything back up, keep checking to see if the Tech disappeared. Or maybe just to tear out whatever I found there.

"Breathe, love," Teyr said gently. "Remember those exercises I taught you."

I squeezed my eyes shut. In, hold, out. My lungs inflated like they always had, tugging at the edges of the wound and sending sparks of pain skittering up my spine. Panic flickered at the edges of my mind. How could my mates look at me like this, tend to me like this, when I was an impossible monster?

Zelimir cleared his throat. "Give her a minute to wake up."

Bash and Teyr pushed a few inches away from me on the mattress. I managed my first real, deep breath. Until I remembered the burst of hate that slipped through Zel's iron control last night. My chest squeezed.

"Shade brought down a padena this morning. I've got it cooking." Zel approached, wearing a black silk and velvet robe that didn't fit him. The hem brushed his knees, a triangle of his chest lay exposed where he couldn't quite pull the sides together, and someone had hacked off the sleeves, so his muscular arms bulged out of the armholes when he offered me a cherrystone mug of water.

A crazed giggle escaped my lips. "What the hell is happening?"

Teyr chuckled and stroked my hair. Shade slipped into the room in wolf form and hopped up onto the bed. He settled his body across Bash's legs and pillowed his head on my feet. His wolf mind brushed mine across the bridge. The thoughts felt a little alien, but his simple contentment with being alive and surrounded by the people he loved filled our bond. For the first time, I understood why he spent so long as a wolf. I wished I could crush all the complication out of my brain too.

Bash levered me up telekinetically, and the blanket slipped down, exposing the tops of my breasts. I flushed before the reality of the situation smacked me in the face. They probably saw me naked already, and anyway, my modesty hardly mattered when they'd all seen what lay under my skin. I grabbed the water and drank greedily.

Why was a thing like me thirsty?

I dove for the calm of Shade's wolf mind. My mates had collected in a way I knew meant Zelimir planned a conversation, and for the months we'd spent together, I owed them a few minutes of listening before I disappeared into the forest to destroy myself.

As Shade's calm slowed my racing thoughts, I looked around for the first time. I lay in a large bed in the center of a triangular room. Arching glass windows bracketed with cherrystone sat in bare, deep-blue stone walls. Open doorways led to two other rooms. Dust blanketed everything but the bed.

Bash sat up, and the moth-eaten blanket pooled around his hips. The Kinnia I was yesterday would have noticed how the shape of his lilac, scale-speckled muscles led her eye to his nearly exposed cock. Now, however, I could barely tolerate looking at my mates.

I turned to the other side of the bed to find Teyr had completely emerged from the blankets, exposing his whole naked body with a smirk. I didn't think about the kiss before Shade's trial, or the incident in the baths. I didn't wonder what he might be able to do to me. There was no me to do things to.

I faced my commander, and the instinct to laugh rose incongruously again. "What are you wearing?"

"This is Shade's tower." He scowled. "We could only find a chest of his old robes."

"So, we're all going to look like that?" I asked.

He nodded sullenly, and a laugh burst from my lips, wild and halfway to sobbing. Bash laid a hand on my shoulder. I didn't know whether to lean into the contact or flinch away.

I picked out a special one for you, Shade told me.

That only made me laugh harder. What the hell was a special necromancer robe for a mechanical monster? Tears leaked from my eyes. I didn't know if they came from laughing so hard or the gulf that opened in my chest when I thought too long about leaving. Everything, everything hurt.

Abruptly, my laughter became sobs that churned my empty stomach and made the edges of my wound sear. All that fighting, all that effort, and for what? So I could lose my family all over again? Somewhere deep in my gut, I hated Rydel. She made me believe I could have more, could get the happy ending. She said I could save the world from some fated doom, but I only ever wanted to stay with the people I loved, and now, I couldn't even have that.

The bed creaked under Zelimir's titanic weight as he sat and put a hand on my knee. Teyr rested his head against the side of my arm. Shade snuggled closer to my legs, and Bash rubbed his thumb softly across my shoulder.

Slowly, my sobs abated. None of them moved.

I sniffled. "What are you doing?"

Zelimir sighed. "We made a promise. We're mates, a team."

"I'm a monster," I said.

Bash shook his head. "You are who you've always been."

"No, I—I should leave." I struggled painfully to sit up under my own power. "You're better off without me."

Never say that again. Shade sank his teeth lightly into my ankle. *My Kitty, I will not let you leave.*

Teyr bonked his head against my shoulder. "We've been over this whole 'I'm a problem' thing already. Don't think I won't dunk you in mud to make you remember."

Emotions warred within me. A part of me—the part that had been Kinnia, I thought—sparkled with their statement of faith. Words meant nothing unless backed up by action, and by choosing to stay at my side now, they were taking the ultimate action. The rest of me, the new me who couldn't escape the bite of a broken cable under my fingers, didn't know how to listen.

"Shade has a healing potion cooking for you," Zel said. "It will hopefully knit your side back together."

I swallowed. "Unless I need something different." My mind raced with memories of every injury I'd gotten, every time I'd healed faster than my fellow mercenaries.

"Fae healing has worked," Zelimir said steadfastly, like he was repeating a mantra to himself. "Shade can sense your life signs."

I met his gaze. "Shade can raise SpiderTech—"

He put up a hand, and I stopped.

"Fine," I said. "What next, then? Are we just on the run now? Where the hell are we?"

Zelimir ran a hand through his copper twists. "We're in a forest where Shade used to live. As for everything else—"

"We haven't talked," Teyr cut in. "We didn't want to agree on anything without you."

Zelimir shot him a look and turned back to me. "We proceed with caution. We need to understand...what we saw."

I shivered. I didn't want to understand. I just wanted the Tech gone.

"We'll figure this out together." Teyr wrapped his arms around me.

The four of them opened their Caras, letting me feel the simple honesty of Teyr's words. Whatever else I was, I wasn't alone. I couldn't imagine anything worse.

4

SHADE

A<small>FTER BREAKFAST</small>, I <small>LADLED THE COMPLETED HEALING</small> potion into a bottle and turned to my Kitty, who leaned against the back of the bed.

She took a deep breath and set her jaw. "I want to look again."

Determination and disgust flowed across our bond, and I flinched. I didn't like how furious she was with herself.

"Are you sure?" Teyr asked.

She crossed her arms and winced in pain. "What's the point of talking if all of us are too scared to face what's going on?"

Zelimir sighed and nodded. "I want you patched up as quickly as possible, in case we have to run, so I suppose we should take advantage of the opportunity we have."

Bash sat on the bed in one of my thick, black robes, tucked into a pair of pants for his much shorter frame, and began to unwind the makeshift green bandage around her chest. My pack clustered close. I handed Zelimir the potion bottle. Bash pulled away the last of the fabric, and we leaned in. I hadn't yet seen the Tech.

Her tanned skin already seemed calm, perhaps beginning to knit, but under that lay the metal and cables Teyr had described to me in a whisper. Like her skin, the cables had begun to heal. While a few looked frayed, only one remained truly broken.

I'd felt my pack leader's surge of hate and disgust that first night. Everyone now handled my Kitty like a spell about to explode. But as I studied her, my gaze strayed more to the char marks on her skin than the cables inside. They looked painful. She prodded the wound, and hate rebounded across our bond. I winced.

Zelimir grabbed her wrist. "I know you're curious, but that's only going to worsen your injury."

A cloud of black rage covered her bond, but the anger dissipated quickly. I took a deep breath. She was trying not to fight us, at least.

"It all seems...functional." The corners of my pack leader's mouth tugged down. "Not something I thought I'd ever be happy to say."

Panic and hate clouded her mind.

"But he is." Teyr took her hand. "We all are."

I nodded and realized only my pack leader, my Kitty, and I still looked at the wound. Bash and Teyr had averted their eyes quickly. Why?

Steely determination stole over her Cara. "Pull the cables out."

I flinched. My mind swam with memories of my time inside her head. "No."

Bash raised a tattooed eyebrow. Just the one meant questioning, not surprise, I thought.

"I shared her mind, her injuries." I crawled around Bash and placed my head in my Kitty's lap. This close, I could almost hear her thoughts racing behind those beautiful blue eyes. Everything had been so clean in her mind, so neatly networked, like a confluence of rivers. I could have floated along those paths forever.

Teyr nudged my shoulder. "You shared her injuries?"

I brushed her beautiful face. "I shared her injuries."

"Shade." Teyr nudged me harder. "Focus. You said that for a reason. Why shouldn't we pull the cables out of Kinnia?"

As her disgust rose, so did my panic. "They are important. You could kill her."

She blanched. "I don't need any of this if I'm some monster. Please take them out."

The disgust in our bond cut me. I recognized the familiar bite. Her self-hatred bubbled over, and I watched it register on each of my mates' faces in turn.

"You are not a monster," Bash said sharply. "You can't be a monster because of something someone did to you."

"And what if this wasn't done to me?" She plucked one of the cables and winced. "What if this *is* me?"

I winced with her as her pain rebounded into me.

"Then we always loved this," Teyr answered quickly. "That means nothing really changed."

She scoffed.

I cupped her face. "I thought we were learning to trust ourselves, my Kitty."

She rolled her eyes. "That was when I was human."

"I never thought you were human, and I never cared what you were." I smiled softly. "I trust you as I did before, and I can't let you hurt yourself because you're afraid." I sat up and pressed a kiss to her forehead.

She flinched. Panic and bone-deep shame reached me.

"I love you, I will always love you, and so the cables stay." I nodded.

She shook her head. "I don't care what you say. You can't fix this."

"I spent six years thinking I couldn't fix things after I lost Light," I said. "Just heal for now."

A flicker of frustration ghosted across the bond, but she allowed Zelimir to pour the healing potion into her mouth. The casing grew back over the frayed cables, and the severed one inched toward its other half until it could do the same. The plastic stretched and thickened like skin over a wound. My Kitty was even more beautiful and miraculous than I had known. She panted, and the healing slowed. Her skin didn't reach for itself across the open wound.

Teyr frowned. "Shade, do you have another potion?"

I shook my head. "I'm not a healer. Those were the last of Light's prepared components. For me, it would be like embroidering with a sword."

She slumped into unconsciousness as the potion drained the last of her energy.

Bash brushed hair out of my Kitty's face. "We should carry healing potions. We should have been better prepared."

"Really?" Teyr barked a laugh. "We're a Cara. Even broken, we heal faster than a potion. I haven't touched one in seventy-five years."

I closed my eyes. She needed rest, not more sour, angry air.

"Bash," Zelimir said, "sew her up. I found some clear liquor in the kitchen."

Light and I had slaved over those liquor barrels, trying to get the herbal flavor just right for me to cook with. My skin itched at the thought of him, and I prepared for a shift to take me. But my fae form remained stable, as it had except for the times I'd chosen to shift since arriving here.

I smiled. "Light and I fermented that liquor."

My pack leader inclined his head, a gesture which had no meaning to me. "Teyr, put on some clothes. We're foraging for berries, grains, anything we can eat." He looked at me. "We are secure here?"

I nodded. "Light and I reported our previous residence as Bittermist Thicket but gave no further details. These woods are dense and only inhabited by those wanting to be left alone. The area is plagued by disturbances in the natural flow of magic." I scowled. "Caused by the Thicket's wilder inhabitants."

Wild magic always sounded out of tune with the rest of Thrae's song, a sour note in a perfect symphony. I hadn't missed that in my years away from the Thicket.

Teyr rolled his eyes. "Great, sounds like a super safe place to forage."

I glanced out the window at the thick, dark trees. "Stay alert for the shimmer of wild magic and shadows with no origin."

He sighed. I smiled as the old rhythms of conversation overtook us.

The ember leaned down and kissed my sleeping Kitty on the forehead. "We'll figure this out."

Zelimir stood and tossed Teyr a robe. The ember slid it on, though he had to use the belt to tie the bottom up so he could walk without dragging. He looked like a pup desperate to grow into his wolf pelt. I wanted to point that out to my Kitty so I could hear her laugh, but her mind had already descended into nightmares.

I closed my eyes and sank closer to our bridge. She'd reach for the contentment of my wolf earlier. Perhaps I could offer some solace now. Bash's presence intruded on her mind, ready to kick me out at a moment's notice. My Kitty was power, love, forgiveness, and most of all, mine. I put my hands on her upper arms and opened my eyes to glare at Bash.

He met my gaze steadily. "I'll tend the fire and keep an eye on Dee."

Zelimir grunted, *pulsed* a confirmation, and pulled Teyr out behind him. Seconds ticked away as I held Bash's gaze.

"I am trying to trust myself," I said finally. "As she told me to. Can you trust me?"

Bash sighed. "Spending all this time in her mind is just another way to hide yourself." He rubbed a hand over his scalp. "Did you even notice that? That you're more attuned to her emotions than your own?"

I wanted my Kitty to be the center of my universe. Tracking her mood shifts was easier than managing mine.

"Dee's bridges have given us all abilities we weren't prepared for." Bash covered my hand on her arm. "Work on control with me?"

I stared down at her sleeping face and nodded.

5

TEYR

ON THE THIRD DAY AFTER THE HEALING POTION, BASH AND I sat in the small living area near Kinnia's bedroom, playing the card game we'd invented for the partial deck I'd found under a floorboard and listening for any sign she'd truly woken for the first time in days. I dropped a card on the pile and picked up another. Bash grunted.

Her Cara stirred to consciousness. Bash and I froze. By the speed of her thoughts, she might even get up this time. I shot to my feet and spun toward the bedroom.

Wait, she said.

I halted.

I need...a little time. Let me get dressed. Her mental voice sounded heavy with exhaustion, and that same dark cloud of emotions swirled in her Cara, strung along a thick thread of hate.

I understood that. I would hate to have no idea what was going on or what had happened to me. I'd hate to have everyone talking about me behind my back while I slept, coming to their own conclusions about something inside me. I *pulsed* agreement and sat heavily back down on my chair.

Fire, I wished everybody would stop waiting, though. We just needed to sit down and talk, and the hate would fade. Well, I didn't need to talk. I'd figured everything out already. Between the wires and the glitchy memory I saw when she built the bridge between us, I'd deduced she'd been captured at some point in her time on Earth and some Tech monstrosity had jammed a machine under her skin to mess with her. If Shade was right, and removing the Tech would kill her, we needed to figure out how to disable it. Then, we could all quit worrying.

I hadn't been worried at all, except about her waking up, because I still loved and trusted her. I was also worried about Zel's new habit of disappearing into the woods for hours at a time, especially when Bash helped Shade and I train our bridges. I wasn't worried about her Tech. I'd given thought to the possible explanations for the Tech under her skin. She could be an escaped Jalan who lost her memory. Or she could be a full fae with illusion magic I'd never seen before, trying to convince us of her Tech. Or—

Shade portaled in wearing his wolf form and ran a few quick circles, excitement dripping off every muscle. Even I had to admit he'd been the second most normal since we got here. He spent more time cleaning up the tower than stared moodily out the windows, which I couldn't say about my other two mates.

Zelimir emerged from the staircase. His careful twists had grown ragged, copper hairs frizzing out of place, and his robe looked truly goofy. I smiled and opened my mouth to tease him, but he didn't look at any of us as he plucked one of Shade's spell books off the table and began reading. I grimaced. He was wasting his time. Kinnia's slightly pointed ears made her one-sixteenth fae at most, and that had nothing to do with Tech. Not that I thought she was really, truly Tech.

Kinnia stepped through the curtain Shade had hung over her doorway for privacy and froze. Her navy silk robe dragged on the floor behind her, and the massive, the frilled sleeves almost did as well. She had cinched the waist with her weapons belt, but she left a large triangle of her tanned chest bare. The fabric barely hid the tempting swell of her breasts. If I only pushed the silk aside a little, I could reveal her pert nipples—

And the jagged, partially healed wound that hid the tangle of wires and metal. Which was fine. I'd have no problem with that if I got to touch her.

Shade raced across the room and leaned against her hip.

She shoved him away. "No, Shade. More than ever, no. I could have been created to infiltrate you guys and bring you down, like Cordelia said, or any of a million other bad options."

I seriously doubted that. The Councils wouldn't choose someone with as little fae blood as her, and I couldn't think of anyone else who would want to infiltrate us.

Zelimir sighed and set the spell book down. "My sister was trying to manipulate the situation for her own benefit when she said that."

"What about the rest of the options?" Kinnia shook her head. "No, there's no way around it. You guys are being really...nice, but there's Tech inside me. You can't trust me."

I looked at Zelly. Bash, Shade, and I had all disagreed with her in the brief moments of consciousness she had over the last few days, but nothing seemed to change. He had to try now.

"We trust you," Zelimir said slowly. "But we can't trust the unknown."

I crossed my arms. "Zel."

Heartbreak ached through her Cara, but she just sat in the rickety wooden chair at the desk and nodded. "Finally, someone said it. So, where does that leave us?"

Shade laid down and pillowed his head on his front paws. I looked at Bash and opened my Cara, showing him how her reaction worried me. Just like every other time over the last three days, the dragon kept his Cara tightly closed. I huffed out a breath. Even in the worst likely hypotheticals I could imagine, I still trusted Kinnia. Zelly needed to relax. I snapped my Cara shut.

"The only way to fix this is to make the unknown known." Zel tugged on the end of one of his frizzy twists. "We need to understand how our magic and your *energy* mixes and learn how to control that." He swallowed. "And we—you and I—need to keep our distance. I am the only one not tethered to you. It seems prudent to maintain that until we understand exactly what you're doing to us."

"What *we're* doing to *each other*." I glared at him.

Rifts formed because magic and Tech clashed. If that same principle applied to our Cara, that meant we bore at least as much of the blame.

Zelimir kept his attention on Kinnia as emotions tumbled through her Cara. I whipped a furious *pulse* in his direction. He ignored that too. I sank deeper into my seat.

Kinnia nodded. "If it's some kind of infection, we should keep you clean. But how can we learn more? The...injury closed up."

"Experimentation." Bash stared at her. "Like we did with Drax."

She grimaced and stood. "That seems—"

"Kinnia, we trust you." I pressed a hand to my heart. "I trust you. You could be some lost orphan Jalan or somebody's science project or anything else. I don't care. I know you, and I know you're not a monster."

A hint of gratitude peeked through her haze of negative emotions. Shade stood, shifted smoothly into his fae form, and wound his fingers into her hair. He kissed her, opening his Cara full of love and trust. She remained stiff as a board, barely meeting his lips. Eventually, he pulled back, though he didn't let go.

"We'll figure this out." Zelimir smiled, but the smile didn't reach his eyes.

That shred of warmth in her disappeared. She nodded and disentangled herself from Shade. "I'm gonna take a walk." She put her hands up with a wince before any of us could interrupt. "Not far. I just need to stretch my legs. Been in bed too long."

She headed down the stairs without another word. Shade melted back into his wolf. Silence crowded the air between us.

Zel crossed to one of the windows with his hands folded behind his back like we were in the Lower Council's audience chamber and stared outside. I shook my head. He really blew that. Kinnia needed love and support, to hear we still believed in her like we did before. My explanations obviously helped, where his weird distance only hurt. If we ever wanted to be a Cara again—and I definitely did—I had to intervene.

I bounced up out of my seat. "I'm gonna go forage."

Shade nosed over to my side as if to tag along.

Zel scrubbed a hand over his face. "If I ask you not to do this, will you listen?"

"Nope." I popped the 'p' and dug my fingers into Shade's fur. "But this is a solo mission, so I'll catch up with you guys later."

I bolted down the stairs before anyone could stop me.

Training in an hour, Bash said as I opened the door at the base of the tower. *You need to work on your control.*

I shrugged him off. Control could wait. Kinnia needed to hear my latest theory.

Outside, she paced the edge of the clearing under a dull gray sky that never seemed to change, her robe flapping around her ankles. Frustration, fear, and hate roiled through her Cara.

I plastered on my brightest smile and strolled up to her. "So, I'm thinking this probably happened on Earth," I said. "Metal might not grow, but you probably didn't grow much after you turned seventeen. Maybe some Tech captured you and jammed something into your ribcage, which means you're not really Tech, or"—I paused for dramatic effect—"you were frozen there before humans came through the rifts, unfroze in a natural disaster, escaped to Thrae, then escaped back to Earth, and back again, so you're just an old human."

Kinnia grimaced. Her Cara didn't lighten. Something hadn't worked.

"Either of those would be totally fine." I grinned. "And there are a bunch of other options that would also be seriously fine, no problem, because you're fine and I'm fine and this is all gonna be—"

"Shut up, Teyr." She shoved me.

I stumbled back a pace and stared at her. Her dark curls tumbled over her eyes, hiding her expression, but I could feel her irritation. She was going through a tough time, even though everything would be fine, which meant I had to choke down on my flaring temper and the sparks dancing over my fingertips.

"Okay." I sucked in a deep breath. "I love you. I trust you. That's what matters most. Um, I think there's a chance this is some kind of illusion. If you just let Shade take a look—"

She threw her hands in the air and stormed away. "What about 'shut up' don't you get?"

I trailed after her, my temper burning brighter. "The part where you're not listening. I'm telling you I love you, and everything is fine, and I've got it all figured out, if you'd just let me explain."

"Not listening?" She spun to face me. "Do you hear yourself? Do you believe half of what you're saying?" Kinnia grabbed my hand and pulled it under her robe so I could feel the jagged scar tissue that had been a gaping wound less than a week ago.

Nausea twisted my gut.

I'm a goddamn metal monster, Teyr, she said across the bridge. *I am everything you hate and fear—everything I hate and fear. If you really loved me, you'd at least show me the respect Zelimir is and stop lying to me.*

I yanked free of her grasp. "I'm not lying."

"You're doing what you always do." She shook her head, suddenly quiet like one touch had sucked all her energy away. "You're pretending to be how you want the world to think you are. I can't deal with that right now too. Quit it or piss off."

She walked away again. I stood still and rubbed my wrist. Rain spat down from the gathered gray clouds. Her Cara rang with hurt and anger, always underpinned by that current of hate.

I am everything you hate, she'd said.

I didn't care. I loved her.

My flesh burned where the thick, healing scar had touched me. My stomach churned again. If Kinnia really was Tech, could I hate her? Emotions flooded through my body, so intense they danced out of my skin in bursts of flame, hotter and brighter than anything I'd called since we'd arrived. Rain hissed into a swirl of steam around me.

Maybe she had a point.

6

BASH

Two days later, I worked through my morning exercises alone in the gray light of the clearing around Shade's tower. The plush purple robe I'd tucked into loose pants fluttered as I moved.

Without Dee's panting and grunts harmonizing with mine, my mind wandered. Zelimir would be awake already, starting the fire in the pit on the first floor of the tower and drinking coffee until he heard someone stir upstairs or I returned. Dee's Cara hummed with awareness, but she'd taken to remaining in bed until I involved myself in some other task. Then she'd rouse and stretch privately. The distance stung.

I spun and slashed out with my axe, the bright-red cherrystone dull under the thick clouds. With Zelimir gone most of the day, I had to manage our mates. I needed these moments to myself.

When I finally finished, I wiped the sweat from my brow with the robe sleeve I used as a belt and headed inside. My commander leapt off the low, stone bench next to the fire and closed the handwritten recipe book he'd been reading.

"Bash," he said.

"Commander." I inclined my head.

He set the book down and grabbed the two burlap sacks we'd found with the least mold on them. "I was just heading out."

I grunted. "Dee will be up soon."

Zelimir went slightly ashen, pulled his twists up into a simple bun, and left without another word.

I shook my head and shuffled around the circular fire pit until I had my back to a solid stretch of the wall and a view of the stairs. I hadn't had a full conversation with my commander in days, but he had still been kind enough to leave coffee warming on the grate over the fire. To hear Teyr tell it, the coffee grounds had been one of our greatest finds. I grabbed one of the heavy cherrystone pans, a handful of edible mushrooms, and the seasoning cellars I'd been most pleased to stumble across in the abandoned tower.

Dee wandered down the stairs with a big, dramatic yawn as I sliced the mushrooms with a razor-thin thread of telekinesis. Shade's foolish robe displayed her breasts and hips, and my dragon roared. Knowing only the flimsy blue fabric separated me from her body drove him wild.

"Morning." She peered out the window at the gray skies. "Another day in paradise, I guess. Zel already gone?"

I grunted and dumped the slices of mushroom into the pan with some seasonings and a bit of fat from one of the beasts Zelimir killed, then set the pan on the grate. I didn't know why she asked—she could feel him as well as I—but she had asked every morning so far.

"I'll, uh"—she grabbed a handful of jerky from our dried food stores —"I'll eat this."

Dee walked out the door just as our commander had, and her soft panting filled the air not long after. My dragon grumbled. Pain lanced through her Cara. I didn't need to look out the window to know what I'd see. Her left arm didn't respond as well since the injury, but she worked it and worked it as if she could will her arm back up to its previous performance. Were I exercising with her, I'd tell her to go slow, focus on other muscles to support the weakness. But she made it very clear she no longer wanted to train with me.

I sighed and grabbed the eggs Zelimir had stumbled across yesterday from the enchanted cooling chest along the wall. Dee reminded me too much of him. They both stubbornly refused not to perform at their best, and her remaining in bed served the same purpose as his endless foraging.

Naturally, Zelimir had insisted that Dee should be allowed space and time whenever we weren't experimenting. She needed to process this at her own speed, he said. That sounded too much like his party line at the Academy, but I struggled to disobey orders when Dee kept choosing isolation over company. Last time, she'd sought us out. Perhaps she really needed the space now.

I cracked the eggs over the sizzling mushrooms. Perhaps we all needed space to adjust to whatever we'd learned. My dragon snarled. He hadn't so much as blinked when I saw the glittering metal peeking out through her blood. Every time I considered the repercussions, he grew more irritable, insisting that nothing mattered beyond her being ours.

I breathed deeply and tried to think around him. When I pictured the metal under her flesh, my scales shifted to accommodate goose bumps. In some regards, I agreed with my commander. We had no idea what the Tech inside her meant.

My dragon paced, feeding me images of my night between her legs. She'd tasted so alive, burning up underneath me.

I shoved him aside. Where Zelimir turned the unknown into a threat against the Cara, against magic, against himself, I could only think of Dee. If the metal had been installed later in her life, would they use her up like the batteries we found in dead Tech? If she'd been born with it somehow, what did that mean for her lifespan, her hardiness?

Shade padded down the stairs in wolf form with a groggy Teyr holding onto his tail like the ember would collapse otherwise. I pushed my worries to the side and smiled. I didn't know if my dragon drove my thoughts toward concern for her, but I wouldn't learn more in the chaos of breakfast.

Somehow, I got enough food and coffee into Shade and Teyr that they both used full sentences before half an hour had passed. I scraped my plate for the last few bites of my own third of the eggs and patted my full stomach. Shade might surpass my cooking skill, but I excelled at volume after the tight rations of the civil war.

Teyr stood and poured himself another mug of coffee. "I'm gonna head out a little early."

I looked up at the ember. His sleep-mussed hair slumped over one golden eye, but his gaze looked steady and certain, with none of the frantic energy I'd seen in him over the last few days.

Training shortly, I said.

"I'll do my best." He ducked out the door.

Shade pushed his half-full plate of eggs toward me. "I ate a kill on my run last night."

I nodded and scraped the eggs into the waste bag we kept in case we remained here long enough that fertilizer became useful. "Ready to head out?"

The necromancer hopped up. He'd taken surprisingly well to my training, though he tended to modify my exercises. At first, I thought he was avoiding doing any of the hard work, but I'd realized his modifications simply worked better for him. That ever-circling mind of his, still adjusting back to the full spectrum of fae concerns, needed a special approach only he seemed to understand.

We trooped into the clearing to see Teyr and Dee talking near the tree line. Neither seemed to be yelling, and Dee even smiled, if a little ruefully. I led Shade far enough away that even I couldn't overhear and took a wide stance in the dark mud.

"Have you been working on your mental shields?" I asked.

He nodded. "Even when I'm paying attention to my Kitty's emotions, I do not touch her mind. Most of the time."

I'd never known the necromancer to lie, but a strong offense would build a stronger defense to Dee's passive effect on him.

"I'm going to read your surface thoughts," I said. "Prepare yourself."

Shade took a deep breath and closed his eyes. When he opened them, a thin film of dark blue magic stretched over his irises. "Ready."

I reached out. I bounced off of most shielded minds. Shade's mind felt surprisingly permeable, but when I tried to pull anything out, I found myself in a labyrinth, chasing the tail-ends of a dozen half-heard thoughts. Snippets floated toward me, vague impressions, but nothing concrete.

I pulled back and smirked. "Better."

Shade nodded slowly.

"Now, I'm going deeper." I widened my stance, pushed my hands forward, and pried.

At first, I found myself in his labyrinth again. My dragon growled. I pried harder and felt the strange bounce of the bridges. The walls of the labyrinth crumbled, and Shade's memories opened for my perusal with a faint taste of decay on the back of my tongue.

"Hey!" Dee called. "What are you guys doing?"

I released my hold and turned to her. Shade sank to the mud, panting.

"What do you mean?" I asked.

She frowned and rubbed her stomach. "I...felt that? I think."

The bounce. I'd reached into Shade's mind over the bridges and shattered his defenses that way. All of us had only ever interacted in Dee's mind, assumed the others' bridges would be impassable to us. But if I could reach his mind, what else could I reach?

"We should experiment with that." I took a step toward Teyr and Dee. "Perhaps we can use each other's magic as you can use ours."

Dee blanched. "Right. You won't even need to bring me into battle to keep me from contaminating anybody else. I'll just sit nearby like a generator."

My dragon roared. Nobody insulted our girl, not even her. After I escaped the church, I'd lost years to thoughts like that. Shade and Teyr had disagreed with Dee's statements about herself, but gently. That yielded days of sulking silence. Everyone had forgotten Dee was a warrior.

I stormed toward her. "You will never move on if you keep wallowing."

"Move on?" Her eyebrows shot up, and disdain poured through her Cara. "How am I supposed to move on from this shit? What else is there?"

"Life!" I bellowed.

She dropped her gaze to the ground. "I'm not even alive."

"I thought the same thing for three decades." I stopped mere inches from her, grabbed her chin, and forced her to meet my gaze. She alone knew what happened before those decades, how I had barely breathed in the church. "Until someone smacked me in the back of the head and reminded me that I wasted the effort of getting out if I died believing I deserved nothing more than the life they gave me."

"But I'm not out." She stepped closer. "I have nothing to escape but myself."

The exposed skin of her chest made contact with mine. My dragon begged me to take her in my arms, to convince her with my mouth and my fingers. I ignored him.

"What difference does that make?" I growled. "Right now, you're surviving. Fuck that. Live or die."

Dee's blue eyes burned into mine. Fury coursed through her Cara instead of hate. "That's your advice? That I should just kill myself?"

"I want you to live." I cupped her face. "I won't have you just survive."

A thread of desire wound through her anger. She ripped herself away from me and stormed off. My dragon roared his disappointment, his desire to chase after her. I lowered myself to the mud, crossed my legs, and took a deep breath. Shade crept to my side in wolf form and laid down with his head on my knee. Teyr stared at me.

"I was just making progress." He shook his head. "Dragon in a china shop."

"She's not weak." I exhaled slowly. "Treating her as such will not help."

No matter what our commander said. He wouldn't remain long enough to disagree with me. Shade *pulsed* a muddled mix of agreement and disagreement, then huffed a sigh.

Long minutes passed. Teyr finished his coffee and started searing patterns into the mud. Shade dozed, his snout still resting on my knee. Dee's Cara swirled through rage, hate, disgust, frustration, and eventually, determination.

She returned with her shoulders squared. "We're here to experiment. Let's experiment."

I stood, dislodging Shade's head, and thick mud dripped down the back of my pants. "Teyr's fire has the smallest focus. I'll attempt to wield it."

The ember snorted. "Good luck. Elemental fire takes years of training to master."

I breathed in the simple pattern he taught Dee, then extended myself across the bridge into the familiar flow of her mind. As always, three paths stretched away from her, including the one behind me. I tested each until one hummed a bit like Teyr's *pulses*, but with an overtone of something light and bright I didn't understand. Dee shivered. With another breath, I stretched over that bridge and delved into the warmth I found there.

Heat engulfed me but didn't respond to the gentle pressure of my mind. How did Teyr describe it? His emotions were his flame. I leaked my frustration with my mates into the heat.

A fireball sprang to life in my palm. The air pressure remained stable. Teyr scoffed. I met Dee's gaze, and she offered me a small smile.

7

KINNIA

Every night, I told my mates I wanted to sleep alone. Every morning, I woke, terrified, with some combination of Bash, Teyr, and Shade on either side of me in the large bed. I might hurt them in the night. I hadn't yet, but I couldn't stop myself from checking them for injuries every morning. On the morning after Bash yelled at me, I forced myself to breathe through the panic.

Shade lay on my left, Teyr on my right. My chest tightened. Fear clawed its way up my throat. They snored in easy unison. Low conversation issued up the stairs, almost certainly Bash and Zelimir before our commander disappeared into the woods for the day. Nobody's Cara showed fear or pain.

My chest grew even tighter. What if they hadn't noticed I'd hurt them? What if our mental connection meant I could numb them somehow? I bolted upright and checked my mates with careful hands. No injuries. And no scars on me that looked like what I imagined the cables might have left behind, if I had skin that could scar. The pressure in my chest released enough that I could breathe. I had lasted a moment longer than yesterday.

Teyr draped an arm across my waist in his sleep. Shade curled into me as unflinchingly as he always had. I took a deep breath as the door to the tower creaked open and slammed closed. That would be Zelimir leaving, which meant I could go downstairs without watching him flee. Loneliness expanded in my chest, but I stood and readied myself to face another day as a monster.

MY MATES STOOD IN A LOOSE TRIANGLE AROUND ME IN THE drizzly afternoon light. Under the watchful eyes of Shade's crooked tower, we explored the boundaries of the revelation Bash had yesterday. He reached for Teyr's magic, and Teyr, Bash's magic.

Their power rolled through me like a thunderstorm just about to break. Stretching across my mind like this, Teyr tasted like a light-dappled forest, beautiful on the surface but with brilliant, messy life peeking out from every corner. Bash tasted like an underground river that had been wearing away at the rock for millennia to reveal gemstones and veins of ore. The pressure soothed my panicked *energy*. I closed my eyes and let myself enjoy the sensation. How could Tech have created something this wonderful?

My chest squeezed, suddenly airless. I wrenched my eyes open. The fire in Bash's palm wobbled. Teyr dropped the clump of mud he levitated over Shade's head.

"You are safe." Bash met my gaze. "We are safe."

Shade swiped mud out of his eyes. "This *was* beautiful."

Teyr grinned. "No, I think you look beautiful with a mud mask."

Bash's Cara danced with humor. Shade laughed. I inhaled shakily. I still couldn't laugh with them, not without summoning that manic laughter that always collapsed into tears, but knowing they felt normal enough to smile helped some. Despite the cables inside me, the world still turned. I took a deep breath and focused on the flow of magic. Bash's flame stabilized, and he smiled at me.

Shade plucked at Bash's magic. His power rushed through me with a taste like flipping over a decayed log to see a whole thriving world underneath, but he released the tether just as quickly.

I turned to him. "You're supposed to be practicing each other's magic."

He smiled, and a skeletal humanoid hand darted out of the muck to chase a bone-rodent that sprang up just as quickly. "Why would I be interested in that?"

The hand came down hard, flattening the little rodent into the mud.

"I haven't needed their magic before." He prodded the dead rodent. The bones glowed blue-black, and the skeleton stood on hind legs for a grisly dance with the hand.

I shuddered. Teyr's presence washed through me once more. The ember splayed his fingers and knit his eyebrows as he sculpted Bash's telekinesis. A wad of mud lifted into the air. The brown goop slowly formed into the shape of a penis, complete with grassy balls.

Teyr grinned. I rolled my eyes. He twisted his hands, clearly trying to spin his creation, but he lost control. The whole mess squashed on the ground. Teyr clapped a hand to his mouth in elaborate horror and whirled on Bash in accusation. Bash raised a tattooed eyebrow and tossed two fireballs into the air, expanding them before he caught them again.

"Why are you so good with my fire?" he grumbled.

Bash let the fire wink out of existence. "Meditation, control, focus."

"All right, smartass, keep your secrets." Teyr wrinkled his nose.

The dragon shook his head.

I steadied myself amidst the currents of their power. Their tastes on my tongue

felt almost more intimate than my encounter with Bash and Shade in Drax's apartments. I could easily let myself fall into them. But I had to keep my distance. For their safety. For everyone's.

Over the last few days, I'd managed to pull details about our escape out of my recalcitrant mates. Like all the other times I'd formed a bridge, joining with Shade had opened a rift, but we'd disappeared before they found out what happened. Fae had to be dead. The only question was how many. How many deaths did I have on my hands? How many rifts had I opened without knowing? How much blood had I shed out of sheer, reckless ignorance?

My *energy* surged to meet another flow of magic, and I ripped it back. I couldn't risk doing anything I didn't know would be safe, but could I know what was safe? I had to make up for what I'd done, but I didn't even know the full scope. My chest started to tighten, but nausea arrived first. I stumbled back a step, grabbed fistfuls of *energy*, and crammed it into the bridges to stop my mates from harming themselves. They deserved better than me. Bile burned my throat.

I turned to bolt for the woods and found myself face-to-face with Shade. Along the half-blocked bridges, I could feel Teyr and Bash, just out of arms' reach.

My legs wobbled. "I have to—"

My Kitty, it is a part of you. It has always been there, and you have always been you.

Breathe, love, or I'm going to come over there and distract you, Teyr said.

You are stronger than this, Dee. Focus, Bash added.

I swallowed down the bile and tried to regain control. The drizzling rain pattered softly against my skin. I plucked soggy silk off my legs and curled my toes into the cool mud. I would stay until we figured out if any good could come of this, of me. If nothing could, I'd disappear in the night before any of them could stop me. Otherwise, I owed the world payment for what I had done.

I took a deep breath and opened my eyes. "I'm fine, sorry."

Slowly, they all stepped back. They knew as well as I did that experimentation was the only way forward. I unblocked the bridges.

Shade crouched and rocked gently. He seemed at home in the crumbling tower. He often reached for the bone he wore around his neck, Light's bone, but he also told stories of how they'd built this place together. In a quiet moment, Teyr had said he'd never seen Shade so comfortable with himself, maybe not even before they lost Light.

Teyr's power whisked across our bridge. "Kinnia!"

I started to turn to him. "If you're showing me another cock—"

Zelimir emerged from the trees, clutching a sack Shade had scribbled "Eating Mushrooms" on in one hand and the legs of a dead beast I didn't recognize in the other.

I froze. I hadn't seen him in more than glimpses since the conversation that first day I truly woke up. He met my gaze, then turned quickly away. My heart ached. I didn't want him contaminated by whatever lurked underneath my skin, but I missed him. Everyone else did too.

A fireball lanced across my vision. Zelimir hurried toward the tower in my moment of distraction. Teyr caught the fire, scattering another load of mud. I turned over my shoulder to find Bash juggling two others smugly.

"Show-off," Teyr grumbled.

I raised an eyebrow at the ember's newest pile of mud.

"It was a cock." He frowned at the lump. "I'm not used to being bad at things."

Teyr opened his Cara, and frustration flowed into me. He wanted to keep the mood light, but magic had always come easily. Baby steps irritated him. I swallowed. Honesty. That was all I'd asked of him.

"You're learning something totally new." I closed the distance between us and bumped my hip against his. Safe enough. "That takes time."

Teyr wrapped an arm around my waist. "I want to be learning something else new."

Like this morning, I forced myself to tolerate the touch a moment longer than I thought I could. "We don't know it's safe." And, for all their talk, I couldn't quite believe they still found me attractive.

Teyr pouted. "You, Bash, and Shade are acting no differently than you did before your little rendezvous." He caressed my hip, then the curve of my ass. "It's what's inside that counts. Yours are just a little flashier. Literally, sparking."

I jerked back out of his grasp as my chest squeezed, tight and hollow. Teyr grabbed me and pulled me to his chest. I struggled against his hold even as he pushed calm though our Cara. Distantly, I realized that also tasted like the forest now.

"Pretending stuff doesn't exist doesn't help anyone, right?" he murmured. "That means we have to face this Tech or get rid of it, and you can't get rid of this. As much as Shade can't bring Light back, as much as Bash can't change his past, as much as Zelly can't escape his birthright, this is yours." His arms hung warm and heavy around my waist.

I stopped squirming. "What about you?"

"Oh, I'm special." He grinned. "There's nothing to me a bar of soap and a bit of water can't fix. Especially if you're naked, letting me run that bar of soap over your breasts and between your legs."

My cheeks burned. A single laugh burst from my lips and echoed in the silence of the clearing. I clapped my hand over my mouth and peered over my shoulder to find Bash and Shade looking away quickly with smiles on their faces. Teyr turned my face back to him. I dropped my hand from my mouth. He grabbed my ass and leaned in slow. I could break his hold and flee. He might have given me the option on purpose.

I had to find a way to do more than survive. I wrapped my arms around Teyr's neck and pulled him in. He licked the seam of my lips, and I parted. He twisted his tongue with mine. I searched my reactions for anything out of place, anything cold or metallic. Fire kindled between my legs. His lips warmed mine. Pleasure sparked as he kneaded my ass with one hand and played with the collar of my robe with the other. I gasped into his mouth as he exposed another inch of skin to the rain.

A ray of hope burst through my blackness. I could live like this. Mud squelched, and I hoped Bash or Shade were coming to join us. Maybe both.

"Teyr," Zelimir said.

We jumped apart. Teyr kept an arm around my waist.

Zel stood a few feet away with his jaw set. "We need to stay objective." He looked over both of us before snapping his gaze back to Teyr's face. "There could be a threat we're not seeing."

"Fire, Zel." Teyr tightened his hold on me. "If you felt the bridge, you would know. Tech couldn't create something pulsing with that much life and love."

"I can't be objective. Nor can any of us." Shade bounded up next to Teyr. "We love our Kitty, and she loves us."

"My experience with Tech runs even deeper than yours." Bash

stepped next to them. "Whatever happened or is happening, it's new. And we aren't a Cara without a commander."

My breath caught. The Tech inside me might be only part of the puzzle. The bridges, and maybe other things, might be just me, whatever I was outside of the cables. The ray of hope I'd felt kissing Teyr bloomed into something I might be able to hold onto.

Zelimir crossed his arms. "Whether we're dealing with Tech or something we haven't heard of, the protocol should be the same. Sex is too big of a variable. If you want me to be more of a commander, then it's my say."

Teyr stepped forward, only a few inches from Zel. Shade and Bash fell into formation, so I stood behind the three of them.

"I don't know how certain you think you're gonna get from fifteen feet away," Teyr said. "Treating her like she's going to destroy us at any moment won't discover shit. You're just pushing her away again, like you have been since the fucking Councils told you to."

The air around my mates grew thick with tension. If I was the monster I feared, Zelimir was right to keep away. They all should. But I wanted to cling to that ray of hope. I wanted to believe I could be more than a machine.

Zel frowned. "I'm not trying to push anyone anywhere. I simply believe an outside perspective would be valuable, and I'm as close as we can get."

"You can stay away from my Kitty if you want," Shade said. "But I can't."

Bash shook his head. "You can't either, Zelimir. We've barely seen you in almost a week."

Zelimir shook his head and opened his mouth, but Teyr poked his chest.

"We are tested over and over, broken over and over." Steam rose off Teyr's robe as his skin heated. "Kinnia is our fifth. She could be filled with oil and griffon shit for all I care. I'm not breaking again. I'm not bowing to the unknown."

I wrapped my hand around Teyr's bicep. He trembled, and my hand burned, but I needed him to know I heard him this time.

Zelimir put his hands up and stepped back. "I'm not saying she isn't our fifth." He towered over Teyr and met my gaze. "I'm not pushing you away. All I'm asking for is caution. If you mean us harm, you clearly aren't aware of it. That's why we can't let our guard down."

For a moment longer than I would have yesterday, I held onto Teyr and my ray of hope. Then, reality crashed back over me. Tech buzzed under my skin. Its *energy* powered my body. Of course, I couldn't be trusted. I released Teyr. The ember stepped closer to Zel.

Bash shoved in between his taller mates and put a hand on each of their chests. "Using Dee to vent your insecurities isn't helping anyone." He pushed them away from each other. "Shade, are there bodies of water nearby safe for fae?"

The necromancer hummed behind me. "There's a lake a half hour's walk away. But it doesn't belong—"

Bash waved his hand. "We need to get on the same page. Teyr, Zelimir, go get that batch of soap we rendered and anything that needs to be washed."

The ember blinked. I frowned. Bash made sense—I hadn't bathed since before Shade's trial—but since when did he take charge like this?

Shade clenched his fists and gritted his teeth, muttering something about troggles.

I slid to his side and laced my fingers with his. "You'll keep everyone safe."

Shade looked at our twined fingers and smiled. "I will."

8

TEYR

I TRAILED BEHIND, LUGGING THE BUCKET OF SOAP WE'D rendered out of spare fat and trying not to feel so irritated that I ruined the prospect of seeing my mates naked when we reached the lake. Shade led the group as a fae, but he jutted his nose into the air and sniffed aggressively. Kinnia walked between Bash and Zelimir. At Zelly's prompting, they were talking about the fucking Tech thing again.

I heaved an aggrieved sigh, but none of them turned. If I couldn't figure out the secret of Kinnia's Tech over a week, they wouldn't figure it out on a half-hour walk. At least the rain had stopped. When the sun came out, the jewel tones of the Thicket looked almost pretty.

"The Tech called out to sister when we fell to Earth," Kinnia said. "I have to be sister." We looked at her in unison and she shook her head. "No other woman was there. It sounded like... they recognized me. So, however this stuff got into me had to happen while I was on Earth, which means, I'm Tech."

"You could still be a particularly advanced Jalan," my commander pointed out. "There are still some communities on Earth right?"

I threw my hands into the air, whacking myself with the bucket of soap. Thankfully, no one saw.

"Yeah. And Jalan are just modified humans." She twisted a curl of dark hair almost long enough to reach her shoulders around one finger. "I mean, they don't grow up with those Tech parts."

Bash hummed. "But they tend to start their modifications as teens."

She slowed, and all of us slowed with her.

"You can always see Jalan modifications." Kinnia rubbed the side of her face. "There's nothing on me."

Zel's Cara flickered open so briefly I couldn't separate the emotions, but he didn't seem happy.

"Exactly." I surged forward before they could head down a darker train of thought. "And you're talking in circles. Bash, what is the point of a change in scenery if we don't change the topic?"

He grunted in agreement. That was all I needed. I darted forward and snaked an arm around Kinnia's waist, then pulled her out from between my too-serious mates. She yelped in surprise. Zel pursed his lips but didn't say anything. For the first time in days, I sent my commander a wave of gratitude.

With a smirk, I began tickling her. She shrieked, wrenched out of my grip, and sprinted away. I let her go as her Cara filled with joy. I'd missed that feeling. But I could only give her so much of a head start. I raced after her. Bash and Zel parted to give me an opening. It wasn't an apology—those were still hard-won from the titan—but I could live with acceptance.

I caught up to her as she reached Shade, and we ran in a circle around the confused necromancer until he stopped and pointed. Through a break in the trees, a small, clear lake sparkled in the late afternoon sun. We overlooked the water from the top of a rocky outcropping. A jewel-toned pebble beach marked the far shore. I smiled. I'd been washing in the well, which kept me sane, but a true bath had eluded me for too long.

"My Kitty, you must stop squealing." Shade crossed his arms and peered out over the water. "Troggles are small. They can appear as rocks—"

I dropped the bucket of soap, flashed Kinnia a brilliant grin, and dove for her. We both careened over the edge of the outcropping into the water below. She shrieked and twisted in my grip, balling her body for maximum splash. I released and followed her lead. We hit the warm water in unison, and I surfaced quickly. I loved baths, but my fire muffled underwater. Kinnia popped up a moment after and splashed me.

"Shithead." She smiled.

I floated on my back and waved up at Bash and Zelimir, leaning over the outcropping with Shade. The three of them turned and began walking down the small cliff to the beach.

"C'mon, we gotta catch up." I backstroked lazily across the water.

Kinnia laughed and ducked under, quickly outpacing me. By the time I caught up with her, our other three mates had already reached the beach and begun stripping off their robes. The bucket of soap I abandoned on the outcropping bobbed gently in the shallow water next to them. For the first time in Fire even knew how long, nobody seemed angry or upset.

I allowed myself another moment of aimless floating, then grabbed the bucket of soap from the shallows and drifted up to Kinnia.

She spun as I approached and she held out a wad of dark-blue cloth. "Wash this for me?"

Her bare, tanned shoulders peeked above the water, but I couldn't see any detail below the surface. She'd slicked back her hair, which reached her shoulders without the curls, and her slightly pointed ears poked clearly out. I hadn't seen this Kinnia since the mud trap. My cock sprang to attention.

I tried to paddle around the bundle. "Do I look like your maid?"

She dodged, keeping the robe between us, but grinned. "You look like you're hoarding the soap."

"Teyr!" Zel barked.

I whipped around to glare at our commander. "What?"

Water splashed. I turned just in time to see Kinnia's ass disappear under the water in a dive. She resurfaced a few feet away, her sculpted shoulders glistening, and I ground my teeth. She'd left the sodden robe.

"We need hands." Zelimir called.

I licked my lips. "I'll wash your robe if you let me wash you after."

Kinnia blushed. "I don't think Zelimir would like that."

"He'd be more jealous than anything else." I drifted closer and traced my fingers down her bare arm.

Her brows furrowed, and alarm ghosted through her Cara.

"You have no idea how beautiful you are." I moved to kiss her again.

"Teyr!" Zelimir underlined his shout with a *pulse*.

Kinnia snagged a glob of soap and waved me away with a laugh. Grumbling, I joined my mates on the beach to wash clothes. All of them had stripped, so I got naked as quickly as I could. The washing took nearly half an hour, partially because all of us kept stealing looks at each other's naked bodies, Kinnia included. She stared, occasionally, at Bash, Shade, and I from the safety of the lake, but Zelimir she watched only in glimpses.

Eventually, we got all the robes laid out in the sun to dry. I waded back into the lake. Bash strode into the water, his purple and white scales catching the light, then he began swimming laps. Zelimir tested the temperature with one dark hand, then pulled his twists up in a bun and dragged the soap bucket in to begin his bath.

Shade joined us last, slowly backing into the lake with his eyes on the forest. His wolf ears twitched, and blue magic misted over his tense shoulders. He might never be built like Zelimir or even sculpted like me, but his pale, toned legs and trim waist cut a striking figure against the dark backdrop.

He turned, his tail thumping against his hamstring, and his sizeable cock swung into view just before he ducked under the water. Kinnia blushed. She'd felt that cock against her ass and loved every minute of it. I could relate.

He resurfaced next to her. "My Kitty, may I wash your back?"

My mates, all naked and brimming with sexual tension, had scattered to separate parts of the lake. We had other stuff to figure out, sure, but if I could get all these stubborn assholes in bed, we'd all be better off. I floated toward Shade, then smirked at Kinnia and slipped under the water. I swam directly into the necromancer's legs and barreled him over.

With a flourish, I stood. "Allow me, fair maiden. I am known far and wide for my back-washing skills."

I flexed but didn't make it another inch before Shade popped back up, spluttering.

"Gentlemen, I'm not so fair." Kinnia rose slightly in the water, the tops of her pale breasts bobbing into view in contrast to the rest of her tanned skin. "And I believe you'll find I'm more than capable of washing myself." She swept a huge wave over both of us.

That meant war. Kicking, splashing, squealing, sputtering war.

Shade used his magic first, sending an undead fish into Kinnia's face. She shrieked and punched the thing away just as Bash joined us. He telekinetically shoved a massive wave into Shade and I that sent us tumbling to shore.

By the time I got my bearings, Bash had Kinnia on his shoulders, clearly intending to catapult her into the deepest part of the lake. They laughed and grappled, but I stared. Her muscular thighs, pale like her breasts, tensed around his lilac neck. Her hips curved softly into her toned stomach, and her breasts would each fit perfectly in the palms of my hands.

Zelimir beat me to her rescue by shooting Bash in the face with a stream of water pressurized between two force wedges. The dragon sank into the lake to escape the blast. Zel swam forward and grabbed her, lifting her into the air like a prize. Water dripped off her breasts and down her sides. As she squirmed in his grip, desperate lust burned to life in her Cara. All the blood left my brain. I opened my Cara to meet hers, all joy and desire. To my surprise, our mates followed suit.

"King of the Lake," Zel roared.

Kinnia laughed. He cradled her against his chest. Fire, they looked amazing together. Zel leaned forward as if to kiss her, and I did too. They needed this. We needed this.

His Cara snapped shut. He froze mere inches from her lips.

"No, no, no," I whispered.

Hurt sparked through her Cara, but before the feeling could crystallize, Shade emerged a few feet away with a small army of undead fish. Zelimir yelled and scrambled backward, dropping Kinnia in his panic. Shade grabbed her and started to lift her, but she kissed his neck. He froze with a dopey smile on his face. Rookie mistake, but one I knew well.

She kicked his legs out from under him and lifted him above her head. "Queen of the Lake!"

The army of undead marine life went still, floating and sinking as they should have. I whistled and clapped. Fire, we didn't deserve this woman. Smart, sultry, and strong. She should have been the center of our world from day one.

Shade's voice cut through my enjoyment. *Troggles.*

Kinnia dropped Shade back into the water as her eyes widened. Her Cara radiated curiosity instead of the fear Shade was trying to instill in all of us. Bash and I turned to see what held her attention. Zelimir stared blankly as we reacted in unison. I tried to point at the shore, but he just scowled. I rolled my eyes. If he didn't want to be left out, he should get a bridge.

On the shore, a little group of short, gray humanoids stared at us through round, pupilless, bronze eyes. Small, jagged teeth poked out from their thin lips, and coarse, bronze-and-gold hair topped their round heads. Their wispy golden clothing fluttered in the breeze.

Bash? Maybe the dragon could read some thoughts, get an intention.

One troggle, wearing a floor-length dress and holding a staff of glimmering blue wood, stepped to the front of the group. A voice I didn't recognize, low and gravelly, echoed in my mind. *Queen of the Lake?*

Shade tried to push Kinnia behind him.

She pushed back. "You judge too fast."

Shade gritted his teeth. Kinnia ran her hand down his arm and murmured something that made him step aside. She crossed her arms over her breasts and walked forward.

Bash? I asked again.

They were waiting for this, he said slowly. *They are unarmed and afraid of Shade.*

I nodded, but I couldn't relax. Kinnia seemed too calm. But her every confident step displayed more of her creamy curves, and my attention wavered.

Tonight, we honor the full moon, the lead troggle said. *A night of forgive-*

ness and punishment, of ends and new beginnings. Will you join us in our celebration, Queen of the Lake?

Kinnia stopped in waist-high water. "I'm not really the queen of the lake."

You declared yourself such, the troggle said. *And you controlled the monster that stole our ancestral land.*

She glanced over her shoulder, checking to see if we would stop her. I swallowed but kept my face neutral. She wanted actions over words. If I wanted her to believe I trusted her, I needed to show it. Zelimir pursed his lips. Bash folded his arms.

"My Kitty," Shade whined.

She took a deep breath. "Everyone deserves a second chance."

He ducked his head. She dropped her arms.

Completely bare, she strode out of the lake. "My four mates and I will join you, on the conditions that I'm not really a queen, and there will be no conflict."

I would have dropped to my knees and worshipped her like any royalty she chose.

There will be no conflict. The head troggle frowned. *But how are we to know who you are when you do not?*

Her confidence wavered in our Cara. A little of the shame and disgust of the last few days crept in.

For tonight, be our queen of the lake. The troggle nodded. *You won the title. We bestow it upon you.*

I opened my Cara, full of love and trust. She glanced over her shoulder at me and smiled. The lead troggle stepped forward. They only came up to Kinnia's knee, but when they dipped their comically long staff, the carved, smooth point pressed against her shoulder.

The air around her rippled, and the same wispy golden clothing that clung to the troggles grew over her chest and hips. Euphoria shot through our Cara, and the air around her shimmered bronze with wild magic. One of the troggles offered her a hand.

9

ZELIMIR

HAZE SHROUDED KINNIA'S FIGURE AS SHE TOOK THE troggle's hand and stepped through what she wouldn't recognize as a wild portal. Shade threw back his head and howled. Teyr raised an eyebrow. I launched *pulses* after her, requesting with increasing intensity that she return.

The troggles remained on the edge of the lake, watching the portal fade out of view. Her Cara didn't dim, or even flicker, but she didn't respond. Her emotions grew distant.

My second splashed through the lake and pulled the lead troggle's smooth staff to his chest. As with Kinnia, soft, golden cloth wreathed his hips. The portal returned, and he disappeared through it. Shade snarled and crouched to pounce, but I *pulsed* a quick stop. We might not be able to get to wherever they sent her without them. The necromancer glared at me.

Teyr walked forward. "If we really want to support her, we have to follow her lead."

I gritted my teeth and met the lead troggle's soft, bronze gaze. "Will you take us to the same place you took them?"

Your queen secured passage for all, they said. *We dare not cross her.*

They pressed their staff to Teyr's chest without any further prompting. Shade howled and leapt forward, but only to receive his own passage. I stood alone with the troggles. Vague emotions rolled through my mates' Caras, just out of reach. They didn't seem negative. I needed to be at their side, come what may. I strode forward, and the little creature pressed the smooth tip of their staff to my chest.

Wild magic washed over my damp skin, warm like all pockets of magic. Golden cloth ringed my hips. A bronze wild portal shimmered around me. I stepped onto soft moss in a misty, green-lit clearing. A massive, orange moon rose on my left as day became night. Frantic drums and trilling horns pierced the air. Troggles spun in wild rhythm. My worries melted away in a hazy, pleasant tingling.

Shade appeared out of the crowd and grabbed my hand. I laughed as he pulled me in, and the music caught my feet. We jumped, swayed, and spun in perfect time with the drums while our Caras hummed to a new rhythm.

A chill ran down my spine. I didn't know how to dance, or at least, not like this. Something else drove me.

My Cara skipped in time with the drums played by troggles around the edge of what seemed to be the dance floor. The green bonfire at the center of the clearing spit sparks like any other would, but I'd never seen fire that color before. Every dancer moved around the flames. Wild magic hung so thick in the air here that I couldn't tell what cast the spell. I stopped, and Shade stopped with me.

Confusion filtered through his Cara. "Zelimir?"

"We're being enchanted." I shook my head. "Let's find the others and go."

He cupped my face. With the rhythm still beating into the soles of my feet, his touch didn't feel as uncomfortable as usual.

"A little enchantment might soothe you," he said.

I grimaced. "But I don't know *why.*"

"Troggles are many things, but they aren't liars." He spun in a circle, his arms wide and his tail wagging. "It is simply a party. Dance with me!"

Couples danced around us, mostly troggles. Bash twirled toward us with one in his arms.

I grabbed my second. "Do you feel this? The compulsion?"

He and the troggle both blinked up at me.

"You can stop," he said slowly.

Just a little mood-setting. The troggle nodded. *After the harvest comes new life.*

An aphrodisiac. Teyr would laugh.

"It will relax you, if you let it." Bash patted me on the shoulder and whirled back into the dance.

Shade stared at me, then swept up a troggle partner and moved away as well. I stood alone in the chaos. Relax. Relax. How could I relax with everything going on around us? With Kinnia in here somewhere, and no way of knowing how wild magic would interact with...whatever she had inside her?

Like they heard me, the crowd parted so I could see her, swaying in silhouette in front of the emerald bonfire. Her hands on my chest had been softer than I expected from her years as a mercenary. She threw back her head and laughed. Every curve of her body sang to be touched. My fingers itched.

Bash appeared next to her and caught her in his arms. The rhythm pounded through my feet, up my legs and into my heart, stoking desperate feelings. The sting of leaving every day. The sting of seeing her in Teyr's arms earlier, smiling like she hadn't at me in far too long. The sting of hate and fear and worry blurring over days in the Thicket.

I could relax. The troggle's drumbeat swept me up. My feet danced in patterns I could never replicate. Seconds or days passed. Rhythm filled the clearing with color and life. I changed partners over and over. My body never tired, and the beat never slowed.

Through the blur of my Cara, I sensed my mates in the crowd. One rotation took me mere feet from Bash and Kinnia.

He held her against his chest. She stared up at him with flushed cheeks, taut from grinning. He grabbed her ass and crushed her closer. She claimed his lips in a bruising kiss as he parted her thighs and ran a hand under her diaphanous skirt. She moaned.

I turned away. Worries pressed against the music, the rhythm, the smoke. We couldn't...shouldn't....

Bash smacked into my back. When I turned, he spilled Kinnia into my arms. She caught herself on my bare, dark chest and smiled up at me. Her curves brushed my skin, barely hidden by the golden cloth. She ran a hand up my tense arm as the rhythm melted everything away but how she might feel beneath my hands. Her smile turned into something hungry as she trailed her hand on my bicep over my chest and lower.

I folded my arms around her. Her hips fit perfectly beneath my hands, and I dragged her closer to feel how the rest of her body matched. She made a low sound in her chest and pressed herself against me. I buried my face in her neck and inhaled her leather-and-honey scent.

The drums demanded I take her, make her mine in front of everyone. I fought them back. Now that I knew how she felt under my hands, how she moaned, I couldn't let her go if I wanted to. But I wouldn't rush this. She stared up into my eyes, want and wonder and worry blurring in her Cara. I ran my hands through her dark, curly hair, now long enough to truly sink my fingers into, and cradled her face. She deserved everything I could give her.

I took her hand in mine, draped my arm around her waist, and led us like the music couldn't touch me into a slow dance I learned as the prince I never wanted to be.

10

KINNIA

ZELIMIR SPLAYED HIS FINGERS OVER MY ABDOMEN. HIS chest hair scraped against my back as he leaned down to lick along the shell of my ear. My cheeks flushed hotter. The world spun. I bounced on the balls of my feet, unable to contain the excitement that thrummed through me. Zel jerked away from my head just before I clipped his chin. I ducked to apologize, but he brushed a thumb over my lips, forgiveness already threading through our bond.

I leaned back and ground my ass against him. Finally, instead of holding me at arms' length, he pulled me closer. He grazed his hands up over my breasts and back down to my hips.

A troggle handed each of us a small cup. I tipped the contents into my mouth. The thick, sweet liquid coated my tongue in licorice flavor and rain. My face tingled as my body caught fire. My own heartbeat filled my ears. Zelimir spun me, sending our cups flying.

I twirled once, twice, a third time before coming to a stop facing my titan commander. Like me, his cheeks darkened with magic and excitement. His massive chest rose and fell. His twists had fallen loose from his bun ages ago, glittering in the firelight. A bead of sweat rolled down his abs and disappeared into the cloth riding low on his hips. He started to lean in, and even through the haze, I froze. He would realize I was a monster and flinch again.

Instead, he crushed his mouth against mine. My heart soared, and I arched into him. He ran his tongue along the crease of my lips, demanding entrance. This wasn't a kiss. This was a threat, a glimpse of his dammed flood of passion and need. I would happily drown for another taste.

Zelimir pulled back, his eyes hooded. I didn't need to ask. My commander threaded his arms under my ass. I leaned in, and he lifted me. I wrapped my legs around his waist. My throbbing center met the defined muscles of his hips, and I moaned. He began walking away from the troggle party.

The world dulled. The orange moon shrank with every step he took, turning back to its normal color and size. Instead of arriving back at the beach, we appeared at the edge of our clearing. Shade's tower loomed against the night sky.

The troggles' wispy clothing vanished last, and suddenly, there was nothing between us. Just the warm pressure of his cock underneath me. I moaned. Zelimir captured my mouth. Shivers of pleasure rolled over me, and he savored every one. My back hit something solid. I opened my eyes to see the soft purple glow of force magic reflected in his eyes. He'd put a shield up to protect me from the rough bark of the tree he'd trapped me against.

"I knew your magic had to be good for something." I giggled.

Zelimir's eyes twinkled. He pulled me in for gentle kiss, then dragged his erection across my folds. I drew in a sharp breath, but he didn't move. I pouted.

"Are you ready for me?" He pressed his erection against my clit.

I arched with pleasure. "Yes."

He pulled back and gripped my hips, holding me in place. He met my gaze and, slowly, pushed into me. I gasped. He was even bigger than I thought. Pleasure mixed with the feeling of being full to bursting. He never looked away from my face, as if he were memorizing every moment.

I squirmed. He hesitated, but I reached forward and sunk my nails into his hips to pull him the final inch. His hips met mine. I let loose a howl of need that would have put Shade to shame.

Zelimir held me with one hand and cupped my head with the other. "I've dreamed of this." He trailed his hand down my body and pressed his thumb against my clit. "Of filling you, my mate, my heart."

I closed my eyes. He pulsed his hips slowly as my body adjusted to being so utterly full. When I groaned and chased him with thrusts of my own, he sped up. I wound my fingers into his twists.

Finally, he withdrew entirely and re-entered, faster than the first time, pressing down on my clit and a spot deep inside of me I hadn't known existed. White-hot pleasure shot through my body. A scream tore from my lips. We rolled our hips together, and the real dance began. He clutched my ass. I matched his rhythm and bit my lip to swallow down another scream, in case our mates got scared.

Zelimir leaned forward and sucked my lip out from between my teeth. "Sing for me."

He thrust harder, faster, shaking the tree. Blinding pleasure and building pressure became my world. I didn't hold anything back. The need inside me built, love and pleasure cresting into a crescendo that pushed me over the edge. Stars burst behind my eyelids. I sang for my commander as my body shook. He pressed me into the tree and fucked me softly through my orgasm, drawing the feeling out as long as possible.

I opened my eyes to find a depth of passion and intensity in his purple gaze I'd never seen in him before. My *energy* reached for him. Zelimir pulled me away from the tree and dropped to the ground, barely cushioning the blow with his force. He pushed my legs apart to kneel between them as I arched to meet his still-hard cock. My curls spread out around my head. I felt beautiful, feminine, *wanted*.

He devoured the flushed skin of my neck, then kissed down to my breasts, licking and sucking like a fae possessed. I poured more of my *energy* into him as he lavished me with attention. Something in my brain whispered that I hadn't wanted this. I batted the thought away as he twirled his tongue over my nipple.

He entered me again, suddenly, and I screamed his name. His thrusts became frantic, uneven, but he kept hitting the spot deep inside me. He kneaded my other breast with his hand, plucking harshly at my nipple.

Zelimir spasmed, and I became impossibly fuller as he came inside me. Magic, *energy*, and lust turned my world blinding white. A spike of searing pain split my head, burning down to the Cara in my gut. Zelimir grunted and pushed back up on his arms, his cock still quivering inside me.

Our bond widened. I looked up to ask Zelimir when we could do that again but found him staring past me, through me. His uncontrolled thoughts thundered across the bridge in furious fragments.

We never should have—What about the—How could I have—The cables, the Tech—

Unconsciousness threatened at the edges of my vision, but I made myself into the warden of my mind, like Bash so often was. I didn't need to fall unconscious. I could handle this. I reached for Zelimir across the bridge, but he recoiled. My stomach flipped. I fought to remember my ray of hope. This might not be Tech. This might not be bad.

"Zel." I put my hand on his cheek and tried to force him to look at me. "Trust me."

His face remained blank, his thoughts still swirling. I fought through the troggle magic, the desire to fall into him and let him fall into me, to find a memory of my favorite day as Declan. The bridge waited, ready to share whatever I wanted with my mate, my commander, my love. I extended a tendril of the memory. Zelimir jerked. His purple gaze cleared. He pulled out of me and sat back on his heels.

I sat up as well, feeling suddenly exposed. Words spilled off my tongue. "I love you."

He squeezed his eyes closed and ran a hand through his hair. "I can't do this."

My head swam. "What?"

"I need...." He stood and backed away slowly with his hands up, like he needed protection from me.

I got to my feet. "Why can't you just trust this? Trust me?"

"The cables—we can't—" He shook his head. "It's not safe for the Cara."

My stomach roiled, but underneath that, I felt something I hadn't since I found the cables. The bright, hot burn of anger.

I advanced on my commander. "You know, Teyr's right about you. You've been pushing me away since we met."

He took a titanic step back for every one I took forward and kept his hands between us, getting ever farther away. "What if I did? You were an unknown quantity. You still are. The commander puts the Cara above all else."

I scoffed. "Worse than that, you're a fucking coward. You go around handing out these stupid platitudes, then hide behind your responsibilities every time someone calls you on your shit."

"I'm doing the best I can in unforeseeable situations—" He glanced over his shoulder at the tower and moved a little faster, now almost halfway across the clearing.

"I told you I love you!" I shouted.

The air pressure dropped behind me with a telltale *pop*. The ground became unstable. I shrieked and wheeled my arms, fighting for enough balance to run.

"Kinnia!" He lunged for me.

I teetered. Zel stretched his arm out. My fingers brushed his. His gaze burned into mine, desperate with fear. The ground shook with mechanical footsteps, and I fell.

11

BASH

I teetered out of a wild portal mid-spin and blinked in the sudden dark as cold air brushed my naked body. A bronze shimmer caught my eye to my left. I jumped out of the way as Shade and Teyr twirled into the room, the tall necromancer's arms locked onto the ember's hips. Slowly, I recognized the dark stone of Shade's tower, the layout of the third floor. Where were Dee and our commander?

Shade and Teyr disentangled themselves reluctantly and stared around the tower. I fought through the troggle magic humming in our Cara to find them. Hazily, I found rage, shame, guilt, disappointment, but I couldn't tell what came from whom. Someone began shouting.

Along the bridge, I felt Dee storming across the clearing. I stumbled to the window that would give me the best view. Zelimir stood halfway across the clearing with his hands up. Dee stalked forward, waving her hands like Teyr did when he got upset. A few words cut through the drumbeat still pounding in my ears. Trust. Cara. Coward.

The air pressure dropped. A rift tore through the air behind Dee. Zelimir sprinted for her. I leapt through the window, softened my landing with telekinesis, and hit the ground running. Zelimir stood at the mouth of the rift. I couldn't see Dee. A swarm of BeeTech, rare, tiny, flying machines, teemed out of the rift. My commander roared as they knocked him to the ground.

Shade! Teyr! I sprinted across the clearing. *Dee!*

She didn't answer.

By the time I reached Zelimir, his dark skin glistened with the thin cuts BeeTech's razor wings left on their targets. I gathered a fistful of Tech with my telekinesis and slammed them into the searing edge of the rift. A few dropped, but many more buzzed back into the air and circled for another attack.

"She fell, she's gone." Zelimir roared in pain and launched himself at the rift.

Teyr exploded out of the window I'd jumped through with Shade in his arms and caught himself with jets of fire. I grabbed my mates with my telekinesis and pulled them to the ground. We needed them. The smell of burning flesh tinged the air.

"Kinnia!" Zelimir leaned against the edge of the rift, searing his naked skin.

I didn't know what happened between Dee and my commander. I didn't care. If Tech wanted Kinnia dead, she was already dead. If they didn't, we couldn't get her back through this rift. BeeTech only arrived if the rift appeared too high for earthbound Tech to reach. I raced forward and yanked my commander away from the burning silver rift.

Troggle-sized skeletons rose from the muck with grey flesh still hanging off their bones. Two BeeTech blasts hit the spot where Zelimir had been, drying the muddy ground. He struggled against my grip

I shoved him to the ground and straddled him. "We have to get this closed. We need you."

"Kinnia is down there," he shouted. "I didn't tell her I love her back. I can't leave her."

Another cloud of BeeTech swarmed out of the rift. A bright red fireball exploded over them. Hydraulics hissed through the rift. Five? Ten? A hundred?

"We close this, or we die." I stared down at Zelimir.

My commander blinked. His eyes cleared, and he nodded.

I climbed off and extended a hand. "We won't leave her."

He clasped my hand, and I hauled him to his feet.

Teyr, Shade, hold them off, Zel said in our minds. *Bash, help me close this.*

Kinnia had made a bridge with Zelimir.

I darted for the other side of the rift as a third swarm of BeeTech poured out. While the rift remained open, we had the power of a complete Cara. The runes spilled fluidly from my fingers. With a little telekinesis, Zelimir and I reached the top of the rift.

It sealed with a *pop*. The final few BeeTech melted away under Teyr's fire. Silence fell over the clearing. I reached Dee's bridge and found only a drifting nothingness.

Teyr bent over and panted. "What in Fire just happened? Why was there a rift here?" He put a hand to his gut and narrowed his eyes. "Where's Kinnia?"

Shade straightened, power billowing around him. "My Kitty is on Earth."

Zelimir stared blankly at the spot where the rift had been.

"Hello? Thrae to Zelly?" Teyr crossed the clearing and grasped Zelimir's shoulders. "What the fuck did you do now?"

Zelimir twisted out of his grip. "I didn't do anything."

Teyr rolled his eyes. "Fucking shocker. Nothing's your fault, you self-ish, blame-shifting—"

"I didn't do anything," he repeated. "I couldn't."

My dragon bellowed. I had given Dee to my commander, trusted him with her, and he lost her. Worse, he hurt her before he lost her. Zelimir stared into the distance, somehow less than the fae I'd known. He'd been disappearing little by little the longer we stayed in the Thicket. Maybe since Dee joined us. I handed the reins to my dragon.

"What happened?" I asked quietly.

"We had sex." He stared at the empty air. "The bridge formed. She asked me to trust her, told me she loved me, and I just...couldn't." He took a deep, shaky breath.

I took a step closer. "What did you say?"

He raked a hand through his twists. "That it wasn't safe. We couldn't be sure. I had to put the Cara first—"

I roared like I had never roared before, my dragon's voice becoming mine. Zelimir, my commander, the fae I'd looked up to for seventy-five years, flinched.

"You cannot keep relearning the same lesson!" I bellowed.

His mouth fell open. My dragon cocked my fist back to hit him. My neck grew cold in two spots. A familiar burn spread from the coldness, a poison I hadn't felt since Zelimir's trial.

"What in Fire?" Teyr muttered.

Zelimir swayed and collapsed. Three green globules of Gorar's poison slid down his neck. I stumbled. To my right, Shade melted into his wolf and braced. A wave of freezing water crashed over us and hardened into ice. My vision darkened as Lir stepped forward with a frown.

"Dee," I gasped. "On Earth."

"Kinnia is where she belongs." Lir's gaze darkened. "And you need help."

Somebody slammed something dull and heavy into the back of my head. Blackness clawed for me. Two people in rainbow Lower Council robes circled into view.

"Hit him again," someone said in a sharp voice I almost recognized.

Pain blossomed, and the darkness swallowed me whole.

12

KINNIA

IN FOR FIVE. HOLD FOR FIVE. OUT FOR FIVE.

I pressed my bare knees against one side of the plastic tube where I rode atop the HoldTech that had scooped me up as soon as I landed on Earth and braced my back against the plastic behind me. Eyes on the rift the Tech was fast leaving behind, I pounded on the plastic.

The rift snapped shut.

I frantically brushed my hand over the bridges between myself and my mates. The strong, braided ropes sagged like they'd been severed from the line. Panic clawed my throat. One of their stupid lectures said Tech couldn't retain power after a rift closed. Did that make me—my bridges—Tech?

The Tech's stride jostled me. I scooted around to face forward and braced my feet on the other side of the plastic dome. This was as close to sitting as I could get without touching the telescoping entrance below me. The position kept me from rattling around like a naked bead in a shaker, at least.

The gray and white hills around me distorted through the thick plastic. Jagged shapes dotted the landscape, likely some of the partially destroyed buildings that coated Earth.

Earth.

In for five. Hold for five. Out for five.

Last time I walked Earth, I had needed every drop of my *energy* to escape. It didn't matter if I was a metal monster. It didn't matter that I showed the most vulnerable part of myself to a man I loved, and he'd run away. I couldn't let any of that matter. I had to survive.

The cold mantle of rationality which allowed me to survive Earth the first time welcomed me like an old friend.

MY HEAD KNOCKED AGAINST PLASTIC. I BOLTED UPRIGHT AND blinked sleep from my eyes. The world outside the HoldTech was dark except for a few tiny red and green lights in the distance. We had stopped. I shoved to my feet, ignoring the way my bare skin clung to the plastic. Pressure buzzed against my skin in a way that reminded me of a goblin's leering smile.

I reached for my bridges. Limp ropes slipped through my fingers. I gritted my teeth. The HoldTech would only have stopped if we'd arrived at our destination, or if it had to charge. The floor under my feet hissed and spun open.

I fell through and hit cold, smooth floor. The HoldTech stepped back into the doorway opposite me. I sat up and felt around in the dim light. Metal floor. Metal walls. The HoldTech lowered itself and blocked passage through the doorway.

Bright lights flickered on, revealing a small metal room with a narrow hallway beyond the HoldTech. At the end of the hallway, bright light spilled from the open door of a room. I scrambled to my feet.

"Welcome home." A man broad enough to block my view of anything beyond stepped into the hallway from a room to the right.

Not man, Jalan. Metal plating consumed most of his head and covered his right eye, where a dim red bulb burned in its place. What little skin remained on his face sagged with age. Three thick ropes of cables sprouted from where the skin of his forehead met metal and dropped into the collar of his long, pristine white coat like hair. He smiled but wouldn't quite look me in the eye. Several metal teeth glinted in the bright light.

He strode to the room and the HoldTech scooted out into the hallway to allow him entrance. I stepped toward him.

"Ah, ah, ah," he said, and I halted.

He stepped inside and pressed a red button on the right side of the wall. A thick sheet of metal slammed down in front of the HoldTech with a resounding *clang*, trapping me in the little room with the Jalan. Other *clangs* sounded farther away, as if that one button had shut every door in the building. I went cold.

He took two paces toward me. "It's been too long."

Welcome home.

I flicked a glance at the red button.

Freedom.

I poured *energy* into my legs and leapt at him. Colliding with him felt like hitting a wall, and he didn't topple. I wrapped my legs around his waist and yanked the *energy* into my arms to pummel him out of the way. My elbow jarred as I hit his face, and he smiled. My stomach sank.

A metal arm shot out of the wall to my left, clamped around my waist, and yanked in an effort to pull me from the Jalan. I clung with all my strength, all my *energy*, but the metal arm pulled harder. I lost my grip and slumped back to the metal floor.

"Far, far too long." He backed away several paces. Still far, far closer than I ever wanted a Jalan, but out of arm's reach.

A small, stitched label on his white coat read *Elijah*.

"Histrionics won't help anyone. Come now." He backed up and hit the red button. The door slid aside and he turned and started down the hall. The HoldTech was gone.

I swallowed down a scream of frustration.

Elijah reached the end of the hallway, then turned. "Do I need to be clearer? Follow me."

He waited. I took a deep breath and followed.

When I neared Elijah, he entered the room, and I continued inside. The room looked like other labs I had seen on Earth, except for one glaring difference: everything was whole, well-maintained, and working.

Bright lights blared off the smooth, white plastic floor and the slim, sterile metal bed near the right side of the room. I remembered days and weeks of waking up to the chill of a similar bed, always the first sign Tech had captured me again, even before the ache of cables having been detached from my joints registered in my brain.

On the righthand side of the room, slivers of white wall shone between banks of computers with extendable screens and devices I didn't recognize. The wall to the left shimmered with the same clear plastic as the HoldTech and half a dozen small rooms with matching metal beds were visible. A metal tube jutted from the farthest righthand corner of the nearest room.

The wall directly ahead wasn't a manmade wall at all but was the side of a mountain where dark, jagged rock flaked off, leaving a heavy coating of dust on the floor. This lab had been built into the side of a mountain. In the middle of the stone facing hung a heavy, metal door with the number 43278 painted on it.

Elijah chuckled. "Home is where the heart is."

I fisted my hands at my sides. "Where am I?"

"I thought you might have some latent memories, but...." He turned to a computer and raised his voice like he needed an audience to hear him. "Total retrograde amnesia related to the events of the reassertion."

One of the computers in the biggest bank beeped.

He turned back to me. "Why do you care where you are?"

"Because I have something to get back to." The words slipped from my lips before I realized I believed them.

Even with the Tech inside me, even with Zelimir's freakout, that truth burned in my bones. I had something to get back to. And I wouldn't let a few half-dead cables or an insane Jalan keep me from that life.

He crossed his arms. I put my shoulders back and my chin up like I'd seen Zelimir do so many times.

"If it will relax her...." He spoke like he wasn't accustomed to people hearing him.

"This is my sanctum sanctorum, one of my greatest achievements." He swept his hand around the room. "An Earth lab, restored to its former glory. I reprogrammed all the Tech myself. Took years of hard labor, but I am now equipped with the particular tools I need for my work. One of a few labs I maintain, but certainly the best. After all, you're here." He grinned, still not quite meeting my gaze.

I shivered.

"Now, you can relax. That will make the next steps easier." His red eye rotated. A wide, red beam landed on my feet.

I scrambled backwards and hit the plastic wall.

"Fantastic, isn't it?" He swept the beam up my body. "I can see things you wouldn't believe. Heart rate's a little high, but that could be related to the spike in cortisol." He smiled. "I'd have given it to you, but I only cracked this one a few months ago."

My heart stuttered. "Given it to me?"

The Jalan laughed like two pieces of metal banging together. "Ah, don't worry, my girl. You'll catch on soon."

My mind raced. I had no memories of an Elijah. But the way he talked, the familiarity in his smile...I might not know him, but he spoke as if he knew me. As if he created me. My stomach flipped. Memory of the cables crawled through my mind's eye. I grasped for the certainty I had something to live for and found it just out of reach.

The beam clicked off. He turned to a whirring computer bank behind him. "First scan shows no significant abnormalities," he said in that same loud, clear voice. "But, of course, only a deeper examination will reveal any true flaws."

The biggest bank of computers beeped again.

"I'm fucking out of here." I swung toward the we'd entered through.

"I'm almost certain I didn't teach you that language."

From the corner of my eye, I glimpsed the cable that shot out of the underside of his wrist. Time slowed. I swerved. The cable followed. With a slick, familiar sound, the cable plunged into my abdomen.

"Let's see if you're ready." He raised his voice again. "Computer, download memory."

I tried to run, but my limbs didn't obey. My feet marched forward under someone else's will to the table near the bank of computers. I tried to scream, to cry, to do anything else. My feet kept moving, one in front of the other. I sat on the metal bed, then laid down.

Elijah pulled a small stool from the computer area and sat next to my head. He pulled the nearest screen with an extendable arm down to him. Incomprehensible ones and zeroes scrolled across the screen, followed by flashing images. My memories, I realized with a jolt, starting with my first escape on Earth, over seven years ago. My cycle of capture and liberation, then my time as a mercenary whipped by faster than I could process.

Realization burst through my mind. The cables. The glint of metal on my ribs. My scarless skin and *energy*. The ease with which I learned. I'd lost my family seven years ago, right before I was captured for the first time. Elijah must've found me then, experimented on me, and claimed me as his own.

A tear slipped down my cheek. The pictures slowed as I journeyed back through the wilds. The moment I used my *energy* to shield my budding Cara from my new mates rewound and played again.

Elijah's eyes glowed with reflected light from the screen. "You've grown far past my projections."

My memories sped again. At Bash's trial, he slowed.

"K1NN14 displays the ability to channel the energy indigenous Thraens call 'magic' with access to a Thraen," he said in his computer voice. "Though doing so causes significant activity in the nociceptors, syncope, and a limited comatose state. This 'magic' seems to function as if the originating Thraen wielded it. This is an extremely promising stride for Project 43278, but further data collection and potential interviewing of K1NN14 may be necessary." He glanced down at me. "Goodness, it's nice to have a face around to explain things to again."

The process repeated at every trial. Each of his speeches grew denser with terminology I didn't understand, but one thing made perfect sense. I was K1NN14. Kinnia.

My stomach roiled. He made up the number to distance himself from the awful things he did to make me like this.

Elijah pulled down two more screens, bracketing the first, as he replayed what I realized was Shade's trial. One screen showed a table of numbers, the other a bright-green line that waved up and down, then flattened.

He stopped my memory in the blackness of drowning and pointed to the line. "Do you know what that is?"

I couldn't answer. He pressed a button on his wrist, and the memory began moving again. The line he directed me toward scrolled across the screen. It stayed flat as the screen remained black. The screen turned a searing white, and the line began bobbing up and down.

My voice returned to me. "No."

He patted my shoulder. I flinched inwardly, but my body remained still.

"That's death, my girl." He grinned. "I forgot Thrae still has water. Didn't plan for a drowning." He laughed, high and triumphant. "But I built a machine strong enough to compensate. Shocked back on by its very own material! I daresay you're unkillable."

My stomach heaved. Bile bubbled in my throat, but I couldn't vomit. He built me. He built me? The way he said that didn't sound like he found me and installed Tech in my body.

Memories continued to play across the screen until I saw myself, reflected in the monitors like a three-headed monster. Elijah snapped his wrist, and the cable withdrew from my abdomen with a sickening *slurp*. Control of my muscles returned. I shut my eyes and willed myself to get up. I could almost picture it. I would rush for some weapon, wield it against his precious machines, and force him to take his words back. To admit he lied. He didn't build me.

Something in my chest thumped hollowly. He knew things about me I'd never guessed and moved around this lab with the certainty of a man who knew every crook and crevice of the room. All of Teyr's hopeful predictions, all of Shade's promises that I couldn't be anything he wouldn't love, all of Bash's soft smiles tumbled away, leaving nothing but cold truth.

Elijah built me. Nothing kept me going but machined metal and a Jalan's mad hopes. Every choice I agonized over meant nothing. If they hadn't been chosen for me, they'd still all led me here, to whatever he needed me "ready" for.

I rolled onto my side and vomited.

"By Earth's light, I wish you needed fewer organics to work," he muttered. "Computer, clean up."

A panel in the wall slid aside to reveal a small, dark metal cube on wheels. The machine looked like no Tech I'd ever seen. It wheeled over and eviscerated my vomit with a small green laser. I rolled onto my back and stared at the white ceiling. The hollowness expanded, consuming my chest, my limbs.

My limbs? Could I call them mine?

I shifted my attention onto Elijah as he pressed a small button under his metal ear. The charger returned to the port. He crossed the room to a wheeled small cart filled with vials and small tools and pulled it toward me.

"No sign of anything from your side." He sat down at the stool beside my bed. "I want everything they know, however you have to get it."

His words drifted in one ear and out the other. I couldn't care.

He pulled a bright light from near the computers to over the bed. "As thrilled as I am that you're up and running, I have to make sure Thraen foolishness caused no permanent damage." He rolled me onto my side, and I glimpsed the flash of something silver he picked up from the cart, then he sliced into the thin scar that was all that remained of the gaping wound in my side.

The pain shattered my haze. I screamed and jerked away.

He frowned. "Nociceptors."

Elijah sifted through a rack of vials on the cart before selecting one filled with a thick, white substance. He scooped a dollop out with a metal tool and spread the gel around the edges of the wound, which numbed instantly. When he brought the knife back down, I only noticed the slick sound of my flesh parting. I would have cried if it seemed worth the effort.

"Lucky only cable seven was cut," Elijah murmured. "Six connects your brain to your spine." He clicked his tongue and put on his computer voice again. "Aging strains cables, exponentially increasing likelihood of drift. Cables six, seven, and eight visible in flesh of K1NN14. Compensate in future designs with increased elasticity."

Elijah leaned in and pulled the light closer. "What the...." He called to the computer, "Cable seven shows signs of mending previously believed impossible by any means other than surgical. Thrae lacks surgical understanding, and memory indicates no treatment beyond a concoction of herbs and Thraen energy known as 'potions.' Further examination necessary to determine if ability originated from K1NN14 or represents a new property of Thraen energy."

Elijah rambled as he worked, speaking to me and his whirring computer bank with the same level of dispassion. Eventually, he smoothed the contents of a different vial over my side. My skin reached for itself across the gap. Another wave of sickness rocked me, but I had nothing left to throw up.

He flipped me onto my back and smiled at a point next to my head. "I'll figure out what made you so nervous and solve it. Then"—his smile grew broad, fanatical—"you'll help me save Earth."

"No one can save Earth," I mumbled. "Give up. Only Thrae is alive."

"It really is charming to watch you try to think." He trailed a finger down my cheek. "Thrae is simply an echo of reality. A bump in the cosmos. A place of fairytales and make-believe. To abandon Earth would be to doom myself and all future Jalan to nothingness." He smiled. "But myth, belief...now that's a power source you can do incredible things with.

"When you first left, I was worried all my work—all Dr. Miller's work—would go to waste. I thought I might've been wrong about the simulation." He shook his head. "But the longer Farquin couldn't catch you, the prouder I grew. And now that you're back, I intend to return Thrae's power to Earth, where it belongs."

"Simulation?" I choked out.

He frowned. "You don't know?"

I shook my head.

Elijah gestured at the clear plastic wall. "Computer, rotate amniotic sleeve three."

The metal tube in the closest room beyond the wall rotated to face me, exposing a clear panel. My abused stomach screamed. Yellowish liquid shot through with veins of blue filled the tube, and the pale body of a dark-haired girl of about thirteen floated limply within. Thick, black letters at the top of the tube read, "K1NN13."

"Your predecessor in the SISTER line." He looked at me out of the corner of his eye.

I'd seen the ones and zeroes that scrolled across the screen before, on computers and readouts on Earth. They were what made the Tech run. My family. My childhood. Everything that made me who I was. He invented it all.

With a cry of anguish that didn't reach my lips, I sank into the oblivion of unconsciousness.

13

ZELIMIR

Someone jiggled my arm with a warm hand. "Zel, wake up."

I sucked in a painful breath. Memories flashed through my mind. Kinnia's perfect body beneath me, offering me her trust, her heart. The burst of euphoria, strange and sharp. *Please, Zelimir. I love you.* Backing away with my hands up. Her fingers, just out of reach as she fell.

I had a list of excuses. None of them mattered. I'd failed. A rift formed every other time she fused Caras, but instead of planning for that, instead of telling her I loved her and I was afraid, I ran.

"Zel." Whoever it was shook my arm harder.

I blinked my eyes open. Teyr's face swam into view above me.

"There he is." He sat back, allowing me a view of my surroundings.

Dim, red fifs reflected off smooth, darkly rainbowed stone walls. The ceiling disappeared into the dark above us, but I didn't need to see more. I would've known the place just from the comfortable ache of surveillance. The Academy. I closed my eyes with a groan.

Teyr huffed. "What happened, happened. Slaughtering yourself and stewing in your entrails doesn't fix anything."

"Could I reanimate someone who had slaughtered themselves and stewed in their own entrails?" Shade asked. "And what would those remains be capable of? Is the body in pieces? Slaughter is a vague term, as is entrails."

"Fire, Shade, it was an expression," Teyr muttered.

I opened my eyes and shoved into a sitting position. The cool wall met my back. Someone had clothed me in a pair of rough, loose brown trousers and nothing else. My mates all wore the same. Teyr alone laid close enough to touch. Shade lolled against the wall directly across from us. Bash sat with his legs crossed and his palms on his knees in the middle of the room, away from any of the walls. I couldn't see a door.

"How long have you all been awake?" My voice sounded scratchy from disuse.

Teyr snorted. "There aren't exactly clocks in here."

"Nearly an hour," Bash said quietly.

Seconds before the Council descended upon us, my second had yelled at me about getting over my fears, once and for all. Now, he kept his eyes so stubbornly closed I wondered if he was avoiding my gaze. Stewing in my entrails wouldn't help anyone. If I had leapt through the rift after Kinnia, I would be dead. A voice in my head surprisingly like my father's reminded me it was better to tuck tail and live than die for pride.

I sucked in a bitter breath, then pushed my father and Kinnia from my mind and stood. I had to solve the problem in front of me.

"Did you discuss escape in all that time?"

"Somebody"—Teyr glared at Bash—"thought we should wait for our fearless leader."

I sighed. "Well, I'm here. What do we have? Shade, portals?"

The necromancer shivered. "Can't you feel it? They are crushing our magic out of us. Maybe, with my Kitty's strength...."

I palmed the haft of a spear to check and, for the first time in my life, my magic didn't reply. My gut twisted. "No magic at all."

"Yup." Teyr popped the 'p' in the way he knew I found irritating.

No magic. No weapons. No door. No Kinnia.

"Is she alive?" The words spilled from my lips before I could catch them back.

"Yes," Shade growled.

Bash readjusted his hands. "We don't know."

"I won't think any other way." Teyr crossed his arms.

I nodded slowly. The quiet path to her felt the same as it had in the moment we connected, aside from the emotionlessness. "I won't think any other way either."

Teyr clenched his jaw but nodded. I rolled my shoulders. Tiny scratches and cuts twinged across my skin.

Bash's voice whipped across the room like a blade. "You won't be fully healed for another few hours yet."

He opened his eyes. His gaze swirled with emotion I couldn't quite parse. He opened his Cara to me. Regret, not for what he said but the way he said it, tinged with lingering frustration. I shared my own bone-deep regret for everything that led up to losing Kinnia. He snapped his Cara shut.

"Our Anam Cara is not complete," he said.

Before I could respond, a circle of rainbow light glowed on the far wall. A door appeared and rolled to the side. The fifs changed from red to purple to brilliant white, and Councilor Odhrán entered with Councilor Ambrocio at his side. The short elf bounced with every step, but the old fae's beard dragged on the ground behind him. The door rolled shut behind them and disappeared.

"Commander Zelimir." Councilor Odhrán opened his little arms, flourishing his rainbow robes. "I'm so sorry for your accommodations, but in light of recent events, I'm sure you understand."

Part of me wanted to pounce on the councilors, throttle them, and demand answers for everything they'd done in the last couple months. The part of me that my father raised folded my hands behind my back, and nodded. "Of course. This is a stressful situation."

"Stressful?" Councilor Ambrocio cried. "Your mate almost killed a full Cara, that was just doing their duty during the trial. He summoned a beast that—"

"You tried to kill our mate." Teyr took a step forward with fire in his slitted gaze.

"She's a freak, an unknown, an abomination." Yellow mist poured from Councilor Ambrocio's ears.

I winced. In someone else's mouth, those words finally sounded as cruel as everyone said they were.

Councilor Odhrán stepped in front of his colleague. "Calm yourself, Ambrocio. I allowed you to accompany me. I can send you away just as easily."

Councilor Ambrocio grumbled but stepped back. One knot loosened in my gut as another tightened. The Councilors were no more united than they had been, but I didn't like how easily Councilor Odhrán handled Councilor Ambrocio, as if he outranked him.

"We understand you are an esteemed Cara without a blemish on your seventy-five-year record before recent events." Councilor Odhrán smiled. "I'd like to bring you before the Councils to tell your side of the story. As a show of good faith"—he flicked his wrist—"I'll even loosen up on that pesky magic suppression so you may use your natural Cara communication to discuss."

The pressure lightened ever so slightly. I *pulsed* to each of my mates. They each responded in the affirmative, clear and comfortingly steady.

I inclined my head. "Thank you, sir. I understand how frightening this must seem from the outside, but I feel certain we can explain everything sufficiently."

Teyr *pulsed* his offense and a repetition of Bash's words at the base of the tower, but I ignored him. With the Councils' resources, we could rescue Kinnia before anything worse happened.

Councilor Odhrán clapped. "Wonderful. Before we do that, though, I want to understand the extent of Kinnia's effect on you."

My smile froze on my face.

"Will you submit to a little test? It's really just an interview with a few extra measurements." He leaned in with a small smile.

Shade and Teyr began furiously *pulsing* their refusal. Seventy-five years—more—of obedience pressed me forward.

I will not submit to anything additional, Bash said.

I glanced at my second. He met my gaze with steady gray eyes. I knew little of his past, but I recognized the intractable set of his shoulders when something brushed too close to that past. I wanted to be the leader he wanted me to be.

"Forgive me, Councilor," I said. "I'm not sure why we would need to be interviewed before the interview."

He smiled sheepishly. "Well, you know how special these circumstances are, don't you? I have to ensure there's no danger to the councilors."

My stomach roiled. He knew something, something he wasn't certain we knew. We had kept only one secret from the Councils that would make a fae holding us prisoner speak that slyly.

"Kinnia is special," I said slowly, "but I'm not sure I know what you're referring to."

Councilor Ambrocio scoffed. I ignored him. This was clearly Councilor Odhrán's show.

The short elf took a step closer and lowered his voice. "I didn't see it myself, but a handful of your fellow Anam Cara units reported cables and metal inside Kinnia's injury." He raised his eyebrows, an expression somewhere between shock and excitement. "We have to know the extent of the effect the Tech had on you before allowing you back into the audience chamber, of course."

Every instinct I had told me to run. Behind me, I felt my mates fall into ready stances. A tidal wave of *pulses* rocketed through my Cara, too fast to understand, but the feeling of the vibrations conveyed their meaning well enough. Panic. Fury. Panic again.

"I see," Councilor Odhrán said evenly. "Perhaps I should be clearer. You're deep inside the Academy. Each of you has a complete Cara dedicated to suppressing your magic. In addition, Geminai's Cara watches the door, with orders from Councilor Ambrocio and the Upper Council to do whatever it takes to keep you in this room. I would dearly love to report back that you offered your help gladly, but I'll have my answers one way or another."

A wave of intense, almost malicious curiosity radiated off the short elf. He would do awful things to learn more about Kinnia. Should we fight and maybe die, or submit and live to see another day? I began running the permutations in my head before taking a deep breath. My mates needed me. I *pulsed* the question to them.

Shade answered quickly that he would bear up under any pain to see his Kitty again, with an undercurrent of certainty that he could resist questioning. Teyr hesitated, then sent an uncharacteristically short *pulse* that he would like to live. After another moment, he shared an aching fear of what she would think of us for answering the Councils' questions.

Bash took the longest. Scales twisted and writhed across his face. He snarled to himself more than once. *I do not wish to submit.* His mental voice resounded with echoes I somehow knew meant he spoke to Shade and Teyr as well. *But neither will I die for this ridiculous fae's amusement.*

To me alone, he thought, *Thank you for the choice.*

I swallowed and faced down the short elf who held our fate in his hands.

"Well?" Councilor Odhrán asked.

"We will undergo your testing," I said.

He flicked a thin stream of magic out the door.

"But"—I drew myself up to my full height—"on no account are you to tell the others we helped gladly."

My mates stepped up beside me, forming a united line, as the door glowed and rolled open. Farquin strolled in, pushing a cart laden with pieces of metal that gleamed like Tech as the fifs dimmed to red again, and Councilor Xerxes entered after him.

Councilor Odhrán grinned. "Your wish is my command."

14

BASH

I STOOD BEHIND THE CHAIR ODHRÁN SUMMONED AND gripped the back so tightly my knuckles turned white. A flat, silver disk adhered to the center of my abdomen just above my Cara and displayed a scrolling line of numbers the Jalan seemed to be able to understand. The disc didn't hurt, but its weight kept me aware of its presence. The Jalan had attached the same sensor to all my mates. Zelimir and Shade both sat in their chairs, but Teyr stood on my left with his arms crossed.

Shade poked at the little sensor curiously. "What does it do?"

"Basic energy readout," Farquin answered.

Odhrán shot him a look. "But we have many other tools to use if this becomes difficult."

The cart of gleaming metal tools behind Farquin promised the truth of his words. In Bittermist, Dee had confessed to her strange training session with the Jalan and the way his gaze always followed her. We couldn't trust him. My dragon bellowed at me to rip through the three councilors and the Jalan between us and escape. Ambrocio had little more than his divinatory magic, and Xerxes' sensory tricks would be no match for us in a fair fight. But I had made my promise to my commander. I gripped the chair hard enough that the wood groaned.

"So, let's get started." Odhrán clapped his hands. "Councilor Xerxes, would you like to lead the way?"

The spymaster inclined his head and stepped forward. "Did you see the sparks inside your mate?"

Zelimir gritted his teeth. "In the colosseum? No."

Odhrán tapped his foot. "After?"

"No," Shade replied. "I never saw any sparks."

"Because you were too busy committing treason!" Ambrocio shouted.

Farquin put his human hand to his mouth to cover a small smile.

Xerxes inhaled slowly. "Gentlemen, if I could conduct the interrogation?"

Odhrán nodded and stepped back, dragging a scowling Ambrocio with him.

"When did you realize she had Tech inside her?" Xerxes asked.

"No sooner than you did." Zelimir crossed his arms.

"But you suspected something." The spymaster circled around us. "Or you wouldn't have lied to us so often."

I turned with him. I would not allow him unrestricted access to my back. Tension knotted my muscles, and the red of the fifs reminded me too much of light filtering through stained glass.

"We suspected she wasn't human," Zelimir said. "But the ears made us think fae influence caused the changes, not Tech."

Teyr's sensor beeped, and he jumped. Xerxes and Farquin smiled simultaneously.

"And you, ember?" Xerxes said. "What did you think?"

Teyr scowled. "I thought she was weird."

"Why?" Xerxes leaned in. "Your academic records indicate you wouldn't formulate theories without some prompting."

Teyr stared at the floor and remained silent. Gaze still on Teyr, Xerxes extended a hand toward Farquin, and Farquin handed him a thick metal band.

"The sensors will tell us if you're holding something back." He slipped the band around Teyr's head and twisted a fixture at the back until it wrapped snugly around his skull. "This will produce the truth, if you will not."

Teyr groaned. My dragon threw himself against the walls of my brain, fighting for control before they could use that against me. I squeezed my eyes shut and devoted every thought to keeping him down.

"I saw a weird memory," Teyr said tonelessly. "When she built the bridge between us. It stuttered and seemed to be missing pieces. It reminded me of a broken Tech." He gasped for breath and dropped into his chair.

The Jalan smiled openly now, just a small smile, taunting and certain.

"Good." Xerxes inclined his head. "Now, what is a 'bridge?'"

I stared at the spymaster. A moment of silence passed. All our sensors beeped.

Odhrán tapped his foot, but Xerxes merely clucked his tongue and gathered more metal bands off the cart.

"These will sap your energy, so I don't prefer them." He settled one on Zelimir's head. "We need to know much from you." He put the next band on Shade and turned to me. "I'd rather not conduct multiple sessions."

He started to put the band on my head. Manacles clicked into place in my memory. Rage flooded my system, and my dragon exploded out of my grasp. We roared in one voice. I slammed my fist into Xerxes' jaw, then launched the chair at him and bolted for the exit.

White-hot pain like nothing I'd ever felt before crashed over my body in waves. I collapsed to the floor before I even reached Farquin and his fucking cart. By the time the pain abated, a heavy circle of metal ringed my head. I hadn't even felt them put it on.

"Pain is a sense, you know," Xerxes said quietly. "I don't like wielding it, but rest assured, I will if you continue withholding information."

I sat up. The band pinched my skull, and my muscles ached with exhaustion. Despite that, I stood and walked back to my spot in line without a flicker of emotion. My dragon lay quiet in a corner of my mind, licking his wounds.

"The bridges," Xerxes said. "We have other methods of testing, but I'd like to hear it from you."

"They replace our normal Cara bonds," Zelimir said in the same flat tone Teyr used.

"They're bigger," Shade said equally dully. "Wider. More flexible and more beautiful."

"And we can reach each other across them." The words wrenched themselves from my throat, sapping something from me. At the end of long nights on the altar, I often laid there long after the priests had finished with me, too tired to move. That same feeling seeped through me now.

"We'll run more tests on that," Odhrán said. "Beyond the interrogation."

Xerxes nodded. "Let's talk a bit about how these bridges feel. You're being controlled by something Tech-like right now. How does the feeling compare?"

"Completely different," Teyr spat with his usual fire. "Kinnia's bridges are like nothing I've ever felt in seventy-five years of fighting Tech."

"My Kitty ebbs and flows like Thrae itself." Shade shook his head. "You walk in Earth's straight lines."

My sensor didn't beep. No words poured from my lips. The spymaster seemed satisfied. My muscles shook with the effort of standing.

"When did the feeling change?" he asked.

"Immediately," Zelimir said in his normal voice. "The effects of the bridge are instantaneous."

Xerxes hummed. "And before the bridges? Did you notice anything about your Cara that made you suspicious?"

"That she was strange?" My commander shook his head. "We thought her human. Any strangeness had to be that."

The spymaster clucked his tongue. "Your diplomatic upbringing shows itself, commander. Did you notice anything that feels more salient now that you know the truth of her?"

My dragon snarled. These fae knew no truth. They knew third-hand reports and torture devices. Dee could never be contained by the likes of them. But my sensor beeped, and words squirmed past my lips. "She healed fast and never scarred. And she spent years on Earth, often captured by things there."

The scent of violet alcohol teased my nose. The first time I ever touched her flawless skin, and I'd turned the memory, the information I'd learned then, over to these monsters.

Odhrán cleared his throat. "I said we'd do the technological inspection later. Please refrain from muddying the waters of this topic with that one."

Xerxes hesitated for a split second. If I hadn't spent years looking for openings, for the one priest who didn't have the stomach or the one weak link in my chains, I might've missed it. The spymaster answered to Odhrán now as well, and he resented that fact. I tucked the information in my dragon's claws as another wave of exhaustion swept over me. Centuries disappeared, and the church surrounded me once more.

Questions swam past me. Some, I answered. Others, my mates answered. Information spilled like blood across the floor that I sank onto, too exhausted even to sit. Dee's past, her habits, her secrets. What we thought she might do in an emergency, if she managed to make it back to Thrae. The "if" lodged in my side like a blade. We told them everything about a woman they doubted any of us would ever see again.

Xerxes paused in front of me. I stared up at him. His hooked face melted into that of Father Isaack, the man who took me in, taught me my lessons, and tore me apart as a curiosity once night had fallen.

"One last question," Father Isaack said. "Before we begin the...scientific part of the afternoon. How do you feel about Kinnia?"

The sensors beeped. My mates and I spoke in one flat, affectless voice.

"We love her."

15

KINNIA

THE SHARP SMELL OF ANTISEPTIC WOKE ME. MACHINES whirred nearby, but no telltale hiss of hydraulic legs greeted my ears. Bright lights blared through my closed lids. The surface underneath me was familiar, slickly cool. Nothing obvious restrained me.

I opened my eyes and found myself still in Elijah's lab. I remembered the Jalan, the cable, the revelations that followed, but I could no longer trust my memory. I had to be certain. I slid my hand across my hip and the smooth skin of my abdomen until I found the place the biggest cables always connected, where my Cara vibrated when— No. I couldn't think of them now. I pressed down. My skin squished like it always had. I poured *energy* into my hand and pressed harder, ignoring the ache of my bruising skin and empty stomach. There. Something hard. Rectangular, with a divot in the middle. A plug.

I yanked my hand away and sat up. A cable in the back of my neck pulled with a spark of pain. I reached for the cable, intending to tear it out no matter what it did, and realized with a low moan that Elijah had shaved my head while I lay unconscious. A dry sob racked my body. I pulled my knees into my chest and rocked. I had nothing of my own. Not my body, not my memories, not even my hair.

The wheeled cart covered in tools still sat next to me, bearing the bloody knife he'd used to slice me open. I didn't have to exist. It wouldn't even be killing myself—I'd have to be alive in the first place for that. I laughed in a short, hysterical burst and grabbed my bald head. The metal door in the dirt wall clanked aside. Elijah stepped into the room and stared at me as the door closed behind him.

"Hm." He shook his head and crossed to the biggest computer bank.

I trailed him with my gaze and discovered the cable in the back of my neck led into those machines.

"Your vitals are all over the place." He walked to me and pressed a hand to my breastbone, urging me to lay down.

Some useless instinct deep in my body resisted the pressure. Rainbows of cables sprouted from a metal plate on the back of his hand and fed into the webbing of flesh between each finger joint. A piece of clear tubing ran blue liquid between his pointer finger and thumb. He pressed harder, alien strength in his metal joints, and the instinct collapsed. I lay back and stared at the ceiling. Did people feel a similar metallic power when I touched them?

Elijah shuffled to the computer bank. "Your caloric intake is disastrously low, likely related to that emetic episode. Computer, SISTER nutrient compound four."

A clear cable spooled out of the table I lay on and sank into the flesh of my inner arm with a sharp pinch. Something thickly red oozed along the plastic toward me.

"I suppose I'll get used to that in time." He chuckled. "I've got some tests to run on other equipment, unfortunate timing, but after that, it's all you. I want to try toning down the activity in your amygdala, see if that reduces this pesky stress response." He grinned, not quite meeting my eyes again. "I can't wait to figure out what's making you tick. Five's gonna need it."

He whirled, white coat flaring, and strode back through the same metal door he'd entered from. The door shut automatically behind him, leaving me alone once more. I took a shaky breath in the quiet. The red stuff calmed a little of the worst pangs in my stomach. Terminology bounced through my brain, a pile of nonsense adding up to the same conclusion. I wasn't real. He'd built me for some purpose—to fix Earth,

I blearily remembered him saying—and he saw me as nothing but equipment to achieve that goal. He'd crafted my memories, my abilities, everything to achieve his ends.

The knife gleamed. The blinking lights of the computer bank turned into a set of orange eyes, a set of pink ones, both asking me if I loved life. I snorted. I couldn't love life if I wasn't alive. Elijah's manic rant chased the apparition's words. I might not be real, but what I did was. And I knew deep in my bones, that Tech destroyed. Thrae couldn't be the mistake he claimed. Not when it thrummed with life and love, not when it held my only real, good, memories.

The computer screen in the bank that the cable in my neck led to remained lit. I sat up slowly. The screen displayed a series of boxes, each tracking different numbers and lines. Only the steadily bobbing line Elijah had pointed out to me when he watched my memories looked familiar. I took a deep breath, and a different number skyrocketed. I stretched, despite the way the clear cable pulled, and a third line dipped. This was some kind of physical readout.

When he'd watched my memories, he hadn't made a single note about feelings or even the Cara. I reached for my limp bridges, then snatched my hand back. How dare I reach for that? Zelimir had been right to run. I was something worse than any of us had imagined.

In for five. Hold for five. Out for five.

My thoughts steadied, and I studied the screen again. The line that moved when I moved had reacted, but all the other numbers stayed steady through my panic. Elijah didn't calculate for emotion. The small, hopeful piece of me I had assumed was dead warmed.

I grabbed the slim, clear cable in my arm and pulled. As expected, it left my flesh easily, with nothing but a little blood and trail of the liquid in its wake. The readout didn't react. I took a deep breath.

There had to be a way out of this place. I faced the hallway of clear rooms.

My stomach revolted, attempting to expel whatever sustenance I'd gained through my arm. I clapped a hand over my mouth. I would just keep my eyes down, ignore new and old horrors alike.

I touched the cable at the back of my neck and found it to be about an inch thick. Plastic-coated, but I could feel the metal within. Too new and well-reinforced to pull out. The thin, bloody knife wouldn't help me. I needed something stronger. A few tools he hadn't used lined the bottom tray of the cart. My blood chilled as I spotted a long, fine-toothed saw with a circular handle.

The wrongness of everything here tightened my gut like a vise. Nothing on Earth should be new. And Elijah shouldn't use these instruments of torture on anyone else. I pressed thoughts of what use he might have for the saw to the back of my mind as I hefted it, scooted back to get a little slack on the cable, and placed a length of the cable on top of the cart. I had nothing to lose. I pulled *energy* into my arms and ran the saw along the cable. The teeth sank through the metal and cables, sending up sparks that pulled at my memories. I drew the blade back, then drove it forward. In two back-and-forths, the cable severed. The computer blared a high-pitched alarm.

"Shit." I leapt off the table and tore for the door in the clear wall.

The plastic floor offered little grip to my bare feet, and the feet of cable still dangling from my neck bounced against my naked spine.

I burst through the plastic door and poured *energy* into my legs as I raced past the rooms. I reached the last room and the brilliant white lights died to nothingness. Only the slap of my feet on the floor made me certain I was still running. A heavy metal door clanked open behind me. I expected yelling, more alarms, the door blockers, Tech.

"Why?" Elijah sounded genuinely confused.

His voice emanated from the darkness behind me.

Up ahead, a sliver of light seeped through the gap under a door. Electric lights began turning on behind me. Hydraulics hissed, but nothing moved around me. I gritted my teeth and coaxed a little more *energy* into my legs. The strip of light grew closer and brightened.

The electric lights caught up to me, searing my eyes. I stumbled and caught myself against a wall. On the other side, a tube empty of liquid held a slumped body with my coloring. The engraved label read, "K1N-N11." I choked back a scream and shoved away from the wall. Scant feet away, a dusty wood coatrack bearing a single white jacket stood next to a metal door. I sprinted forward.

"Stop!" Elijah shouted.

I skidded to a stop at the door and grabbed the dusty white coat off the rack. A metal panel began to descend over the door. My stomach dropped. I poured *energy* into one leg and kicked the door. The hiss of hydraulics grew louder as the door splintered away. I flung myself into the hot, dusty daylight and stumbled to a halt, breathing hard. I shoved my arms into the lab coat as I spun to face the rundown building I'd emerged from. It didn't look familiar. I scanned my surroundings but couldn't spot a single landmark in the gray hills.

Shit.

Running and hiding, capture and escape, an endless game of cat-and-mouse which would only end if I found an open rift. That had been my life for five years. I couldn't do that again.

The hydraulics grew louder beyond the slow closing door. Elijah didn't think I could escape. He didn't think I could feel or want to know. I owed Shade, all of my mates, more than finding my broken body—if they ever found a body at all. I owed them an explanation and a chance to save Thrae from his maniacal plan. I closed my eyes and reached out with my deadened Cara.

A tingle, like my mates' magic across the bridges but flavorless, pulled my mind to the left. I opened my eyes and turned. Nothing but lifeless gray landscape. The tingle could be some sort of homing beacon for Elijah or other Jalan. It could be the location of the rift I came through and a way back home.

A SpiderTech arm shot through the tiny opening at the bottom of the door the metal plate hadn't closed off yet, but the Tech missed me by a foot. A DogTech appeared at the small opening and began scrabbling to get through. The metal plate ground to a halt, leaving only three or four inches of broken door exposed. I smiled bitterly. The DogTech had jammed the metal in place. That might be the head start I needed.

I set out at a ground-eating pace in the direction of the tingle. The pull grew stronger, then familiar. The goblin's smile rose in my mind's eye. The buzzing in the air behind Punaky's Pub felt a little like this. And a little like my mates' magic, when they worked through me.

I raced up a hill, then careened downward. Unease filled my limbs, and I shortened my stride. What did Punaky's Pub and my mates' magic have in common—beyond the feeling on my skin and the sinking sensation that everything was about to change?

Hydraulics hissed in the dead Earth air. I raced forward and prayed the tingling led somewhere useful. I reached the top of a rocky hill with a sheer drop on the other side. I pressed my hand against the ground there. Warm, like pockets of magic.

What did I know about rifts? They spawned randomly. Councilor Ambrocio had insisted that anybody who said they could predict rifts was a liar. A thought struck, and I wondered why I'd never considered it before. Rifts only formed in or near the wilds. If they were truly random, they should pop up all across Thrae, even in human lands. Which meant rifts were somehow connected to the wilds.

To magic.

My heart hammered even harder. I touched the spot again. If rifts needed magic from the wilds, maybe they needed something specific from Earth too.

The hiss and whir of Tech sounded in the distance. Panic sent a tremor through me. Elijah had sent Tech after me. By the closeness of the sound, I would soon have anything Tech-specific I needed to open a rift, if I survived the encounter.

My heart skipped a beat. I didn't need Tech. Rifts formed in the wilds or around *me*. I touched the faded white line on my side and closed my eyes. In Drax's living room, I'd pulled Teyr's fire into me and pushed it into my palm across our bridge. But my bridges dangled limply, still unconnected.

"Shit."

A bead of sweat rolled down my face. I pressed my free hand to the warm ground. I couldn't rely on my mates. Instead of looking within myself, I sent my *energy* toward the ground, through the warmth. Magic danced, faint and wavering. I reached for it. My *energy* snapped back.

The hiss of hydraulics filled my ears. Far too close. If they caught me again, I'd never escape. I slammed my palms against the ground and tried to shove my *energy* out. The *energy* fought me. Elijah hadn't intended for me to use my *energy* like this. But Elijah had no idea what I was capable of. I had to find my own limits. When I built my bridge with Zelimir, my *energy* sank into his magic, penetrating him more deeply than he did me. I pushed into the ground with every muscle I had, every drop of determination. Nothing changed. I needed more fuel.

Too-even metal footfalls pounded against the ground like a rainstorm of boulders. Close and closer. I glanced over my shoulder. The vanguard of the Tech crested the hill. Elijah, in a HoldTech modified to carry a plastic chair, led them, his red eye dim and useless in the sunlight. Hate burned deep within me. My maker didn't care that I was a monster. I was just a tool he could use as he wished. Tears streamed down my cheeks. I screamed, pouring my rage and pain into my *energy*.

The power clashed with the magic's heat in a brilliant vibration that reminded me of something. The fresh tingle of magic danced. I opened my eyes. A thin, silver rift cut into the world to my right, barely wider than my shoulders. Going through would burn me. Worse, I might plummet off a cliff when I got through.

"Good luck finding me again." I pressed my hands together above my head and dove in.

16

SHADE

MY BODY VIBRATED. MY HAIR STOOD ON END. THE JALAN'S tests made my insides ripple with unknown power. Even the fur on my tail defied gravity and pointed toward the ceiling. Ambrocio and Xerxes had left when the technological inspection began. With that complete, Farquin loaded his tools back onto his cart and rattled out the only door to our prison, leaving only Odhrán behind. The door rolled shut behind him.

"I am satisfied that you are yourselves. No Tech has infiltrated your minds or bodies." The small elf almost sounded sad. "Though your Cara bonds look like nothing I've ever seen. It's as if the heart of them has been yanked out, and new, smaller connections have formed." He hummed. "Like the inside of a cable."

I licked my lips. My Kitty changed me, expanded our connection into something more, but I would never compare our bridges to cables. Magic and life bloomed in my gut.

A goblin appeared in the room and tapped Odhrán on the shoulder. I narrowed my eyes. The little gray creatures always seemed to pop up next to things I wanted to destroy. The two exchanged a few words before Odhrán turned back to us, shaking his head.

"Unfortunately," he said, "you still tried to kill us. You abandoned your duties. You hid a possible Tech from the establishment."

"Because you would have killed her," Teyr snarled. "Why would we trust you?"

I itched to call up a pack of skeletons to reinforce his point.

Our pack leader crossed his arms. "Is this our sentencing, Councilor?"

Councilor Odhrán hesitated for the briefest moment. Only my wolf ears caught the stutter in his breath. "No Cara in over half a millennium has behaved as you have. Deciding on the proper sentence will take time."

I didn't know why he might hesitate before a sentence like that, but my pack leader would know.

"Fine," Zelimir said. "When should we expect to hear?"

Councilor Odhrán threw his hands in the air. "Do you think yours is the only problem in the wilds? Rifts have become so concentrated here that all Caras are being recalled to the Academy. The Upper Council has never been so busy—to say nothing of us on the Lower Council." He smoothed a hand down his front. "You will be held here until told otherwise. I would not expect to hear soon."

He turned on his heel, and his robes swung out around him. The scent of old magic and wash of rainbow colors called to mind their smug faces as my Kitty lay drowning. Thrae's song stuttered, off-beat. The door rolled aside. I dropped to a crouch and tried to rip magic out of the ground.

I choked on dirt and crumpled to the floor as he started toward the door. Once, I'd misjudged the location on a portal and appeared deep in the ground under Bittermist Thicket. The oppressive magic of our Cara guards raced in and filled the void where mine should be instead of that crushing dirt in my lungs.

Bash placed a hand on my back with a small static shock. I jumped, and all my hair relaxed. He helped me stand and kept an arm around my shoulder. I studied my trembling fingers with mild surprise.

Breathe, Bash said in my mind. *Run through the exercises I taught you.*

My knees knocked together. I closed my eyes and imagined myself as a single brick, then a wall of bricks, then a tower of the same, all sturdy and impenetrable. Slowly, my shaking calmed. When I opened my eyes again, Odhrán stared at me. I snarled.

"Don't make any more trouble for yourselves." He called up a ball of rainbow light, which scattered into four low cots grown out of the stone floor. He smiled, then sprouted a fifth cot and left.

The fifs dimmed back to red. The door rolled shut on our prison, then disappeared. Teyr screamed and threw his hand out as if he were launching a fireball. Nothing happened.

"Fire!" Teyr spun to face our pack leader. "What now, oh leader of great leaders? Any more amazing ideas, like fucking Kinnia and dropping her into a rift?"

Zelimir frowned. "I didn't fuck her."

"Of course, you did!" Teyr shouted. "In the dirt, both of you pumped full of troggle jizz and high on magic. Don't—"

I tuned out his shouts and wrinkled my nose at the sour air. He needed the release of yelling, but little would change until quiet came. Bash's arm remained heavy and warm around my shoulders. Light often held me like this. A whine slipped past my lips. I'd awoken without his bone, and the loss ached more than my unreachable magic.

I'd never asked Light if he liked Bittermist Thicket, but I didn't have to ask if he liked the Academy. His joy showed on his face, in the way he moved, in his smile when he looked at Teyr, at all of us. In my years of memories from the tower, he helped, guided, even joked, but I didn't know if I'd seen him truly smile until we met our mates.

Teyr stepped forward, gesturing wildly. The sour smell rose until I could see it swirling around my fighting mates in crackling neon streaks. I palmed the space where Light's bone should be. I didn't need Light's bone to do what he would have wanted me to.

I patted Bash's hand in thanks, then glided between my two mates. The swirling, angry light vanished as they both stepped back and went silent.

"Light did not like the Bittermist Thicket." I stared at the ground. "I never asked because I did like it." The weight of my mates' gazes grew too heavy. I sank to the floor. "Before the pack, I thought I could do that.

Ignore things for my benefit. Make my world small. And Light"—I swallowed—"Light let me."

Teyr opened his mouth, then shut it and sat next to me.

"When I killed him, I thought I could shrink my world until there was no space for pain." I met each of my mates' gazes in turn and ached. "Thank you for keeping me. For giving me warm places to sleep. For feeding me. For petting me when I sat at your feet."

Bash sat on my other side and patted my knee.

"And...I'm sorry." I stroked my own tail. "I don't want my world to be too small for my pack."

Zelimir sat across from me, completing our circle. "I missed you."

"You will never miss me again." I got to my knees and leaned forward to capture my pack leader in a hug. I *pulsed* to Bash and Teyr.

They shuffled forward, and I crushed my mates in my arms. Most of them. My heart pinched. I let tears run down my cheeks and opened my Cara. Grief and worry, hope and joy swirled into my mates. I had never cried fae tears in front of them before.

My mates opened their Caras, and we bled together. For Light. For memories each of us would never be able to let go. And for my Kitty, on Earth without us. I didn't know how long we sat like that, but Teyr extracted himself first, and we all released one another. I settled back against the floor.

"I'm sorry." Teyr wrapped his arms around his own waist. "She's gone, and I feel so helpless." He released his waist to put a hand over his heart. "What I felt from you that night wasn't nothing, Zel. Your passion and love overwhelmed my thoughts." Teyr grinned. "Fire, seeing you through her eyes—"

Bash groaned. "Focus."

"I am focusing." Teyr's gaze slid down to my pack leader's dark chest.

My ears twitched. Zelimir's hard pectoral muscles wove together under his dark skin. His heart pounded against the side of his chest, just visible through the ringlets of copper hair there. I wanted to cup my hand over that place, feel his heartbeat in my palm. My pack leader crossed his arms, and his cheeks darkened.

Teyr grinned. "Are you blushing?"

I sighed. "I'm unsure what in Zelimir's chest I'm supposed to be looking at."

Bash grunted something that sounded like a laugh. I wagged my tail. My Kitty made us laugh, but the four of us didn't laugh alone anymore.

After a long moment, Zelimir shook his head. "She gave me the bridge, connected us. It overwhelmed me and I"—his voice broke—"I couldn't stop thinking about everything we learned in this fucking place. How Caras have always progressed according to certain rules."

I flopped, belly first, into my pack leader's lap like I would have as my wolf. He ran his fingers through my tangled hair and took a stuttering breath. I didn't think he'd apologized, but neither had Bash. Perhaps that was all right, even if it ached a little in my chest.

My bridge sprang to life. Pain seared my Kitty's sides. Her Cara swirled with hope and determination.

I shot upright. "She's alive."

17

KINNIA

I SAILED THROUGH THE RIFT INTO COOL, SWEET, THRAEN air. I opened my mouth to suck in more and got a mouthful of neon yellow-green leaves as I collided with the tree canopy. Smaller branches whipped across my face and body, but a few larger ones sent me spinning. I landed in a small clearing hard enough to lose my breath.

Muted birdsong teased my ears, and not much farther away, low conversation. I lay still and drew in deep, wheezing breaths. Then I reached for my bridges. Taut. I grinned. They stretched away from me in the same direction but turned fuzzy before I could feel their location.

I had used up most of my *energy*, but I pulled some in to push against the fuzz. Instead of the tastes I'd come to associate with my mates, I received new, strange flashes. A dandelion, blown away by the wind. A mushroom, growing and dying on repeat. The leap of a frog so brightly colored it had to be poisonous, even in the wilds.

I rubbed my eyes and pulled my *energy* back. Had Elijah broken something in me? Could I no longer reach my mates?

Like a bell in a quiet room, Zelimir's voice rang in my mind. *You're alive.*

His breathless relief lit something within me. *I missed you. Where are you? I can't feel you. I'm coming.*

My message rebounded off the fuzz. I grimaced. The more I touched the fuzz, the more it tingled like magic. Foreign magic, but magic. Whatever was wrong had nothing to do with my time on Earth.

I shoved into a sitting position. The length of cable still attached to my neck hit my back. I'd made it back to Thrae, but I remained a soulless monster with nothing to my "name" but a stolen lab coat, some cable in my neck, and an unheard-of power to create rifts. I couldn't save Thrae on my ass. I needed to find my mates and warn them before I went into hiding somewhere Elijah would never find me. He couldn't blow up Thrae without me, right? I laughed bitterly. Did he intend to blow up Thrae? Oh, why hadn't I asked more questions?

Low conversation still whispered through the trees, promising at least a first step to finding my mates. If the speakers would talk to me. I pushed to my feet, reached back, and tugged on the length of deadened cable. Without the machine powering its attachment, the cable released with one good pull. I nearly cried. A thin stream of blood dripped down the back of my neck. When I wiped the blood away, smooth skin already covered the plughole. The cable ended in a perfect rectangle, about the diameter of my thumb with four prongs. In the calm of the forest, it almost seemed silly that such a little thing had ruined my life. My existence. I wasn't alive.

"Elijah thought I wouldn't leave," I murmured.

Hearing the words out loud slowed my heartbeat a little. He couldn't control my every move, or he wouldn't have asked why I fled. Declan had been real. My mates were real. Thrae, every light and sound and color I'd loved in the years since I returned—arrived, was real. I didn't care what Elijah said about myth and belief. The colors here were brighter, the pain sharper, the emotions deeper than anything I experienced in his simulation. I wouldn't let him use me to destroy Thrae.

I pulled the white coat tighter around myself and noticed a name embroidered on the front pocket beneath the thick layer of gray dust that covered almost everything on Earth. Dr. Beatrix Miller. Whoever she was, I thanked her for dying without her coat.

I started walking through the woods toward the voices. The white coat stood out against the bright leaves and rich earth. The hem just reached my thighs, barely covering the essentials. My weapons belt sat in Shade's tower, somewhere else in the wilds. I should have taken Elijah's knife, or the saw, or anything. I didn't look like anything I'd ever seen in the wilds. Maybe I should turn back, try to find my own way instead of making contact. If something attacked, I might be able to pull on my mates' magic, but if I opened a rift right next to me—

A pub I'd never seen before that looked like a hill with walls and doors came into view up ahead. The voices issued from within. My stomach rumbled. My tongue stuck to the roof of my mouth. I'd just fought my back from Earth for the third goddamn time. I could barter or trade for something to eat. I walked into the pub. Low, yellow gemstone lamps illuminated dirt walls and chunky, neon wood furniture. A matching bar lined the back wall. Every one of the fifteen or so fae turned to gape at me.

I channeled Teyr's confidence and met their gazes,. Maybe I could find a friendly face, or an inattentive one with a pocket to pick. Not that I'd ever gotten good at that. Elaine— No. Elaine was a figment of my imagination. Or Elijah's. They were all imaginary, down to their last screams and the coppery scent of their blood in the air. Knowing that didn't stop the hole from opening in my chest. I swiped at the tears that filled my eyes. Stupid, to be crying over ones and zeroes. Stupid to think I could save or change anything anymore. I stumbled toward the nearest empty table.

Someone wrapped a warm, large hand around my upper arm and pulled me into a darkened corner booth. I started to scream, and they pressed a matching hand to my mouth.

"Declan? Or is it Kinnia now?" the woman asked in a pleasant, teasing voice.

I swallowed my scream. I knew that voice. Cordelia, Zelimir's older sister, released my mouth and arm. The gemstone light that should have shone above her table lay broken next to her cherrystone mug. Shadows draped too heavily over the booth for me to have spotted her and her dining companion, a titan wearing layers of green and yellow fabric that tumbled off his shoulders like a plant. The other titan scowled at me, but with no real heat. He didn't know me. That comforted more than I would've thought.

I faced the titan princess, and my mouth fell slightly open. I remembered her resplendent in fine gowns and royal condescension. Here, she looked the part of a warrior. Her long, copper braids coiled in a tight knot on the top of her head. Molded purple leathers clung to her body, revealing the corded muscle her gowns hid. A sword hilt, drenched with gold and gemstones, glittered at her waist.

"What are you doing here?" I demanded.

She looked me up and down, suddenly the princess I'd met. "I was going to ask you the same thing."

My mind swam. Exhaustion and hunger wound aching fingers through my body. I wanted to spill my troubles at her feet, as if she would simply whisk me back to Stoneheim, and I could return to the days before we ever arrived at the Academy. Another voice—which sounded suspiciously like Zelimir—reminded me that Cordelia had political aspirations of her own. She allied herself with Zel's father, whom he fought with constantly, and she had suggested I was some kind of spy. Which I might be.

I dropped my shaved head into my hands. I barely understood fae politics when full and rested. She touched the dried blood on the back of my neck. I jerked my head up. Cordelia pulled her hand away with a curious expression. My stomach growled louder than Shade's ever had.

"Nip," she said. "Return to the treants with my proposal. As long as it takes. Their healers would be invaluable." She tossed him a pouch of herbs.

"It's safe to leave you now, Princess?" Nip shot me another glare.

Cordelia looked me over. I couldn't imagine what she saw.

"On your way," she said. "Order us some stew on your way out, please."

Nip thumped his fist against his chest, then stood and walked to the bar.

"So." Cordelia sipped her drink. "That coat makes your legs look amazing."

A choked, hysterical laugh escaped my throat.

"You've bled on it, though." She tutted. "And white is so hard to remove stains from."

Through my haze, I recognized a bid for information. I could convince her to help if I played my cards right. "I, ah, found myself in a place I couldn't stay."

"With my brother's Cara?" Cordelia turned to press her back against the wall and stared at me.

I blanched. "No, no. I wanted to stay with my mates."

She quirked an eyebrow. "Past tense?"

Nip returned and placed two bowls of steaming stew on the table with cherrystone spoons, nodded to Cordelia, then left. I dug in, both to sate my aching stomach and to give myself a moment to think.

Past tense. Could I possibly still want to stay with my mates? Could I want anything? I needed to reach them, to save them because they shouldn't have to pay for my existence. But every time I thought about what came after, I imagined living out the rest of my days in solitude.

Elijah's delighted laugh echoed in my mind. *Unkillable.* The rest of those days might be extremely long, but that would be no more than a monster like me deserved.

I scraped the bottom of the bowl. Cordelia shoved hers in front of me. I offered her a small, grateful smile.

"It's a really long story." I poked the stew with my bright red spoon. "I just...need to find them. Do you know where they are?"

"What happens after?" She crossed her arms.

I spooned up another bite, tasting it this time. Warm fae spice and thick gravy danced on my tongue.

"That's up to them." I met her purple gaze, just a shade lighter than her brother's. Maybe they'd need me a little longer to save the world. Maybe they'd help me hide somewhere better than the dank caves I'd been imagining. Maybe—

I swallowed. I couldn't let myself think they might still want me.

A muscle twitched in Cordelia's jaw. "I have reason to believe they're being held in the Academy, a few days' ride from here."

My heart soared. A few days.

A male fae walked past our table in a cream tunic a deep red pants. A member of an Anam Secca. I inhaled sharply and choked on a bite of stew. Cordelia thumped on my back as I coughed.

The Secca officer glanced at me, and his eyes widened. I grabbed for him, but he darted away with a shout.

"Shit." If my mates were at the Academy, that probably mean the Council was looking for me. I shoveled a few more bites of stew into my mouth and washed them down with the cider. "We've got to go. Now."

Cordelia stared after him. "You're wanted by the Councils."

"And a lot of other people." I stood and stepped out of the booth. "Let's go."

We hurried out of the pub as someone began yelling. I blinked in the sun. Cordelia put two fingers in her mouth and whistled. A roc's screech pierced the air. I flattened myself to the grassy pub wall. I'd seen the birds from the caldera of the volcano. Bash told me the only way to survive a roc was not to be noticed.

Cordelia stood calmly as its shadow grew darker and darker. Maybe titans had some camouflage I didn't know about. The roc dove.

"Shit, run!" I grabbed her hand and tried to pull her away.

At the last moment, the bird spread its scintillating blue-green wings and landed softly on the ground.

She laughed. "Relax."

The massive bird shuffled its feathers back into place. As it moved, I noticed a purple leather saddle on its back. My jaw dropped.

"This is Rocky, my roc." She pulled me forward. "Forgive the name. Rocs are trained for decades, so I've had him since childhood."

I froze mere inches from the razor-sharp curve of a beak longer than my body. He bent down, and I glimpsed my reflection in the huge, dark pupils of his green eyes. I looked desperate and young.

"Rocky, this is Kinnia." She turned to me. "You go by Kinnia now?"

I blanched, the black writing on the tubes stark in my memory. "Um—"

The door to the pub slammed open. Cordelia grabbed me around the waist and lifted me like I didn't weigh a thing. The roc lowered its beak to the dirt, and she stepped on. Rocky launched us over his shoulder. I shrieked, clinging to her arms as she flipped gracefully. As one, we landed on the hard leather of the saddle with me in front. Five fae in Secca red poured out of the door, firing arrows and bolts of magic indiscriminately at us.

"Fly, my friend," Cordelia cried.

Rocky flapped his wings a few times and lifted into the air. My stomach dropped as the ground shrank away below us.

Kinnia? Zelimir said.

My breath caught. His taste exploded over my tongue, neatly tilled and tended fields in the wake of a flash flood that brought needed hydration.

We're being suppressed. I don't know if you can hear me, he said. *But I'm sorry. I knew your bridge was good the moment I felt it, and I panicked.* He paused for a long moment. *I love you too.*

Cordelia clicked her tongue. "Are you all right?"

Where are you? Zel asked. *What is your situation? Did you hear what I said earlier?*

I bit my lip. *I'm on my way,* I said. *With Cordelia. Talk soon.*

The bridge grew fuzzy again. I relaxed as much as I could.

"Now," Cordelia said. "We have some catching up to do."

18

TEYR

I SAT IN THE CENTER OF OUR STONE CELL WITH MY MATES IN a circle around me. The Caras suppressing our magic distorted communication across our bridges, but if we all focused on one bridge, we could push back enough suppression for one of us to speak. A purple itzal squeaked as it ran along one wall.

"How many rifts are being left open because the Council is wasting its resources on us?" Zelimir said, not for the first time, and put a hand on my shoulder.

We didn't know if touching helped, but it could hurt.

"We can only hope just a few," Bash answered, also not for the first time, as he grasped my other shoulder.

Shade sighed and put his hands on my knees. "I would like to talk to my Kitty directly."

After weeks and months on different pages, coming together like this to try to reach Kinnia warmed my chest. I mimicked Shade's sigh with a smile. "We drew straws, and you lost. Stop moping and focus."

He twitched his ears unhappily but closed his eyes. A moment later, I felt his earthen essence hovering at my bridge. Zelimir and Bash joined him, and I reached toward Kinnia.

Love?

Teyr. She sounded so tired. Pain and sorrow ached through her Cara, as they had since her first rush of excitement at hearing from us had died out.

How are you doing? I asked.

I'm fine, she responded tightly. *Camping with Cordelia. We're two days out now on her roc.*

Zelimir gripped my shoulder tighter. My mates could hear but not speak, so we'd discussed priorities ahead of time. We needed to get facts. What she knew, what happened to her. Hearing her flat, resigned voice, I didn't care about facts. I just wanted her to be all right.

Is Cordelia actually being helpful? I asked.

Cordelia agreed to get you guys out of there in exchange for bringing you to King Zephyr. Her voice sounded as even and sure as Zelimir's did when handing down his orders. *The Councils have gone silent, and the wilds are terrified. Cordelia says the rebellion's numbers have almost tripled since Shade's trial.*

I waited for her to ask a question, rave about the bird, repeat something Cordelia taught her. The Kinnia we lost would have told us everything about her new experiences the second she could. Silence stretched between us.

Bash shifted, his knee brushing my back, and his hand trembled. His mind magic bore the brunt of the effort to make this happen. He'd be exhausted before long.

Love, I know something's wrong, I said. *We can feel how upset you are.*

I'm not upset, Teyr. I'm destroyed. Her voice broke. *But I can't tell you like this.*

Her emotions went blank. She couldn't close her Cara, but I could picture Declan's mask slipping over her features. Numbness covered everything.

It's not a secret I'm trying to keep, but I need you safe first, she said. *We need to talk in person.*

Tears slipped down my cheeks. That sounded an awful lot like goodbye.

I love you. I wished I could hold her, show her. *Whatever's going on, we are a Cara. A family.*

She sighed. *We need to focus on getting you out. I need as many details as you can give me about your situation.*

Zelimir squeezed my shoulder. I opened my eyes to meet his purple gaze. We both knew how stubborn Kinnia could be. If she needed to focus on getting us out, I'd only be wasting time trying to talk around her.

They've dedicated a full Cara to each of us to suppress our magic, I said. *We've been told we're in the heart of the Academy, but the true heart is full of crystals jutting up from Thrae's core, and there aren't any here.*

The door rolled open. The fifs floated upward, their red glow brightening. Something impacted my shoulder with a burst of pain, and I toppled forward. My connection to Kinnia shattered. Shade growled. My commander stepped in front of me.

"I told you to hold your fire!" Drax bellowed.

I sat up and ran my finger across the tip of the bolt sticking out of my left shoulder. With gritted teeth, I reached around my arm and yanked the bolt out. Pain seared through my shoulder, but I shoved myself toward Kinnia's bridge, trying to reach her. Like every other time I'd tried to use magic in here, phantom water filled my mouth, choking and airless. I drowned until I pulled back and smashed my hand against the ground.

"I'm sorry, Councilor, but they pushed past our restraints." Chrysophylax's oily voice seeped in the door. "They could have been communing with anyone."

I groaned and turned to face the worm. He remained perfectly coiffed, as always, but still in trainee greens. I smirked. Next to him, Quin clutched a runed crossbow.

"You know exactly who they connected with," Drax hissed. "There is no use in vagaries."

Chrysophylax snicked.

Zel stepped forward. "Councilor Drax."

Our old mentor turned to him. "Commander Zelimir, the Councils have reached a verdict. They declared your Cara guilty of the uptick in rifts, the destruction of the colosseum, and an assassination attempt against the Councils." He sighed. "Arrangements are being made for a public stripping of your Cara."

I rocked back. Stripped of our Cara? Stripped of the thing that made us whole. We'd all go insane and die while the wilds watched.

"The Upper Council is in agreement?" Zel asked.

"The Upper Council did not disagree." Drax pursed his lips. "In fact, they said nothing."

"I knew you sympathized with Zelimir and his mongrel." Chrysophylax's forked tongue slipped out of his mouth. A set of leathery, red-and-blue wings burst out of his back.

I tried to push to my feet. My legs didn't respond. Bash charged. Chrysophylax sent Bash flying against the far wall with a single flap and wrapped his wings around Zelimir.

Shade leapt forward. Drax whipped two pink vines around him and pinned him to the ground, then mouthed *don't* like a warning. I looked at the bolt in my hand, glistening with runes. I never learned the language of magic beyond what I needed to close rifts, but I thought one rune looked like the symbol for "lock." Bash struggled to a sitting position. Gray blood leaked from his forehead.

The sound of fists colliding with skin and scales resounded from inside Chrysophylax's winged cocoon. A bruised and bloodied Zelimir burst from his wings. Chrysophylax took flight, panting slightly. He pressed his thumb to his split lip and looked at the golden blood there.

Bash roared, charged across the room, and rammed his head into Chrysophylax's stomach. Chrysophylax recoiled but caught himself after a few feet with his powerful wings. I snapped the bolt, felt my left side return to me, and leapt to my feet.

"I think we've had our fun." Bash grinned.

Scales crawled over Chrysophylax's entire body, and he doubled in size. Long, pointed teeth sprouted from his mouth. His ears morphed into pointed fans the width of my chest. He roared a true dragon's roar, and the walls shook. Bash stumbled back a step, and his eyes went red and blue. My stomach sank as I recognized the impact of a true dragon's mental magic.

"I had this ready for just such an occasion." Chrysophylax shrank back down to humanoid form and strutted over to Bash while pulling a leather strip from his pocket.

I launched myself at him. Drax pinned me to the ground with tingling pink whip of magic. I glared at our old mentor, but he only shook his head with that same air of warning. I fought anyway. It didn't matter if submitting might be smarter, I couldn't let my mates say I hadn't done everything I could for them. Chrysophylax fastened the collar around Bash's neck and stepped back. Bash sagged to the ground.

"I'll tell Councilor Odhrán you used the collar," Drax said solemnly.

Chrysophylax rounded on him. "Councilor Odhrán—all the councilors—recognize the dragonkin's strength, the power of our mental magic. You ought to as well."

Drax sighed and retracted the pink whips of magic from around Shade and me. "Let's give Zelimir and his mates time to adjust." Dark purple bags hung under his eyes.

Zelimir caught my gaze and *pulsed* something incomprehensible through the pressure of magic. I stood and walked over to him while rubbing my bloody shoulder. I might've broken Quin's magic, but without Cara healing, my left arm would be worthless for days. Shade joined Bash on the floor.

Chrysophylax sauntered to the councilor's side, still smirking at Bash. They stepped out and the door rolled shut, then disappeared. The fifs darkened to a low red once more.

We rushed to Bash. Shade had already begun helping the dragon to a sitting position. Bash groaned and pressed a hand to his bald head. Softly glowing crystals of all colors studded the scaled green leather strip around his neck. Deep yellow moss covered the back, holding sides of the leather together. I reached for the collar with my good arm, but a bolt of red magic lanced out and shocked me before I could get close. Bash and I groaned in unison. My hand went numb.

"Great, now neither of my arms work," I said.

"Chrysophylax wouldn't have wasted the components if we could simply remove the collar." Shade rubbed Bash's shoulders.

I took a calming breath. "At least you haven't lost your ability to state the obvious."

"Like you lost your arms?" he asked.

Fire licked along my fingers until I noticed the smirk on Shade's lips. "You're messing with me."

He nodded. "I'm trying. Is it working?"

Zelimir rubbed his face. "That's hydramoss holding the collar together. A magic plant that only grows in dragonkin territory. They're very private about its uses, but I know it's supposed to be stronger than cherrystone when sealing something."

"I can't feel my dragon." Bash said.

Zel ran his hands through his increasingly frizzy twists. Bash leaned back on his arms. Shade scratched one of his wolf ears.

Somebody had to say it. "I don't want to lose our Cara."

Bash scooted closer. The edge of his knee pressed into mine. Zelimir sent me a wave of understanding, then sat. Shade put his head in my lap, placed my numb hand between his ears, and nodded until it felt like I was petting him. I laughed, and the fear coursing through my veins eased.

"I think," Zel said slowly, "the Councils' plan will create one of two problems for us."

"I was starting to worry we didn't have enough going on." My voice cracked, betraying my bravado. I twitched a tingling thumb over Shade's head as the feeling returned.

"In one scenario, we lose our Cara," Zel said.

The words shivered down my spine. Madness. Death. Total, soul-crushing loneliness.

"In the other...." He sighed. "I don't know if they can take the Cara from us. When Kinnia filled our bond with her *energy*, it became something more. We became something more." He shook his head. "The moment the Council realizes they can't make us an example or control us...."

Relief and worry surged through me. Stripping our Cara meant they intended kill us. All the wilds knew that. And if they couldn't strip our Cara, they might as well kill us the old-fashioned way.

"Then we have to escape," I said. "And fix whatever happened to her on Earth."

Zel nodded. Shade squirmed deeper into my lap. Bash took a deep breath.

I forced my tingling hand into a fist in Shade's hair. "Whatever it takes."

19

KINNIA

SITTING ATOP ROCKY, CORDELIA AND I TORE OVER THE MUD Pits of Saltair. My frozen fingers ached from gripping the saddle. The wind whipped through Cordelia's golden sleeping pants and tunic I'd belted to my smaller frame and the white coat I wore around me for warmth in the high, cold air.

My mind drifted back to the battle in the Mud Pits that had started me on the path here. If Shade had never saved my life, Zelimir had never let me cover him, Teyr had never coaxed me into sharing some of my history, Bash had never patched me up, would I have ever loved them? If the rift had never opened in the Mud Pits, would I have simply been split from the Cara and returned to human territory, never to know what lurked inside me or how beautiful life could be? Even now, with programs in my head and cables in my chest, I couldn't quite bring myself to regret that. If I'd never known, I might not fight to save Thrae.

Cordelia clicked her tongue twice, the signal to Rocky to land. I shamelessly wrapped my arms around the princess' middle and closed my eyes. The world whistled past me as Rocky dove. She whooped. Heights hadn't been a problem for me until I tasted clouds on the back of a beast who could eat me in one bite. My heart raced.

Did I have a real heart? Elijah said something about too many organics. I'd seen flesh beneath and around the cables in my side. What about my brain? Something lab-grown? Harvested like a SpiderTech? Or nothing organic at all? The girl I'd seen in Elijah's lab, the other *sister*, did she have a computer brain? Maybe I had a computer brain for my computer memories. A shiver that had nothing to do with the cold ran through my body.

We landed, and I jumped from the bird's back into the high, dark brown grass.

"You didn't seem so skittish a couple months ago." Cordelia landed next to me. "What happened?"

A couple months ago, I'd been real. I swallowed that answer down. Cordelia had been kind so far, but if I were her, I'd kill something like me. I wouldn't even begrudge her for trying.

"Big bird go high." I flapped my hands like wings, bitterness filling my gut.

A corner of her mouth ticked up in a sarcastic smile.

I flopped onto the ground. The dirt under the grass shifted a little under my weight, but I didn't think I would punch through like in the Pits. Stooped, swampy trees brushed the ground with their blue leaves, and a small, jagged pond stretched fingers through the high grass toward us. Rocky hopped over to the pond and stuck his head in the water. Cordelia sat down next to me with a waterskin and two sticky buns.

"All right, I've let you stew long enough." She handed me a sticky bun. "You have to snap out of whatever this is if we're going to save my brother."

Anger flared brightly in my veins. "Where do you get off telling me it's been long enough?"

She scoffed. "I'm your ride, and you haven't even told me what happened. I think I'm well within my rights."

"I told you—"

"You told me you 'fell' into a wild portal and emerged naked next to the pub with that coat. No in between." She met my gaze and raised an eyebrow. "No offense, human, but you don't know nearly enough about the wilds to lie to someone who grew up here."

I held her stare. "So?"

"So," she said, "I know that look on your face, like death rides on your shoulders." She put the sticky bun on her knee and rolled the waterskin between her palms. "My mother had that look before she died."

I looked down. "Zelimir said she died when he was little."

"He was," she murmured. "But I'm older." She set down her water-skin and toyed with the ruby pendant around her neck. "Fae rarely die of sickness. Nobody knew quite what to do, but we kept him away."

Pieces began to fall into place. A sudden reminder of the fragility of life. A young son. An inheritable title someone had to accept. Zel couldn't have grown up in higher-pressure circumstances.

I grasped for the dregs of my anger. "And because of that, I should tell you all my secrets?"

"Tell me whatever you please." She dropped the pendant. "I'm telling you I'm not going on a suicide mission. And trust me"—she grabbed my chin and forced me to meet her eyes—"this will be suicide if you don't get it together."

Rocky trundled back over and settled down with his head tucked under his wing.

I jerked my chin out of her grip. "What if I don't trust you?"

"Then why are we here?" She threw her hands up. "I've made deals between warring fae clans easier than this."

I let silence reign for a moment. I just kept remembering that moment in Stoneheim when she waltzed in, set all my mates on edge, and called me a leech.

"Why?" I asked. "Why broker deals? Why help me? Why do any of this rebellion shit in the first place?"

Cordelia sighed. "If I tell you, will you promise to get yourself together?"

I stuck out my hand.

She laughed and clasped my hand. "Deal."

I took a bite of the sticky bun. Sweet bread melted in my mouth, along with meat and warm spices I couldn't identify.

Cordelia rested her weight on her hands and stared into the trees.

"My father wants to unseat the Councils because he believes they're not handling the rift problem correctly. There are many other things in this world that need to change. Everyone says fae don't work well together by nature, but I think that's an excuse. We manage it every time we need to. A little cooperation would improve the wilds for everyone. The Councils are the first thing in the way, because nobody clings to tradition as much as them, but our world is bigger than the human scourge of Tech." She shrugged. "Sorry."

I swallowed the sticky bun with a suddenly dry throat. She'd stumbled on a perfect description for me.

"I don't know if that makes sense to you, but that's what Ar-a-mach is supposed to fix." She shrugged again.

"What?"

She puffed out her chest. "Our rebellion's finally gotten big enough to need a name."

I nodded slowly. "Why do you still work with your father, then?"

She smiled a little sadly. "He was ruthless, brilliant, and unparalleled in strategy."

"Past tense?" I popped the last bite of the bun in my mouth.

She smirked but nodded. "He's still brilliant, and I believe armed rebellion is the only way to unseat the Councils, but...I've begun questioning some of his decisions, his aims. He's well over four hundred. " Her tone grew a bit softer. "I've spent a long time paving the way for Zelimir to follow in his footsteps. After everything with our mother, I wanted to be a good big sister. And now, those footsteps have been in the sand for so long that both of them are too scared to step anywhere new." She shook her head. "When you've been doing this long enough, it's hard to believe anything new isn't bad."

She met my gaze, and I heard the meaning under her words.

"I was new." I met her gaze.

She knocked back a sip of water and held the skin out to me. "Drink up. I want to be in Stoneheim before—"

The air pressure dropped with a familiar *pop*. I shot to my feet and grabbed for the sword at my—shit. Still unarmed. I spun toward the sound and found a rift nearly my height splitting the air behind Rocky.

He scrambled away awkwardly, unable to take off through the low trees. I pushed *energy* into my legs and raced forward. If I could open rifts, maybe I could close them. If I survived long enough.

A SpiderTech arm shot forward, cracking Rocky's beak. Cordelia screamed. I launched myself into the air and reached across the bridge for Zelimir's magic, picturing the one-handed sword I might be able to lift and praying two rifts couldn't open in the same place. A glob of sticky purple nothing filled my hands. Instead of bringing a blade down on the cables, I landed a completely ineffective two-handed punch.

Cordelia followed me with her slim, decorative sword and just managed to lodge the cherrystone blade in SpiderTech's arm. A laser blast grazed my shoulder.

Another SpiderTech arm whipped out and slammed into Cordelia's stomach. She flew back and landed with a *squelch*. Rocky screeched and pounced on his princess. Blaster fire sank uselessly into his wings.

Her sword remained in the SpiderTech arm. I glanced at the sick-looking magic in my hands. Bash carried an axe, but Zelimir and Teyr always coated the head in magic before he used the weapon on Tech.

I lunged for Cordelia's sword, shoving *energy* into my arms, and yanked the blade from the metal before running it across my force-covered palm. The red blade took on a patchy purple hue. I screamed and hacked at the Teck trying to crawl out of the rift. No showy moves, no perfect stances. Cordelia's fancy sword became a hatchet in my grip, but the Tech fell. The ground at my feet turned into a scrap pile.

My elbow jarred. I wiped more force onto the blade. Bad things kept happening to me, and I kept taking them. Alex and my family died, and I'd shut down. Zelimir commanded me to be alone, and I'd shut my mouth and fell in line. The Councils tried to goddamn kill me, and I'd just hoped for the fucking best. Tech followed their programming, right?

I might not be alive. I might not have a soul or a past. But I *felt*. I took a deep breath and realized the Tech in front of me all lay dead. Through the rift, I spotted a swarm of backup Tech racing toward me.

Calm filled my mind. Tech or not, I wouldn't be following anyone's orders anymore. I stepped closer. The heat of the rift licked my face. Like on Earth, I reached out with my Cara and my *energy*. Unlike on Earth, something vibrated in answer, more like my own power than the magic of my mates. I cupped my hands, gathering magic, *energy*, and my own furious determination into a ball.

With a cry, I shoved my hands into the rift. The edges wobbled and threaded with a clear, light blue. I pulled my *energy* back, and the rift surged toward my hands. But instead of burning me like usual, waves of silver and blue washed down my arms. As they reached my chest, the waves cooled me like ice water on a hot day, soothed me like a warm bath on sore muscles, welcomed me the first time Zelimir kissed me. My view of Earth shrank.

Tech needed something vital, the very life force of worlds like Thrae's magic, to survive. They bled Earth dry of that something until only Thrae remained. And I stood on the cusp between the worlds, sucking the Tech's life force into me. The edges of the rift wavered, mere inches from my wrists. I pulled my hands out and smoothed one palm over the remaining hole. A final wave of power rippled along my arm, and the rift closed.

The air pressure didn't change. No sound accompanied the rift's absence. *Energy* thrummed in my arms, my legs, everywhere. I buzzed like I'd just pounded three cups of coffee, and I couldn't keep the triumphant smile from my lips. Maybe I could save Thrae.

Cordelia cleared her throat. I turned. Rocky held her carefully down with one taloned foot. I nodded to the bird, and he released her. He'd protected his princess from harm. So had I. I guessed I'd earned the thing's respect.

She stood. I couldn't read anything in her expression, but she didn't run screaming. I reached into the pile of Tech scrap at my feet and hoisted her sword. Rocky screeched as I approached, ready to cut me down with his wings if I made the wrong move. With a flourish, I flipped her sword and extended the hilt to her.

"I'm not gonna lie," I said. "I am going through some unbelievable shit. But I intend to save your brother, and I'd like to do that at your side."

"You closed a rift. You *absorbed* a rift." Her gaze held more naked emotion than I'd seen from the princess before. Shock. Fear. Deep and true confusion.

I could wrap my arms around myself and disappear. Let hazy complaints about my origin sweep me back into their embrace. But the anger in my chest wasn't dead, only banked. It flared as I considered fleeing.

I held her gaze. "I didn't ask for this. And I can't explain it now, but I'm going to use it to fix everything I can."

She nodded slowly. "Will you tell me someday?"

I laughed. "If we survive long enough."

"I think you might be crazy." She stepped forward and grabbed the sword hilt. "But okay."

I snorted. "Would you believe you met me at a weird time in my life?"

Cordelia laughed, and I took my first full breath since that moment Zelimir backed away from me.

20

BASH

I SAT CROSS-LEGGED ON MY COT WITH MY HANDS ON MY knees and my eyes closed, listening. There remained nothing to hear. The bellowing, shifting, and prodding of my dragon had all fallen silent. He lodged in my throat, smothering me even more than the chainlike pressure of the Cara suppressing my magic.

Humans believed you couldn't miss something until it left. Not once in my life had I felt the truth of that so acutely. My dragon had voiced all the desires I spent my life repressing. Though I battled him down more often than not, I needed someone reminding me what it was to crave something so badly I hurt. I had told Dee life was about finding a way to do more than just survive. Perhaps I had forgotten that in my years of careful quiet.

The thick leather collar didn't cling tightly enough to restrict my breathing, just tight enough that I could never forget about it. Old memories fought their way forward when I dwelled on the feeling too long. At least Chrysophylax lacked any restraint. His magic lay on the piece so thickly I could nearly taste it, and that kept me grounded in the moment. I ran my finger along one of the crystals. Despite our many failures, I reached for my power and pulled. My body froze, taut against the cold chains wrapping around my limbs. I released the pull of magic and caught my breath as the chains melted away.

"Stop playing with it," Teyr said. "It has to be dragon magic, and those flying worms hoard knowledge even more than wealth."

I dropped my hand back to my knee and opened my eyes. A physical restraint like the collar couldn't be permanent. I had destroyed enough of them in my life to know.

"Chrysophylax remains a trainee." Shade fell back onto his cot and pillowed his hands behind his head. "Why wouldn't they use a fully trained Cara?"

"I asked around when Kinnia got assigned to him." Teyr sat on the floor in front of his bed. "They're stuck on their final test because their oozekin, JoJo, won't settle into a final form. Been here almost eight years. That's why he had so much time to train Kinnia."

I growled.

Shade huffed. "How do you learn all these things?

"Everybody wants to talk to me." He sighed. "Or at least, they used to."

"Is any of your information actually helpful?" I asked.

Teyr scoffed. "If we can get out of here. Slavica, a sneaky little urander-shifter I met, told me her best friend is Chrysophylax's uncle's wet-nurse. She can get us dragon milk whenever we want. It's supposed to be spicy and help prolong sex."

I exhaled slowly. "So, no."

"She also told me where his suite is." He plucked a pebble off the floor and hurled it across the room. "Just down the hall from Gnuq's wing. I'd bet gold they're working together—which means your collar belongs to one councilor, not all of them."

"It serves the same purpose." Zelimir sat on his cot with his back against the wall, picking at his fingernails.

I couldn't imagine what Gnuq wanted with me, and Chrysophylax seemed to trail Odhrán around. Perhaps Teyr's information was out-of-date.

Shade sat up. "A skeleton could pull the collar off. No one considers the undead." The necromancer turned to me with a wild, desperate look in his eyes, as though asking me for permission to dive however deep he needed to find his magic again.

"We want to avoid hurting our fellow Caras," Zelimir said quickly. "We're still all fighting for the safety of Thrae. They are following orders, just as we have in the past. Right, Shade?"

He nodded, though he clutched his blankets in one tight fist. "Chrysophylax?"

My commander glanced at me. "That might be different."

Shade bounced up and bounded over to Zelimir's cot. Though the magic suppression kept him in fae form, Shade dropped onto the cot. Zelimir scratched his head.

"Geminai's Cara delivers our meals," Zelimir said.

We'd been planning like this for hours or days, always starting there.

Teyr picked up the next refrain. "They don't seem thrilled with babysitting duty, either."

Zelimir sighed. "And they wouldn't be delivering our meals if we weren't still a secret from the public."

"And they wouldn't have been chosen if they didn't belong to someone," Teyr said. "If that Chrysophylax is in Gnuq's pocket, who does Geminai belong to?"

Finally, a new avenue to explore. "Xerxes would want nothing to do with the troll."

"Geminai is less subtle than most landslides." Teyr snickered.

Zelimir nodded. "Councilor Drax would not ally himself with such fae."

"Councilor Drax may have no allies but us." I stared at the distant ceiling. He had given us what he could with the dragonkin nearby, and one thing seemed clear. He did not support the Council's current behavior, and he would do what he could.

Teyr shook his head.

"Geminai shares Councilor Ambrocio's dully regressive attitudes about humans and everything else interesting," Shade said. "Perhaps they are aligned to make boringness reign over the wilds."

Teyr started laughing, but Zelimir put up a hand.

"Shade, we need to focus." My commander sighed. "When Geminai wanted to impress someone, he used to tell that awful story about felling a Tech when he was young. Orders or not, I doubt he'd swear himself to Councilor Odhrán, given how closely the councilor has aligned himself with Tech. You saw the free rein he gave Farquin with us."

I nodded slowly. "That leaves Councilor Ambrocio."

Zelimir pursed his lips. "Unless he's jumped the line to ally directly with the Upper Council."

"All we need to know is that it's not Odhrán." Teyr leaned forward. "Everyone else cares more about appearances. Do you think they'd send them down unarmed to keep trainees from getting suspicious?"

Zelimir stroked Shade's hair and smiled. "I think that's something we can figure out next mealtime."

I WOKE EARLY THE FOLLOWING MORNING, RAN THROUGH MY exercises as best I could, then sat and waited. Last night, we'd watched Terris bring us what we believed to be dinner. He didn't even carry the hilt he usually summoned his air blade into, so at breakfast, we would strike.

I touched the moss at the back of my collar. My mates knew nothing of the particular agony the collar caused. In the morning quiet, loneliness ached through my bones.

Dee, I called across the bridge. *We're coming for you.*

I couldn't reach her through the suppression, but trying eased the ache.

I will do what I must to break these shackles and return to your side. Nothing on Thrae or Earth can stop me. I took an unsteady breath. *Not even myself.*

As expected, no answer. I threw myself into fitful meditation until my mates rose.

When even Teyr sat blearily upright on his cot, I strode to the middle of the room and began working through one of Dee's morning routines. My commander stood and stretched with me when he recognized a particular slash. Teyr shoved out of bed at a slow point in the routine and took the space on my left with much grumbling. After a particularly furious combination, Shade joined us carefully, marking the moves his still-unsteady fae muscles couldn't replicate.

We'd moved like this when we left the Academy the first time, like five limbs attached to the same body. Once we had Dee back, we would be unstoppable.

The hour approached. Teyr and I took position on each side of where the door kept appearing. Shade joined me. We hoped the magic suppression would fade as we exited our cell, but if not, I was prepared to carry the necromancer for part of our flight. Zelimir stood in the middle of the room. We only needed to get far enough for Shade to portal us out. Battle-clarity tingled through my fingers. I growled in the space where my dragon's bellow should have sounded.

"Open," someone said on the far side of the door.

I nodded to Zelimir. The moment a crescent of light cracked into our dim red space, Zelimir charged. No magic, no tricks, just blunt force. I grinned, savage and pleased. The door had rolled half-open by the time Zel reached it, and he hit the Exilis, Geminai's fairy healer, square in the stomach with his head. Food flew across the room. Exilis skidded on his ass down the hall. Zelimir sprinted into the hall. Teyr, Shade, and I took off after him.

As I passed Exilis, he sat up groggily and opened his mouth. "Hel—"

I kicked him in the head, and he slumped to the floor. Doors rolled open on each side of the hall. I ignored them and raced behind my mates toward the T-intersection at the end of the hall. The farther we got from the prison, the more the chill of the chains slipped away. My magic returned, though my dragon remained trapped.

A few feet ahead of me, Shade melted into his wolf with a howl and pressed his nose to the ground. Zelimir and Teyr paused at the intersection until Shade's loping stride brought him alongside, and they all pelted to the left. I roared and followed.

By the pounding footfalls, legions pursued us. A constant, backward flow of air slowed us. Something sharp dug into my calf. The stone under my feet shook. Spikes drove upward into my bare soles. I grunted in pain.

Zelimir reached back, grabbed my hand, and yanked me forward. Shade swung two sharp rights. The wind disappeared as we vaulted up a flight of stairs. We burst into a mostly empty lecture hall. I checked the room's four doors, two at the bottom of the rows of desks, one behind us, and one across the upper deck. Exactly what we needed, except for the trainee Secca sitting at desks in the middle with books spread in front of them, gaping up at us.

"Run," I growled.

One fae jumped to his feet. The rest remained frozen. My magic flowed through my veins, begging me to loose its power. I slowed and began wrapping tendrils of telekinesis into every crack of the collar.

"Fuck them," Teyr hissed.

Shade melted back into fae form and began muttering. Hoofbeats pounded the floor behind me. Something massive collided with my back, and I crashed through several rows of seats.

Someone landed on top of me. With a breath, I recognized the barnyard scent of Brettrus, Geminai's second. I tried to tear him off, but my focus split between him and the collar. Without my dragon, I couldn't do both. He kept his hold easily.

"Bash!" Zelimir shouted.

I craned my neck to see him a row down and a few desks over. Geminai pinned Zelimir with his massive troll body, and Lir's Cara clustered around him, wielding all the elements of the world to keep him down. It took six fae to stop my commander. I would make them use at least as many for me.

I turned to Brettrus and grinned.

A full Cara I didn't recognize circled Brettrus and me. They closed their eyes as one, and the chains landed on me once more. A roar tore from my throat, and I searched for my other mates.

Teyr stood halfway down one set of amphitheater stairs, trapped in a column of Terris' whipping wind. Every fireball he summoned fizzled into sparks. Another Cara burst onto the stairs and extinguished even those. Shade remained at the top of the stairs, trying to summon his portal while dodging the golden bhelrian I knew to be Xerxes. Gnuq,

Odhrán, and Ambrocio stepped through one of the lower doors and closed it behind them.

"You test the limits of my kindness," Odhrán growled.

Shade howled. Odhrán summoned a rainbow cage around him. Yet another full Cara approached, and he shrank back against the wall.

I scanned the Caras holding us, memorizing faces. They would not get away with this. My dragon's roar of agreement would have given me the strength to fight. The silence drove me half-mad.

"It's not right," Zelimir ground out. "The Councils have decided to blame us instead of learning the truth."

Geminai stood and hoisted Zelimir to his feet.

"Kinnia isn't your enemy," he said. "The councilors tried to—"

Odhrán waved a hand. A rainbow gag appeared in my commander's mouth.

"The councilors tried to kill her!" Teyr hollered over the whipping wind. "They thought power was more important than—"

Another gesture from Odhrán, and Teyr, too, was gagged.

"More important than progress," Shade said. "Than magic. Than lo—"

Odhrán gagged Shade. Only I remained.

"Than love!" I bellowed. "We are prisoners for nothing!"

Thick, rainbow fabric filled my mouth. Silence fell. The trainee Secca stared back and forth between the councilors and us with wide eyes. Brettrus lifted me to my feet. I made myself dead weight and watched his arm muscles tremble.

Gnuq clapped. "This room is no longer open to trainees."

The Cara ducked their heads and scurried out the far lower door. In their haste, they left it open behind them. Xerxes transformed out of his bhelrian and landed next to Ambrocio. The old fae looked more ancient than usual. He lifted his arm at an odd angle with especially aching slowness to reveal a slim, leather bracelet with a shifting, dark oval on it. Even without my magic, I recognized the oval as a miniature of the Upper Council's portal, which Ambrocio had positioned to view the room.

Odhrán tutted. "I don't know why I expected you to follow orders, except for your seventy-five years of training."

"We should've expelled them the moment they crossed our threshold with that—that *thing*," Ambrocio hissed.

Odhrán didn't even twitch in his direction.

"I wouldn't go that far." Gnuq ran a hand over his lower stomach. "I've so enjoyed watching them struggle."

Odhrán rolled his eyes. Xerxes said nothing. He looked from one of my mates to the next, studying each of us in turn. When he looked at me, I saw no malice or pleasure in his eyes. Merely slight disappointment and sharp interest.

"Regardless." Odhrán straightened. "The date is set. Make your peace with each other. In three days, we strip you of your Cara."

A few of the Cara mates in the room gasped. I met my commander's grim gaze. We had three days to be ready to fight again. Fae began dragging us out of the room. I remained boneless, making Brettrus struggle as much as possible while I watched the room. Gnuq and Odhrán fell into conversation. Ambrocio stared blankly at his bracelet. Xerxes' gaze never left us.

Through the door the trainees left open, I spotted a swath of blond hair and a bit of metal plating. Farquin. He leaned into the doorway and watched us with the same small smile he'd worn during our testing.

One of the Cara mates suppressing my magic drifted a little too close. I kicked him in the back of the knee, sending him crumpling to the ground.

In the brief loosening of the chains, I thought in Farquin's direction, *We love her regardless.*

The Jalan cocked his head to the side and smiled wider.

21

KINNIA

ROCKY LANDED ON THE ROOF OF ONE OF STONEHEIM'S enormous towers. Cordelia began hustling me inside as soon as our feet touched stone.

"Everyone knows your face," Cordelia said. "Father has made you the symbol of Ar-a-mach."

"Okay?" I batted her hand from my arm. "So what?"

She paused on the narrow staircase leading off the roof and crossed her arms. "So, you need to hide if you don't want him descending on you before we ever reach my brother. My quarters await."

I'd been worried the return to her palace home would turn Cordelia back into the condescending princess I'd first met. Instead, she baldly announced we were flouting her father. I hurried down the staircase behind her.

Her quarters covered the top two floors of the tower we'd landed on and bore the same rich purple and gold decorations as the room where my mates and I had stayed. Instead of five beds, she had one, along with a massive desk. She devoted the whole top floor to a closet, but the effect was strangely homey.

She pulled aside a tapestry and pressed her hand against a line of runes etched into the stone wall. "That should keep us hidden." She sighed. "Rocky's not the subtlest with his arrival, but we'll be all right for one night." She glanced around. "Father can't enter without my knowledge, nor can anyone else."

"Okay," I said. "And tomorrow—"

Someone knocked on the door. She waved me up the spiral staircase, then started toward the door. I ran up three stairs, then flattened myself against the wall where I could just peek around the edge of the stairs. A male titan I didn't recognize stepped in, wheeling a food cart.

"Rizon." Cordelia accepted the cart and sat on the chair at her desk. "You're too good to me. What have I missed?"

The titan clasped his hands behind his back. "The treants are interested in the deal you proposed, but they need a firmer timeline. Movement is, for obvious reasons, a concern for them."

One of the books I'd read in the library had explained treants were an extremely long-lived clan of gifted, treelike healers who rarely moved more than ten or fifteen feet in a year in order to protect their root systems.

Cordelia nodded. "Tell them we've got a guild of portal mages who wish to speak to them about the possibility of transmitting them or their magic across the miles needed to reach the battle."

Rizon quirked an eyebrow. "We do?"

"Working on it." She smiled tiredly.

He nodded. "Nothing more on the movements of the dragonkin, but rumors have surfaced that they believe the Council are a problem for other fae. The dragons' only interest lies in the girl and her potential."

Cordelia scoffed. "I told Father that would happen. It's the embers we need to keep an eye on."

"I'll reassign some people." Rizon paused. "There is news of your brother."

My heart pounded.

"Several new Cara-trainee recruits report he's being kept at the Academy, which we knew, but he and his mates made something of a jail-break yesterday. Four councilors—the ones you'd expect—appeared to stop them. Apparently, there was some rather convincing yelling about falsely assigned blame and the Councils superimposing their will on the magic of Thrae."

It took all my will not to launch myself down the stairs to question the man. Did my mates survive? Were they hurt? Which councilors? Was Drax on our side? I couldn't imagine the kindly old man I'd lived with thinking my mates should be imprisoned for any of the things we'd done. I forced calm. Cordelia hid me for a reason. I couldn't save anyone if I blew my cover now.

"Their Cara is set to be stripped two days hence, in the nearest caldera because the colosseum remains ruined," Rizon said. "King Zephyr is invited, with entourage."

I blanched. Two days to save them, and we had to rest tonight. Not a lot of margin for error.

Cordelia nodded. "This is all good to know. Total recruitment?"

"A little over two hundred."

She grinned. "Thank you, Rizon. That will be all."

Rizon exited her room. I stepped from the staircase, and she turned to meet my gaze.

"Nosy," she said. "Want to eat?"

"Do you think they're hurt?" I demanded. "Should we still rest? What about—"

Cordelia put up a hand. "We've been traveling nonstop for four days. I'm going to eat, shower, and put on something a little less grimy. After you've done the same, we can discuss."

I huffed. "But—"

She touched a rune on the surface of her desk, and the wooden behemoth transformed into a few low couches around a table. "No buts."

Cordelia had the same stubborn set to her shoulders as Zelimir. I obeyed.

When both of us had eaten, showered, and donned matching sets of soft, well-fitting purple pajamas, I collapsed onto one of the couches. Cordelia took the one across from me.

"Well?" I muttered. "Can I ask now?"

She chuckled and pressed a small rune in the corner of the coffee table the couches surrounded. "I think it's time."

The top of the table dissolved into a map of the Academy grounds. Along one side, five small, reddish stones labeled with each of the councilors' names floated. On the other, floated a single stone, slightly darker in color, labeled "Upper Council."

I sat up. "Whoa."

She shrugged, but she wore a small, proud smile. "We can't go up against the Councils without knowing them."

"The stones?" I asked.

"Information." She frowned. "Everything we've got on them, though it's never enough."

I stared at the single stone for the Upper Council and wished I could tell her something new about them. "Do you have a plan?"

She ran her hand over the golden scarf she'd used to tie her hair up. "I get us in. You get my brother and get us out."

I pursed my lips. "Any hows in that plan?"

"I've got one," she said. "But you're not gonna like it, so let's talk through yours first."

I grimaced. "Not very encouraging."

She grinned and said nothing.

"All right, exits." I sighed. "No Rocky, I'm assume?"

Cordelia shook her head. "Solo missions only."

I pointed to the stables on the map. "Then that's our best chance. We left our mounts when we fled."

She nodded. "It would be strange for me to arrive without a guard, so we'll ride in and get stabled there as well."

"As for getting to them...can we send a message ahead?" I couldn't believe Drax would imprison my mates, and if he wasn't doing that, maybe he would help.

"It's a risk." Cordelia wrinkled her nose. "Anything out of the ordinary draws attention to us."

I scrubbed a hand across my face. "Then I need to know your in."

She smiled primly. "A member of my royal family was recently involved in a public incident. It would be strange if we didn't ask to check on him."

I frowned. "What about me?"

"I'll arrive with a small entourage and be ushered into the audience chamber as quickly as they can gather the Lower Council." She chuckled. "If they have their way, I'll be ushered out just as quickly."

If I could see Drax, I could get him a message. I just had to believe he really was the fae I thought. "So, I'll be one of the guards?"

"Father only employs titans." Cordelia touched a rune in the arm of the couch, and a dress floated down from upstairs. "You'll be my attendant."

Glittering, soft purple fabric fizzed out of the ridiculously low neckline, down over a fine-boned corset, and into useless, off-the-shoulder swags. The long skirt had less glitter, but I could tell by the way the fabric shifted that it would cling to every crevice of my body. Just as I was reassuring myself the dress had okay coverage below the waist, it juddered to a stop a few feet from me, revealing twin slits stopping at—I hoped—midthigh.

I gaped. "What is this shit?"

Cordelia pulled a long, golden wig from a drawer in the coffee table. "I go everywhere with an attendant."

I crossed my arms. "Except to pubs to meet with informants."

She laughed. "Rocky ate my last attendant."

I narrowed my eyes. "You literally threw me onto his back."

"You both got over it." She grinned. "I think he even likes you, now that you've saved my life."

I ran my hand down the silky fabric. "I can't picture myself in this."

"Exactly." Cordelia shook out the wig. "Tylwyth teg are a rare species of fae known for weak illusion magic and seductive tendencies. Even suspicious councilors won't look twice." She chuckled. "Can you imagine one of the Lower Council getting ensnared by such a middle-power fae?"

The skirt gave me plenty of room to move. I could probably hide a dagger in the bodice. I frowned and ran a hand over my shaved head. I'd never worn anything this feminine in my life. What few skirts I had in childhood were ragged, and I wore them over a few pairs of tights or leggings to keep warm.

No. I had no childhood, no skirts.

Cordelia peered at me. "What's going on in your head?"

I bit my lip. "Do you think I'll look pretty?" It kept me from spilling my whole inner monologue, robotics and all.

She stood. "Let's find out."

"What?" My face went hot. "Now?"

She smiled, and her gaze softened. "What's a sleepover without a little dress-up?" She swept the dress out of the air and strode up the stairs, the wig in hand.

My stomach flipped, but I followed her. Better to know now.

At her instruction, I stripped down. My cheeks burned even hotter. She loosened the corset, then dropped the dress over my head. The fabric settled softly against my skin.

She circled behind me, pulled the corset into place, and tightened the laces. I caught my breath at the first pull, but once fully tied, it didn't restrict my breathing as much as my tighter bindings had. Lastly, she offered me a pair of silvery-purple heels. I slipped into them and laced the ribbons up my shins.

"How does it feel?" she asked.

I swallowed. "Soft."

"Good." She walked over to a flat panel of wall with another rune. "Come here."

I wobbled across the room. She laughed and pressed her hand to the rune. The panel faded into a mirror. I stumbled back a step and looked away.

"Uh-uh," she said. "You have to see this. I'll stay up all night if you don't look."

I clenched my teeth and looked. In the mirror stood someone I did and didn't know. I slowly straightened. The person staring back at me had my own eyes, my broad shoulders, my hand twitching for my absent weapons belt. But the rest....

I'd seen myself in pools, in baths, in the tiny hand mirror I carried as a mercenary to make people believe I shaved, but never a full-length mirror like this. Lean muscle corded my bare arms and the flashes of leg. My stance reminded me of Bash's, wide and ready for anything stance. I had Declan's set to my shoulders and Kinnia's grace.

I'd always expected to look strong. I didn't expect the softness of my cheeks, the curve of my hips, the way the corset pressed my breasts forward as if asking to be touched. Tears slipped from my eyes. The person that stood in the mirror looked like someone my mates could love, dress or no dress. Maybe even Tech or no Tech.

I met Cordelia's gaze in the mirror. She'd pressed a hand to her mouth, but I made out the curve of a fond smile.

"Thank you," I murmured.

"You can keep the dress, if we don't destroy it tomorrow." She straightened her hair scarf. "Now come on. I'm exhausted."

22

TEYR

My mouth tasted like dirt. Sleep clouded my mind. I rolled onto my back on one of the thin cots Odhrán had conjured up for us, and something pressed into the back of my neck.

I rolled over and stuffed my arms under the pillow. A tug at the back of my neck cut through the haze of sleep. I remembered that stupid lecture hall, finishing each other's sentences, and being escorted out. Nothing about getting back here. I rolled over and rubbed my eyes. The skin on my neck tugged again.

I sat up, opened my eyes, and stared down at my hands. Wooden cuffs, rough like bark, encircled each of my wrists. They didn't connect to each other, but long strings of braided copper and rich, purple vines wound out of them and up my arms. What in Fire? These didn't look like anything I'd ever seen before.

"We all have them," Zelimir said.

Nausea chased a bit more grogginess away, and I looked up to see each of my mates wore the same new accessory. Shade lay on the floor in a wolflike ball with his fae head on Zel's foot. Our fearless commander sat upright on his bed, staring at his own cuffs. Bash faced the wall, his hands on his knees. The twists of copper and vine from his cuffs sank into the skin on each side of his neck just below the leather collar.

"What?" I said.

Despite my requests, we had never gotten coffee in here, and the only thing that kind of woke me up was remembering Kinnia out there, coming for us. I reached for Kinnia's Cara like I had every morning since she'd landed back on Thrae. My Cara ended in a short, fuzzy haze. A silent haze. My heart thundered. I stared at Zelimir like he had the answer.

"I can't feel any of you either." Shade sat up. "You are well. We must assume my Kitty is too."

I sucked in a deep breath, my sleep-addled mind struggling to keep up. "Is this because we escaped?"

"No one has explained." Zelimir sighed. "But I must assume so, given *that*."

He gestured to the door, and I shifted to look in the direction he indicated. A thick wall of iridescent magic shimmered in front of the door they hadn't bothered to make disappear.

Shade blew out a long breath and slumped back to the floor. Zelimir didn't explain any further. Bash didn't even move. Which meant my sorry mates had been sitting around since they each made the same series of discoveries. They needed me to be an early riser, or all their mornings would be dismal.

I hopped off my cot, yawned, and faced the door. "So, what have we tried?"

"To understand it. The wall is several feet thick, and powered by, as far as Shade can tell, four additional Caras." Zel raised his wrists. "These will maintain an even more intensive magic dampening effect no matter how far we run. There is nothing to try."

I faced them. "There's got to be something. They haven't brought food yet, right? We don't know what they might've missed there."

Shade shared a shred of hope, but Zel shook his head.

"They won't leave us the exact same opening. I'd be surprised if the magic even dropped for food." Our commander leaned back on his arms.

"We've got one day until they strip our Cara. We don't have time for another plan."

My heart thudded unevenly. I tried to pull my worry into fire, but water filled my lungs and blended with that dirt taste.

"We're not just going to let them do that," I said. "We don't know what *Dee-saster* might strike the Councils."

Bash ground his teeth so hard I could hear it across the room. No one else replied.

"Fire, do you really just want to roll over and die? After all this?" I threw my hands in the air. Maybe a little anger would motivate them where excitement wouldn't. "What kind of commander are you, Zelly?"

Zel only shook his head. Not even a reproach for the nickname I knew he hated.

I sank back down onto my cot. The despair in the room seeped into my bones. Even during the bad months, just after we lost Light, I could usually get Zel or Bash to say something. But this? I had no idea what to do with this.

The door rolled aside, and I straightened. I wouldn't miss our opening. The ember from Chrysophylax's Cara, Oisin, stood in the doorway behind the shimmering wall of magic with a tray full of food. His long, golden hair fell in a perfect ponytail down his back, and both his ears glittered with earrings, despite the trainee greens he still wore. He looked like a perfect ember, the kind they printed pamphlets about. My temper warmed my veins.

"How's it feel, being reduced to cafeteria lady?" I called. "Bet you didn't expect this when you left Emberhold."

He snorted and set the tray of food on the ground near the barrier. Like Zel guessed, the barrier didn't move. Instead, it reached shimmering fingers of magic out and began pulling the tray into itself like an ooze.

"What, Councilors got your tongue?" I stood and smirked. "How does their asshole taste, by the way?"

"You don't threaten me." Oisin pulled his ponytail over his shoulder and stroked it. "You're a heathen. You abandoned our ways as soon as it became difficult to keep them. I consider this a kindness to a fallen brother."

My face heated. Anger flickered in my chest, and I itched for my fire.

"I didn't abandon them." My voice came out higher than usual. "They're wrong. I reject them."

Oisin smiled. "I suppose that would be a comforting thought in your position."

I scrubbed my hands over my pants. We hadn't been offered so much as a bucket of water to clean up with. Grime coated my skin, and I could feel Oisin noticing it.

Zelimir appeared at my shoulder, towering over me. "We are all ordered to give ourselves over to the Cara and the Councils as our highest arbiter. It seems you've failed this basic requirement."

His warmth reminded me of when he pushed calm over the Cara, but I didn't want to calm down. I didn't want to be saved.

"And I would've rejected them anyway!" I yelled.

Oisin laughed and started to turn away as the food tray ejected out of the magic barrier on our side with a clatter. My ears rang. I'd heard that laughter enough times. All through school. When I first entered the dueling pits, scrawny and ink stained. I knew how to make people like him stop laughing.

I fell into a fighting stance, and the rush of drowning when I pulled on my magic reminded me I'd lost everything that mattered. I couldn't even feel my mates through the Cara. I snarled. I'd learned a lot of information around the Academy this time around, and about Chrysophylax's Cara most of all.

"I hear the priests never let you into the temple before you left," I called. "Don't you ever wonder what you missed?" I leaned forward with a grin. "Because I could teach you with my heathen lips."

Oisin turned back toward me, his composure shattering down the middle as rage contorted his features. "They told you—" He stopped himself and straightened, though he couldn't quite regain his poise. "Door close."

The door rolled shut as he turned on his heel and stormed away.

I grinned, not even bothering to look at my somber mates to cele-brate. I didn't need them. Not to fight my battles, and not for this. I knew the best way to crush an ember was his pride. Though I wished Kinnia could've seen me.

23

KINNIA

Five guards accompanied us to the Academy. Cordelia chose four, and her father assigned the fifth. Her four guards paid me no attention, but her father's, Tellis, always had one eye on me. Either he knew, or daddy titan really didn't like new things. I ignored him.

When I woke this morning, I'd strummed my bridges, as had become a morning habit since my return to Thrae. Foreign images still clouded my mind, the same I'd grown used to over our days of travel, but something new underpinned them. A thick grittiness in the back of my throat. My *energy* sank into the feeling almost like the frisson of power I'd found on Earth, but the grittiness tasted like dirt. In all my experimentation, I'd never felt anything like that before.

I toyed with one of the other two crystals we'd strung onto Drax's necklace to disguise it as we crossed the grounds to the main door of the Academy. According to Cordelia, both stones gave off enough magic that any suspicious onlooker should read me as fae. A cool morning breeze kissed the top of my breasts. My skirt swished with every step. I felt airy and exposed at once as trainees turned to stare at us. The attention had been just as bad in the Academy's town, which she insisted we ride through for practice.

"Stop playing with them." Cordelia kicked my ankle. "Poised, aloof, doting on my every whim after I saved you from a violent allabat shifter."

I dropped my hand back to my side and tried to relax my fingers instead of readying to grip my nonexistent sword hilt.

She sighed. "Think cloud. It's time."

Cordelia continued across the Academy's burnt orange grass. Her long-sleeved dress of dark purple velvet floated just above the dirt, powered by more of the runes I'd learned she wrote. The bodice dripped with gold, and she'd braided a thin tiara into her copper hair. She looked regal and powerful. Everything she really was.

She stopped in front of the massive, rainbow-toned door of the main Academy tower, and after a moment's hesitation, they swung open. Cordelia strode in. I trailed behind. Cloudlike. Confident, puffy, and ready to drown the world.

A small, naked pink pixie flitted up alongside us. "Princess Cordelia! We are honored by your presence. The Lower Council awaits you in the audience chamber, as requested."

I struggled not to frown. This certainly wasn't the same pixie I knew. Had Gnuq replaced his assistant once I gave her the dress?

Cordelia nodded icily, every inch the princess I'd met months ago.

"However, in exchange for the immediacy of this meeting, the councilors have asked a small concession." The pixie watched her. "No more than three may accompany you."

Cordelia stopped. "Why was I not informed of this ahead of time?"

The pixie squeaked and cowered. "Not sure, Princess/ Communications of that nature fall outside my purview. But I'm afraid I must insist, or the Councilors will bar you from the chamber."

Cordelia looked over the guards and me as if deciding between us. "Rizon, Tellis, Maia. Wait by the horses."

Her father's guard, Tellis, gritted his teeth but left with the other two.

The pixie led us to the waiting room before the audience chamber and pressed her tiny hand to the door. "They'll be just a moment."

Cordelia sat with her ankles crossed, and I stood behind her. The guards took positions by the door into the audience chamber. She gestured for me to lean down, and I did.

"Rizon and Maia can distract Tellis and ready the horses at a moment's notice," she hissed into my ear. "Laugh like I told you a joke."

I giggled, trying to channel Slavica's laughter in the baths. Cordelia nodded approvingly. The door rolled open. She stood sinuously, I walked at her shoulder like I'd been trained my whole life to do.

The Councilors sat on their thrones on the dais like usual. No, wait. I blinked and peered closer, scraping my memories. Normally, Councilor Odhrán sat on the left end, and Ambrocio in the middle. They'd swapped seats. What the hell did that mean?

Cordelia strode forward. I kicked into gear and followed her to the center of the room.

"You detained my brother secretly and without explanation," she began in a clear voice. "We had to learn this secondhand from student gossip. I understand the Councils have their own justice, but surely you understand this is far beyond what the titans can be asked to tolerate."

I tried to thrust my chest out without seeming ridiculous. Gnuq looked at me, then away. Councilor Xerxes rested his chin on his hands and stared at Cordelia. Councilor Ambrocio lifted one arm like the action hurt him and cupped the back of his neck. A dark bracelet I hadn't seen before glimmered on his wrist. Councilor Odhrán leaned against the back of his chair, less interested than I'd ever seen him.

Drax fidgeted. He seemed uncomfortable, the corners of his mouth tight as if holding back disagreements. He looked at my face, down to my chest, then stared at Cordelia. I hadn't taken his necklace off since he gave it to me. He might not recognize me, but I knew he would recognize the necklace. I just needed to find my moment.

"Good morning to you too, Princess Cordelia," Councilor Odhrán said. "How can we best address your grievance?"

"This is far more than a grievance, Councilor Odhrán." She stepped forward. "This is an infringement on the rights of not only titans, but all of faekind. We allow your Anam Seccas to roam our wilds and settle inter-clan squabbles, but the Councils' justice has never before extended to secret imprisonment of fae who've committed no known crimes. Ember-hold has informed me they will be sending their own delegate in a few days' time to discuss the harm perpetrated on one of their own, and I would not be surprised if the dragonkin sent someone for Bashu. As the first, I speak for all four of the fae you hold captive, and the wilds at large."

Councilor Xerxes smiled just a little.

"Can this be resolved by the assembled fae, then, Princess?" Councilor Odhrán asked tiredly.

She scoffed. "I certainly expect you to try. At the barest minimum, I expect to see my brother today, whole and hale. If I find him in any other state, my father the king has expressed interest in seeing what a coalition of titans, embers, and dragonkin would look like." She shook her hair back. "This is merely the latest in a series of decisions that represent your failure to prioritize the good of Thrae and faekind above the good of yourselves. I have a number of grievances to that end"—she leveled a look at Councilor Odhrán— "which I'm happy to explain as well."

Zelimir warned me she had a silver tongue, but she had more than that. Cordelia's speech delved deep into the intricacies of fae politics. I understood a few parts. Demands for information about the increase in rift activity, why so many Caras had withdrawn to the Academy, if they had a plan to move Caras and Seccas without the colosseum, which had apparently previously served as a locus point for a network of portals. Despite my confusion, I couldn't tear my eyes away from her. I believed her every word.

I looked to the Councilors to see if any of them believed. None of them had so much as shifted position, except Drax, who'd begun running his finger over the green lava flower pin he wore. Rydel's mark. I knew Drax. I could trust him. I met his gaze and set my hand on the center crystal in my necklace. He nodded minutely and offered the tiniest smile. Something in my chest released.

"Stop." Councilor Odhrán put up a hand. "There's no audience here for you to perform for, Princess. If we let you see your brother, will you put your other concerns to rest?"

"For now." Cordelia inclined her head. "But I intend to let the wilds know that you would fell the most powerful Cara to walk this land since Varsina's time because they responded to a threat *you* created." She lifted her chin. "Our magic chose her, as it has chosen every other Cara mate before. She has shown no signs of betraying that. You may not like her human blood, but you cannot hate it enough to turn away an ally in these times of turmoil."

Councilor Odhrán leaned forward with a spark of interest. "And what if the problem is more than just her human blood?"

Councilor Ambrocio shot to his feet. "She's filled—"

"With human emotions," Councilor Odhrán cut in smoothly.

I fought to keep my expression steady. None of the councilors looked surprised. They knew I wasn't human.

"Everything alive is filled with emotion," Cordelia said. "Human, fae, rational or not, those emotions are what makes us different from Tech." She pursed her lips. "Why do you bring such a thing up?"

"A mere thought experiment, Princess." Councilor Odhrán leaned back in his chair. "You will see your brother in a neutral location for ten minutes, observed."

Cordelia scowled. "How gracious. I will make sure to report your generosity to *everyone* under my father's sway." She turned and swept out of the room.

I dodged, bowed slightly, and tried to sway my hips as I followed her. Hopefully fae-aloof looked a lot like human-awkward.

We waited in the same small room, until the far door rolled aside to reveal Brettrus' minotaur bulk.

He looked us up and down. "Come with me."

Cordelia's scowl deepened. "I'm sorry, does the Lower Council intend to leave me in the care of a mere Cara mate?"

He snorted. "This or nothing."

She strode from the room ahead of him, a thundercloud darkening her brow. Brettrus and I followed, though I tried to keep Cordelia between me and his horns. I couldn't quite forget the stabbing pain of them puncturing my stomach. Even though none of the injuries I'd received in Zel's trial had been real. They'd felt as real as anything else.

After a few turns, someone called, "Wait!"

Cordelia and I turned to see Drax exiting a door several feet behind us. He stepped closer, his rainbow Council robes shimmering around his shoulders. I'd never seen him wearing them outside the audience chamber before.

"Ah, Councilor Drax." Cordelia smiled. "Much more like it. I knew the Council didn't intend to snub me during such a precarious time."

Drax inclined his head. "I'll take them from here, Brettrus."

Brettrus frowned. "My orders—"

"Are overruled by mine," Drax said. "I am not only a councilor but also tactician of all Caras." His pink gaze grew hard. "I do not want a repeat of what you allowed yesterday. Fetch your Cara and bring them to my apartments."

Brettrus scowled and scuffed a hoof against the ground. "As you command."

Drax held out his arm for Cordelia as Brettrus hurried away. She slipped her hand into the crook of his arm, and he swept her in the opposite direction of the retreating minotaur. The guards and I fell behind. No one spoke. An itzal scampered out of our path, and Drax stared at it. My heart hammered. We rounded a few more bends, and Drax opened his golden door for us. Cordelia's guards moved to flank the entrance with their burly titan arms crossed. She swept ahead, and he followed. I joined them inside.

The moment the door rolled closed, Drax opened his arms. "Kinnia?"

I threw myself into his arms so hard he stumbled two steps back. He wrapped his arms around me and rubbed my back in comforting circles. I'd never had a father. Not in my fake memories, and not in my real ones. Elaine used to whisper stories about her father, whom she loved until sickness took him. My month living with Drax was the closest I'd ever gotten.

"Drax, I'm—" His chest muffled my words. I forced myself to release him and step back.

He raised a brow.

"I'm Tech." I clawed at the bare skin of my chest. "I'm a shell filled with cables and programming." I swallowed. "And I'm still hoping you'll help me one more time."

I dropped my gaze, unwilling to see hatred transform his features. He would yell now, or attack me, or turn me over to the Councils. I was the thing that killed his family. I deserved nothing better, but he needed to know before he helped me.

He chuckled. "I don't think so."

I looked up, met his kind pink gaze. "What?"

"What do I always say?" He laid a warm hand on my bare shoulder.

"Lessons learned through trial-and-error stay with a student longer than any lecture," I answered automatically.

Drax nodded. "And I've watched you learn those lessons. The one thing Tech can't do is learn, no matter how many times they fail or who teaches them."

Tears spilled down my cheeks. "I met the Jalan who built me."

"And I met my father, and my daughter met me." Drax pulled me back to his chest. "We all come from somewhere. It's what we do with our lives that matters. You choose every day to face your fears and rise above them. There is nothing but life in that."

I drank in his words, letting them sink into my metal skeleton with the warmth of his hug.

Eventually, Cordelia cleared her throat. I stepped out of Drax's embrace and faced her. She stared at me, shoulders square and arms crossed, radiating power and disappointment. Despite the dress, she looked like the warrior I'd met on the road.

"'Weird time in your life' might have been a bit of an understatement." She looked me up and down as if trying to confirm my story. "Is this what Ambrocio was trying to say?"

I met her gaze straight on. "I'm not going to apologize for not telling you. I'd do it again. I'd do anything to save my mates."

She grabbed one of my hands and turned it over. "You cry like a child and eat like you've never been full."

I shrugged. "Organic shell. No idea what's in my head."

"No one really knows what's in there, I suppose." She sighed. "You could've killed me half a dozen times or more." A corner of her mouth lifted in a small smile. "I suppose this'll make life more interesting." Cordelia released my hand and stepped back.

Far from a ringing endorsement, but better than I'd gotten from her brother. I'd take it. At the very least, I could be certain she wouldn't want her father to know.

She faced Drax. "Kinnia lied about needing your help one last time."

My mouth fell open. Drax raised an eyebrow.

"It's not just her," Cordelia said. "I need your help. My brother does. All of faekind does."

Drax turned to the hearth. "The Lower Council is tearing itself apart. I am outvoted in every matter. Xerxes has disappeared into his networks, hoarding information the more other councilors ask for it. The Upper Council demands constant oversight, riding Ambrocio halfway to the grave, but they say nothing. Gnuq and Odhrán are half-mad with power, but I don't believe they truly sit on the same side." He sighed and faced us. "I don't know about your rebellion. I make no future promises, but you have me for this, today."

"I would love to discuss the aims of Ar-a-mach further and see if we can't come to some understanding." Cordelia straightened the tiara in her hair. "But we need a plan, and we need it fast."

"Let's see what potions I've got on hand." Drax started toward his kitchen. "And I have a little surprise for you."

24

ZELIMIR

GEMINAI AND TERRIS MARCHED ME DOWN AN INDISTINCT hallway toward an unknown fate. When the two of them showed up in our cell, I'd been shocked. I figured they'd been sent to the border for the massive mistake of nearly letting us escape. Perhaps, despite everything, those in power didn't think the four of us that important.

I tugged at my cuffs. They seemed to pull magic from our own bodies, transmute it into something new, and feed that back into us on an endless loop. The vines and copper looked too much like the cables of Earth. I thought of Farquin but doubted he'd bother using this much Thraen material.

Rumor was, Councilor Odhrán had an undue interest in Thrae-Earth designs, though I'd assumed that to be an insult directed at his goblin wife. But he'd been so different since our return. Lir said the goblin guards were his idea, and he'd welcomed Kinnia the most vocally of all. If he'd known, or suspected....

Previously, I would've thought any kind of serious Thrae-Earth hybrid designs impossible, but between these cuffs and the thrumming, magical life of Kinnia's bridge, nothing felt impossible anymore.

Through the hazy fog of the cuffs, my Cara hummed as if it expected to find something around the next corner. We rounded it and arrived at

Councilor Drax's golden door, flanked by two armed titans in Stoneheim purple and gold. Geminai opened the door and strode in as if expected. Terris prodded me, and I stumbled inside. Someone caught me with strong, dark hands. I looked up to find my sister gripping my arm. Councilor Drax stood at her shoulder, tall and proud.

"What are you...?"

The guards. Had she somehow arranged for only my release? I would turn back and rot with my mates before I left them behind, nor would I let Father control me again.

Cordelia released me and placed a hand on her hip. "A prince makes a very public escape attempt, revealing his capture to the wilds, and you thought we wouldn't check on you?"

I took a deep breath. "Father knows I am a Cara commander first."

"He's our father," Cordelia said softly. "He doesn't want to see you hurt."

My Cara flipped, tumbled, hummed. I only barely noticed through the haze.

Councilor Drax lowered himself into his usual armchair next to the roaring fire. Next to the other chair stood a tall fae with long, blonde hair. A soft purple skirt, the same color Cordelia always dressed her attendants in, framed her long, tanned legs and melted up into a glittering corset that proudly displayed her breasts. My blood stirred. I swallowed. She wasn't my Kinnia. I shouldn't even give her a second thought.

Her gaze caught mine. Kinnia's blue eyes shimmered with emotion. I lunged for her without a thought.

My sister caught me in a hug. "There, there, brother. Every eye wanders sometimes."

Geminai snickered. "So weak even a tylwyth teg's got you in knots."

Kinnia had snuck in undercover to save us, and I needed to maintain control of myself long enough for her plan to work.

"It's been too long, Geminai." Cordelia released me but kept a hand on each of my shoulders. "Tell me, is it still true that if I cut off all five of your cocks and stuck them together, they wouldn't satisfy a pixie?"

Geminai growled.

"The Council ordered you to observe." Councilor Drax summoned himself a mug of shining melony. "More, Geminai, and I will happily toss you out."

The troll scowled and leaned against the wall. I trained my gaze on my sister, focusing on the weight of her hands on my shoulders. I couldn't look at Kinnia, couldn't run to her, couldn't hold her or apologize. Not now.

Cordelia asked me a few simple questions. Any injuries. If I was being fed. If I needed anything. She hadn't arranged for my solo release, just a welfare check. I answered frankly, struggling to pay attention with Kinnia just inches away.

"What sort of torture devices are these?" She gestured to my wrists.

"I don't know," I replied.

She wheeled on Councilor Drax, who peered at my wrists. Behind them both, where I couldn't look, fabric shifted. Kinnia was looking as well.

Cordelia released me and turned to her. "We need to report home urgently. Tell the guards outside to have the others ready the horses." She tossed her braids over her shoulder and handed Kinnia a lumpy cloak. "My father must hear of this."

Kinnia started to stride across the room, and I smiled. Despite the disguise, she still walked with a warrior's tread. She seemed to catch herself and slowed. The airy dress made her look fragile, like something I should have known needed nothing more than love and protection. She disappeared through the door. I clenched my fists.

Councilor Drax looked up. "In all honesty, Princess, I have no idea what those are. There was talk of additional security measures after the recent escape attempt, but I've never seen them before."

Geminai snorted.

Councilor Drax leveled a steady glare at him. "Councilor Ambrocio is in charge of much of their day-to-day care, but Councilor Odhrán offered to take personal responsibility for their security."

Cordelia smiled tightly. "I'm sure we don't need to point fingers, Councilor. I'll get to the bottom of this."

I heard the tone of coded language but couldn't parse the meaning.

My thoughts drifted to my muddy Cara. I could feel Kinnia through the door.

Geminai grunted. "That's ten minutes."

Cordelia released my wrists. "Be strong, brother. The Council changes like the wind. Your predicament may shift any moment."

That made perfect sense. Kinnia was here. We needed to be ready.

I nodded. "I'll be ready."

Geminai grabbed me by the shoulder and shoved me into the hallway. One of the titan guards had disappeared, but the other nodded to me as I passed. Geminai led the way, and Terris dropped behind. I forced my mind into my Cara. Blurry, hazy nothingness. I stumbled. Terris swore and sent a gust of wind to push me upright.

There, under the pain, I found Kinnia. Following close behind us.

I mustered every ounce of control I had to keep my head facing forward. Despite everything I'd done, every time I pushed her away, every stupid thing I said, she still came back for us. I didn't deserve her, and I certainly wouldn't ruin her plan with something as simple as my all-consuming desire to see her.

Geminai took the same circuitous route back as he had here. I slowed in every doorway, playing up my weakness just long enough for Kinnia to be able to slip through behind us.

"Rotten fruit on a log, Zelimir," he growled. "You didn't have this much trouble getting out here."

I bent my arms and tugged on the cuffs with my teeth. "Do you have any idea what these are doing to me?"

Geminai swallowed and averted his gaze. "No one does. They're experimental."

Interesting. We continued forward until we reached the door to my cell.

Terris knocked on the door next to ours and called, "Open!"

Our cell door rolled aside to reveal the thick layers of multicolored magic.

"Zel!" Teyr yelled. "You're okay!"

Geminai stepped up behind me and knocked again. The layers shimmered and reached for me. My heart sank. If Kinnia entered, she would be just as trapped as us. I had to do something. I rammed my head backwards. The troll's nose crunched under my skull, and he bellowed in unison with my mates' shouts. I cupped the shaft of a magical spear, but my magic fizzled. A wave of air flattened me to the ground. I tried to rise, but the air kept me down.

Let them cage you, Kinnia whispered.

I couldn't tell if I heard her in my mind, or if I wanted to hear her so badly I summoned her out of Terris' air, but I went limp.

"Fucking traitor." Geminai spat a wad of grayish-yellow phlegm onto the ground inches from my head.

Terris hauled me to my feet with the air. Geminai pummeled my ribs until something cracked. More than enough time for her to get inside. Worth the pain.

"Traitor?" I wheezed. "You stand with this Tech digging into my skin." I shook my manacled wrists at him.

"You drove the Council to this." Geminai tore me out of Terris' hold. "When you're gone, the rest of it goes with you."

I laughed mirthlessly. "If you believe that, you're even dumber than I thought."

He tossed me into the room. I sank through the warm layers of magic and landed on my back. I smiled up at him through blood-stained teeth.

"We'll be back in an hour. You won't be a stain on the good name of Anam Caras much longer." Geminai smashed his fist against the other door.

Our door slammed shut. I coughed as my natural healing, not our Cara healing, began to work on the broken bones.

"Zelimir?" Shade said.

"Wait," I whispered.

"Shit."

Like blinking Kinnia appeared in the middle of the room wearing the same purple dress and blonde wig I'd seen earlier, but now with her weapon belt around her waist. I needed to tell her I loved her face-to-face, needed to watch her blue eyes light instead of dim.

"Kinnia?" Teyr sat up in his cot and stared at her.

She only tapped a quick inventory of her weapons belt, like she always did when nervous. My stomach sank.

"Dee?" Bash turned from the wall for the first time since we'd woken with the cuffs.

She didn't respond.

I took a step forward. "Kinnia, please."

She turned just as Shade launched himself across the room and bowled her over. He caught her mere inches from the floor and pressed a kiss to her lips I could almost feel through our muffled Cara.

She pried herself out of his grasp. "Just wait. I don't want you to do anything you regret."

"What could we possibly regret?" Teyr asked.

Devastation ripped through her Cara, sharp enough to cut even through the haze.

25

KINNIA

I RAN MY HAND THROUGH THE WIG, SHAKING OFF THE LAST of Drax's potion. A leftover from the civil war, the slightly out-of-date invisibility tonic had gotten me where I needed to be. Back in prison. But this time, with my mates staring at me, and mysterious, multicolored magic at my back.

I grabbed the faded golden charm on my weapons belt. Drax's surprise was that he had gone himself to retrieve everything we left in the Thicket after he'd heard my mates' story. The guard I'd sent to the horses had Bash's bright-red axe tucked safely in a holster that hid its true nature, and Shade's bone necklace in an interior pocket.

Here, now, facing them, I couldn't confess the truth of what I was. What I'd been created to do. The dark walls pressed in on me, and those sick cuffs glistened around their wrists. I'd tell them. I would. I just needed them properly safe first.

I shook my head. "Later. We need to get these cuffs off you."

Zel frowned. Shade nuzzled against me, and nausea clawed at my throat.

"They are somehow powered by our magic." Bash clinked his together. "I couldn't discover more."

"Right."

I took Bash's hands in mine and looked at the wood like that would help. Bash also wore a collar, but when I looked at that, he hunched his shoulders as if to hide it. Another problem for later.

Magic. Power. *Energy*. They weren't the same thing, but they were overtones of the same instrument.

"I think I can fix this."

Zel crossed his arms. "Our connection to you—"

I waved a hand. "Is partially blocked." I met his gaze and found an ocean of love within. "But you can still feel me. Otherwise, how would you have known to stall at every door?"

He smiled fondly. I couldn't look at him. I grasped each of their hands and placed them on my shoulders. Their skin, warm and cool, callused and smooth, against mine sparked another wave of nausea.

"Do you remember before Bash's trial, when I was trying to figure out what kind of a team we were?" I asked.

Teyr shook his head. Zelimir frowned. Shade toyed with the strap of my dress. Bash stared at a point behind me like he couldn't quite look at me.

I sighed. "We were three hard-hitters and two people kind of okay at dodging."

Teyr snapped his head up, dislodging his hand. "Yes!"

"Well"—I repositioned his hand back on my shoulder—"now we're four hard-hitters with Tech connecting us."

Zelimir sucked in a breath. I tried not to flinch. Not a good sign.

"Trust me." I laid my hands over as many of the cuffs as I could reach and tried to sound confident. "This will work."

To my surprise, they relaxed. No, I shouldn't be surprised. They didn't know the truth. Not all of it, at least.

I closed my eyes. In for five. Hold for five. Out for five. Branching piles of cables sprang to my mind, and I shoved the image away. Shade said something about my mind feeling like a river. I pictured all the channels and streams of the islands around the Academy feeding into a larger body, becoming stronger. I reached for their bridges, dammed with the foreign magic I'd been feeling for days and the grit of the cuffs.

In for five. I pushed my *energy* toward the grittiness.

Hold for five. I wrapped my *energy* around the cuffs' tingling, buzzing hooks and curves.

Out for five. I pulled my *energy* back.

My bones warmed. My stomach tingled. Power filled me, and the only thing that didn't fit was that grit. It clouded my system and fought to escape. Wood splintered, and the cuffs dropped off my mates like dead leeches.

I smiled.

The air pressure dropped, and the silver of a rift bloomed in front of my closed eyelids. I snapped my eyes open.

Zelimir yelled. Shade crumpled. Teyr leapt away. Bash grabbed my arm and shoved me behind him.

I stepped around Bash. My mates froze. This time, I gathered *energy* and guilt in my hands and thrust them into the rift. Soft hydraulics hissed. Heat rippled over my skin. The rift softened blue, and I pulled the edges along my arms, into my chest. The power filled my already-full *energy* reserves to the bursting point and clashed with the grit collecting around my joints. I breathed through the pressure and smoothed the rift away.

"Kinnia?" Zel asked.

I shook my head. I couldn't look at them. I turned to the door. Magic and *energy* didn't mix. Maybe, with all the power built up in my system, I could put out enough *energy* to disrupt the shield.

I strode forward and thrust my hands into the multicolored magic. It tingled warmly over my skin. I shoved the overflowing *energy* out, trying to send the grittiness with it. My arms shook. The ground split under my feet, rumbling wildly enough that the whole Academy must have felt it, and I stumbled. The block of magic shattered like glass, and the door exploded into splinters. The air pressure dropped again. One more trick before my show ended.

"I got this." I whirled for the new rift with my hands still out. "Get to the stables!"

My mates raced past me. I could let them leave, stay behind. I sucked in a breath. I owed them better. I closed the next rift even more easily than the last and sprinted for the door.

I skidded to a halt at sight of my mates frozen and staring at Farquin. The Jalan raised his hand and blaster with a curious smile. My stomach flipped. No.

"You know and love her still." He stared past them at me. "She is a machine. Test tube body, hand-designed infrastructure."

Bash growled. Zel held up a hand. My world turned on its head. The world stole my secrets from me every time.

"Built, born, or conjured, you have no control over her actions," Zel said.

Teyr nodded.

A door to my right started to roll aside but caught on a short cable connecting the wood to the stone of the frame. They couldn't open the door more than a few inches. I glanced down the hall. Every door for the first fifty feet of the hallway had those closures, and several were struggling to open.

Farquin chuckled. "I personally worked on the stem to connect her partially crafted brain to her mostly organic body. How would you know what is or isn't controlled?"

I had recognized him. I forced aside my swirling thoughts and strode up beside my mates. "How come I remember you and not Elijah?" I crossed my arms to hide their shaking. "No more riddles."

Zel whipped a look at me. I kept my gaze on the Jalan.

"We will find plenty of time to talk later." Farquin grinned. "But for now, I think the whole Academy felt that blast. Get running. I'll find you again before long, SISTER." He pressed a button on his neck. The air around him shimmered, and he vanished.

I yanked my gaze onto my mates. Would they ask why he called me sister? Should I say something?

A thin beam of fire shot out of the nearest door and sank into the cable holding it shut. Zel grimaced. Shade melted into his wolf.

I called up Rydel's map in my head. "Follow me." I bolted down the hallway.

My mates pounded after me.

A full-fledged Secca stormed into the narrow hallway in front of us. I yanked my sword from its sheath. Bash grabbed two of them with his telekinesis and tossed them against opposite walls. I charged.

An unarmed short elf tossed a globule of orange magic into my path, and when I stepped into it, my heel stuck in place. I couldn't get close enough for a proper jab. Teyr knocked another to the floor with white-hot fireballs.

I poured *energy* from the last rift into my arm and backhanded the elf with the flat of my sword. After all this effort, I wouldn't be caught again. He slumped to the floor. A door rolled open behind us. I took off again. The shortest path to the stables led me up a short staircase, along a hall, and down again to a totally average round, red door. Rydel's map promised the hallway we needed sat behind the door.

"Bash, anyone there?" I asked.

No life signs, Shade answered across our bridge.

I glanced at my dragon while I pushed my hand against the door. He stared back at me. If I didn't want them to ask about me, I couldn't ask about him. The door rolled aside.

Five, from the left, Shade said.

I bolted forward. We needed to hide. The first door led to a suite, the next, a study room. I shoved that door open, we all piled in, and I quietly rolled it shut just as fae thundered by in the hallway.

Clear, said Shade.

I opened the door.

We hid in rooms three more times. Twice, I caught glimpses of Geminai's gray skin through the closing door. I skidded to a halt at a T-intersection. The left path would get us there faster, but fae shouted from all directions.

Two right, Shade said. *Five left*.

"Shit." I wheeled right and came face-to-face with two fae in trainee greens with level two badges.

All seven of us froze.

One trainee with rounded, fuzzy gray ears on the top of his head peered over our shoulder, then motioned for us to follow. "This way. Quickly."

Things couldn't get worse. We followed the shifter into a Cara suite with a large window overlooking the archery training grounds. His mate, a tall, thick fae whose dark skin dripped mud, rolled the door shut behind us.

He looked at me. "I'm sorry we threw food at you."

Bash stepped to my shoulder, radiating a willingness to destroy the trainee if he lied.

I rubbed my hand over my wig. Second chances. "It's all in the past."

The trainee brightened. "Ar-a-mach!"

He and his friends thumped a fist against their chests just like Nip had in the tavern. I breathed a sigh of relief. We could trust rebels.

"Best we can do." The one with the ears threw open the window. "Put in a good word for us with Princess Cordelia?"

Zelimir groaned. Someone pounded on the door. Bash grabbed me and dove out the open window. I wrapped my arms around him and squealed. We landed softly on the orange grass. He buried his face in my neck and held on, filling me with rightness and safety. But he didn't know the truth about me. I scrambled out of his arms and yanked my skirt back into place. Teyr, Zelimir, and Shade landed around us with varying degrees of grace.

Bash stood and looked over the archery field to the stables beyond. "Straight shot."

Zel nodded. "Final stretch."

We ran. Shouts split the air as trainees spotted us. Some urged us to go faster. Others bellowed our location. Wind chased our back, pushing us faster. A deep red portal opened on my left, and Zel threw up a purple wall to block the armed fae stepping through.

A group of Cara and Secca trainees gathered on our right and fired as one. The first arrow hit the ground just behind Shade's back paws, a few others throughout our group. Bash grabbed two out of the air and launched them telekinetically back at the shooters. Teyr washed the second wave with a wave of flame.

Zel fell behind. His bulk wasn't built for speed. Bash and Teyr slowed with him. I poured *energy* into my legs and matched Shade's breakneck pace. If the titans didn't have the horses ready, I'd make sure they were by the time my mates reached the stables. We skidded into the wide door·together to see five titan guards and Cordelia, already mounted next to our saddled horses.

"You sure know how to make an entrance," she said.

I laughed breathlessly and vaulted onto my roan. "Ride on ahead."

She eyed me.

"I'll hold the mounts for my mates." The well-trained horses wouldn't move without their masters. "I need a moment."

"You owe me." She shook her head, then addressed the guards in a language like tumbling stones before turning back to me. "We'll take the main path, try to mislead them. You cut through the forest."

They rode out. Shade planted his wolf butt on the ground and stared up at me.

"I know you're a fae now." My voice shook "That doesn't work anymore."

He huffed. Bash, Teyr, and Zelimir sprinted into the stable, breathing heavily.

"Mount up," I said. "Cordelia's waiting for us."

They leapt into their saddles, and we pounded out the open door toward the tree line. More trainees pursued on foot. Bash yanked clumps of muddy earth out of the ground with telekinesis to slow them. Teyr cackled and launched fireballs. Zelimir tossed purple boulders with his free hand as he leaned low over his horse.

We disappeared into the trees and pelted off the path, slowing to avoid trees. The pounding of booted feet on the ground quieted. I took a deep breath and guided my horse around a large tree. This was as close to privacy as I'd get.

"You should know." I tore the wig off and threw it to the side.

Teyr glanced at me, then looked again. Bash stared at my shaved head.

"You were the human we saw in the wilds," Teyr said. "Before...."

My heart skipped a beat. They were the fae I saw when I came through that first rift, three years ago. I'd never known Thrae without knowing Teyr and Bash, at least.

"I thought you forgot about that," I murmured.

"Never again." Bash looked away.

Zel *pulsed*, wondering what we meant, but I frowned. I needed to know why my dragon had barely looked at me during our escape. I rode up to him and put my hand out to touch the scaled leather collar around his neck.

He grabbed her wrist. *You can't touch it.*

What is it? I asked.

Teyr answered me instead. *Some kind of dragon magic. That worm you like so much put it on him.*

Chry? He wouldn't. He was my friend, my only friend when my mates abandoned me.

"We watched it happen," Zel said.

My chest burned. "Stop. I have to get the collar off."

Zel frowned. "You—"

I whipped toward him. "After everything, are you really gonna tell me I can't do something?"

If we stop, we'll be caught, Bash said.

I narrowed my eyes. "N—"

Horses pounded down the main path, not far through the trees.

Bash met my gaze. "I'll wear this collar for the rest of my life in exchange for keeping you safe."

Nausea tore through me. He didn't know. He didn't know.

"I'm not real," I said.

Cordelia trotted up to us. "Cut through the trees doesn't mean dawdle. We have to move."

I stared at the trees in front of my roan and ignored my mates' questions as she whirled her horse around and led us away.

26

ZELIMIR

We slowed our panting mounts as we neared the golden walls of Stoneheim, Cordelia in the lead. Kinnia's roan, least used to hard running, frothed slightly. She sat so quietly on his back. Although she had taken off the blonde wig, her cheeks remained rosy and dotted with fake freckles. Her breasts bounced with each of her horse's steps.

Not real. What did Kinnia mean? What could have changed to make her say that?

My sister's guards surrounded us. I was too tired to figure out if that was meant as an honor or an insult. The gates creaked open, and we entered the town of Stoneheim to thunderous cheers. Hastily erected banners of every color ran from house to house. Titans lined the streets, waving and cheering. As she entered, the crowd began chanting Kinnia's name.

Shame, disgust, and embarrassment roiled through her Cara. I *pulsed*, and we closed rank around her. When we reached the castle gates, fae rushed out to take our horses, A young, silver-haired titan almost fell over himself to get to Kinnia's horse.

"It's good to have you back," Cordelia said over her shoulder to me as she dismounted.

I climbed down and patted my horse's neck. No doubt, Father had designed this display to feed our ego and further his plans, but I still didn't know what role my sister played.

I turned to face my dismounted mates. Shade, in wolf form, leaned against Kinnia's legs like she was the only thing holding him up. Her grip on Bash's hand turned her knuckles white. Teyr wrapped his arm around her waist, though she remained tense. We needed to talk. Alone.

A titan in house colors hurried up to me. "King Zephyr requests his children's presence in his study posthaste."

Exhaustion washed over me. Of course, he did. I *pulsed* for my mates to head to the baths and get some sleep. I would join them when I could.

No, Teyr said in my mind.

I flinched. I'd forgotten they could reach me that way as well now.

We're not abandoning you to face your father alone anymore, he said. *We never should have.*

Shade howled.

Despite my fatigue, I smiled. *You never abandoned me. My family isn't your problem.*

We're a Cara. Teyr squeezed Kinnia's waist. *That means we share all our problems, and Fire, is your father a problem.*

Bash *pulsed* agreement.

Suck it, Zelly. Teyr kissed the side of Kinnia's head. Her emotions didn't shift. *You can't out-logic yourself.*

I grimaced. The ember had a point, however irritatingly he chose to make it. My mates didn't have families of their own to face, so I'd never thought of mine as a problem that could be shared. We started toward the door.

Cordelia grabbed Kinnia. "Not yet. We need a moment."

They hurried into the stable, leaving us staring after them. Kinnia's Cara became confused, then focused. I exhaled. If she didn't distrust Cordelia's plan, neither did I.

They re-emerged after a few moments, and Kinnia had been transformed. All the makeup had been scrubbed away, leaving my mate fully visible. The skirt of her dress had been tucked up and folded into shorts, and a simple stablehand's tunic covered the top.

I raised an eyebrow.

Cordelia shrugged. "Ready to go."

Yet another secret. I smoothed out my dirty pants like it would make a difference and led my mates to my father's study. The door opened without a sound. The lacquered purple and gray wood walls hadn't changed, nor the high-backed leather chairs in front of his desk. My father taught me to always look for the meaning under words here, the hidden, selfish motive. Sitting behind his massive desk, he, too, looked much the same. I'd gotten my build from him. My square jaw and thick hair. My eyes. Only the copper and silver curls he wore in a topknot had changed since my childhood.

Cordelia slipped around us to stand at Father's right. He frowned as the rest of my mates filed in. My father's silver curls weren't all that had changed, I reminded myself. More than a century and a half had passed between when I'd first been allowed in here and now. I finally felt like a different fae.

Kinnia took her place on my left. Teyr still clung to her like she'd disappear if he let go. The call to the Cara had felt like an escape from my father's world of mistrust and politics into one of order and acceptance under the Councils.

Bash joined me on my right. Shade's power enveloped his wolf body, and he rose to stand next to my second as a fae.

I laughed mirthlessly. Despite claiming to want freedom, when I'd answered the call of the Cara, I'd happily fallen in line and danced to the tune of my second piper as well as I had my first. I should have known from the first moment I stood with all five of my mates that the Councils hadn't given me the acceptance I needed. My mates accepted me.

I locked eyes with my father.

"Son, I'm glad to have you home." He rose, pressing his fingers into the map on his desk. "All of Ar-a-mach is."

Despite the years of distrust, Stoneheim remained my home. I'd grown up walking these halls. Broken my first bone, had my first kiss... I'd even brought my injured mate here when I had no one else to trust.

I released a breath. "I am glad as well."

He smiled and turned to Kinnia. The light in his eyes sharpened. "And you, my dear, are most welcome. Anything you need, my staff is at your service."

Kinnia nodded. I met my sister's gaze with a smile. She glared at me. One secret unraveled.

Cordelia laid a hand on my father's shoulder. "I crossed paths with her"—she nodded to Kinnia—"on the way to the Academy. She was bent on rescuing her Cara by herself. I provided the in she needed, dealing a blow to the Councils while keeping Ar-a-mach personnel as far out of direct confrontation as possible, in exchange for them all returning here after the fact."

He patted her hand. "A brilliant move, my daughter. And how did your attendant fare in the commotion? I didn't see her among the returning heroes."

"Felled, unfortunately, in the crossfire." Cordelia hung her head in mock grief, but I caught the wink she sent Kinnia.

"Ah," he said. "She will be well-remembered among the heroes of this war."

War? asked Teyr.

I *pulsed* to him to keep his temper for now.

"But how are you? How did the Councils treat you? What did they want to know?" Father walked to his liquor cabinet. "Please, find a seat. Would you like a drink?"

"Father, it's been a very long day—a series of long days—ending with a very public and unasked-for reception." I grimaced. "We would like to rest."

My father faced me. "You wouldn't refuse a bit of hospitality, would you, Zelimir?" Centuries of power and command rolled off him in waves, daring me to refuse.

I quailed and started to take a step back to sit. Kinnia appeared at the end of our bridge, radiating her warmth, her curiosity, everything about her I loved. My mates joined her, not saying anything, just lending the silent support I needed to remain strong.

"I would never refuse an offer of hospitality. I thank you for your beds, your baths, and your healers. But I will not sit down and allow you to interrogate us to your heart's content before we've breathed a day's free breath."

My father turned away from me, back to his liquor cart. "I suppose you'll do what you want, as always." He waved vaguely. "Kinnia, dear, would you do me the honor of joining me for a drink? You seem whole and hale, and I'd love to hear more about how you saved my son's life."

"Uh...." Kinnia's Cara filled with uncertainty.

My father turned back, jovial once again. "Wonderful, I've got a liquor you'll simply adore—"

I stepped into his eyeline. "Ask the question you want to ask."

He smiled, fake confusion in every line of his face. "What?"

"Ask it," I said. "The more games you play, the less you'll get out of us."

His smile faltered. "I think you might do well to remember whose house you stand in. A guest's respect goes far."

"That is a lesson I know well. And I think I'm giving you the respect you've earned. Ask."

He ground his teeth. "Is she Tech?"

"She is our mate, and I will not let her be viewed as anything other than that, no matter the rumors. True or not, she fights Tech at our side. She risked her life to free me with every expectation that I would reject her from my side." I locked gazes with my father and allowed my force magic to crackle in my eyes.

He'd taught me everything I knew about saying something without saying it. And, thanks to his little display, Kinnia was a celebrity. A hero. If he didn't like her Tech, too bad. He'd made her untouchable.

Kinnia's emotions swirled like a storm through her Cara. I opened my Cara, letting my confidence spill into her.

I love you, I said. *You once told me being human is about getting to decide what that means to you. Choose what your history means, and I will listen.*

"She saved my life." Cordelia pressed a hand to Father's arm, pulling him back slightly. "She brought your son home."

"But she is...." He left the sentence dangling, expecting me to fill it in.

"My mate, my lover, and a part of your family." I smiled. "I will get you what report I can tomorrow. Today, my mates and I will retire to our suite." I jerked my chin at my sister. "I'm sure Cordelia can help you adjust."

My father clenched his jaw, the stubbornness Teyr always accused me of settling into his stance. But I was done arguing, done playing his games. I turned and left. My mates followed.

I'd never left before being dismissed before. An unseemly grin pulled at my lips. I peeled Kinnia out of Teyr's embrace and settled her at my side.

"We better be heading to the baths." Teyr clung to Kinnia's hand. "I smell like day-old donkey."

Kinnia raised an eyebrow. "Day-old donkey?"

Teyr grinned. "And the questions are back."

27

KINNIA

I sent my mates into the baths with the promise that I could get the dress off by myself. I'd never been more wrong. Cordelia's carefully tucked "shorts" came apart easily enough, but the top evaded me. I spun in yet another circle behind the privacy screen that blocked me from the mineral pool I'd shared with Teyr on my last visit to Stoneheim in an effort to grab the stupid ribbons at the back of the corset.

With a low groan, I stopped and faced the partially fogged mirror. My own eyes stared back at me from the only clear section. The frustration in them morphed into the cold rationality I knew all too well from facing legions of SpiderTech. Farquin said my brain wasn't quite organic, that it needed a special fixture to connect to the rest of me. Could I really be anything more than an advanced SpiderTech in a human body?

"Kinnia," Teyr called. "Stop stalling and get your perfect ass out here."

I blanched. I shouldn't be here. I should've told them already. They needed to know. Zel had no idea what he was talking about when he told me to decide for myself.

Teyr rounded the screen through a ray of sunshine, fully nude. He wrapped an arm around my waist and rested his chin on my shoulder.

"I know you said you didn't need any help"—he pressed a kiss just under my ear—"but I decided I do."

I grimaced and started to push him away. He tightened his grip on my waist.

"No." He grabbed a handful of my skirt and cleared the rest of the mirror. "Watch me. Watch us. I want you to see this."

I squirmed. "Teyr, I'm not—"

My breath caught as he kissed down the line of my neck. With his free hand, he untied the bow at the top of the corset and began loosening the laces.

"Look at yourself," he whispered. "The blush staining your cheeks. The way your eyes flutter when I"—he nipped the tender skin of my neck—"do that. How could you not be real?"

My eyes fluttered, and my cheeks blushed, but I shook my head. "That's not proof, that's biology."

Teyr loosened the last tie and unhooked the ribbon from the corset. It fell away, dragging the skirt with it. I faced myself in the mirror wearing nothing but a pair of panties.

"What makes a person real, then?" He ran both his hands up my front and cupped my breasts, burying his face in my neck again.

My nipples hardened. Goose bumps shivered across my skin. I could've broken his hold easily.

"Real memories," I whispered. "A Jalan built me, programmed my childhood to make a perfect machine to use against Thrae. I'm not even really alive."

I'd said it. He would leave now.

Teyr pulled back to meet my gaze in the mirror. "Kinnia, I can make you feel so goddamn alive."

My chest squeezed. "Don't call me that."

He furrowed his eyebrows and stopped caressing me. "What?"

"That's his name for me," I said. "The Jalan, Elijah. I don't want it."

He ran his thumbs over my nipples, and they hardened again. "Whatever you want, love."

I exhaled. "Feeling alive and being alive are different."

He dropped a line of kisses along my shoulder. "At least let me try before you dismiss the idea."

A zing of need shot through me. I trembled, and my toes curled. Had he really heard me? Did he understand? Teyr slid his hand down until the tips of his fingers rested against my panties just above my covered clit. I forced my hips to remain still, though my chest rose and fell with my needy breaths.

"What do you see?" He opened his Cara. Lust, love, and support rushed into me.

I shook my head. "Seeing doesn't mean anything. I saw a whole fake life."

"Hm." Teyr pulled me against him. His erection pressed into my ass. "Then what do you feel?"

I opened my mouth to respond as he slipped his fingers into my underwear and caressed my clit. I moaned. He wrapped his other hand around my waist and rubbed my abdomen. My muscles fluttered under his touch. I rocked into the pleasure and dropped my head back against his shoulder. Elijah had no idea what I felt.

"You gotta look, love," he murmured.

I smiled as I picked my head back up. The spot on my stomach Teyr caressed so gently that caused such a reaction in me, lay right over the socket where Elijah plugged me into his computer.

Teyr froze. "You just got scared. What's going on?"

"I have a socket there." I pressed where I'd felt the sharp outline. "What if that's why I'm sensitive?"

He nodded seriously. "Sounds like we need to find a second sensitive spot." He kept his fingers nestled against my clit as he dropped his other hand to my legs.

I leaned against him and spread my legs. If he found somewhere else that caused the same reaction, would it make a difference? Could I believe a rectangular jut of metal didn't exist below that area of skin as well? Would any of this make me more real?

He grazed his palm down over the top of my left thigh, then up the inside. No reaction. My stomach flipped. He repeated the process on my other leg, and halfway up my inner thigh, my muscles twinged. Pleasure rippled through my body. I exhaled.

"That seems like a very weird place for a socket." Teyr grinned at me in the mirror. "Though, Bash is better at anatomy. We'll get him to confirm next time."

He stroked his thumb softly over the spot, setting off a cascade of tingles. He'd found another spot, and it wasn't even symmetrical. Elijah jammed cables into my wrists, my elbows, my neck, my stomach. In one of my many captures on Earth, I'd even woken with them in the backs of my knees. But never, never in my thighs.

I spun, threw my arms around Teyr's neck, and pressed my lips to his. I was tired of looking, tired of thinking, tired of taking apart every memory and experience for some clue. I just wanted to feel.

He met me with the same intensity, all teasing gone. When I started to pull away, he cupped my ass and lifted one of my legs to hook around his trim waist. His erection pressed into my needy core.

I managed to disentangle my lips. "What if I'm too heavy? There's metal—"

Teyr crushed his mouth against mine and thrust his tongue inside. I made sounds I didn't know I could, and when he leaned back, I struggled to catch my breath.

"You have the same perfect body you had when we first met." He brushed his nose against mine. "And if you're implying I can't handle you because I'm not a mountain like our commander, or a musclehead like our second, then you've not paid attention during training."

Teyr grabbed my ass with both hands and lifted. I squeaked as my feet left the ground, and I wrapped my legs around his waist.

He nipped my earlobe and murmured, "Can I tell you a secret?"

I nodded.

He leaned back, and his molten gaze bore into mine. "No one truly knows if they're real."

I shook my head. He thrust his cock against my still-clothed pussy. I groaned, and he smiled.

"My parents died for a system that claimed to be blessed by an element of Thrae itself." His eyes darkened. "I didn't realize until I got out that the system only worked because people believed that. Belief is all there is." He cupped my breasts and kissed the top of each. "And I believe in you. You're my goddess, the most real thing in my world. I don't care what came before. All that matters is your blush when I tease you, how you laugh at my jokes, the sparkle in your eye. The way I love you."

I swallowed. Teyr's honesty, his total belief coursed through his Cara. Elijah said Thrae was powered by belief. Could that be enough? Could I stop asking, stop wondering, stop worrying, and just choose to be real? Tears welled in my eyes, and he released one of my breasts to wipe them away.

"I don't need you to say anything." He ground his hips into me. "Except yes, if you want me."

Need and hope swirled within me. I didn't know if I could believe like he did, could just decide like Zel wanted me to, but I knew I wanted Teyr. I wanted to be more than a cold body on a slab, waiting for someone else to give me purpose. I wanted to choose my own.

"I think I feel empty."

He frowned. "Love, I can feel your emotions. *Empty* isn't the word I would use."

I ground my hips against his, savoring the friction of his pubic hair even through my panties. "No, I'm far too empty."

He groaned, pressed a hand between us, and burned away my only remaining clothes. I gasped as his flames licked my skin, sharp but not painful. He lined himself up and slid into me.

Fire seared through my veins as we moaned in unison. I rocked deeper onto him, and my hips met his. He pulsed forward, grazing that spot deep inside me, and I clenched my thighs around his waist.

"You are perfect." He huffed out a breath.

I clung to him and sank into our shared emotions, the need echoing through our Caras. He drew back to thrust again and released my ass entirely, trusting me to hold myself in place. With dexterous fingers, he teased my nipples to attention, drawing brilliant pleasure from my body.

His thrusts quickened. He pulled away from my mouth and peppered my neck and collarbone with kisses. Between each, he murmured praise to my strength, my beauty, how beautiful and good I was.

I dropped my head to his shoulder and moaned. He threaded his hand between us to rub frantic circles around my clit. My orgasm raced forward.

At the last moment, he buried his face in my chest, sucked a nipple into his mouth, and dropped his other hand to that spot on my abdomen. I cascaded over the edge, his name on my lips, and he followed me a thrust later. We held each other, breathing hard.

"You're one of us." Teyr kissed me so sweetly it hurt. Then he lowered me to the ground. "Never forget that."

I nodded, *pulsing* an affirmative through our Cara.

He smiled softly. "Now, what do you say we go clean up? I can still feel dirt on my back."

We walked buck naked from behind the privacy screen to where our mates floated in the tree-lined mineral pool. Teyr whooped and cannon-balled in. I took a slower path, feeling my mates' gazes on my skin. They'd heard and felt everything that happened behind the screen. I slipped into the pool. Zelimir floated over and caught me around the waist. My heart fluttered.

"I mean what I said while we were apart." He gazed into my eyes. "And what I said to my father."

"I believe you." I smiled at Teyr over his shoulder. "And someday, I'll decide what all this means. But, for me, I need you to know everything first."

My mates drifted closer. I touched each of them in turn and took a calming breath.

"A HoldTech caught me after I fell through the rift."

28

SHADE

I WOUND MY FINGERS INTO MY KITTY'S TUNIC AND PRESSED my head against the book in her hands. The fabric on this couch in Stoneheim's library scratched my cheek, but she preferred it here, so I did as well. She lifted the book with a small smile, and I dropped into her lap. The soft fabric of her brown pants felt much better against my skin.

The palace tailors had worked overtime to outfit all five of us as we preferred, and she looked more like herself than ever before, like who she'd always been to me. Her light-blue tunic dipped low at the neck, exposing the tops of her breasts, and tapered in at her waist, but her brown pants had the same cut as the armored Cara pants. Her hair had already begun to grow, darkening her scalp.

I nuzzled deeper. Her scent embraced me like I'd embraced her last night, amongst the old-book smells and small-rodent smells of the library. My navy satin sleeve slid off the couch until the green velvet at the hem touched the floor. She'd been so gentle, so kind, so responsive. Alone, we lacked the raw heat of our experience with Bash, but I'd been free to brush her mind, to run my magic across her body and our Cara. And she'd let me. I gripped my brother's bone, resting on my pale chest. She trusted me, as I had to trust myself.

My Kitty brushed the hair out of my eyes and gave me a quick kiss. I wagged my tail, making the dark, billowing cloth of my new robe flutter. She turned back to her book, and I closed my eyes.

We'd spent the last three days resting, talking, cuddling, and healing. Sometimes together, more often one-on-one, finding a balance that eluded us in the stifling confines of the Academy. She'd explained everything she knew about Elijah and her memories, which I agreed with Teyr changed very little. I sometimes suspected I had memories invented of pure magic, and I knew my Kitty never wanted to destroy Thrae.

My Cara informed me the rest of my pack was entering the library. Their voices echoed over the shelves and, after a moment, they stopped directly in front of us. I kept my eyes closed. If I pretended to be asleep forever, they would never make me move.

"Shade, it's time. We can't sleep the rest of our lives away," my pack leader said.

I huffed. I could transform and disappear faster than any of them could catch me. I could do it and bite Zelimir on the way out the door. My Kitty stroked my hair. I didn't really want to do that. I sat up and opened my eyes.

Bash squished himself between her and the other arm of the couch. Her hip bumped mine. Teyr and Zelimir dragged over chairs and sat.

My pack leader and his second both wore brown, practical pants with simple, cream tunics, painfully similar to full Cara uniforms. Zelimir, at least, added bracers studded with metal, though I couldn't imagine where he'd gotten that. Perhaps he'd picked it to subtly support my Kitty.

Teyr chose tight, dark leather pants that left nothing to the imagination and drew all our gazes on occasions. Today, he paired them with a deep red tunic that laced down the front and sides. A new gold earring sparkled in his ear on the shaved side of his head.

"We need to discuss what we're doing next." Zelimir started to run his fingers through his newly redone twists, then stopped. "I've had a few meetings with my father, Councilor Drax via the communication bowl he gave Cordelia, and Cordelia herself. Father made us heroes for surviving the Councils' torture, and his little rebellion is no longer little.

The numbers swell daily. He's even hired a full Cara as Stoneheim guards." He scowled. "Father won't give me numbers until I agree to join his side, but I know there are too many to house in Stoneheim village."

I growled. Zelimir's father kept circling my Kitty, trying to entice her into meals or drinks to talk about her future. I hadn't bitten him yet for fear of being thrown out and losing all the wonderful places to sleep here.

My Kitty worried her lip. "What about the Councils and Farquin?"

"I actually wanted to talk about that." Zelimir met her gaze. "You mentioned Elijah during our escape."

Her Cara filled with disgust and rage. "Yes."

"I know him."

My Kitty's mouth fell open. Betrayal chased the disgust from her Cara as she stood. I stared at my pack leader.

"Not personally." He put his hands up. "By reputation, mostly. He's the leader of the Jalan in the wilds, the man Farquin liaises for."

"Then you know where he is." I grinned. The song hummed in my ears, waiting to be called on.

My Kitty met my gaze and nodded.

"Not exactly." Zelimir frowned. "The Jalan have gone silent. Nobody's cleaning up the scrap metal from rift fights anymore, and Farquin disappeared from the Academy the same day we did. I knew where their home base was—or where they claimed it is—but some reports say that's empty now."

I stood. "We should destroy what he left behind and discover where he went."

Bash grabbed my wrist. "Not without a plan."

The song soared.

My Kitty stared at us. "I'd love to go."

I grinned and let the power in my eyes show me glimpses of the space between.

"But I don't know if he would make the mistake of leaving anything behind." She dropped back onto the couch. "His lab was spotless."

I scowled. "We can check—"

"She said no, Shade." Zelimir underscored his words with a *pulse* to sit back down.

I sank back to the couch. The song sputtered into nothingness. When one of the pack disagreed with me, I lost.

The Upper Council, not the Lower, has put a bounty on you"— Zelimir nodded at my Kitty—"in the form of a favor."

Teyr sucked in a breath through his teeth. "When was their last favor? Three hundred years ago?"

I nodded. The favor had gone to a Cara commander, but none knew what the man had asked for.

"They want her returned alive to the Academy." Zelimir frowned. "Several other fae, including the dragons, have offered hundreds of thousands of gold pieces and protection if she's brought to them instead."

My Kitty's Cara burned with guilt. I glanced at the collar still encircling Bash's neck. I imagined his dragon was much like my wolf, the part of me born of magic and at ease with the world. My heart would ache without my wolf.

"It's not your fault." Bash caught my Kitty's chin between his fingers and forced her to look at him. "With or without my dragon, my feelings remain the same."

She nodded, but her mood remained low.

Zel sighed. "Last of all, Councilor Drax says that even with the Caras called back, goblins nearly outnumber all other fae at the Academy, and Councilors Odhrán and Gnuq seem equally happy to let them run wild with—he believes—unpowered blasters."

"Do you think one or both of them are working with this Elijah? It seems too lucky we're careening toward war with hybrid Thrae-Earth designs everywhere." Teyr conjured a fireball and tossed it up in the air.

A horn blared. A titan woman sprinted around the corner, and her face went red when she saw Teyr. "You're in a library full of flammable texts."

"Don't you have fire-proofing runes everywhere?" Teyr pointed. "I can see one right there."

"Don't tempt fate," the woman hissed.

Zelimir stared at him, and Teyr put out the fire. The titan librarian exhaled a sigh that certainly meant something, though I didn't know what, and she left. The library returned to its quiet hum. My Kitty curled the book she'd been reading to her chest. I didn't know what volume she held today, but I'd asked yesterday, and she admitted to tearing through every philosophical text in here.

That didn't seem right. My wolf lived in the moment, which freed me from my constant overthinking. She dove into these books, which only made her think harder. Her emotions had been more settled over the past day—as much as hers ever were—but dark fear floated over her like an angry spirit.

"I don't know if the Council is working with Elijah," she said. "But I know we have to stop them both. I don't want to destroy Thrae, and I don't want to fight a war. I just don't know how to stop either on our own."

"So, what, we join up with Zelly's father?" Teyr shook his head. "He's setting this war off as much as"—he glanced at my Kitty—"anything else."

She sighed. "I don't know anything about war, and I don't want to, but it seems to me we can't really turn down any hand extended to us right now."

"Is stopping the war your highest priority?" Bash asked quietly.

My Kitty's Cara turned worried. "I want to know more about myself. Elijah doesn't know everything I can do, but neither do I."

"Joining a rebellion is gonna suck up any time we have to do our own stuff," Teyr said.

"I know." She sighed. "But we can't exactly do our own stuff if we have no idea where to go or how to get there. Cordelia has information networks that would be really useful."

I whined. "Can't we get help somewhere without King Zephyr?"

My Kitty stroked my hair. "No one else is offering." A look I couldn't decipher crossed her face. "Well, almost no one."

My pack leader leaned forward. "What do you mean?"

"I need you all to be reasonable."

She met each of my mates' gazes in turn and held them until they nodded. She turned to me last. I didn't like the intensity in her Cara, the danger it implied. I wanted to refuse. I wanted to be able to do anything I needed to keep her safe. I gripped Light's bone and nodded. I trusted her.

"When we were on the road, I made a deal." She extended her wrist, revealing two small, pale orange spell circles.

I went cold.

"You—" Zelimir clapped a hand over his own mouth and took a deep breath before he lowered his hand. "You made a deal. All right."

She inclined her head. "A bard named Rydel offered me two summons in exchange for my life story on my death bed. I've already used one." She swallowed. "I'd like to use my second for this."

Panic gripped my heart. I snarled. "Your second question could kill you if she wants you at death."

Bash exhaled slowly. "Short elf, older, orange eyes?"

My Kitty nodded.

"I know her." Bash met my gaze. "She saved my life."

I scowled. "But—"

Zelimir shook his head. "It could be that Kinnia will die if she does this, or Rydel could have simply felt her uniqueness, as we did, and marked her. I've heard tell of the bard, and my instinct leans toward the latter."

"Mine as well," Bash said.

Why couldn't they see that any risk to my Kitty's life could not be tolerated? We needed to be equals in danger, as in all things, but no one else had a death sentence on their hand. I looked at Teyr, trying to channel the expression my wolf wore when I begged for attention.

"I don't know." He rubbed the back of his head. "You said you already used your first one?"

She nodded. "And I felt fine. You didn't even notice. If we don't want help from King Zephyr, this seems like the only way forward."

All my mates made various noises of assent, and I bit my tongue to keep from running out of the room howling.

29

KINNIA

I SAT IN THE MIDDLE OF ONE OF THE MOST LUXURIOUS picnic blankets I'd ever seen in my life and breathed through the tension in the little clearing in the woods surrounding Stoneheim Castle. My hands shook, and I placed them into my lap.

To escape King Zephyr's surveillance, Zel had convinced him the five of us wanted to go for a picnic in the woods. It took nearly an hour to talk the king into allowing us to go without guard, but finally, we'd been provided with a huge basket full of food and a communication bowl to check in if our trip lasted longer than an hour.

The bowl lay abandoned at the base of a tree nearly a hundred feet away. King Zephyr shouldn't be able to activate the bowl without a response on our end, but we felt safer with it at a distance.

Despite my mates' agreement that we contact Rydel, they encircled me like they were waiting for something to leap out and attack. Bash leaned against the trunk of a thick, ancient tree, for once the most relaxed. His history with Rydel made him confident the little seer wouldn't yank my soul from my body once I asked a question.

Zel stood bolt upright next to a tree exactly a quarter circle from Bash and scanned the trees. Even across the bridge, I couldn't tell whether he worried about his father sneaking up on us, or summoning

Rydel. Shade lay along one edge of the picnic blanket in wolf form with one paw over his snout. He kept looking up at me with emotion too heavy for his wolf's eyes to convey. Teyr paced the final side of the clearing, muttering.

"You know this is safe?" Zelimir asked.

We'd spent the rest of yesterday afternoon and some of this morning debating that question. I couldn't keep talking in circles. Before anyone could respond, I rubbed the spots on my wrist and chanted Rydel's name. The forest darkened as if a heavy storm passed overhead. The temperature dropped a few degrees. A swirl of orange dissolved into a flickering projection of the little bard with her arms high in the air.

"—and so it came that—" She dropped her arms with a scowl, layered robes I recognized as her storytelling dress falling down around her wrists. "I really need to put office hours on this spell." She brushed off her wispy form and crossed her arms. "Speak, child."

Bash chuckled, and the bard spun.

"An audience this time. Wonderful." She scowled at him. "Drax's piss boy?"

I flinched. Rydel might treat me like a dumb kid, but my mates deserved some respect.

Bash smiled. "If that's all you think, you've lost your touch, seer."

I swallowed. Maybe he had a different relationship with her than I thought.

"You've come a long way." A reluctant smile crept across her lips. "Don't worry, you'll be back to fighting that dragon of yours soon enough."

Guilt roiled in my stomach as Bash touched his collar. Despite what I'd said, I didn't know if I could take it off. The dragon magic felt totally unique.

Rydel peered at the rest of my mates.

"The wolf doesn't frighten me," she told Shade. "And I don't think it comforts you as much as it used to."

He melted into his fae form and sat up, fingering Light's bone. I patted his knee, but he didn't seem to notice.

"And you." She glared at Zelimir. "Haven't you heard the human saying about letting things go?"

He shook his head and clenched his jaw.

She scoffed. "Look it up before you kill the best thing that ever happened to you."

I frowned. Rydel was supposed to be here to answer my questions, not say vaguely cruel things about my mates. I cleared my throat.

She looked at Teyr with a sigh. "This isn't your precious duel arena. Start acting like it."

He flinched as if hit and stopped pacing. I reached for him across the bridge.

Rydel finally addressed me. "If you seek more relationship advice, I will bill you for every coin I lose tonight."

"I'm not, I swear." My face went hot. Despite my mates' questioning, I hadn't told them any more about my first question to Rydel. She just had to bring it up.

"Hmph." The old bard tapped her foot. "What is it, then?"

I glanced at my mates and found them all watching me intently. Great. "Last time we spoke, you mentioned knowing all sorts of secrets. King's war plans and stuff like that."

Rydel waved her hand to hurry me along.

"I want a location," I said. "I think. Or I want to know where you think I should go to learn more about...well, me. And a Jalan named Elijah, and where our paths intersect."

I'd spent the last three days in the library, trying to figure out where Teyr's belief in me fit into the philosophy of centuries past, and they all circled back to self-knowledge. I needed that if I was ever going to be able to believe.

"Better." Rydel hummed. "Elijah's been leading the Jalan for almost thirty years, and he was a player before that. I know an awful lot about him." She grinned. "I'm going to need a little more information on what you want."

I huffed. "I don't know anything about him. That's why I'm asking you."

Rydel clucked her tongue. "You know something you're not telling me. Something connected to him."

Zelimir stepped forward to intervene, and Bash *pulsed* to all of us to let Rydel continue. My commander frowned but stepped back. I crossed my arms and tried to decide whether or not I wanted her stopped. I only knew one real thing about Elijah, and that was me. As I thought that, Rydel smiled. She already knew. The anger I felt in Drax's apartments bubbled up again.

"He built me," I spat. "Is that what you want? Me to tell you that you were right all along, I'm one-of-a-kind special, the sort of nightmare people tell their kids stories about to scare them into obedience?"

Shade whined. Teyr started toward me, disagreement on his lips. Rydel sighed and flicked a wrist. A dome of pale orange magic flickered into place around us, blocking my view of my mates.

My pulse jumped. Maybe the little bard did want to hurt me. She laid a hand on my wrist, and I knew that the block was only visual. My mates would be able to hear us and even charge in if they wanted to, but a little distance would keep them from interrupting.

Just like in the tavern, a sliver of calm stole into my chest. I shook my head. I couldn't take down her dome if I wanted to, but I didn't intend to be led around by her again.

"I don't need to be told I'm right," she said. "And you know that. Just as you know you're wasting energy on this campaign of self-hatred."

Her words landed like rocks in the lava of my anger and melted. I didn't know anything. I was tired of people telling me what I knew.

I threw up my hands. "How can I not hate myself? I was built to destroy a world I love in order to save a world I hate."

"So, you self-destruct? How lucky for those who want you gone." Rydel shook her head, her orange eyes sparkling like she knew a joke I didn't. "If I had enemies like you, I'd lead a much more peaceful life."

"What the fuck would you do in my position?" I crossed my arms.

"I'd look for answers without assuming what I found would be the worst, most awful options on the table." The old bard leaned back. "You've already made up your mind. Nothing I give you now will change it."

I leaned forward, about to argue that would be a breach of our deal. Rydel met my gaze coolly. Bash said she found him at his lowest point and told him what he needed to hear to pick himself up. Could she be trying the same thing on me now?

Three days with my head buried in philosophy books hadn't gotten me anywhere. The philosophers argued back and forth with each other across the centuries. One idea would look promising, only to be smacked down by the philosopher's own apprentice a decade later or his own words on the next page. I took a deep breath and forced myself to uncross my arms.

"I haven't made up my mind," I said. "Or I've unmade it just now."

Rydel patted my cheek. "Good. A little light will ease your way." She closed a thin, partially translucent set of sideways eyelids.

The dome around us grew brighter.

"Elijah keeps a lab on Thrae." Rydel's voice deepened and folded over itself. "You've been there, or almost. I can feel it on you. You will find your answers there, in the dark, in the clave. Patience yields what you need most of all."

My mind whirled. Had she given me a prophecy or a map? A guess or the truth?

She opened her second set of eyelids and put her hand out to steady herself on something I couldn't see. The pale orange dome faded away, and color began leaking out of her body, just like last time. "Next time I see you, she of three worlds, will be both our last."

When only her orange eyes remained, she winked at Bash. Then, her eyes disappeared, along with the darkness in the sky.

I rubbed her wrist and tried to smile. "Well, at least it wasn't 'she of the evil Tech who's gonna kill everyone.'"

Bash snorted. Zel leapt across the clearing and pulled me against his chest. I turned her words over in my mind. How could I find a lab I'd never seen?

"Seers speak in riddles, my Kitty," Shade said. "You can heed their guidance but not take their advice."

I cast back through my memories of Elijah's lab on Earth, leading up to my escape. The perfect clarity with which they came back to me made a little more sense now, at least. But that place hadn't reminded me of anything here. None of Earth did.

"Who the hell does that old broad think she is?" Teyr muttered. "Talking to us like that."

No, that wasn't right. Something did feel familiar. That buzz when I opened a rift. Punaky's Pub. But we'd need to get out from under Zel's father's thumb to even think about going there.

"Rydel is not known for her social graces, but I've found her advice invaluable." Bash tugged on his collar.

Maybe I could kill two birds with one stone.

Teyr snorted. "Anybody have a clue where she's talking about?"

I wriggled out of Zel's hold. "I have a guess. And maybe a plan. You said your father has a Cara as guards now?"

30

BASH

FULLY ARMED AND ARMORED, MY MATES AND I CREPT through the halls toward Stoneheim's tertiary courtyard early the following morning. According to Zelimir, the courtyard was close enough to important things that people would notice the rift Dee had to create but not populated enough that someone would stop us and was located right on one of the Caras patrol routes.

I scratched at the collar and forced myself not to rush because I wanted it removed. My dragon would usually fill me with surety, but he remained nothing more than a blockage in my throat. I'd lived over two hundred years alone in my head. Never again. Chrysophylax's face appeared in my mind's eye, but I chased the image away with a deep breath. Dee sent me a wave of calm. If she truly had been programmed, her childhood some kind of computerized image, I couldn't imagine that much different than the time before I escaped the church.

A door swung open in our path. I froze as Cordelia stepped out with a knowing smile. She would turn us over to her father. I would have to wear this collar until the choking drove me mad.

"Why do we keep meeting like this?" she asked. "It's like you're trying to avoid me, brother."

Zelimir straightened. "I have no idea what you're—"

Dee stepped in front of him. "I have to do something without your father knowing, so we're gonna create a distraction and leave."

"See?" Cordelia looked over her head at my commander. "It's not that hard to tell the truth." She patted Dee's arm. "Anything you need is yours. What kind of distraction?"

She glanced at me. "A rift."

Cordelia raised her eyebrows. "I'll make sure the Caras are awake."

Dee nodded and started walking away.

"Wait!" Cordelia leaned into the room she'd exited, then turned back with a heavy, glass communication bowl.

"Take this." She pressed it into Zelimir's hands. "If you're in trouble, call."

My commander swallowed. "The same to you."

She smiled teasingly and waved us on. My heart started keeping time once more.

We walked a few minutes longer, and Zelimir led us out into a small, unoccupied courtyard surrounded by golden stone walls. I'd done my exercises here a few times during our last stay. The flowers bloomed only in direct sunlight, and the high castle walls kept the garden shaded until nearly noon, so it remained empty most mornings. An itzal squeaked and bolted through a crack in the wall as we entered.

"Stables are through that archway." Zelimir pointed to the only other exit, an open stone doorway with a dirt track leading out and around.

Dee gestured the rest of my mates into a circle and faced me. "Are you ready?"

Teyr smirked. Shade nodded gravely. Zelimir offered me a rare, genuine smile. Dee held out her hand.

"So, we do this and bolt." She tapped each of the weapons on her belt in turn.

Tension wound through my mates' Caras. I stared around at the fae I'd spent nearly a century with and the woman who'd changed my life. All of them about to cross one of our most sacred boundaries, intentionally abandoning a rift, to help me. And I hadn't even told most of them why I hated the collar so much.

"Not yet," I said.

Dee frowned. "Are you okay?"

I nodded. Long-buried memories of my days in the church flooded my mind. Not the worst of the worst, but nights chained to the altar, their slick blades, scratching quills, and strange potions. The pressure of the cuffs, present even when they released me. I closed my eyes and rolled the memories like a boulder over the bridges.

"Oh." Teyr sounded like he'd just gotten the wind knocked out of him.

"What is that—" Shade asked.

Dee shushed him.

My commander put his large, warm hand on my shoulder. Thank you."

I hoisted my memories out of their minds like water from a well. Dee opened her Cara first. Love and support poured into me without a trace of judgment. The rest of my mates did the same, until their love chased the taste of honey from my mouth.

My commander patted my shoulder and stuffed his hands in his pockets. "Are we ready to get started now?"

I smiled. No questions, no pressure for more. My mates knew me well. *Yes.*

Dee put her hands on the collar. Zelimir and Shade each put a hand on one of her shoulders and held one of Teyr's hands.

"On my count. Clockwise from me." She hummed a human riding song she'd insisted on teaching us on the way back to the Academy for Shade's trial, a call-and-response where people joined in one by one, then all at once.

She reached the part of the song where the first singer joined in. The earthy smell of turning over leaf litter kissed my mind as Shade joined Dee and added his hum to the song. The next came. Zelimir's power joined Shade's with the scent of dirt after rain. His deep, resonant hum echoed off the walls.

Dee's breath hitched.

The last. Teyr rushed forward, smelling of sun-warmed bark, and took up the lyrics.

Dee groaned, low in her throat, without breaking the rhythm of the song.

My mates reached the chorus. Goose bumps prickled across my skin. She pushed her *energy* across our bridge. It ghosted down my neck and tangled with the magic of the collar. I shook with the weight of the pressure around my neck and remained standing only through the knowledge that my mates controlled the pressure.

Dee pulled back. The leather of the collar heated. The crystals sank their jagged edges into my magic. Pain shot down my spine, and my knees quivered. I slipped my axe out of its holster and buried the cherry-stone head in the ground to keep standing before Dee could lose her grip.

A *crack* split the air. The heat fell away. My dragon roared to life, and the emptiness around me filled with color. My mates. The twitch and rustle of wildlife. The thrumming minds crowding the castle behind me. My dragon curled and coiled, begging that we take Dee here and now.

The air pressure dropped, and I opened my eyes. A silver rift, taller than any I'd seen before, parted the world behind Dee. Her breath came in quick pants. Fear and excitement warred in her crowded Cara.

I reached for her. A soft hydraulic hiss whispered through the rift. A bell rang in the distance. Thoughts from strange fae poured into my mind.

The warning bell? Who's attacking?

Take toast to the second floor, and juice to the third.

Five more minutes….

If Ar-a-mach won't move, it will die.

Probably that Tech spawn Zelimir won't let go of.

MOVE! My commander's yell cut through the clamor.

My mates sprinted away. I'd lost every barrier I'd constructed between my mind and the world. Dee bent to grab the collar and pulled me away. I barely remembered to yank my axe out of the ground.

I stumbled after her with my eyes closed for focus, erecting my walls one by one. The jumble of thoughts eased. I managed to open my eyes just as Dee tugged me around the corner of the castle wall, outside the courtyard. Shade had transformed into his wolf and took the lead while

Zelimir ran a scant few feet ahead of us with Teyr. More and more bells sounded. Footfalls pounded behind us.

I pulled Dee close enough to kiss her cheek. With my dragon back and my woman by my side, I knew we'd make it out. The next corner revealed the low wooden stables. Zelimir had asked the stable hands to tack our horses for a sunrise ride last night, so they should be ready.

"Hey!" one of the titans at the front door of the castle shouted. "Where are you going?"

My dragon urged me to attack, to subjugate the guard so he never rose against me again. I fought the impulse. My relief at his return couldn't overpower my reason. I plucked the guard off the ground and lodged him safely in the upper branches of a nearby fever boxwood. My dragon rumbled a chuckle through my chest, and I grinned.

We pounded into the stables and found four titan teenagers in stable garb holding our mounts' reins.

Zelimir skidded to a stop in front of them. "Go to Princess Cordelia. She'll keep this from landing on your heads."

The teens nodded, wide-eyed, and dropped the reins to race away. Our battle-trained horses remained steady as we mounted. Zelimir thundered out of the stable, Shade on his heels. My dragon purred and begged me to take Dee again. I wrapped an arm around Dee's waist and pulled her from her mount onto my saddle, in front of me like we had ridden so long ago.

Bash? Her brow furrowed.

I tied her horse's reins to my saddle and urged both beasts into a gallop. She laughed and bounced with the rhythm of the horse's gallop, her curves sliding against my chest. I grabbed her chin and tilted her face up to claim her mouth in a victorious kiss.

My dragon nodded as if I'd finally made a good decision.

31

SHADE

We raced toward Punaky's Pub. Days disappeared under my pounding paws, and my mates pushed their horses as fast as they could go. We poured healing potions into the animals' water to coax a few more miles out of them, though Teyr told my Kitty the trick only worked on short rides like this. Zelimir expected his father to pursue, but she insisted he had no way of knowing our destination.

I didn't care. Panting alongside my Kitty eased something in my chest even my wolf no longer soothed, though I wished worry would stop marring her Cara. The closer we drew to the pub, the heavier our destination hung over her. Last night, when we made camp a scant mile from our destination, I curled into her bedroll in the hopes I could chase away whatever nightmares plagued her.

If the bags under her eyes this morning were any indication, my efforts had been for naught. I rose to find her sitting on a log in front of the fire next to our pack leader. Bash ladled breakfast out of a bubbling cookpot, and Teyr snored behind him. I shoved up off the ground and took the log across from her. We wouldn't discuss anything significant until Teyr woke.

I made myself stone and sank into her Cara. A cloud of worry covered every other emotion, but underneath it, threads of pleasure from the warmth of the bowl Bash handed her, from our pack leader at her side, hummed. I exhaled and tried to smile comfortingly at her across the low flames. Bash took the seat next to me and handed me a bowl. We ate in silence until Teyr finally rose.

"So, what do we know about this place?" Zelimir asked.

Teyr grimaced and took the seat on the other side of my Kitty. "Already?"

"We've been awake for hours," Bash answered.

The ember rolled his eyes and downed his coffee.

My Kitty swallowed. "Not much beyond Rydel's prophecy, or whatever that was. I could just kind of feel…something in the air when we were there. And I felt it again on Earth."

"Can you tell us about his lab on Earth?" Teyr held out his mug for a refill.

Bash frowned and filled his cup. My Kitty grimaced, and real fear darkened the worry in her Cara.

"You don't have to do anything you don't want to," I said.

That earned me a smile as she spooned a bite of oatmeal into her mouth. I warmed down to my toes.

Zelimir put a hand on her arm. "I understand this might be painful, but it will keep us from walking in blind."

She set her bowl on her lap. Worry and fear danced in her Cara until she pulled a blanket of determination over both. I frowned. Our pack leader shouldn't push her so hard. She rarely refused him so direct a request.

"The building was full of Tech." She took a deep breath. "Heavily guarded and reinforced in the main sections, but not as well guarded in the places he didn't go as often."

Bash nodded. "Short-sighted. A little egocentric."

"Try a lot." She exhaled a laugh. "I don't think Elijah knew I could disobey him. I don't think he knew I was…someone."

Wonder wove through her determination. A bright, powerful wonder, like she'd never said those words out loud before, or at least never considered their implications. The same wonder I'd been feeling since I met her. I wagged my tail. Finally, my Kitty began to see just how spectacular she could be.

Zelimir put his empty bowl on the ground. "What sort of guards and reinforcements?"

"Big metal plates over the doors." She fidgeted with the faded golden rune-charm on her belt. "Tech, but I doubt he'd be able to hide that here."

Teyr raised his eyebrows. "Tech? Like, Tech that obeyed him?"

My Kitty ran a hand over her close-cropped hair. "It seemed like they did."

Her words settled between us like stones dropped into a still pool. The Academy taught that Tech obeyed ancient programming, mostly patrol circuits their human masters gave them before the fall of Earth. Centuries of strategy depended on that assumption. I hadn't believed anything the councilors said since they tried to kill my Kitty, but our pack leader went ashen in a way I thought implied shock.

"All right," he said slowly. "Anything else we should know?"

She chewed her bottom lip. "He seemed to be storing all his information about me in big computer banks and playing it on little screens. That might be a good place to look."

Teyr finished his second mug of coffee, wrapped an arm around her shoulders, and knocked his head gently against my Kitty's. "I'll pull them apart by hand if that's what it takes to get the information we need."

The emotions in her Cara didn't shift, but she laughed. "They'll break."

He scoffed. "I knew that."

I barked a laugh, and my mates joined in. Mirth filled the morning air, but the dark feelings muddying my Kitty's Cara lingered even as we finished our meal and packed up camp. Fear and worry, worry and fear. With Bash's voice in the back of my thoughts, I kept her feelings from infecting mine, but I couldn't deny worries of my own as her distress built. She needed a moment to gather herself.

"I can create a portal for my Kitty and I to scout around the lab before we all go," I said.

My mates looked up from their various organizational tasks.

Our pack leader frowned in a way I knew meant he did not intend to allow me this. "I don't know if that's—"

I crossed my arms. "I will go with my Kitty and return. Together, we would be able to give a comprehensive report. She remembers a feeling, but we haven't been there in months. If Elijah was there, he may have moved."

Her Cara darkened as pre-emptive disappointment leaked in. "Rydel said the lab was here."

"Rydel said it would be somewhere *like* here." I dipped into the realm between, and power beaded in my eyes. "Only you and I can be certain before we all enter a location full of goblins."

That, too, only spurred her fear. My heart ached. In attempting to assuage my Kitty's concerns, I seemed to be worsening them.

"All right." Zelimir ran a hand over his intricately woven twists. "But no more than five minutes, or we're coming after you."

I nodded and submerged myself in the magic of Thrae. Its song wound through me, and I grabbed my Kitty's hand. Together, we stepped through the space between life and death. Up ahead, one area sagged, even more lifeless and gray than most in the realm between. I led her toward that colorless region.

Purple and orange foliage bloomed around us as we stepped out into life once more. My Kitty stumbled slightly, but I held her upright. I stretched my magic into the clearing around us. Above, below, beyond. Frantic heartbeats winged through the trees, likely birds or rodents. Similarly small death signatures reached out of the dirt, begging for my power to make them dance once again. Past a worn path, a dozen slow, early-morning humanoid pulses wandered. None reacted to us.

My Kitty scrubbed her hands over her arms. Fear and relief danced in her Cara equally. "Still here."

"Good." I rubbed away the goose bumps that still pebbled her skin. "Let us take these five minutes of quiet."

She looked up at me. Her lips shone in the morning sun. I bent to kiss her.

"Can I ask you something?" she said before my mouth touched hers.

I leaned back. "Anything."

"How are you so...." She waved her hands in a way I could glean no meaning from. "Okay with all of this? With me?"

I frowned. "I love you."

"How?" She pulled out of my grasp and paced the clearing. "You even trusted me at the beginning, when the other guys didn't—couldn't."

Concern whirled through her, on the heels of the same dark fear. A profession of my love wouldn't be sufficient. But she'd come to me for reassurance, when she usually turned to one of our other mates, and I would not fail her.

"I love you like I love my magic." I sank to my knees and dug my fingers into the dirt, pouring power into a fine-boned gisvin skeleton. "Many find my magic unsettling, ghoulish." I frowned. "When we first trained at the Academy, some trainees even went so far as to call my necromancy evil."

The bones clawed up out of the dirt. My Kitty sat onto the ground across from me and rested her chin on her hands. That signaled attentiveness, I thought.

I spun the gisvin into a jig, the miniscule bones of its rotted gliding membrane clattering. "To me, it is like touching a private part of Thrae. There is no less beauty in that which no longer lives as that which does." I met her gaze. "I have spent too long loving things others hated to even falter in my love for you."

"That makes sense, I guess." She watched the gisvin intently, but a bit of comfort surfaced in her Cara. "Trust is different than love, though."

"Trust has...many meanings."

All my secrets swirled through my mind, things I'd kept from my mates, from even Light. Many called total transparency trust, and I had never managed that. The gisvin collapsed back into a pile of bones as worry snuck between myself and the magic. I couldn't talk around my Kitty, not when she chose to rely on me.

"How do you trust me?" I asked.

"I've been hurt a lot by people I thought I could trust." She blew out a long breath. "But they always showed themselves in little ways. So, for me, it's about patterns. The longer someone goes without those red flags, the more I'm able to trust them." She smiled softly at the pile of bones between us. "And you've been putting in your time since the beginning. We had a few bumps along the way, but you always try not to hurt me."

Her words glistened in the sunlight, set to the easy rhythm of her heartbeat. Patterns, I could understand. My Kitty trusted me because I thought of her, prioritized her comfort and safety. She didn't need every stone overturned. I trusted her because of the warmth in my chest when I saw her, the wholeness from the moment we met. But that didn't translate out of my mind well.

"You treat me like Shade," I said slowly. "Not my wolf. Not a powerful necromancer. Not part of Shade-and-Light. Shade."

She frowned. "Have the other guys—"

That's five minutes, Zelimir said across the bridges. *We're leaving now.*

No need, I replied. *I will portal back and collect you.*

I stood, and my Kitty stared up at me.

"You really do trust me, don't you?" she asked.

"Of course."

Bright emotions overwhelmed the dark for the first time since we set out toward the pub. I reached into the space between again and pulled our mates toward us.

32

KINNIA

I swept my hands through the leaves covering the ground as Teyr, Bash, and Zel appeared through Shade's blue-black portal. The wolf's certainty warmed me even as my skin buzzed with the presence of...whatever it was that caused the buzzing. It felt stronger here than it had when I spoke with the goblin, so assuming Elijah hadn't figured out how to turn things invisible, I'd put money on his lab being underground.

"Did you check for anything below us?" I asked.

Shade paused for a moment, then shook his head. Bash grunted in agreement.

"You think it's down there?" Teyr asked.

I looked around at the empty forest. "Do you have a better guess?"

"Brace yourself." He spread a thin layer of flame across the ground of the clearing, dodging all our feet, and incinerated the top layer of forest debris.

A chipped metal double-door became visible against the charred dirt a few feet from me. Whatever comfort I gained from my talk with Shade melted away.

Zelimir put his hand up. We waited and listened. Nothing.

I walked to the doors. Each bore a small, inset handle, and the number 4263 had been etched in the middle. I tugged on one handle, and it popped out.

Bash put a hand on my shoulder. *Let us.*

I stepped back. I didn't really want to open the doors. They reminded me too much of the door in the mountainside in the lab where Elijah held me captive. Zel and Bash each grabbed a handle and tore the doors off their hinges to expose a ladder dropping away into darkness. Nothing surged out. No sounds echoed up.

I swallowed. "I'll go first."

"Let me." Teyr frowned down at the darkness. "Better crowd control."

"I can help up here."

Shade flattened himself to the ground. Blue-black power crept toward the tree line, and a few more tiny skeletons scraped their way out of the ground. They scampered over as Shade sat up, and I recognized them as a type of winged tree rodent I'd seen throughout our travels. Teyr once called them gisvin.

Shade gestured to the skeletons proudly. "They'll keep watch and warn me."

Zelimir nodded. Teyr grimaced and began climbing down the ladder. We followed. Zelimir and Bash sandwiched me between them, and Shade brought up the rear. My heart pounded in my ears as the buzzing intensified. Entering a lab, even for answers, even with Rydel's promise at my back, felt a little like suicide.

Artificial lights buzzed to life as Teyr hit the ground, and light illuminated the remainder of the ladder as I grabbed the next rung. My grip slid. When I pulled my hand back, something green and metallic smelling coated my fingers. Nausea clawed at my guts. I knew blood when I saw it, whatever it came from.

Bash, continuing at the same pace, nearly stepped on my other hand, and I descended the rest of the ladder without looking. Teyr and Zelimir stepped out of the narrow landing area as I dropped the last few feet. No alarms. No doors slamming shut. Just...quiet. I turned and saw the Jalan bodies on the floor. One to the left, and two more to the right. I would've heard my mates fighting, would've felt it.

Bash landed, and I watched him run through the same train of thought. I drew my katana and entered the hallway. A gray, artificial stone I'd seen neat squares of on Earth made up the walls, ceiling, and floor. I ran my hand along its rough surface to feel the bite. Farther down the hall, a ruined Tech I didn't recognize lay on top of a crumpled, bleeding goblin. More goblin bodies, a few collapsed Jalan, and a handful of doors lay in the other direction.

Finally, Shade arrived. He and Bash stepped into the hall together. Shade gasped and sprinted down the hall toward the goblin.

Beware. Bash lurched after him.

My stomach flipped, but I followed with Teyr and Zel at my sides. *Beware* meant Bash recognized that this carnage, this utter silence, had come recently—and that the perpetrator might still remain.

Shade skidded to a stop on his knees, heedless of the metal and broken glass. He pried the goblin out of the tangle of Tech with careful hands and cradled the small body. Green blood smeared the front of his robes. The goblin coughed weakly.

Bash squatted next to Shade and pressed a hand to her small head. "Nothing useful. She can only think of the pain."

"She's dying. If I catch her in the exact moment of death, I might be able to ask something." Shade looked up at us, looking more like the wild necromancer who exploded out of his wolf to save me than he had in a while.

I frowned. "Put her out of her misery." The goblin Might have tried to kill me an hour ago, but I wouldn't stand around watching someone else suffer in one of these labs.

Bash drew a small dagger from Shade's belt and slashed the blade across her neck, severing the flesh almost to bone. Shade leaned forward, a cloud of power crowding around him and the body in his arms.

"Who did this?" His voice reverberated with command.

The goblin's last breath rasped out of her throat. "Him."

"Ah!" A pleasant voice echoed off the walls behind us.

I spun on my heel, expecting to find Elijah.

Farquin leaned out of a door down the hall with a small smile on his face. "I hadn't quite finished cleaning yet. My apologies."

I gaped. Previously, I'd seen him in simple but neat black clothes. Now, he wore rough brown pants like I'd seen on the goblins in Punaky's Pub and a long, white coat buttoned up to his neck, both coated in a thick layer of grime. His unshod feet, though covered with metal on the bottom, were nearly black with dirt. The coat bore countless splashes of brown, red, and green. Tech oil, goblin blood, and Jalan—human blood.

His gaze shifted to the goblin in Shade's arms. "I suppose I can finish up later. Not much to hide now that you're here."

"You...." I shook with rage. "You did this. You killed everything."

"Yes." Farquin shucked the white coat and folded it inside out so none of the blood got on his filthy cream shirt. "How else were you going to get a look at everything?"

Zelimir stepped forward and raised his hand to grab a weapon out of the air. I shook my head.

He's a killer, Zel hissed. *We should at least restrain him.*

I don't trust him as far as Shade can throw him without magic, I replied. *But I want to see what he's talking about.*

Zel's lips thinned, but he nodded. I returned my attention to Farquin and found him grinning.

"For a while there, I thought the Cara communication would be the limit of your power." He watched me with wild eyes. "Talking to a computer is one of the hardest things. I thought your code would simply be too fundamentally dissimilar. But now look at you." He laughed. "Elijah is a moron."

"How did you know we'd be here?" I asked.

He frowned. "You're not going to like the answer. Can't we get settled first?"

I looked at my mates. Shade gently laid the goblin's head on the floor and stood with a little help from Bash, his knees dotted with blood from the glass he'd knelt on. Teyr scowled. Zelimir simply stared back at me. I'd asked for this. I had to make the decision. I nodded.

Farquin strode down the hall, and we followed. Broken glass and oily

Tech crunched under our booted feet. Blaster fire singed a few walls. I slowed and peered into the door he'd emerged from. A pile of bodies lay in front of a squat metal machine that hissed and emitted a thin stream of smoke. I flinched and noticed the label next to the door in that same black writing. Autoclave.

The high, metallic squeal of a rusty door drew my attention forward. At the end of the hall, Farquin held open half of a swinging double door, the other side of which hung askew. We jogged up to him and stepped inside the room.

Unlike the sleek, bright whites of Elijah's lab on Earth, this lab had walls of that same gray stone, crowded with dingy equipment. Instead of a massive, whirring computer bank and wall of monitors, he had a few cracked screens and a patchwork-looking main computer. Rough-hewn shelves held vials and silver tools that made me shiver. A monitor hung on a swinging arm over the slim metal table in the middle, but only one. Cables snaked across the floor. I didn't remember this place any more than I had the lab on Earth.

"So," Farquin sat in the rolling chair in front of the computers, "how I found you is a bizarrely complicated question, the answer to which stretches back a few months."

I frowned. "Tell me."

He sighed. "I gave a little tracking device to an urander-shifter Xerxes sent to get eyes on you. Elijah's idea."

I ripped the small charm I'd been carrying since the *Cross Roads* off my belt.

Can we kill him now? Teyr asked.

Not yet. I had to know what the charm meant, what else he knew.

He nodded. "I've been following you more or less since then. Boss's orders." He smiled apologetically. "I didn't report anything that would get you in trouble."

"Did you know we were in Bittermist Thicket?" I asked.

He frowned. "Do you really trust me so little? Of course, I did, but I said the wild magic there disrupted my ability to track. I even left you alone to come to terms with your destiny."

I stared at him. He really, really thought he was helping.

"You opened the rifts along our route," Zelimir said.

"I can't open rifts. Almost no one can." He smiled at me. "I reported your location, Elijah sent Tech to the corresponding spot on Earth in case a rift opened, and I suspect that confluence opened them."

I bit my lip to hide a sigh of relief. The last thing we needed was someone who could open rifts. Someone other than me.

"What else can I answer for you? Or would you rather look around yourself?"

My heartbeat roared in my ears. I'd come in search of answers, and he offered them up on a silver platter? Everything in me screamed "trap," but I couldn't deny the allure of my first simple answers.

I ran a hand over my head. "How about a little of both? My mates look around while I sit here and talk with you."

Farquin's grin widened. "Perfect. All I ask in return is a few answers. I want to know how it feels to be you."

No, Teyr hissed. *Don't tell him anything. And I'm not going anywhere.*

He's right, my Kitty, Shade said. *I won't leave you alone with him.*

I sighed. *One of you can stay, but I really do want the rest of you searching this place. We have to be able to confirm what he says.*

Zelimir nodded. *I'll stay. Leave no stone unturned.* He met my gaze. *And leave no creature suffering.*

"I'll take that deal." I set the tracking device on the desk where most of the computers sat.

Bash, Teyr, and Shade stalked out of the room. Farquin gestured to a low stool overturned in the corner of the room. I grabbed the stool, set it on its legs, and sat well out of arms' reach. Not that that would make a difference with his blaster.

I grimaced and faced the Jalan. "Tell me everything."

He smiled playfully. "Now, where's the fun in that? I want to know what you're wondering. What that brain of yours thinks to ask."

I thought about punching him. "Fine. How do you know Elijah?" I wrinkled my nose. "I mean, what's your relationship with him? I want the whole thing, back to front."

"I'm no fae looking for loopholes out of your questions. I want you to know everything I do." He chuckled, but his eyes burned with that furious intensity I'd seen in all our other interactions. "I want to help you, SISTER, more than anything."

Zelimir put his hand on my shoulder, and I leaned into his warm weight. I didn't have to face this alone, at least.

"I begged him not to build you," Farquin said.

I started. "What?"

He grinned. "Elijah is a genius, but he's always been greedy." Farquin waved his hand to indicate the room. "Every Jalan in the wilds would kill for a lab like this, but he needed something old-Earth-quality." His gaze returned to me. "Any Jalan would be thrilled to build a simple new Tech, but he wanted you. He wanted to save Earth."

Farquin hummed. "An old Earth scientist, something with an M, created the first few SISTER models. Elijah found a half-burnt notebook with designs and plans that led him to her lab, which housed her final prototype, K1NN11." He shrugged. "After that, I couldn't deter him."

I'd seen that prototype in the dusty tube and had stolen a white coat with an M-name on it. Zelimir began massaging my shoulders.

"Why did you try to stop him?" I asked shakily.

"Oh, every model she made went violently insane within a few hours of release from the amniotic sleeve." Farquin grinned. "Clearly, Elijah managed to improve on her design."

I rocked back into Zelimir's bulk. For a brief, strange moment, gratitude for Elijah washed over me. If he'd made a few different tweaks to a centuries-old design, I could've been nothing more than a footnote. A mistake, to be smiled over with whatever version of me managed to survive.

"You stopped talking to Elijah after he decided to carry on her work?" I asked.

"Certainly not." Farquin chuckled. "People in our field disagree all the time. I stood by his side as he made every iteration. I even pursued you when you escaped." He shook his head. "Elijah was dead set on having you to himself, but the more I followed you, the less the idea appealed to me. Eventually, I...well, I wouldn't say I *let* you escape." He smiled. "I simply stopped looking in the right places."

Memories clicked into place. A bit of blond hair peeking through a shattered window. The glint of metal where I knew there was no Tech. Blaster shots coming out of nowhere. That was why he looked so familiar.

Teyr entered the room. "There are cots in two of the other rooms, and a pretty big kitchen." He reached my side and handed me a purple-leather-bound book. "I think this is a journal. I found it by one of the beds."

I opened the book to pages of neat handwriting.

Farquin inclined his head. "Elijah's."

I squeezed Teyr's hand. "Thank you."

He nodded and shot Farquin a narrow-eyed look, then left.

Farquin leaned back in his chair, looking perfectly at ease amidst the gore. "When you showed up at the Academy, I fended Elijah off as long as I could, testing your capabilities. The time simply came for me to reveal my true allegiance."

I blinked. "What—"

"Ah, I think it's my turn." He shook his head indulgently. "How do you feel about food?"

"Um." I frowned. "Good? I mean, I eat it. I like it well enough."

"Food tastes good?" He leaned forward.

I glanced at Zelimir, who shrugged.

"Yeah," I said slowly. "At least, the good stuff does."

He hopped to his feet. "As I expected. You weren't programmed with taste receptors."

Zelimir straightened, cupping the shaft of a spear. My mind spun like a leaf in a windstorm. Farquin spit information faster than I could possibly process, and none of it made sense.

"Goodness, you're a little jumpy." He unscrewed his blaster arm, disconnected a couple cables, and laid it on the table. "Better? I merely want to move a little."

"Better." Zel's spear evaporated.

Bash leaned into the door. "Found a permanent portal. Shade's testing it." He sent me a wave of love and support, then ducked back out.

"True allegiance?" I prodded.

Farquin smiled and began pacing. "Elijah thinks Thrae is just Earth's runoff, but I know better. Magic and Tech were never meant to mix. Every time someone tries to combine them, catastrophe ensues. That's why we were put on different worlds and kept apart by boundaries that should have been impenetrable. Ancient humans scraped the very top of achievement, blew holes in the walls between Earth and Thrae. The war that followed was a warning never to try that again."

He whirled to me, eyes burning hotter than ever before. "Until you. You, K1NN14, SISTER, whatever you want to be called, are beyond impossible." He closed the distance between us, and Zel stepped closer to me. "You took an organic shell and turned it into a body. You turned a program into consciousness. You were put here to lead us into a new age, not become—"

He reached to grab me by the shoulders. Zelimir whipped out his one-handed blade and pressed it against the Jalan's neck. Farquin froze, his one flesh hand extended in front of him. I pressed myself back against Zelimir.

Farquin straightened with a small laugh. "Forgive me. I've overstepped."

"Damn right you have," Zel growled. "Sit down."

Farquin glanced at me. I nodded automatically. The Jalan walked back across the room and sat without another word. Zelimir dropped his hands to his side but didn't release the blade. My heart pounded. What did he mean, lead them into a new age? Who was "us" to a person like Farquin?

"I don't mean to scare you." He smiled self-consciously. "Please, ask on, if you wish."

His stare, the way he switched between obsession and obeisance, sent a tingle up my spine. I didn't want to talk to him anymore. "Can you show me how to use those?" I pointed at the computers behind him. They would confirm or deny his story.

"I don't have to show you anything." He plucked a dusty cable off the top. "If you just plug in, you can—"

My chest squeezed. "No!"

Farquin raised an eyebrow.

I took a deep breath. "I want to do it myself."

He nodded. "Simple enough."

Shade bounded in as a wolf and pillowed his head on my lap. *The portal goes to the Academy,* he said through Cara. *A sub-basement I've never seen before.*

His tongue lolled out of his mouth, and he nuzzled my arm. I scratched his head. Farquin stared at Shade for a long moment, then looked back at me.

I nodded at the computers. "Teach me."

In a few moments, I whizzed through the maze of files Elijah left so carelessly unprotected with Farquin hovering a safe distance away. He kept drifting closer, then back away as Zel or Shade blocked him. Bash and Teyr joined us and created a staggered block between the Jalan and me. Their presence eased my nerves a little.

Farquin directed me to a video he'd compiled before we arrived labeled "Before." I stared at him for a long moment, then typed my designation into the machine. Files covered the screen. He made a small, disgruntled noise as I clicked on a file labeled "Birth."

A video filled the screen of Elijah welding my skeleton together on a metal table in the sparkling Earth lab I'd seen. My brain grew in a vat of cloudy green liquid around a metal core. Other Jalan came in and out, including Farquin. Elijah attached the cables and submerged me in the same tube as the others. I looked about four years old. Bile rose in my throat.

"I might suggest the volume." Farquin pointed to a button on the side of the screen.

If I truly didn't have to be what Elijah made me, I needed to know what he'd done. I needed to be able to combat him with everything I had.

I pressed the button Farquin indicated.

"...connecting the brain to the artificial stem," a slightly younger Elijah said in his computer voice.

I shuddered.

"This will officially start the simulation, so her motor functions can develop over time." He pressed a few buttons on a panel attached to my tube. My head clicked a bit down on my neck on the video. "I started too late with K1NN12, too early with K1NN13. This should be the perfect point." He frowned. "I've decreased the amount of indigenous Thraen DNA in the mixture as well, which should prevent over-inventiveness."

He hummed as he wheeled a monitor over and plugged it into a port that attached my tiny stomach to the plastic of the tube. Ones and zeroes scrolled over the screen, just like I'd seen in the lab on Earth.

"And there we go." He clapped. "I've given up direct control over what the simulation produces this time. Too perfect a life leads to quicker rejection. But I've controlled for a few elements." He ticked points off on his fingers, still staring at the screen. "I gave the simulation my knowledge of human towns, for realism.

"I guessed at K1NN14's adult power set and fed that in. Last, I programmed it to encourage her to save Earth at some point and add in human prejudice against Thraens. Should make the transition easier. The rest, K1NN14's brain will fill in. The simulation program only manages scope and continuity." He patted the plastic front of my tube and smiled. "I'll see you when you're twenty."

The video ended. Silence reigned over the lab. I'd invented my whole past myself. Elijah tossed a few elements into the pot, but the years of beatings and rejections, the deaths of my friends? All me. All because I *believed* that was what my world should be.

I stood and pulled away from my mates' hands. "Why did you make me listen to that?"

"What?" Farquin asked.

I faced the Jalan, quivering with emotions I couldn't name. "Why? Why the audio?"

"So you would understand." He grinned. "You have such an amazing mind that you—"

"Amazing?" I threw aside the stool I'd been sitting on.

Shade melted into fae form. My mates cleared a path between us.

"Amazing." I cackled. "I hated myself from conception. Filled my world with abuse. How amazing could I possibly be?"

"But you didn't—after that, you—" Farquin put his hand up.

"I knew you were crazy." I shoved him until he hit the metal table in the middle of the room. "But I didn't know you were so pants-shittingly stupid." My breath raced out of control.

He smiled. "If you just keep watching, Kinnia—"

"Don't call me that!" I screamed.

His eyes went wide enough I could see myself reflected in them. A hairless, senseless, bellowing thing. I sank to the ground. My mates opened their Caras, trying to overwhelm me with love. I batted them back.

"Alex's stupid fucking quest was the first thing I believed in," I mumbled. "We all believed. And somebody else made it up all along."

The lights in the room burned down on me. Everything spun. I hated myself enough to kill Alex, Elaine, David, and Harry. If I had enough hate in me for that, I had enough in me to invent my mates too.

Bash crept to my side, a monster from my own mind, and I swung at him.

33

TEYR

I whirled on the Jalan as Dee crumpled to the floor. "Leave. Now."

Farquin scowled. "You don't understand the science behind her."

"And you don't understand anything else." I took a step forward. Fire licked up my fingers. "She doesn't need science now. She needs us."

He put up his hands with a small smile. "I can't deny she seems to crave your presence. Do what you must. But consider flipping through that journal soon."

I hurled sparks at his feet. "No more sly suggestions. If you really want to help, put in earplugs and guard the entrance."

Zelimir slid to my side, and Bash, my back. Shade growled, standing between her and the Jalan.

He inclined his head. "I will be at the ladder, where I can intercept anyone approaching from there or the portal."

"Can you use the portal?" Shade demanded.

Farquin shook his head. "Unlike your mate, I cannot feel the magic of this place." His gaze drifted past me to where she sat crumpled on the floor. "She is a miracle of magic and an abomination of science. I will do anything to see her goals realized. If you wish the same, I see no reason for us to fight."

I opened my mouth to argue, but Zel *pulsed* for me to stand down. He pulled Cordelia's communication bowl off his belt and handed it to the Jalan, murmuring something about letting him know if it went off. I stepped back with a frown and leaned against the computer desk. Bash grasped Farquin's arm and nearly dragged him to the door, then shoved him into the hallway. Before the Jalan could react, Bash closed the crooked door and faced us.

Zelimir rushed to Dee and dropped to his knees beside her, but when he didn't do anything more than rest his hand on her shoulder, I said, *Pick her up and put her in your lap.*

She hasn't asked me to do that. His gaze remained on her. *I don't think she even knows I'm here.*

She's stuck. We need her to know we're real. I projected my voice to all my mates. *She needs to feel us, not fear the Tech insider her.*

We should get her out. Shade reached for her.

No! I grabbed Shade's arm. *Every time she hurts, you go to her side.* I glared at my commander. *We need to be unpredictable. Pick her up and put her on your lap. Kiss her, feel her. Pretend you're her mate, and she needs you.*

As intended, Zelimir flinched. "I don't need to pretend."

"I'm not the one you need to convince," I said evenly.

Zelimir's eyes blazed, but instead of fighting me, he sat beside our mate and settled her sideways on his lap. He rubbed his hand in comforting circles over her back and held her close. She covered her face with her hands and rocked.

I sighed. *Bash—*

The dragon sat in front of Zel and spun her on our commander's lap to face him. Where Zelimir didn't want to ask, Bash pushed. He ran his hands up and down her front. His scales rippled as he cupped her cheeks and kissed her forehead.

"You're right here, between us. You can feel that, Dee." Bash kissed each of her cheeks.

The darkness threatening to consume her Cara eased. She dropped her hands from her face. Zelimir brushed his lips across the base of her neck. The darkness lightened another shade, and lust crept in. Blood rushed to my cock as I sat beside Bash. Shade licked his lips and sat on the floor next to me. The artificial lights flickered above us, making the fallen Tech glitter like fairy dust.

Touch her, I said. *Feel her.*

Zel paused. *Why don't you do it yourself?*

Because you don't do this. This place is a horror show. You, I assume, have been waiting for a quiet moment in a rose garden to fuck her again.

Zelimir met my gaze over her head. *I want everything to be perfect for her.*

You can't have that, I said. *Nothing's ever going to be perfect, and denying both of you doesn't help anyone.*

He nodded slowly, and I swallowed. Zel listened more these days, but I hadn't seen that intense, absorptive look in his eyes in a long time. He was actually trying to hear me.

A shiver of pleasure ran up my spine. I threaded my fingers into Shade's hair. With him beside me and Zelimir paying attention to me, I felt like a god again. Zel dropped his mouth to the place where her neck met her shoulder, not just kissing but sinking his teeth into her skin. She moaned and leaned her head back against his shoulder. Without prompting, he slipped a large hand under her tunic.

I played with Shade's hair and ears to the tune of rustling fabric, low moans, and panting. His grunts joined the symphony I was creating. Waves of heat and lust pushed back against her despair. I opened my Cara, spilling need and desire into our bond. My mates followed suit. Zelimir remained hesitant, worried but wanting. Bash shared an almost animalistic desperation, his dragon seeping in at the edges. Shade yearned in a more emotional direction, but I couldn't figure out where, as our lust swirled together.

I *pulsed* to Bash to make sure he had a hand between her legs. He stopped kissing her to growl at me and send a mental image. His lilac hand and my commander's dark one caressed the seam of her pants in unison. I grasped my cock and tugged on Shade's hair so sharply he moaned and leaned his whole weight against me.

Pleasure raced through my veins, but when I reached for her Cara, I found darkness still threatening the edges. She needed more. I reached for Bash's telekinesis across the bridges and shuddered. In the haze of want, it felt like touching something more vital than any body part.

With his magic, I tugged Bash's shirt up over his head, exposing her hands on his pale purple body. I removed Zelimir's next. His muscles rippled as he rolled his hips against her. Finally, I took hers. As I revealed the plain black chest support, Bash leaned forward to lick and suck her covered nipples.

I glanced around the room. My symphony needed a crescendo, something to burn out her worries and make this place safe again. The metal table in the middle of the room, so much like the one in that video of Earth, beckoned.

"Up," I said. "Bend her over the table."

My mates turned to me with matching expressions of shock and horror.

34

KINNIA

THE LUST DRAINED FROM MY BODY AS I CRANED MY NECK TO stare at Teyr. I didn't want anything to do with this table, or any table like it. If I never laid on another metal slab, it would be too soon.

Teyr unlaced his hand from Shade's hair, though Shade whined.

"You're worried you're still in that simulation," Teyr said.

I nodded. Zelimir's hand tightened on my thigh.

"You can let that frighten you forever, or you can face it." He pressed a kiss to my lips. "Covering something up with fear or anything else just allows the wound to fester."

I swallowed. The table gleamed in the flickering light.

Teyr whispered in my ear, "I know what Rydel meant. I don't actually think I'm exceptional. And I think if I stop putting on a good show, everyone's going to notice I'm just...me."

My heart broke at the slight tremor in his voice. I gripped his bicep and smiled up at him. If he could do that, I could do this.

"Okay." Despite the fear racing through my veins, I nodded. "Okay, let's do it."

Bash captured my waist and pulled me from Zel's lap to my feet. Teyr took my hand, steadying me as Bash undid the laces on my pants.

If you really don't want this, say no, Zelimir said in my mind. *If you even squeak the word, I'll cover you in force so thick no one will ever touch you again.*

I reached back and squeezed my commander's shoulder. *I need this.*

Zel grunted and stood. He and Bash pulled my pants and underwear down in a single smooth motion. I toed out of my boots as Teyr removed my chest support with one hand and tossed it aside.

I stood and walked toward the table on shaky legs. A wave of purple force swept in front of me, clearing the floor and the table of debris.

My face reflected fuzzily off the table's surface, more the implication of a person than a real image. I'd been constructed on a table just like this, been restrained on one for machines to probe and Jalan to coo over. My non-memories didn't contain a single imprint of those experiences, but I knew the table's cool surface nearly as well as I knew my own skin. Beyond the hiss of hydraulics or the taste of Earth dust, its slick feeling defined my worst memories. But I hadn't invented it.

I bent over the table. The cool metal stung my taut nipples. I hissed and started to lift back up, but Zelimir put his warm, large hand on my lower back.

In for five. Hold for five. Out for five.

I pressed my cheek against the cold metal and closed my eyes. Bash and Zelimir explored my back. Someone swept a hand along my spine. Someone caressed my ass. Together, they palmed my thighs, grazing that sensitive spot Teyr found. I groaned and opened my eyes. Teyr leaned against the table with computers, shucked his own pants, and petted a panting Shade, sitting at his feet. When I met his gaze, Teyr took his erection in his hand.

Someone pressed two fingers against my clit. I rocked into the table as my eyes fluttered shut once more. The cool metal calmed my super-heated body. I stretched my arms forward and grasped the edge of the table, holding onto it like an old friend.

Bash eased my thighs wider. I gasped, and he let go. A needy whine slipped from my lips, but Zelimir replaced him. My commander entered me in one smooth motion. I cried out. He'd been so careful last time, always checking and waiting. Now, he thrust into me roughly, stretching

my walls as far as they could go. My breasts slid across the metal, and I
held on tighter.

Just as suddenly, he slid out and backed away. I choked on the loss.
Bash grabbed my hips and slammed into me. My hips ached as he
crushed me against the table. He bent over my body to suck marks along
my spine. His cock hit me at a different angle, and he lingered at the end
of each thrust, pressing himself fully against me.

He pulled away, and I forced my eyes open. Shade's robes lay
discarded on the floor as he knelt fully nude in front of Teyr and licked
up the length of his erection. I met Teyr's molten gaze.

The metal of the table warmed under my skin. If I were nothing
more than a machine trapped in my own imaginations, I could not have
created four fae so perfect and unique. I wanted to feel all of them, find
their differences and similarities, inscribe this moment in my mind as
proof.

"Teyr," I gasped.

Teyr toyed with Shade's ears. "Yes, love?"

Zelimir entered me once more, smacking my ass as he slid home. A
bright burst of pain sparkled up my spine, combining with the pleasure
into an intoxicating new sensation.

"Please," I moaned.

Shade took Teyr into his mouth, eliciting a low groan from the
ember. I swallowed, surprised at the rush of additional moisture
between my legs.

"I think—" Teyr shook his head as if to clear it. "As much as I'd love
to fuck that pretty mouth of yours, I'm a little busy." He stroked the top
of Shade's head. "I can't just leave him hanging."

Zelimir slipped back out.

I pouted. "You could—"

Zel rammed home again, and this time, he wrapped an arm around
my ribs and pulled me upright. I groaned as the new angle pressed
against something sensitive inside me.

"Bash, on the table. Kneel." Zel thumbed my nipples.

The dragon obeyed, his erection bobbing proudly in front of him.
Teyr grunted. Zelimir lifted me off of him and laid me on the table

between Bash's legs. My heart pounded in my ears. I'd agreed to bend over the table, not put myself back in the same position I kept finding myself in.

My commander caressed my face. "This position is just as safe as the others. Just as real."

I grabbed the edges of the table and shut my eyes. My mates' need still roared through me, and the stale air still lay quiet outside the lab door. I turned my face into Zelimir's massive hand and inhaled. Vanilla, dark fruit, and the animal scent of sex.

I turned back and opened my eyes. Bash knelt before me, scales swarming across his skin. I needed to face this. I nodded. Zelimir smiled. He pulled me up the table until my head fell off the end, and I found myself eye-level with his erection. He tapped my chin, and I opened my mouth. Bash lifted my ankles to his shoulders.

As one, they entered me, and my world shrank to sensation. Bash hit that spot inside me every time and drove me into Zelimir, sending him deeper down my throat. I tried to roll my tongue, my hips, to move, to help, but I didn't need to. My mates pinned me between them and wrung pleasure out of my body.

My orgasm built like a wildfire. My breath came at the end of muffled moans. Bash grunted as his thrusts sped, growing impossibly stronger. I couldn't remember a time before my mouth contained this much of Zelimir. I wouldn't want to go back if I did.

Bash found my clit and rubbed frantic circles around it as his hips began to stutter. He ripped his cock out of me with a growl. His fingers tensed on my clit. Hot liquid splattered across my chest as his Cara exploded with pleasure.

My mind whited out as I came with him. Through the haze, I felt Teyr join us over the edge. Zelimir pulled out of my mouth. He planned to finish himself off now that I'd been satisfied.

I pulled my legs off Bash's shoulders and spun to face my commander. He started to shake his head, but I covered his mouth. I'd spent months waiting for these fae to wake up and do what I wanted them to. Now, on this fucking table, I wouldn't wait anymore. I wrapped my legs around his waist and pulled him into me.

He sank deeper with a low groan. I dropped my face onto his chest and scraped my teeth over his nipples. Finally, he grabbed my ass and began thrusting. My second orgasm built to match the dam of pleasure I felt him holding back.

I leaned back and ran my hands over his chest. "I'm close, Zel."

Shade's Cara dissolved into pleasure behind us.

Zelimir groaned. "K—"

He froze. My lust banked, and I dropped my hands. I couldn't be called that, not on this table, not in this moment. But I couldn't go nameless forever, either. All the people I'd been swam through my mind, none of them fitting quite right in a life spent running away.

I ran my thumb over his bottom lip. "Call me Kay."

"Kay." He tasted the name, rolled it around in his mouth. "I like it."

I shivered. The vibration reminded me of his cock still seated inside me. I pulled him closer, and he groaned.

"Kay, I'm so fucking close."

I captured his mouth, and he returned to his frantic pace. I rocked into every thrust, my orgasm roaring back to life. He grabbed my ass, lifting and dropping me, driving ever deeper and faster.

Bash pressed his lips to my neck. Shade slid his long fingers over one of my breasts, while Teyr teased the other. I moaned into my commander's mouth. Every movement sent a wave of heat from my head to my toes.

Zelimir thrust again, and the waves crashed together in a cacophony of sensation. My moan turned into a scream as my entire body tensed. My commander exploded inside me. I sank into the pleasure. Slowly, my mind cleared, and the table below me filtered back into my awareness.

The table didn't spring to life with cables, didn't bind and trap me. I simply sat on a strange table. A strange, real table. I'd been dreaming of my mates for months, and I hadn't come up with anything half as good as what just happened. I exhaled and smiled at Teyr.

My commander pulled out and pressed a kiss to my lips, drowning me in his love. All of their love. Shade and Teyr moved their hands to my arms. Bash rested his head against my shoulder. We just stood together, panting and feeling.

"Ah, Commander Zelimir?" Farquin called from the door. "Your communication bowl is blinking."

I cursed and crossed my arms over my breasts. Thankfully, Farquin remained outside.

Zel looked at me. "Are you going to be all right, Kay?"

I dropped my hands to my lap. "I don't think I'll ever be the same, but I'm gonna be all right."

35

ZELIMIR

I PRESSED A KISS TO KAY'S FOREHEAD, THEN PULLED ON MY pants. By the time I reached the door, the foggy glass bowl in Farquin's palm lay still. I swore and grabbed the pouch of pre-mixed herbs out of my pocket. He handed me the bowl. I ducked back into the lab, sprinkled the herbs over the bottom, ran my finger around the rim, and waited.

Behind me, my mates dressed. Bash *pulsed* that he would take Kay to the small bathroom he found during his exploration. My gut clenched. I'd never shared with my mates before. Locking eyes with Bash as he had driven Kay into me had been a new level of pleasure, but Teyr.... I hadn't enjoyed the weight of his eyes on me, his orders. They'd felt less like a helping hand and more like we weren't good enough for someone as experienced as him.

"No luck?" Teyr leaned against the table. He had dressed but left his pants unlaced.

The herbs hadn't so much as twinged. A finger of real worry crept down my spine.

"No." I leaned back out the door to Farquin. "Thank you. You may return to the ladder. We'll inform you when we need you again."

I stepped back into the lab and shut the door in the face of the open-mouthed Jalan. Bash and Kay re-entered, dressed and holding hands.

"Whatever my sister needed, she either found elsewhere or I'm too late." I sighed and emptied the bowl's contents back into the pouch of herbs, then put on my tunic. "Bash, can you sense anything from this distance?"

He shook his head. "I think I could have a full conversation with one of you on the opposite side of Thrae, but despite Dee—" He turned to her and raised a tattooed eyebrow.

"All your old nicknames are fine." She smiled shyly.

She'd whispered her own name for the first time with me inside her. I would treasure that memory for the rest of my days.

Bash inclined his head. "Despite Dee's boost, I still can't cover more than half a mile for anyone else."

I ran my fingers through my already frizzing twists. I hadn't cared for my hair on the road. The dutiful part of my brain scolded me, but I ignored it. Kay leaned on Shade, petting his ears and buckling on her weapons belt with a small smile on her face.

"Do you have something to say to me?" Teyr slid to my side and bumped me with his hip.

I scowled. He wanted me to admit he'd been right about us sharing one another from the beginning. I didn't want to see his smug grin.

"That was a threesome with spectators." I swallowed a grimace. By all the stars, I sounded like Shade. "Bash, Teyr, keep an eye on Farquin," I said before the ember could reply. "Kay, are you going to watch any more of the videos?"

She inhaled shakily. "I don't know. They're probably just a bunch of growing, then when he released me."

I nodded. "We have the journal." I looked at the necromancer. "Stay with her."

Shade wound an arm around her waist with a sly grin as my other two mates left with Farquin's abandoned blaster arm. I glanced at the communication bowl again. Cordelia's last words to me—to Kay, in some ways, but she did hand me the bowl—about pulling each other out of trouble thudded against the back of my skull.

"If you need me, *pulse*. I'm going to head to the surface." I glanced around the lab, the strange stone walls. Maybe the walls block the signal. "I want to try to reach Cordelia again."

"Be safe." She kissed my cheek. "Maybe one of these days we'll actually get to have a night in Punaky's Pub. I still haven't tried that liquor." Her Cara filled with wonder. "I don't know what my lifespan is anymore. We might have all the time in the world."

I gripped the bowl and swallowed against a sudden lump in my throat. She hadn't mentioned a future since she rescued us from the Academy. I wanted to take her into my arms and never let her go, but we didn't have time for my silly sentiments. I strode from the room.

At the base of the ladder, I found Bash and Teyr staring at a now re-armed Farquin. I nodded to the three of them and explained my plan.

Farquin grinned. "You know, it's long been theorized that this—"

I waved his words away as fire sparked on Teyr's fingertips. "I'd love to hear about that another time. I have calls to make."

"I'll be right here when you're ready." Farquin smirked. "Or anywhere else she needs me."

I ascended the obviously goblin-built ladder three rungs at a time. I still didn't know what to make of the Jalan's presence. He seemed, at the very least, earnest in his desire to assist Kay. And by Bash's count, he had slain twenty goblins, a dozen Jalan, and a nearly equivalent number of Tech singlehandedly. If his mania didn't overflow again, he might be a powerful ally.

Afternoon sunlight painted the surface in bright colors, but I headed for the place we'd left the horses without seeing. I carried only Cordelia's bowl on me because I expected her to contact me only in a crisis, but I had others in my pack.

The horses grazed happily. I hurried to my bay Shire horse and pulled out Councilor Drax's bowl, then sat in the grass. First, I tried Cordelia again. No answer. Councilor Drax's bowl began glowing. I dumped the herbs from Cordelia's bowl into his and ran my finger around the top with a pounding heart. His thumb-sized form sprang to the surface instantly.

"Zelimir!" my old mentor cried. "It's time, they're going, it's now."

"What?" I shook my head. "What is happening now?"

"Ambrocio and Xerxes." He panted. "They've banded together while Gnuq and Odhrán are too busy fighting each other to 'handle the threat in front of them.'"

"And that threat is Ar-a-mach." My blood went cold.

"And Kinnia." He caught his breath. "They—"

"Kay," I said.

"Kay." Councilor Drax inclined his head. "They just left, but they're taking a force of Caras and Seccas large enough to require some time to move."

I sucked in a breath. "Caras don't fight fae."

"I stood against the plan." Drax shook his head. "So they stripped me of my title with, according to Ambrocio, the Upper Council's approval."

That hit me like a punch to the gut. As my world came apart, as I realized the organizations and hierarchies I put my trust in didn't deserve that trust, I'd been able to hold onto the fact that Councilor Drax was a good man in power. Now, my old mentor was simply a good man.

"I'm sorry," I murmured.

"It's all right." He grinned. "For all their magic, they're too disorganized to bar me from the Council chambers." His pink eyes glowed.

Councilor Drax—Drax would be fine. I needed to figure out how to reach my family. "Are they marching on Stoneheim?"

He shook his head. "They know the main force isn't there."

And Father wouldn't tell me where the main force was because I refused to join his cause. A growl tore from my chest. Even when I wanted to do what he wanted, he conspired to stop me.

"Do you know where my father's force is?" I asked.

"Are you not—" He shook his head. "Yes, but if you're not already there, I don't think you should go."

I clutched the edges of the bowl. My father was the same fae he'd always been, but when we first arrived at Stoneheim, I hadn't recognized Cordelia, my father's new right hand. As I watched her with Kay, as I saw her without him, she reminded me more and more of the firebrand I grew up with. She had the same force of personality, the same determination to follow through on what she deemed right. Even if I didn't have a duty as a son, the world would lose too much if we lost her. I had to go.

"Tell me," I said.

He sighed. "They're at the clearing where the Battle of Light took place."

My heart skipped a beat. I remembered the field with crystal clarity. It was only a day's ride from here, and nearly a week from the Academy. But I never wanted to return, and none of my mates would unless I forced them. I was so tired of forcing them.

"Thank you," I said numbly. "I'll let you know what happens."

"Ar-a-mach is an army, Zelimir," he said. "They may well be fine."

"They're my family. I have to go." I shook my head. "Does this have anything to do with Kay? Were Councilors Ambrocio and Xerxes the ones trying to kill her in the trials?"

"No one wanted to kill her." He frowned. "I never approved anything that would've killed her."

"What?" I furrowed my eyebrows. "You had to know the last trial was too dangerous."

"I...." He pursed his lips. "I remember that trial somewhat indistinctly. What happened?"

My heart thudded unevenly. "Can you tell me what happened in my original trial?"

"That would be the climb, yes? A nearly hundred-foot-tall sheer cliff face with one rest point in the middle, twenty minutes for you to get your whole Cara to the top." He laughed. "You beat it handily."

I nodded as worry wrapped icy fingers around my spine. "And Shade's most recent?"

Drax hummed. "I'm not sure Shade had a trial this time around."

My worry settled into chilling certainty. Someone had tinkered with his memory. Only another Councilor would be powerful enough, and Councilor Odhrán focused on conjuring.

We'll join you soon, Bash said. *Farquin refuses to stay behind.*

"I have to go." I needed to talk to my mates.

Drax nodded, and I dumped out the herbs.

I stared into the dark communication bowl. My mates had their own feelings about Ar-a-mach, and my family in general. If they refused, I would go on my own. I couldn't abandon my duties as a brother, nor as a soldier defending this world, but I couldn't order them to go with me. Not for this. A hollow feeling took up residence in my chest.

I *pulsed* back a simple affirmative. Farquin would complicate the conversation, but I didn't imagine my mates could subdue him now that he had his arm back.

BY THE TIME MY MATES ARRIVED WITH FARQUIN IN TOW, I had a fire crackling and a pot of stew bubbling over it. My frayed nerves bunched my muscles painfully. Bash stood next to me. Kay sat on one of the logs I'd put around the flames. Teyr took the seat on her left, and Shade crowded in on her right. Farquin helped himself to the stew and took the log directly across the fire from them.

We didn't have supplies for six. We'd need to hunt or shop, either of which would slow us down. I shook my head. I couldn't plan for a trip I didn't know my mates would be making. I needed to ask them.

"Did you watch the rest of the videos?" I asked instead.

Kay shook her head. "I turned on the next one, saw myself grow a few inches in that tube, and shut it off." She shuddered, and a softer sort of fear and disgust filled her Cara, something more like being creeped out.

I handed her a bowl of stew. She wrapped her hands around it gratefully.

"You know," Farquin said, "I could tell you what happens at the end."

She frowned. "I don't want to know what you think is important for me to know anymore."

A look of genuine devastation crossed his face. "I will wait to be asked."

Teyr snorted as I handed him a bowl. "I bet. You totally seem like someone who's good at listening."

Farquin pressed a hand to his chest and opened his mouth.

Bash accepted his bowl and said to me, "Did you reach your sister?"

"No." I ladled out stew for Shade and myself. "I got Drax."

Everyone looked at me. I never used his name without a title.

"They stripped his rank as Councilor." I stared at my bowl and sat on the third log. "And perhaps tinkered with his memory over the last couple months."

"What?" Teyr asked through a mouthful of stew.

I explained quickly.

Farquin raised his flesh hand timidly. Kay narrowed her eyes but nodded at him.

"Odhrán has some power to influence the mind, but he's far from the most powerful councilor in that field." He spooned up a bite of stew. "For that, I'd look to Gnuq."

I nodded. The satyr was renowned for his ability to control crowds, which helped him run the Academy, but rumors circulated that he could be even more powerful one-on-one.

Bash handed me a bottle of water he must have pillaged from Elijah's lab. I looked at the clear, smooth plastic, so foreign to this world.

"And there's something else." I swallowed. "Councilors Ambrocio and Xerxes are leading an attack on Ar-a-mach. We're closer, so we can rest the night, but I'm riding for their headquarters in the morning. They need me."

Bugs hummed in the wake of my words. Pink magic from the trees lit the night around us. Kay stood and crossed the circle to sit by my side. She rested her head against my shoulder in quiet support.

"I've been thinking," she said. "Elijah invented Alex's quest to save Earth, but...I liked having something to believe in. A purpose. And when I listen to Cordelia talk about Ar-a-mach, it sounds like something I could believe in."

My heart warmed.

"You want to join up." Teyr scraped a spoon through his stew. "After everything King Zephyr's done."

She shrugged "I don't want to join for him."

Shade whined. "My Kitty, we cannot trust him."

Frustration ghosted through her Cara. "Cordelia wants to build a better world for everyone. Trust her. Shit, trust me."

I trust you, Bash said. *Enough to fight a war at your side.*

She smiled.

"Fire, I'd give just about anything not to go to war. I don't actually need a big, motivating cause." Teyr tapped his feet. "But of course we're going. How many times do we have to say it? We're a team, a pack, a Cara, whatever word you like."

I grinned at the ember. I didn't need to order him, I only needed to ask.

"I will not abandon my pack," Shade said.

Teyr whooped and stood. "Ar-a-mach!"

Shade howled, and a grin stretched his lips. Even Farquin's brown eyes sparkled with excitement. My heart swelled, and I let my joy pour through the Cara. I'd tell them where we were going tomorrow.

36

TEYR

I SIGHED AND LOOKED UP AT THE FOREST AHEAD OF US.
Patches of fog clustered in low hollows and high branches of purple
trees slowly turning blue, and birds sang mournful songs. Even the
wilds conspired to bring our mood down.

Kay stared blankly ahead on her roan, twitching the reins every now
and again to keep in line. Her Cara felt more pensive than anything else,
but she'd shrugged Farquin off when we left in the morning, and she
kept glancing back at where he rode sullenly in the rear of the pack. That
just wouldn't do.

I rode up beside her. "So, are you still thinking about Zel's cock, or is
that just me?"

She blushed, and Zelimir *pulsed* a sharp reprimand.

"Maybe we don't talk about this when we're surrounded by others,"
she murmured.

"Others?" I smirked. "We were all there, except Farquin, who's too
sulky to even listen right now."

Real or not, I 'grew up' in the human world, she said. *One soul mate. One
partner. Now, I have four mates, and I don't even know if I have a soul.*

You have a soul. I put my hand over hers on her reins. *And I know you're
using that as an excuse to keep not talking about what happened back there.*

She wrinkled her nose. "You want to talk about stuff people aren't bringing up? Okay. What about what you said to me before I got on the table?"

I pulled my hand back and looked around. No one turned, but Zelly obviously could hear us well enough respond to my comment about his cock.

I don't even know what made me say that, I replied. *It was just...whatever I could come up with to get you through your block.*

"That's a lie." She met my gaze. "If I have to face myself, so do the rest of you."

"Then you should be talking to Zelimir." I shook my head. "He almost waded into battle against the Lower Council by himself."

She snorted. "Trust me, I will. But you changed the topic."

Fire, when did she get so smart? "So?"

She ran her hands along her reins and sighed. "Let's try this. One of my favorite jobs as a mercenary was relocating this loaded old lady. I don't even remember where anymore, but wow, she treated us like the shit under her oxen's hooves."

I raised my eyebrows. "This was your favorite because...?"

"Because in the middle of it, her daughter showed up." She chuckled. "Reamed her mom out while we watched and gave us double pay to take her back home."

"Ah, so you're a greedy human, as we first expected." I nodded sagely.

Kay wiggled her eyebrows. "Turns out, the woman was trying to move into her daughter's house. They'd been fighting about it for months. After three days of traveling back the way we came, the daughter realized her mom was using anger as a shield for how insecure the world made her feel as she got older. She just wanted to be relevant." Kay laughed. "We ended up turning around again and moving them in together."

The implication landed heavily on my chest, and I scowled. "I haven't treated anyone badly."

"I'm not saying that. I'm just saying I used to use Declan like that. A shield." She swallowed. "Anything that went wrong was my fault, not his. If I'd just been a better him, everything would've gone better. Being him meant I didn't have to deal with all my own bad parts."

I braided a few strands of my horse's golden mane. Kay didn't know what she was talking about. I'd just said that stuff to get her out of her own head. Of course, I was exceptional. I had to be. I fought my way up through the system, and when I got out, I had the balls to look back on that system and realize its flaws. Nobody un-exceptional could do that. Here, with only Kay's judgment-free eyes on me, did I really believe that?

No. I believed that stupid old bard. I didn't know if I'd ever really left the duel arena, primping and preening and winning the crowd's favor any way I could. I knew only vulnerability would have gotten Kay on that table, but that confession tasted sourer in the cold light of day, with all the blood in my head. It tasted like admitting I could only fail my parents. But I'd promised her honesty, at least. I opened my Cara to reveal the nauseating mix of shame and relief inside me for a moment, then snapped it shut.

She smiled softly. "I think you're exceptional."

I clapped my hands to my cheeks and pretended to look surprised. "Really?"

Kay snorted. "Shithead."

Behind her, the trees had turned a true, vibrant blue. The grass beneath them was ruby-red. I knew that combination.

"Zel?" I called. "Where exactly are we going?"

Kay looked at me sharply. Bash shared a matching worry with me.

Zel straightened. "The Ar-a-mach base camp."

"These trees look familiar," I murmured.

Kay looked at Bash as he opened his Cara to all our mates, revealing a mess of distrust and concern that matched my own.

"I'm going to try to send a message ahead to my sister." Zel laid his reins across his thighs and pulled a communication bowl from one of his saddlebags.

I frowned. The brush along the path rustled where Shade loped alongside us in wolf form, scaring half the beasts in the wilds. The way Zel ended the conversation only confirmed my suspicions. I'd heard

Light's golden laugh echo off these trees. But our commander wouldn't bring us—bring Shade—to that place. Would he?

Why are you all being weird? Kay looked at me.

I looked at Bash. *Should we tell her?*

We may be misremembering, he said. *The commander wouldn't do this.*

Ahead of us, the trees grew denser and darker, nothing like the blue we'd been riding through. I exhaled sharply. Maybe we'd ridden past the spot where Light had died. Zel's bowl connected, and he began muttering. After a few moments, he dumped out the herbs, then pulled his horse to a stop and dismounted. We halted as he faced us.

"Ar-a-mach needed to hide somewhere the Councils would never think to look for them," he said.

My stomach dropped. "No."

I slid off my horse and stepped forward. The trees ahead of us weren't just dark, they were black. Like they'd been burned.

Zel held up his hands. "Please, just listen—"

I didn't want to hear anything else. I sprinted past him and shoved through the thick, blackened leaves. My heart skipped a beat. A massive clearing spread out in front of me, surrounded by more blackened trees, with only a few blades of red grass poking up through the dark dirt. Colorful tents crowded around each other in the center, and fae wandered back and forth between them. But I couldn't pull my gaze away from the Tech.

The ChargeTech that had taken Light's life to destroy remained frozen where it had stopped the moment we lost him. Those Fire-damned tents stood beneath its thirty-foot-tall rectangular metal body, as if some of the dozens of blasters sticking out on jagged arms weren't aimed directly at them.

That day, after Drax had given the order for us and every other Cara in the area to ride for the massive rift, Light bet me a drink that he'd take down more Tech than me. After the funeral, when everyone had finally left his grave, I'd taken a glass of his favorite cider and poured it onto the dirt that covered his body.

Zelimir shoved through the trees behind me.

I whirled on him. "Why the fuck would you bring us here?"

He put a hand on my shoulder and shoved calm through the Cara. "I wanted to explain before we entered the clearing. I thought we could support the fight from outside, never actually have to see...."

Kay joined us. Bash crashed through the branches.

She stared up at the ChargeTech as horror flickered through her Cara, then she looked at Zel and me. "Why is this worse than any other Tech?

"This is where we lost Light," Bash murmured.

Zelimir couldn't be this stupid. He couldn't have thought this wouldn't hurt us. He couldn't be this bad of a—

My stomach flipped. I spun. We had to keep Shade out.

He poked his wolf nose past the edge of the tree line.

37

SHADE

MY VISION NARROWED TO THE TOWERING TECH AT THE center of the field. Char and blood crowded the scents of game and forest rot from my nostrils. My skin crawled. The song of Thrae screamed in my ears toward a feverish conclusion. Blue-black magic wrapped around me, and my paws gave way to fae hands. My fingers met the dirt in front of me as my wolf form disappeared. I clawed at the ground in an effort to pull my wolf back into me.

I my mind's eyes, I watched as Light smiled in the instant before he tumbled to the ground. A wild howl tore from my fae lips.

My Kitty knelt at my side and wound her fingers into my hair. She spoke alien words that flowed in one ear and out the other. I sank deeper into the dirt and begged my wolf to take me, but the magic wouldn't obey my call, racing toward its own desperate climax. I had killed him. I stood here while my magic ripped the life from him. I breathed this air in the last moment I had ever truly breathed.

She pulled me into her lap and cradled my head in her hands. One of my ears pressed against her rib cage. Through the screaming char, her life signs beat into my skull. I inhaled one heartbeat, exhaled the next.

Her words dripped out of time with the magic's song, in time with her own heart. A slow, measured pace. Quiet. Other voices echoed around and over and through hers, but I discarded them. Slowly, her voice resolved into words.

"Shade," she murmured. "Shade, I'm here. I've got you. I'm right here."

My Kitty. Light never knew her. He would have loved her, loved her, loved her.

"Can you look at me?" she asked.

My eyes watered. I blinked and trembled with the effort of keeping the Tech in my sight. If I looked away, it would spring back to life, would force me to take another mate from myself and my pack.

"Shade?" my Kitty said.

She wanted me to look at her. She would never ask me to hurt our pack. I wrenched my gaze from the Tech and onto her. Her gaze, the same delicate blue as the lips of an air-deprived body, bore into mine. More sensations fought for my attention. She stroked my hair and softly around my ears. Worry, frustration, and determination warred in her Cara.

"Good," she said. "Just keep looking at me. I've got you."

Her heartbeat pounded in my ear. The music of Thrae slowed to match her rhythm, and finally, finally, I could sink my fingers into my magic again. My wolf wrapped around me with a tingling itch. The cacophony dimmed. My pack stood nearby, yelling at an approaching someone, a cluster of smells I vaguely remembered from my pack leader's home. Other fae, living fae, went about their day in the distance.

No life signs reached me from the Tech itself, but dozens, hundreds of corpses answered from beneath the dirt. I closed my eyes. My Kitty petted my hair. Her heartbeat rang even louder in my wolf's body, a steady drum I clung to with all my might.

"When I landed back on Earth," she said, "I wanted to give up. I'd spent so long trying to get away but ended up right back there." She swallowed. "But I couldn't stay there. I needed to get back to you. I know how overwhelming all this is, but please don't give up on us, Shade."

Her words moved to the heartbeat of the drum. What did she want?

"The Jalan couldn't move the ChargeTech after the battle," said someone in a high, musical voice. "So, they hollowed out the insides and turned it into a livable space."

"That has nothing to do with why we're here." My pack leader sounded sharp and sour.

I shrank. Most often, that tone was turned toward me. My Kitty curled around me and made soft sounds.

"I bargained for the Tech," the woman said.

"You chose this *place* as your headquarters?" my ember shouted.

"Yes," she shot back. "The Councils think the Jalan still own this land. They would never look for us here."

My dragon growled.

"Look, you don't need to like it, but we need to move." The woman's voice grew impatient. "I don't know when the attack is coming."

I forced my eyes open. My ember paced the blighted ground, nothing like his sure, leaping steps when last we fought here.

"You see Shade, right?" He gestured at my Kitty and me. "We can't go inside that thing."

In. In. The word echoed in my mind as I struggled for its meaning.

A cluster of fae heartbeats ascended one of the legs of the monstrosity and stopped just past the shell of its body. No signs of stress. They walked along the inside of the thing without so much as the tiniest spike in heart rate.

"You have to come inside," the woman said. "Father refuses to spend most of our time in there—he says it's not safe, even though I've checked the thing for traps a dozen times—but it's the only place we're certain we can't be overheard. I want to take advantage of what time we have left to plan."

I trembled. In. They wanted me to breach the thing, to walk amongst its guts, to see what my magic had wrought. But I already knew. I'd watched my Light die. My Kitty nestled one hand in the fur of my belly and dropped kisses on the top of my head.

"Shade and Kay will remain outside." My pack leader's voice rang with certainty. "The rest of us can handle the planning."

Emotions too large for my wolf mind threatened. My breathing sped.

Light's bone burned inside my chest. I couldn't allow my pack to leave. I couldn't lose them.

Don't give up, my Kitty said.

I forced my wordless desire to stay with them across our bridges.

"I won't force you." My pack leader shook his head. "Take what time you need."

My Kitty looked down at me with wide, soft eyes. "I'm happy to sit with you. Whatever you want."

They didn't understand. I had to make them understand. I wouldn't give up, not even in the face of my greatest shame.

I...will...come. The words fluttered out of my mind.

My ember knelt on one knee by my head. Moisture shimmered in his golden eyes. "I'd stay out here myself if that didn't mean looking at the nightmare instead. Don't worry about it."

No.

Rest, Bash said. *I will walk it with you later, if you prefer.*

The magic's song swelled again. My fur receded back into my skin. I pulled free of my Kitty and stood to my full height, towering over my Kitty, over everyone except my pack leader and his sister.

"No!" Rotted arms shot out of the ground around my feet in answer to a call I didn't remember making. "We're a pack." I met my pack leader's gaze and let his purple eyes blot out the rest of the sensations, the emotions battering at my control. "I will go with you."

He studied me for a long moment, then turned to his sister. "As he says."

She sighed and led us toward the Tech.

My Kitty pushed to her feet, then took my hand and gently squeezed. *Thank you for not giving up.*

The dirt crunched beneath my feet. If I didn't concentrate on every step, place myself in the here and now, I would lose myself. Only her hold on my hand kept me moving forward. The rest of my pack faded away. The sister laughed, high and mocking.

I dove for her and tore the space between life and death forward to consume her. The song swelled. Blue-black mist enveloped her body, stretched forward in search of the other life signs around the base of the

Tech. What difference would it make if those around her died? Pawns in a war I never wanted to fight, betrayers, takers of my brother's name in vain.

As the cold of the space between seeped into my bones, my Kitty's hand warmed mine. She hadn't let me go. She trusted me. I swam against the song and released the magic. My pack leader's sister rocked back on her heels.

My pack leader stepped toward me, and for the first time in a long time, I could read his expression clearly. Fear. My ember—Teyr, I remembered his name as the song faded—extended a hand to stop me. Bash held a preparatory stance, ready to leap at me if I didn't stop. My Kitty alone remained where she had been before the song, though concern clouded her Cara.

Something dark and cold curled around my heart. I pulled my hand from hers and turned to storm away just as hundreds, thousands of new fae life signs appeared at the far edge of the clearing. A scream split the air.

"Attack!"

38

BASH

I whipped my head away from Shade's towering fury, away from the princess' frozen smile. A mountain of thoughts crashed through the forest on the other side of the clearing toward us, so many I couldn't pull them apart. Repeated refrains floated toward me.

Councilor Xerxes said—

Councilor Ambrocio said—

Before it gets bigger.

"The Lower Council." I unsheathed my axe.

Cordelia frowned and lifted a bracelet to her mouth. My commander nodded sharply and pulled his two-hander out of thin air. Teyr conjured a fistful of fireballs. Dee squared her shoulders. Shade gritted his teeth and stepped to her side.

"Ar-a-mach!" King Zephyr's voice echoed over the fray. "Our enemy descends upon us. Take up arms and fight. Fight for freedom!"

The first attacking fae burst from the trees.

Do whatever you have to do, my commander said. *Survival is paramount.*

My dragon roared, and battle-clarity drowned out the implication of his words. I loosed my own cry and charged the encroaching army. My mates pounded after me, alongside the legions of Ar-a-mach.

A tall, ethereal looking Secca officer in red pants and a cream tunic at the front of the army reached out his hand, and my feet tangled uselessly together. I tripped, and he released his hold. I turned the stumble into a roll and came up with my axe still at the ready in front of a floating oozekin in Cara cream and brown. The councilors had called all Caras back to the Academy.

I swung. The oozekin parted easily around my blade and reformed in the same spot. Zelimir had already fought his way deep into the horde, and Teyr fought a circle of Secca officers.

My dragon snarled at me, and I grabbed Zelimir's power over the bridges. The oozekin spat a globule of glowing magic in my direction. I dodged the magic as I splashed a fine layer of glowing purple force over the blade of my axe, then ducked under a gout of fire spraying from a nearby fae.

A leafy part-treant in red pants swung a bark-covered claw at my head. I cracked my axe into the treant's trunk. My blade sunk deep into his skin, and he groaned as translucent brown blood flowed. A death blow, if he didn't make it off the field fast enough. Something in my chest panged.

A fuzzy-eared shifter nearby screamed and launched a blast of pure-white magic at my chest. I threw up a telekinetic shield, and the magic ricocheted into the fray. With a snarl, the shifter pulled twin cherrystone swords from his belt and lunged at me.

Bash, your six! Zel called.

I yanked my axe up to block the shifter's blades, and a body collided with my back. The impact threw me forward, and the shifter used the momentum to slice into my cheek. The cut burned worse than a single slash should. Magic on the blade. Or poison. I threw my arms around the small shifter and tackled him to the ground.

The person that rammed into me landed next to us. A tinggi elf in vibrant blue robes, clearly Ar-a-mach, and bleeding from a gash to the abdomen. The Secca shifter struggled against my grip, trying to get his swords between us. I snatched his wrists with a band of telekinesis and pinned them to the dirt above his head.

He spit at me. "Traitor."

I slammed my axe into his wrists, severing both with a single blow. He screamed. I shoved to my feet and ignored that feeling in my chest.

The battle swirled around me. Screams split the air. Memories of the civil war fought through the burning pain in my cheek. I'd seen fights like this before, hapless chaos where only uniform color separated one side from the other, but something felt wrong.

Twelve o'clock! My commander hollered.

I looked up just in time to see Brettrus' horns parting the crowd ahead of me. With a burst of Teyr's fire, I shot into the sky and landed on the far side of the minotaur just in time to watch him slam through a huddled cluster of gnomes in bright orange suits. They tumbled to the ground in a bleeding heap. Brettrus didn't spare them a glance as he turned back to me.

Someone shouted, "I've got this one."

"No, I do!" another replied.

Brettrus lowered his head for another charge. I clawed for Shade's necromancy. Decay melted on my tongue, but four half-rotted corpses crawled out of the dirt and launched themselves at the minotaur's horns. A haunting melody wound over the battlefield and called me into its rhythm. I spun in time as I dove out of the way.

Fight. Shade's voice floated like a whisper on the wind against the song. *The music will swallow you whole.*

The corpses dangled off Brettrus' horns. He tore at them, but the music swelled as he batted their hands away. I made myself stone, a fortress, a thing without ears. Slowly, the song tapered off, and the corpses fell still. Brettrus tore them away as I closed the distance between us.

Thank you, I said to Shade.

He didn't reply. Brettrus whipped his hardened fist at my head. I tried to dodge, but a gust of wind forced me into the blow. I glanced around, expecting Terris, but found a sheepish short elf in pink and gold.

"Trying to deflect!" she said.

Brettrus laughed. "You can't stop picking the losing side, huh?"

I swung my axe. He didn't dodge. The blade lodged in his chest, but with his toughened skin, only drew a thin line of dark blood.

Dots of Ar-a-mach color studded a sea of Cara and Secca cream around me. The civil war pitted matched enemies against each other. Even with far more Seccas than Caras, this was a slaughter.

"Fight!" King Zephyr yelled over the fray. "Show them our might! Our dedication! That we will battle to the last fae for freedom!"

"Retreat!" I yelled and *pulsed*.

"To where?" Brettrus swung his massive fist again.

I tossed up a shield, then slammed it out, into his chest. He stumbled back. I stared around the field. Dead trees behind us. Dead trees ahead. None would give us cover.

Ar-a-mach will die, I said to all my mates. *There's nowhere to retreat.*

The Tech. My commander's voice slid over the bridges with hard, cold certainty. *We needed...exceptional magic to get through its shell.*

The ground shook under my feet, and I leapt out of the way of an icy explosion that froze a group of Ar-a-mach fighters in place. Teyr *pulsed* refusal. Zelimir argued back. I pinned Brettrus to the ground with a sheet of telekinesis, handed that hold to my dragon, and began prying members of Ar-a-mach out of the chunk of ice that remained.

"Run for the ChargeTech," I ordered each one. "Tell everyone you see. Run for the Tech."

It is that or die, Shade said.

I'd rather live, Dee replied.

That silenced Teyr. The cry began to echo up from different parts of the battlefield.

"The Tech! Run for the Tech!"

I returned my attention to Brettrus on the ground. My dragon bellowed for me to kill him. One swing of my axe would sever his head as neatly as I severed the shifter's wrists.

That thing in my chest panged. I'd killed fae in the civil war. My commander told me to do what I must. But I'd watched the titan make foolish choice after foolish choice on Council orders, just as the attacking fae did now. If we hadn't found Dee, we would have been these fae. I would not kill them.

I slammed the butt of my axe into Brettrus' skull once, twice, three times. He slumped, unconscious, and I pulled my telekinesis back. My dragon roared his disapproval.

"No!" King Zephyr's disembodied voice cut through the noise. "Show them no weakness! We are Ar-a-mach, and we are strong!"

A group of rebels running past me stopped and stared at the sky like they could see King Zephyr there. Beyond them, Dreng, the earth elemental from Lir's Cara, lined up an attack. I sprinted toward them and threw up a shield of telekinesis as large as I could summon over them. Dirt and mud rained down on the side of the shield as Dreng surged forward. The rebels stared at me, but I glared at Dreng and hefted my axe.

Dee leapt out of the fray and smashed Dreng over the head with her folded bow. My dragon purred. I nodded and dropped the shield. Behind her, a metal globe the size of a human head with a glowing red center floated above the fray. Tech. And Tech I'd never seen before.

I snarled. *Move.*

Dee frowned, but she hurried the group of rebels toward the base of the Tech. The globe trailed after her. I launched a telekinetic net at it, but it sailed out of the way and swerved back toward Dee. A slim, red beam shot out of its core. My dragon placed his own shield between the globe and her, but the beam shot right through. I gathered Teyr's fire and crouched to leap for the Tech.

Bash, my commander said. *At the ChargeTech's legs. Crowd control needed.*

My dragon urged me to pursue the new Tech, to destroy it before it could touch Dee with a beam or anything else. My muscles bunched to pounce.

The complex smell of mingled fae blood met my nose, a smell I couldn't separate from the war. Following orders saved my life. I couldn't deviate now. I locked my dragon away and rushed through the fighting toward the legs of the ChargeTech.

At their base, I found Zelimir and Teyr in front of two of the four legs with their hands out in front of them. They strained to hold shields of force and fire around wooden lifts filled with fae that slid up the legs to openings in the ChargeTech's sides. Secca officers battered their shields, battered my mates. My dragon beat against the inside of my skull. Dee, we had to protect Dee.

A nonmagical arrow flew over my head. Dee stood near the third leg where a lift filled with fae rose upward. She swung her bow at any fae who got within reach. Shade stood at her side, his gaze trained on a blue-black portal fae poured into while a loose ring of bodies fended off Secca officers fighting to reach the two of them. The flying Tech had disappeared.

My stomach sank as I raced for the final leg and shielded its wooden lift. Fae piled into the box from all directions, and one of them pressed a hand to a rune on the inside of the lift to send it up the metal leg.

Lir lunged out from behind a striped tent and grabbed for a pile of stones I'd dismissed as art. A coil of water snaked out of the pile I realized covered a well and jutted toward Dee. I couldn't react while holding the shield. The water slammed into her chest, and she dropped to one knee. My dragon fought for release. He would hold the shield. I could trust him.

Lir spun a small cyclone from the well and it headed toward Dee. I *pulsed* to Shade before my commander could. He dropped the portal, transformed into his wolf, and launched himself at Lir. Zelimir nodded at me.

My dragon roared. With a deep breath, I let him stretch the shield over the lift Dee protected. The crowd around me grew less colorful as the members of Ar-a-mach retreated inside. I took hit after hit to maintain the shields. We had to hold.

Last load, Zelimir called.

I wrenched my head up and looked at the hundreds of advancing Cara and Secca warriors. Gray blood streamed down my bare chest. Pain thrummed along my lilac skin. Fae piled into the lift behind me. Geminai's Cara approached as a unit, though Brettrus wobbled. I grinned.

"Are you kidding me?" Teyr shouted to Geminai. "You'll really follow Council orders this far?"

Done, Dee said.

"I'll follow them anywhere." Geminai tore up a strip of ground below Zelimir, knocking him off his feet.

"You'll follow them to slaughter?" my commander demanded.

Brettrus charged me as the last load of fae piled off my lift above me. I dropped the shield, yanked my axe from its sheath, and raised the flat side level with his head. He slammed into the blade. His horns grazed my ribs, but he bellowed in pain.

Done, I said.

"Without the Council, there is no order," Terris shouted above the noise.

This wasn't order. This was death.

"At some point"—my commander glared up at Geminai—"you have to think for yourself."

Done, Teyr called.

And done, Zelimir said grimly. *Get inside.*

I launched myself into the lift and smashed my hand against the rune as a gout of Gorar's poison lanced through the air. Dee hauled wolf-Shade onto her lift and hit the rune on the side of the box. Teyr bowled a fireball toward Geminai. The troll leapt out of the way as Teyr and Zelimir jumped onto their lifts. Terris took to the air, and needle-thin spikes of wind ripped into my skin. Only the knowledge I'd endured worse gave me the strength to keep my hand pressed against the rune as the lift slid up the leg.

Finally, my lift reached the door, and I tumbled inside. Dee and I rushed to the other two lifts to help Teyr and Zelimir while Shade howled. I tossed a shield just beyond the door to protect my commander from Terris' onslaught, and Zel propelled himself inside on a burst of Teyr's fire. Dee fired arrows through the door she'd entered through as Teyr jumped through his own door.

Every door slammed shut in unison with a heavy, metallic clang. Darkness fell, then artificial lights flickered on. Metal walls covered in blinking panels surrounded a huge, square room filled with injured fae.

Cordelia stepped up to Zelimir and I with a bitter grin and blood matting her copper braids. "Welcome to Ar-a-mach."

39

ZELIMIR

THE MORNING AFTER THE ATTACK, A YOUNG GNOME WALKED up to me in the middle of attempting to find space for my father's thousands of zealots into what passed for rooms in the blinking metal body of the ChargeTech.

"Yes?" I asked, a bit sharper than I would've preferred.

The teenage boy jumped. "Um, King Zephyr wants you in one of the rooms on the top floor. He calls it a war room?"

I ran my hand over frizzy twists I hadn't yet fixed after a night on the metal floor and sighed. "All right. Did he say why?"

"Tactical review?" The boy shrugged.

The floor shuddered as something exploded against the exterior of the Tech. The Councilors hadn't abandoned their attack when we all escaped inside, but nothing had penetrated the thick metal shell—yet.

"Go get a spot to sleep in." I nodded at Kay in the middle of the fray, assigning beds because only she could remember the details of this place well enough.

He nodded and bounced away.

My father needs me, I said across all the bridges. *Bash, would you mind?*

My second *pulsed* an affirmative, and we ducked out of the chaos into one of the many hallways that wound the outer walls of the Tech. Panels blinked red and green in seemingly random patterns. Every now and again, something beeped. Part of me understood why Father kept everyone outside for as long as he did. This place turned my stomach.

"Why are you answering him?" Bash asked once we escaped the crowd.

I sighed. "These people need good leadership. He stands between me and that."

"So, you intend to help him?"

"I intend to help Ar-a-mach, as we agreed."

Bash grunted, and certainty settled in my chest. Kay may have asked us to take up this cause, but when she spoke about the rebellion, it sounded right. I owed the wilds my help.

On the top floor, only one of the doors between the lines of my father's thick, dark purple force magic stood open. I took a deep breath. Bash sent me a wave of calm. We stepped into a long, rectangular room, empty aside from a long, naturally grown wooden table with matching chairs around it. My father sat at the head, with Cordelia to his right, and his three closest advisors from Stoneheim to his left.

"Zelimir." He inclined his head. "Your arrival was fortuitous. Those mates of yours worked wonders holding off the Councilors' horde. I've already begun publicizing knowledge of their vicious attack against innocent fae."

"Father." I took the empty seat at the far end of the table, and Bash stood to my right. "My mates wouldn't have had to work so many wonders if you had taken advantage of the perfect fortified base your daughter placed at your disposal."

Kyrios, an older titan man I'd seen advising my father all my life, said, "Now, that's not quite accurate."

Another blast rocked the Tech.

"We fought this thing." Bash remained standing at my shoulder. "Zelimir's statement is extremely accurate."

Father frowned. "I had no way of knowing the inside of the Tech would be any safer than the outside. You can see how the fae resist the idea."

Cordelia shook her head at me surreptitiously, then turned to him.

"What Zelimir means to say is that he's glad he could help, and even more glad we had somewhere to which we could retreat. This attack only highlights what I've been saying about our combat readiness."

Megare, Mother's silver-haired best friend whom Father accepted as an advisor in the wake of Mother's death, pursed her lips. "I can't disagree. These fae clearly aren't able to face an enemy."

"Steady yourselves." Father studied me with icy eyes. "I called this meeting to discuss the events of yesterday, but also to officially welcome my son into our fold."

Every titan around the table bent their head in my direction. The old shackles started falling into place, tying me to what he wanted.

I locked gazes with my father. "What fold is that, exactly?"

"Ar-a-mach," Cordelia said.

I narrowed my eyes at my sister. She smiled.

Father smiled with her. "I respect that you are your own fae, fear not, but your aid"—he inclined his head toward Bash—"and that of your Cara will be invaluable to our cause."

Bash grunted. "What sort of aid?"

"Whatever you see fit to provide." Father spread his hands. "Theos, what do we need?"

Theos, the sharp-eyed, younger titan Father had begun listening to not long before I heeded the call, folded his hands in front of him. "It would be ridiculous to waste a Cara of such renown on something as trivial as supply runs. Would you be willing to travel and spread the message?"

"No." I scowled.

Theos clucked his tongue.

"Your people need training." Bash eyed Theos.

"We could help with that." I smiled.

Two turns through the Academy surely gave us enough experience, and training would keep Father from trotting us out like pets.

"Interesting." Megare looked at Bash for the first time. "And how would you go about that?"

The fae are disorganized, Bash said to me privately through the Cara.

They need to be sorted by ability, then trained to the peak of their effective potential in the smallest units possible.

"Well—" I began.

"We split them into five groups," Kyrios cut in. "Assign each to one of your son's Cara and see what they can do. Anything else would be unnecessarily complicated."

Father nodded. "Agreed. Zelimir, make it so. Call your mates...oh, commanders or something to make the other fae listen."

I started to stand. My father seemed to have learned less from our last encounter than I'd hoped, but at least Bash and I kept him from walking all over us. Perhaps, as commander, I could steer him away from any disastrous ideas.

"Wait," Cordelia said. "I like this plan, but I worry it's short-sighted."

I froze.

Kyrios scowled. "How so?"

"Zelimir is a competent trainer, but that's a waste of his tactical abilities." My sister looked at me. "He'd be more useful in here with us."

"You mean, make him one of King Zephyr's advisors?" Megare studied me closely.

"He's green." Kyrios shook his head. "King Zephyr has all the tactical skill we need."

Theos frowned at the older titan. "I wouldn't call him green, but I agree we don't need him. A Cara is a blunt instrument and best together. Let it be that."

Their words flowed over me as Father met my gaze. He'd mastered neutrality long ago, so I only saw myself reflected in his eyes. I looked tired and small.

Training the fae would be an easy task. Almost pleasant, removed from the politics I hated. And, realistically, removed from any consistent ability to affect my father's decisions. If I wanted to do all I could for Ar-a-mach, I had one choice.

"Well, son?" he said. "If I offered you the role, would you take it?"

I straightened. "Graciously. Thank you for the recommendation, sister."

Cordelia grinned.

Something bright lit my father's face. "Wonderful. Escort your mate out, and let's get down to real business."

I stood and led Bash out to the hallway. "Tell the others to begin training as soon as they're done with rooms. Just start with Kyrios' way for now." I smiled. "I'll work on the rest."

My second inhaled slowly. *Are you sure about working so closely with your father?*

I frowned down at the dragon. He'd watched me stand up to my father barely two weeks ago. He saw me in there just now. I didn't roll over and let Father turn us into mascots for his cause, didn't let him have his way like I used to. Did my second really trust me so little?

I am your commander, I said. *I know what I'm doing.*

He nodded and walked away down the sharply angled hall. I stepped back into my father's war room.

40

KAY

AFTER ALMOST A WEEK IN THE AR-A-MACH BASE, I SHOULD have gotten used to the way heads turned when I strode down the halls. Instead, as I walked from my designated training area back to the room I shared with my mates, the hairs on the back of my neck rose to attention at the murmurs that chased my path.

Everybody here knew my name and as much of my story as King Zephyr found inspirational. They looked up to me, idealized my resistance to the Councils, and had no idea I contained at least as much Tech as the metal husk we all lived in.

Sometimes it felt like I'd stumbled back into pretending to be Declan, but with even higher stakes. At least I'd started getting the hang of navigating the place and sleeping through the night despite the occasional blinking light.

"Commander, come join us for an after-lesson lesson." The deep, male voice echoed off the metal walls.

I turned and tried not to sigh. When fae weren't staring at me, they were trying to get closer to the symbol of the rebellion. The source of the voice, a half-troll mixed with some shorter species I recognized from training, waved at me from a large, padded room. Before I could answer, Farquin beelined around a corner toward me.

The fae grimaced. "Next time."

I offered him a weak smile and sighed as Farquin stopped in front of me.

"SISTER." He smiled.

I hurried him away from the fae. "I told you not to call me that."

"Yes, sorry." His grin looked utterly unrepentant. "I just haven't been able to catch you in the last few days."

A group of Teyr's chattering students entered the hallway with us and instantly fell silent to glare at Farquin. I didn't know whether the fae of Ar-a-mach hated him for his time with the Councils or his Tech. Regardless, he'd been given quarters on the top advisory level to avoid exactly this kind of attention. I'd hoped that would keep him away from me too.

I steered us into one of the right-angled hallways along the outside walls that led to the top of the ChargeTech to return him there. "What do you want?"

"Oh, just to talk." Farquin waved his blaster airily, and a few fae scattered out of the way.

"About?" I asked.

"How do you feel about living inside a Tech like this?" His eyes glowed with curiosity. "Does it feel strange, like living inside a great corpse?"

"Strange is one word for it," I muttered.

A panel beeped next to us, and only days of practice kept me from flinching.

Farquin smiled like he could tell I was uncomfortable. "It unnerves you. Why?"

"Not because it's a corpse," I blurted.

I shook my head as we stepped onto the much quieter advisory level. The thick walls of purple force magic King Zephyr used to cut smaller, private rooms out of the Jalans' more open floor plan jutted into the hallway. The massive, square window in the outer wall allowed in the sole rays of sunlight into the Tech, and I drifted toward the window despite the density of blinking controls nearby.

"So, you don't consider yourself Tech?" he asked.

I whipped my head in his direction and glared.

He put his hands up. "Asked and answered. How does this place compare to Elijah's labs?"

I pursed my lips. Between Shade's meltdown, the attack, and spending my days running around one of the cavernous training rooms desperately trying to keep ancient warriors on the same page as literal twigs while I taught simple dodges and strikes, I hadn't thought to compare either lab to this place. Shit, I hadn't thought to do much of anything. I hadn't seen Zelimir for longer than a few minutes in days, Teyr came back pissy every night, Shade exhausted himself into wolf form training his students nearly daily, and Bash had been even quieter than usual.

Farquin leaned in, that wild curiosity burning in his eyes. "So, it is different. Have you noticed any physical changes from long-term exposure? Changes in appetite, sleep, digestion?"

"Stop asking about my shits." I scowled.

"As you wish." He took a step back. "But you are far more powerful than Elijah ever dreamed, far more than you realize. You'll never learn the extent of that power without pushing yourself."

I looked out the window over the blighted battlefield. Six years had passed, and still, almost no life had returned. I didn't need to access the sort of power that would do this.

Farquin seemed to get the hint. "I will leave you. But if you get curious, you might read that journal." He walked toward the small room King Zephyr gave him and shut the metal door behind him with a *clang*.

I should head to the room I shared with my mates and collapse on my cot to deal with Shade's exhaustion and Teyr's bad attitude and Bash's silence until dinner. I'd done so every day since we moved into the Tech, and it gave me a scrap of privacy with my mates. But staring out at the blackened ground outside, I found I wanted to know what Farquin kept alluding to. I wanted to be sure I wouldn't ever wreak the kind of devastation I saw outside.

I had hidden the journal in one of the many large pockets of my pants. None of the doors in the ChargeTech locked, when they worked at all, and I didn't like the idea of some curious rebel wandering into our room and blasting my secret all over the rebellion. I hadn't read past the book's first page. In a scrawling hand, it declared itself to be the seventeenth in a series, as well as the "Thrae copy," and the first paragraph was devoted entirely to complaining about the need for analog data, whatever that meant. I hadn't been able to handle the way my brain heard the words in Elijah's lilting computer voice.

Not to mention, privacy had been hard to come by inside the Tech. Even since the army outside slowly left—with rumors flying as to why—King Zephyr insisted time outside was strictly monitored. Even if the Councilors weren't attacking, we couldn't know they hadn't left spies, or some shit. So, I'd found the one spot inside that no one really went. At the very base of the body, below even where the lifts dropped people off, sat a mostly empty space with a burned black spot in the middle. Based on the pieces of the story I'd gotten from Teyr since we arrived, I guessed it was where the blast that killed Light had hit the ChargeTech. Everyone avoided the room, so I could sit down there and flip through the journal.

Several more of my students called out to me as I walked down the Tech, but I waved them all off and *pulsed* to my mates that I needed a little alone time this afternoon. I'd just finished fighting off everyone's— well, everyone but Zelimir, who had been too wrapped up in advising to answer anything lately—questions and requests to accompany me when I reached the door to my destination. I slid it open, and quiet washed out like a wave.

I stepped inside, then pulled the door shut behind me. Darkness crowded the space, and I flipped the switch to power on the electric lights. I sat against one wall and pulled the journal out. Everything Eiljah thought about me, without whatever kindness he might've used when talking to me directly, lay between the pages of the journal. The silence pounded against my ears, and loneliness threatened to swallow me whole.

I brushed my fingers over my mates' bridges, and the tastes of each of them flowed into me. A light-dappled forest and an underground river and a decaying log and neatly tilled fields in the wake of a flash flood that brought them the hydration they needed. I didn't need my mates next to me to have them with me. I didn't have to feel lonely anymore.

I opened the journal.

The first dozen entries covered stuff I basically already knew. My reaction time rivaled K1NN13's, which pleased him. The simulation seemed to be progressing well. The entries read exactly like the notes he spoke into the computer on Earth. No crueler, thankfully, but familiar enough to ensure the bright white lab stayed at the front of my mind. I reached for the bridges a few times to gather the courage to keep going as I read through every year of my life, scant months of his, from four to thirteen.

The next entry, a shockingly short one, began, *Something changed.*

40.789.18927

Something changed. After months of stability, the simulation neurotransmitter output spiked in the middle of the night. I checked every connection three times, but they're all tight. Kayel ran a total physical diagnostic when he saw the spike, and K1NN14's heart rate jumped at the same time, but it's since stabilized, and there seems to be no lasting consequences. An observation of the amniotic sleeve reveals no defects. Biologically, K1NN14 recently achieved fourteen years, just past the point at which K1NN13 failed. I've added hourly total diagnostics, but I don't want to depressurize the sleeve for an inspection unless I have to. K1NN13's early depressurization may have contributed to her demise, and I will not make the same mistake again.

I LEANED MY HEAD BACK AGAINST THE WALL. IN FOR FIVE. Hold for five. Out for five. The jargon was hard to parse, but it seemed like Elijah said the simulation did something weird right after I turned fourteen. Right when I met Alex and the rest of my family. Alex found me beaten and bloody, and offered me a better life with the first people who'd ever really loved me. I'd already been on the street for a few years at that point, and nothing else significant happened then. Or nothing as significant as the day that turned my life around.

It sounded crazy in my own mind. I sucked in another deep breath and steeled myself. Elijah couldn't see the simulation. I'd never know, one way or the other. I just had to read on.

More months passed. Nothing came of the spike, which he started calling a blip. The tight feeling in my chest when I thought about the day I met Alex faded under the weight of Elijah's scientific mumbo-jumbo. Page after page disappeared until only a few remained in the whole journal. My body in the tube—or sleeve, as he called it—turned seventeen.

My heart leapt into my throat. I knew what came next. On Alex's eighteenth birthday, two days after my seventeenth, he'd declared we were going to Earth to try to save the planet. The weeks of planning, of hoping, all led up to the moment where I killed my only family because I didn't believe I deserved them. I didn't want to see the worst moment of my from the outside, through Elijah's dispassionate recitation. I tossed the journal across the room. It hit the floor and slid, then stopped at the burn mark in the center.

My Kitty? Shade asked softly. *You have become distressed. May I join you now?*

I stared at the journal, the black spot. In the lab, Elijah said I'd escaped him. On the video, he said he'd see me at twenty, but the record of my real memories he played back clearly showed me roaming Earth at seventeen. Maybe I didn't have the whole story yet.

Did I really need to know everything? I could decide, like Teyr, that I didn't care. That belief would be enough to sustain me from here on out. I could just go to the room and let Shade crawl into my lap.

The burn spot on the floor taunted me. I'd been pushing my mates to grow, to face the things that hurt them and overcome, and it all came back to this burn mark. The moment they lost Light. Or did it? Lately, I sometimes thought they'd been fighting for far longer.

But I needed to face my own demons. Being human is about getting to decide what that means. I told Zel that months ago, and he threw it back in my face when I questioned myself. I sucked in a deep breath, stood, and crossed to the middle of the floor. I grabbed the journal. I wanted to be Kay. I wanted to live.

. . .

78.228.19399

Farquin has lost access to my lab. While I tended to 43278, K1NN14's simulation monitor started displaying an error message, and he chose not to get me. I should never have left him on observation. He still believes the project to be doomed, whatever he says to my face. Now, I can only hope he hasn't destroyed years of work with one careless choice. Computer, display and record error.

Error 34727837.

Farquin will be lucky if I don't hunt him down. When I modified the simulations to run independently, I added an alert for the rare possibility a K1NN model could lead the simulation too far off-program. Computer, display vitals.

By Earth's light, look at that. Elevated cortisol, oxytocin, racing heart rate. Computer, run a full diagnostic, I need to check on the sleeve.

Observation of the sleeve normal. Connections tight. REM at standard rate. Computer, diagnostic results?

Heart rate even higher, neurotransmitters spiking through the roof, high-power electrical activity—why didn't I build in a way to watch the simulation with her in the sleeve? I have no idea what K1NN14 could have changed. The parameters of the alert are fairly wide to allow her to experience maximum realism.

I'm going to have to depressurize the sleeve. She's grown far past any of the previous K1NN models developmentally, so I can't wake her unless she becomes critical. Too much hippocampus activity. But I may just be able to set off a cascade and bring the simulation back into line.

Computer, restart and re-run the simulation. If the code hasn't reasserted itself in an hour, activate procedure 925387. I have to get inside K1NN14's mind to save this project.

89.178.16037

An hour's passed with no change. K1NN14 has been depressurized and transported to the main lab table. If I lose her for this, I'll have Farquin's head. Initiate sim link.

There's a reason I've never done this before. The simulation bounces back and forth between text and video to best build K1NN14's neural pathways, but to those of us outside her brain, it's dizzying.

All right, she's made it to Earth. Burning passion to save it, good, good. Where has the program diverged?

Ah, there's another oxytocin spike as she thinks about—her friends?

Deviation identified. Computer, reassert simulation, focal point, Alex, Elaine, David, Harry.

There we go. This simulation is good, if I do say so myself. SpiderTech approaching to annihilate the deviant factors. Cortisol spike in K1NN14, but well within standard operating procedures. Enhanced REM. Myoclonus in the limbs.

And…that's the deviation eliminated. Error message shutting off. Fantastic. After a myoclonic episode like that, K1NN14 needs a bit more time in the open air before re-pressurization. Computer, wait another hour, then activate program 468675337.

MY EYES STUNG AS I BLINKED BACK TEARS, AND MY HEART pounded wildly. One entry left. I had to finish this before my emotions overwhelmed me, or I'd never pick the journal up again.

27.678.19076

Wh—where is she? Computer, run search program, target, K1NN14.

Negative? How could it be negative? Computer, run search program, target, open methods of egress for humanoid, six feet tall.

One. Fucking one.

Focus, Elijah. Data is data.

Subject K1NN14, left in pseudo-amniotic stasis on lab table one in the wake of simulation reassertion, has—fuck. Subject has vacated the premises. Last diagnostic showed heightened cortisol levels and decreased GABA to compensate. Heart rate spiked moments before disconnection. If I didn't know better, I'd say this was in reaction to the loss of her "friends," but K1NN14 lacks the ability to experience significant enough emotional dysfunction.

I am going to find her. No, Farquin is. This is his mistake. He can clean it up. I will not lose this specimen. I don't know how she revived from the stasis. I don't know how she changed the simulation that much! I have to get my hands on K1NN14, take her apart, and figure out what happened.

A FEW INCHES OF BLANK PAGE STOOD BETWEEN HIS FINAL sentence and the back cover of the journal. Anything he wrote after that must have ended up in volume eighteen, if he even kept writing. My mind clung to these simple facts to avoid the enormity of what I just read.

After my family died, I had run until my legs gave out. Then, I woke up in a lab with clear plastic walls. I tore all the cords and cables out of me and launched myself back into the world alone. I remembered the burning pain of the cables, how it felt so strangely sharp, and how grief clung to the back of my throat even thicker than it had before I collapsed. I'd always assumed I'd been numb for the first run, then captured. But I hadn't been numb. I'd still been in Elijah's simulation.

Tears rolled down my cheeks. I clutched the journal to my chest and trembled. Elijah killed my family. He killed them for what they meant to me, for how they represented my growth away from him. In a computer program built to make me miserable, I made my own happiness. I believed the world could be better. I loved Thrae despite him. I loved my family. Alex's eyes burned with a fire Elijah might've given him, but Alex made all his own. Elaine cared more deeply than I could imagine on some days, helping other street kids and sick birds and anything else we came across. Harry had a sense of humor and way of looking on the bright side I envy to this day. David kept us out of trouble, reigned in our wildest ideas, made sure we never strayed too far into the dark.

Sobs rolled out of me into the silence of the room. I didn't know how long I sat there, but eventually, only one thought remained.

Were any of them less real than me?

41

TEYR

"WHAT ABOUT THIS, COMMANDER?" A TINGGI ELF WITH WEAK illumination magic scattered motes of light against a target in my training room.

The first day, I had my whole group audition with their most impressive attack or defense. I didn't know enough combat fundamentals to do the dodging and hitting shit the rest of my mates seemed to fall back on, so I could only hope to use my own knowledge of improving natural proclivities. What I didn't expect was so many of Cordelia's precious rebels being completely useless.

"It's getting there." I tried to smile, but the elf shrank.

I shouldn't be teaching these fae. I should be...well, I didn't know. The whole rebellion thing ended up requiring a lot more collaboration than I expected, and I didn't collaborate well with anyone other than my mates, and I kept getting pulled away from them.

"Do those breathing exercises I taught you." I shrugged. "And, uh, think about what it feels like to stare into the sun."

"But that feels nice." The tinggi elf furrowed their eyebrows.

"Then think about something that feels bad." I threw my hands in the air and strode to the next fae in line.

Dee leaned into the door of my training room. "Lunch."

"Thank Fire," I muttered.

My group filed out of the training room with me, headed toward the open room on the middle level Cordelia or someone had converted into a cafeteria. The precious few fae allowed outside the metal monstrosity teleported food up onto low wood tables they'd conjured. I dropped into the seat next to Kay, and Bash soon joined us.

A plate appeared in front of me. Dried meat, some rehydrated punaky mash, and a hunk of bread. Same as yesterday. Same as tomorrow, if I had to bet. I poked at the meat and scowled.

"Are you guys getting anywhere?" Kay asked.

"Nope." I popped the 'p' and tore off a mouthful of bread.

"Some of my weaker members have successfully started along the path of mastering themselves." Bash dug into the chalky punaky.

"I can't even get that far." Kay shook her head. "I'm trying to teach everybody basic attack and defense, but that just means the fae who already know their shit ignore me, and I can't better train anyone with a shot at understanding the basics because I have to spend so much time with the ones who just fart glitter all day."

I rolled my eyes. "Try turning the glitter into an attack. It's like running face-first into a stone wall that gets passive-aggressive when you tell them it hurts."

Bash stared out the window. "Perhaps Shade had the right idea."

I snorted and tried to chew the stale bread. The selfish necromancer had claimed the whole outside to summon up armies of the rotting corpses under the dirt and throw them against his group since the last of the councilors' army left. I wanted to go outside too, but the Lord High King Zephyr had declared it too dangerous to have more than one group down there at once, even though we knew where the half-dozen Secca spies hid. I glared at the flat metal walls, the electric lights that nobody had figured out how to turn off yet. No fae should be in here, much less our Cara. Shade told me he found the burn mark on the lowest floor. I hadn't been to see it, and I told him to stay away. Nothing good would come of that.

Kay patted my hand. "Losing our minds isn't going to help anything."

"I thought you wanted my honest emotions." I pulled my hand back and choked down a mouthful of dried meat.

She frowned. "I do."

"Well, here's honesty." I waved my fork at the room. "We're like itzals in a cage here, and it's really starting to feel like all the grand ideals don't apply to anyone who doesn't spend every waking minute on the advisory level. We know just as little and are working just as hard as we did at the Academy." I dropped my fork into the mash. "It's bullshit."

A hint of agreement ghosted over my bond with Bash, but the dragon kept his gaze on his plate.

"It's...not great," Kay said. "Have either of you been able to talk to Zel since he started working with his dad?"

Bash grunted a negative.

"Of course not." I ignited my frustration on my fingertips. "He can't see a pointless position of authority without throwing himself into it so far he loops back around to being Prince Zelly again."

"I'm worried about him." Kay poked at her food. "He's under a lot of pressure, and you know how pressure tends to make him act."

"We all do." I rolled my eyes. "But what in Fire are we supposed to do, other than wait for him to blow up? He's the commander."

Bash stood and strode away without a word. I sent a half-hearted *pulse* in his direction, but I didn't care when he didn't reply. Clearly, we were just going to fall apart again, maybe for the last time, and I was tired of being the one who fought to keep us together.

I shot to my feet. "The dragon has the right idea. Let me know when lunch is through." I pocketed my hunk of bread and left Kay staring after both of us.

Blinking, beeping halls blurred past me as I stormed through the Tech. Somehow, even in this fucking place, I had to kick an itzal out of my way. I didn't have a destination. I just couldn't stay, couldn't keep thinking about this awful place and my ridiculous commander and everything falling apart. I hadn't seen Shade as a fae in about as long as I hadn't seen Zelly. Bash seemed on edge. Kay barely got a breath away from her adoring public. Fleeing the Councils was supposed to mean we would always be together. Why did I keep ending up alone?

I found myself standing in front of a heavy metal door with a thick seam across the middle and a bent handle. Just like Shade described. If I opened it, I would see the only proof of Light's death. I grabbed the handle and froze.

My first day in the Academy, when I told Zelly to shove his orders up his ass and Light took me drinking, the sun set before I confessed how much being in a Cara scared me. How being part of a whole went against everything I knew, everything I'd fought for. How it felt like spitting on the ashes of my parents' shop. He'd kissed me, soft and sweet in the darkness, and never told a soul. I decided then and there a Cara could be worth my time. My eyes burned and, for once, I let the tears bead and fall instead of igniting them into fire. I hadn't thought about the end of that night since he died. I sank to the floor in front of the door. The memory of his smile, the soft press of his lips, warmed me as much as it hurt.

It took years for us to fully bond the first time through the Academy, and we'd still fallen apart when Light died. And we kept falling apart, like losing him doomed us to a cycle of highs and lows. Every time we got somewhere good, the world intruded. Bash lost his dragon. Shade lost his mind. Kay learned something horrible. Zelimir....

He cycled worst of all, and it affected all of us the worst. He was our commander. We needed him to be our center, the one we could rely on, but he just kept blowing it. If I didn't know any better, I'd say he never should've—

That's lunch, Kay said. *I sent your group back to your room.*

Thanks. I climbed to my feet, scrubbed my hands over my eyes, and chased the thoughts away. I couldn't say something like that, even in my own mind. Zel had kept us safe for almost a century.

The door stared at me. I could open it quickly, get it over with.

I turned away. There wouldn't be any part of Light there. He lived in my memories, all our memories of him. With a sigh, I trudged back up the hall toward my useless group.

42

KAY

SHADE LOPED UP TO MY SIDE IN WOLF FORM AFTER YET another day of training, and I nestled my hand in his fur for a little stability as I turned from the hall into one of the water rooms. King Zephyr had a team of water nymphs summoning fresh drinking water from their home-water into wells sunk into the dead ground, which then got piped into these little rooms for drinking. Two of his titans always watched over the rooms to ensure none of the more excitable fae spiked it. After training, I meandered to one on the middle level to catch my breath and miss the post-training rush.

I hadn't seen Zel in over a week outside of meals. I barely talked to the rest of my mates. Everything they'd been worried about with joining Ar-a-mach had come true.

I poured myself a cup, and the first sip of icy water calmed a little of my irritation. Cordelia had been whisked into the same frenzy as Zelimir, but she seemed more comfortable disagreeing with King Zephyr. I drank three cups and set off toward the advisory level.

My Kitty? Shade asked. *Why do we not return to the room?*

"Because I didn't fight my way here just to fall in line again," I muttered.

Shade sent me a wave of support and kept pace at my side.

When I reached the advisory level, I studied the lines of purple force. The biggest room would belong to the king—even when fighting in the name of equality, he couldn't stop wanting to be superior—but the next biggest would be Cordelia's. I lapped the rectangular level twice, measuring, comparing. Then, I selected my door and knocked.

"Busy!" Even through the metal, I could hear Cordelia's poorly contained irritation.

"It's Kay," I said.

Shade whuffed.

I scratched his ears. "And Shade."

A beat of silence passed. I gnawed on my lip. Of course, a leader of the rebellion wouldn't have time for a random member, even if we were friends. The door cracked open, and the barest sliver of Cordelia's face poked through.

She glanced down the hallway in each direction, then waved us in. "Inside, quickly."

Shade and I squished through as she stepped back.

"I can't let anyone see you come in, or I'll be overwhelmed with meetings," she said.

My mouth fell open as I looked around her room. Her bed rivaled Teyr's for messiness, and clothes spilled out of a large trunk in a corner next to a smudged mirror hung off a rune on the wall. A desk sat along the back wall, though "desk" felt like an understatement and an overstatement. A huge rectangular sheet of metal jutted out of her wall, supported by a line of jagged, glowing runes. On top of it, underneath it, and on the whole wall around it sat more papers than I'd ever seen in my life. A stack of communication bowls, at least eight high, listed dangerously to the right on one corner.

I turned to Cordelia and found her similarly disheveled. She'd abandoned her usual dozens of fine braids in favor of a few thick twists of hair, which she seemed to be in the process of pulling into a haphazard bun. She wore the purple leather greaves of her armor and a soft purple top I recognized as pajamas.

"I need to be presentable enough to face a delegation of brownies across the wilds in twenty minutes, and I was reviewing Bash's progress until five minutes ago."

I frowned. Brownies, according to a book in the Academy library, were tiny, partially feral nature guardians.

"After I'm done with them, I have to lead yet another 'should we really attack the Councils?' strategy meeting. Can you talk while I prep?" she asked.

I knew King Zephyr relied on her heavily, but I didn't know exactly how much he had her doing. I grabbed her shoulders as she finished her hair and turned to race away. "Hey."

She froze and met my gaze.

"Breathe," I said.

She inhaled slowly, then exhaled. I held her until she did that twice more.

Cordelia smiled. "It's good to have you around."

I released her shoulders, and she walked to the trunk by the mirror.

"Did you only come to make sure I hadn't lost my mind, or did you have something else?" She knelt and held up a deep blue, bejeweled dress and an embroidered red cuirass.

"Something else, but I'm glad I got to the first thing too." I pointed at the cuirass.

"Hit me." She dug through the trunk for a shirt to wear underneath the armor. "I'm solving problems you couldn't even imagine a group of adults having these days. Did you know most of the Anam Seccas were called away because Father put out enough information about the Councilors' attack to start other rebellions across the wilds."

I shook my head and leaned against her bed, a slightly larger version of the flimsy cots in our suite. Shade settled at my feet.

"I thought this was a good thing, but not according to Kyrios." She scowled. "No, those are pretenders to our success that need to be dealt with. So, please, by all my ancestors, give me something simple."

My initial reason for coming up seemed ridiculous now. "This training is never going to work." I crossed my arms. "Not only is it shit for accommodating the fighting force you have, you've split up your so-called commanders, and they've all picked their own training methods."

I stared at the mountain of papers. "I'm pretty sure you need an army to work together."

She pulled out a long-sleeved, dark-purple tunic and sat back on her heels. "Nobody's offered a better plan yet."

"You could try organizing groups by combat experience instead of randomly." I shrugged. "Then, at least, there'll be some order. That's why Caras are so strong, the order."

She peered at me. "Do you really think that? It's not the magic, not the bond, not even the damned Councils?"

I fidgeted with the hem of my shirt. "The order is part of it, at least."

"That order is what removed all the Caras assaulting us." She swirled her finger in the air at Shade, indicating he turn his back while she changed. Shade huffed but rolled over on my feet and covered his eyes with one paw. "According to Drax, the Upper Council laid down the law. No Caras to leave the Academy, not even to deal with us.

No leaving? What were they doing about rifts elsewhere in the wilds?

Cordelia shucked her pajama top and pulled on the tunic. "Now, I love you to pieces, but if you don't tell me what you actually want to ask, I'm gonna spontaneously figure out how to explode you with my mind."

How did she know me so well already?

"Zel's not doing great." I gnawed on my lip. "He quit the politics thing for a reason, and I dragged him back into this. But he's never gonna say anything to me. How does it look from your side? Do they really need him?"

She pulled the cuirass on over her head with a sigh and lifted one arm to show me the straps. I stepped closer and began tightening them.

"My father relies on him," she said. "He's the only other one at the table with combat experience. But Zel's irritable. He's clearly not sleeping enough. He's snapped at enough delegates that I have to make social calls on my own now."

I slipped the strap through a cherrystone buckle. At this point, the stone felt more natural than the metal surrounding us. "Could you get him out of anything else?"

She turned to the mirror, frowned, and began fixing her bun. "I don't know. It's a difficult time for—" Cordelia met my gaze in the reflection. "You're really worried, aren't you?"

I looked away. "Every time he gets put under pressure like this, he freaks out and starts making stupid decisions."

Shade barked soft agreement. Cordelia tucked her hair more neatly into place, grabbed a small box of cosmetics, and turned to me.

"A stupid advisor isn't useful to anyone." She hugged me. "I'll get him out of his after-dinner meeting tonight. Talk to him, put his head on straight."

I squeezed her. "Go kick some brownie ass."

She laughed airily, her princess persona already settling over her shoulders. "Go kick some brother ass."

AFTER DINNER THAT EVENING, I PACED WHILE MOST OF MY mates watched me from their cots. Zel had eaten with the other advisors and left with them, but Cordelia had winked at me across the room. He had to arrive soon.

"My Kitty." Shade walked up behind me and wrapped his long arms around me. "Do you need me to fill you with pleasure and chase your worries away?"

Teyr snorted, his mood dark as always at this time of day. "Yeah, seeing your cock pumping into of her on his first break in over a week'll soften Zelly right up."

I patted Shade's arm.

"I did not intend to use my cock," he said. "For the timing, I thought my fingers most appropriate."

Humor ghosted across Bash's Cara from where he sat on his cot with his legs crossed. Teyr laughed a genuine laugh, and I smiled. It had been a while since I heard that sound.

"Not right now," I murmured.

Along the bridge, I sensed Zel turning down our hall. I straightened. Shade released me and stepped back. Teyr leaned back against his headboard in a more indolent pose. The door swung inward, and Zelimir stepped through, looking exhausted.

"Hey," I blurted.

He took a step back and looked around the room. "So, it was your meddling." He scrubbed a hand over his face. "At least I don't have to worry about what Cordelia wants from me now." He crossed to his cot and sat heavily, then pulled his boots off with wedges of force.

I raised an eyebrow at the rest of my mates.

Your scheme, Teyr said. *Your opener.*

Bash *pulsed* quiet agreement. Shade melted into his wolf and trotted over to Zelimir. He nudged the titan's knee, but our commander didn't react. Shade sat and offered me his closest approximation of a doggy shrug.

I walked over to Zel's cot and sat on the opposite side, my back against his. "We're worried."

He laughed bitterly. "Join the club. What about?"

"You?" I said.

"I'm just a little tired." He shook his head. "How is your training going?"

I sighed.

Bash unfolded his legs. "You're working yourself to the bone for your father's benefit."

"He's not the same leader he used to be. If I don't...." Zel ran a hand through his frizzy twists. Usually, he got them fixed every time we saw his family. "If my father doesn't have good advisors around him, he's going to mess up again, like he did making everyone sleep outside, and more fae will die."

"And you're that good advisor?" Teyr snorted.

Zelimir straightened slowly. "Why wouldn't I be?"

"How many answers do you want?" Teyr sat up, fire blazing in his eyes.

Quit it, I hissed.

Shade transformed back into a fae. "Teyr spends every evening angry now because he hates training." The necromancer pillowed his head on Zelimir's knee. "He doesn't mean the things he says."

"I might," Teyr snapped. "You can't just write me off because I'm not making perfect sense to your picky little mage brain."

Shade ran a nail along the metal floor. "I only mean to say you regret most of your off-the-cuff comments these days."

Teyr shot to his feet. "Fire—"

"Seriously!" I shouted. "Can't we have one normal conversation? The point of this was to get Zelimir to take a break."

Bash scowled. His scales shifted across his face.

What didn't your dragon like? I asked.

He sighed. *Nothing to worry about now.*

I rolled my shoulders and focused on the mate I'd set this all up for. "Zel, can you just take a little step back? You don't do well when you get overwhelmed, and it seems like Cordelia's handling things."

He narrowed his eyes. "I'd rather hear more about what Teyr meant before we continue that conversation."

"No," Shade said. "I explained—"

"You're still struggling with facial expressions." Zelimir shook his head. "Forgive me if I don't trust your social interpretation."

Shade shrank into himself, and my temper surged. I stood.

Teyr laughed. "Oh, perfect. You kicked the dog. Bash, you have anything you want to add to this shitshow, or should we all fall in line and do whatever Zelly says? Or maybe Kay is your commander now."

Bash rubbed his wrists, scales seething over his face and lilac chest. "Do not taunt me."

Teyr turned on him, fire in his eyes. I lunged forward, intent on tackling the ember before he made the problem worse, but Bash caught me with his telekinesis.

"What?" Teyr asked. "You finally going to break through that iron control of yours, show us what a dragon can really do?"

"Teyr!" I yelled.

Telekinesis wrapped over my mouth, muffling me. Bash stood. Teyr's glare faltered for a moment, but he didn't move.

"You are a child, screaming because don't know what else to do," Bash said in a low, dangerous voice. "And Zelimir remains my commander, however painful that may be." He released me.

As soon as he uncovered my mouth, I asked, "Painful?"

Bash ground his teeth. "My dragon says words I would not. Forgive me."

"No." I stepped forward and looked at each of my mates.

Zelimir had crumpled in on himself like someone punched him in the chest, but his gaze lingered on Bash. Shade had nearly melted into a puddle on the floor, looking at no one and nothing. Teyr quivered with what looked like rage, but tears glimmered at the corners of his eyes. Bash stood tall and proud, looking anywhere but at Zel or me.

"No, I don't think you get to do that," I said. "We've been in an impossible position for months now. We can't keep waiting for a quiet moment to sort out all our issues." I glared at the dragon. "Talk."

"When Zelimir struggles, our world shifts to accommodate." Bash glanced at the titan, then me. "And your eye—all our eyes—are always on him for signs of the struggle, to catch before the crash. I am...jealous."

My stomach flipped. Did I pay more attention to Zel than the rest of my mates? He resisted every step of this process more than the rest. He needed more coaxing, made me feel worse when he drifted away.

"I'm sorry," I whispered.

Bash shook his head. "We have all contributed."

Zelimir stood. "Is that what you all think? That I can't do anything by myself?"

Teyr shrugged. "In the lab—"

"In the lab, you kept you distance because you didn't want to touch me," Zel snarled.

Shade curled deeper into himself. *I do not know what you can do. I only know no one believes I am any more useful than I was as a wolf.*

Zelimir frowned. "That's not—"

"You listen when I hurt people," Shade whispered. "Or get scary. Never any other time."

Across the bridges, he shared memory after memory of being spoken over, talked down to, or ignored. I pressed a hand to my mouth.

Teyr groaned. "I don't think you guys are going to want me around unless I'm the fire-prodigy sex god, and I don't think I'm that anymore."

"I enjoyed the responsibility I had in Bittermist Thicket," Bash murmured.

I stepped out of the circle of my mates and took a deep breath. All of them had pushed down hurt, maybe seventy-five years of it, to make space for me as I fought to figure out who and what I was. Now, I needed to make space for them.

"Zel," I said, "what's Shade good at?"

He peered at the necromancer on the floor. "He is outstandingly powerful, to the point that he ends conflicts before they start."

I shook my head. "No power. No violence."

"He's...." Zel stared at the ceiling. "A talented chef, who I haven't once asked to cook since he regained the use of his hands."

Shade picked his head up off the floor and nodded.

"Teyr," I said, "what makes Zel a good commander?"

The ember pursed his lips. "He never misses anything in a fight. Doesn't matter how fucked he is. I've never gotten surprised by an attack when he could've warned me." He sighed. "It's less scary to wade into battle knowing he's watching my back."

Zelimir smiled very slightly.

I turned to my dragon. "What's Teyr's worst trait?"

"Dramatics." Bash crossed his arms. "He would irritate me less if he said what he felt without all the...sparkle."

Teyr frowned. "No matter what I'm feeling?"

My dragon grunted an affirmative. Teyr nodded.

"Shade?" I said. "How did you feel about Bash when we were at your tower?"

"Grateful." He nodded as is speaking more to himself than me. "Everything fell apart, even you, my Kitty. Bash ensured we roused, trained, ate. But he left more space." Shade tapped the ground. "It was good if we ate some, trained some. Better than nothing."

Bash opened his Cara. Apology, thanks, and love washed over all of us. One by one, the rest of our mates did the same. I smiled.

"About the lab," Teyr said.

I braced. A flicker of nerves raced through Zel's still-open Cara.

Teyr licked his lips and opened his Cara to reveal pulsing desire. "I very much would like to touch you."

Zelimir blushed and put his hands up. "I don't—I didn't mean—"

Teyr stepped close, his eyes at our commander's lips. "Oh, I heard you loud and clear."

As he leaned in for a kiss, Zel grabbed me by the waist and pulled me in between them. I yelped.

Coward, Teyr whispered across the bridges as he devoured my mouth.

I ignored their petty bickering in favor of falling into Teyr's kiss, mingling my need with his. When Zel grazed his hands from my waist up to my breasts, I groaned and broke the kiss to lean the back of my head against his shoulder. Teyr pressed burning kisses down the column of my neck.

Shade stepped to my side and urged my mouth open with his tongue. He no longer kissed like he was trying to learn me. Instead, he kissed with the easy passion of a man returning to a book he'd read many times. He tangled his tongue with mine like he'd known me all his life. I moaned into his mouth and wound a hand into his long hair.

Bash penned me in on the final side and captured one of my breasts from Zelimir. Pleasure raced to my needy core as Bash kneaded my skin with none of Zel's gentleness. I grabbed his ass and sank my nails into the fabric of his pants. He growled.

Teyr reached the neck of my tunic and drew back. "You have more of these, right?"

I nodded without really hearing his question. Teyr grabbed my tunic's collar and yanked, exposing the utilitarian chest support I'd put on for training this morning. Bash and Zel both used Teyr's fire to delicately burn away the straps. The fabric flopped away from my chest, and my nipples pebbled.

Zelimir cupped one of my breasts in his massive hand and circled my nipple gently with his thumb. Bash dove headfirst, peppering my skin with kisses and flicking his tongue over my nipple.

Pleasure raced through my body, and I closed my eyes. I couldn't tell whose hand caressed me, whose mouth warmed my skin. Pressure built in my gut, my first orgasm already on the horizon from the sheer attentiveness of my mates. Somebody unbuckled my weapons belt and threw it on a nearby bed. I forced my eyes open and pulled from Shade's mouth as they found the laces on my pants.

Teyr knelt in front of me, his gaze burning with the need I felt in his Cara. "You're all taken care of everywhere else."

I threaded my fingers into his hair. Shade put a finger to my chin and pulled my mouth back to his as Teyr unfastened my pants with deft fingers. I gasped as he yanked them and my underwear to my ankles. Cool air brushed briefly against the moisture between my legs before he groaned and covered me with his mouth.

He lapped the whole length of my slit before dancing his tongue over my clit with practiced ease. He traced a finger through the gathering slick, then plunged his finger into me. I lost the rhythm of my mouth on Shade's in the waterfall of moans Teyr drew from my lips. Shade kissed my face, my neck, my collarbone, anywhere he could reach as pleasure gathered like a wave.

Help her, Zel said across the bridges.

I didn't have time to wonder what he meant. Shade and Bash each grabbed one of my legs and hoisted me into a mock sitting position. They spread me for Teyr, giving the ember the space to add a second finger, then a third, and curl them to brush something inside of me that made me see stars. Surrounded by my clothed mates and pinned in place for them to see, I wouldn't have moved for anything.

Zelimir tilted my head back and pressed his mouth to mine while Shade dropped his attention to my breasts. The necromancer tugged one nipple and circled it with his long fingers in time with Teyr's thrusts, driving me to new heights. Zel kissed me like he had in the clearing outside his castle that first time, like I was everything he ever wanted, and he knew it for the first time in his life. Bash sucked bruises into my thighs.

At the same time, Teyr tested a fourth finger at my entrance, stretching me to a pleasant burn, and suctioned his mouth over my clit. My vision went white as I shuddered into an orgasm.

Teyr stood and pulled Shade into a kiss as I caught my breath against Zel's chest. Bash trailed lazy fingers across my breasts, and Zel dropped kisses on top of my head. When I felt confident I could stand, I squirmed to be released. Bash and Shade let me down.

"I'm not done." I put my hands on my hips and stared at my mates. "Are you going to make me touch myself?"

"Never." Zel pulled all the cots together in the middle of the room with Bash's telekinesis and lashed them in place with bands of force.

I shivered at the easy display of power and the hunger in his eyes. He would take me apart if I let him. I strode to the massive bed while the rustle of fabric behind me told me my mates were undressing. Someone telekinetically swept all the sheets off the beds. I sat and turned to my mates. In a line like the world's best buffet stood four beautiful, naked fae with their cocks jutting toward me.

I groaned. "How am I supposed to choose?"

Bash growled. *I think you can take us all.*

A wave of need rolled through me at the thought. I couldn't imagine how, but I had to try. I had to feel them all. I bit my lip and nodded.

Shade approached the bed, and I pulled him close before he could hesitate. Our mouths met, and I could taste myself on his lips. He beat his tail against his leg. I ran a finger along one of his ears, and he broke the kiss to climb onto the beds with me.

He lay on his back, his legs dangling off the edge toward the rest of our mates. I climbed on top of him and straddled his waist. His cock pressed against my ass, and I ground back into it while he sat up to lick my nipples. The wetness between my legs smeared against his abdomen. Bash groaned low in his throat and shared a mental image of how my dripping center caught the light when I moved.

Shade poured his need into me, a desperate desire to be with me while our mates watched. I lifted up and sank down onto his cock. Teyr had prepared me, but Shade was far longer than the ember's fingers. He hit a spot deep inside me, and I moaned. He pressed his mouth back to my breasts and thrust.

I felt Bash approach across the bridges. He smoothed a hand up my back and bent me forward, crushing my breasts onto Shade's face. The necromancer gasped for air, but only pleasure resonated across his Cara.

Bash wrapped an arm around my waist and traced lazy circuits around my clit. White-hot spikes of pleasure raced up my spine. He pulled back. I whined at the loss, but he pressed his lubed fingers against my asshole. I moaned. He rubbed small circles, allowing me to adjust to the pressure.

Bash pushed his finger in, and my breath caught. A whole new kind of pleasure rocketed through my body. He fucked one finger in and out, keeping time with Shade's thrusts, then added a second finger, spreading me wider. My pleasure started cresting into a second peak, but I didn't even have two of my mates inside me yet. I tried to fight it down.

Don't, Zel said. *Come for us. We want you relaxed.*

We want you undone, Teyr murmured.

Bash removed his fingers and lined his cock up with my ass. Shade paused to let him in. My dragon entered my asshole slowly, drawing a long, high sound from my mouth. One of my arms gave out, and I collapsed onto Shade's face. He groaned and dragged his teeth across the sensitive skin of my breasts.

Everyone remained still until I pushed my arm back up underneath me and pressed my hips experimentally back. Both cocks drove deeper into me, and I moaned. Bash grabbed one of my hips, Shade the other, and they started moving in time. Together, they hit places inside me I didn't even know existed. My second orgasm ripped through me on a scream, and only their hands kept me moving.

My mates' Caras rattled with the maelstrom of desire I'd created. It filled me, powered me. When Teyr slid onto the bed, I grinned and opened my mouth.

He shook his head with a small smirk. "We can do better than that, love."

Teyr ran his hand down Shade's torso to where my body met his. I frowned, but any confusion melted away when Teyr strummed his fingers over my clit. I'd let him do anything he wanted if he kept touching me like that. He pulled back. Shade growled as my breasts swung out of his reach.

Teyr stroked his ears. "Patience."

He climbed on top of Shade, slotting himself neatly in between us. His cock pressed into my stomach when I bounced down, and though he needed his arms to keep from crushing our necromancer, he stole a kiss from me.

Shade pulled out, and Bash paused. Teyr's golden eyes rolled back into his head as Shade lined up their cocks up side-by-side while dragging kisses along Teyr's shoulders. The sight of the two of them sent a surge of pleasure and confidence through my veins. I could take them both. How could I not, when so much love underpinned the swirling typhoon of need around us?

Bash eased me down onto them. I moaned as they stretched my walls to the point of pleasurable burning. They groaned in harmony with me. I'd never been so full. I ached with the feeling, but I began bouncing almost immediately, chasing the third orgasm curling in my core. Teyr crushed my breasts against his chest as he hugged me close. I lost myself in the rhythm, the pressure, the unbearable fullness, until the cot shifted underneath us.

I opened my eyes to find Zelimir kneeling, his ass hovering above Shade's head, and his cock at perfect mouth height over Teyr's shoulder. He cupped the back of my head and I opened my mouth as he slid his cock inside. I savored the salty taste of him on my tongue.

He groaned and thrust. I abandoned myself to the rhythm of my mates. My body moved forward and backward as they did, awash in pressure and pleasure. They occupied my every sense, my every pore. Shade wound a hand around Zel's calf. Teyr grabbed Bash's ass and sandwiched me so tightly between them my breath caught. I came again from the sheer fullness of them, and they fucked me through it.

As my fourth orgasm gathered, Shade's thrusts grew erratic, falling out of rhythm with the others. Bash pulled him back in with his telekinesis, but I could still feel the quiver in the necromancer's limbs. He wouldn't last much longer. Bash *pulsed* that he was close, and Teyr responded in kind. Only our commander, last to join, needed a moment longer.

I rolled my tongue over him. *Someone hold me up.*

A soft cushion of Zel's force wrapped around my ribs. I grabbed his hip with one hand, pulling him in and out of me. He groaned, but I could tell he needed more. I squeezed my hand between my legs and gathered everyone's wetness. Then, like Bash had, I pressed a finger against his asshole.

He tensed at the intrusion, but I sent him waves of calm and desire. He exhaled and relaxed. Slowly, I pushed into him. He tensed again, but everyone shared their pleasure, their nearness. Zelimir wanted to come with us. I knew it. He knew it.

He relaxed once more, and I thrust deeper. He groaned low in his throat, and a new rush of pleasure broke through his Cara, bringing him as close as the rest of us.

Our collective orgasm approached like a storm, powerful enough to take us all out. White-hot pleasure ripped through my body as we came in unison. They stuttered through a few final thrusts, and I started to collapse onto Teyr's chest, Zelimir still in my cum-filled mouth.

I swallowed and removed him gingerly. Bash pulled out, and I rolled off Teyr and Shade. I pillowed my head on Bash's chest. Zelimir lifted my legs to slide underneath them. Shade tucked in alongside me, and Teyr lay across both of us. We remained like that trembling through aftershocks for a long time.

Eventually, my commander looked at the enchanted timepiece dangling over the door. I followed his gaze and frowned. If we didn't sleep soon—and somewhere other than a pile—we'd all regret it tomorrow. I brushed Bash's arm to wake him. Like the mornings, his mind came to life without a hint of fog.

"Another round?" He cupped one of my breasts.

"Maybe." I ran my thumb over the tip of his budding erection. "But I think we need to have one more conversation first."

Teyr groaned. "I could converse much more productively after a couple more orgasms."

I elbowed him. "This was your idea."

"I'm listening." He tugged on my other nipple.

I slapped his hand away.

Shade rolled onto his stomach and kicked up his long, pale legs. "Is this in relation to Teyr's denigration of Zelimir's advisory skills?"

Zel leaned up onto his elbow with a frown.

I bit my lip and shrugged. "It didn't seem like a joke."

Teyr sighed. "It wasn't."

43

TEYR

Zel's gaze, the incisive one he reserved for problems he needed to solve, weighed heavily on my shoulders. I swallowed. If we really wanted to put all our problems out in the open and march into the breach arm-in-arm, I needed to say the thing I'd been thinking on and off since we first found Kay.

I trailed a finger over Shade's spine. "You're a bad leader."

Zel twitched an eyebrow. Bash made a small, startled sound in the back of his throat.

"Not a bad commander." I put up my hands. "I—any of us—would follow you into the most doomed battle. But military strategy and leadership are different."

Zelimir stared over my shoulder. "I almost destroyed our Cara at the Academy. And on the ride to the Academy. Here, my advice is sought after and discarded. I suggested you four as trainers, but they cut me off before I could say anything more—"

I covered his mouth with my hand. "All I'm hearing is logistics, the mistakes you've made, and how you intended to improve from them. Commander stuff." I took my hand back. "Leaders look past logistics. Sometimes, it doesn't matter how things get done as long as people are happy while they're doing them."

Bash frowned. "Who are you suggesting as leader? Kay?"

She blanched.

"I don't know about that either." I looked around at my mates, naked and piled on top of each other. "We haven't been a Cara for quite some. Maybe not since Kay joined us. And I don't mean that in the bad, we-haven't-been-talking way. I mean"—I channeled my frustration to find the words into a spark and flicked it from finger to finger—"we're something new. Something beyond that." I shrugged. "Any of us would be a bad leader for what we are now."

Painful silence settled over the room.

"Thoughts?" I asked.

"How would that work?" Shade frowned. "Without structure, I worry...."

"I know you worry." I traced the shape of his jutting shoulder blade. "But we've kind of already figured it out. When one of us is going way off the deep end, Zelly drags us back." I sat up and leaned against his titanic body.

He flushed and stuffed his hands into his lap to keep his cock from touching me. I smiled.

"Bash grounds us," Kay said. "With advice or with training. He keeps us from doing more than we can. Reminds us we have to live our lives."

The dragon smiled softly and ran a lilac finger from the notch in her collarbone to her belly button. She shivered.

"Exactly." I resisted the urge to jump up my excitement. I had no intention of leaving the warmth of the pile.

Zelimir exhaled slowly. "Shade wears all our hearts on his sleeve and faces the problems other people would dodge head on." He ran a fond hand over the wolf's hair. "He'll keep us from getting to this point again because we're going to listen to him from now on."

Shade nuzzled Zel's palm. "The world is often ugly and, of late, trying to kill us." He caressed my leg. "You remind us that we do not always have to be so serious." He smiled. "You give me permission to relax as a fae."

"Kay reminds all us old-timers that we can still change and grow." I grazed the sensitive part of her inner thigh. "And comes like a goddess."

She blushed but didn't smack my hand away. Bash circled her nipples.

"Not fair." She arched into his touch. "Just because I can go again right away doesn't mean you can end every conversation that way."

I ran both my hands up her thighs and started to pull her closer. "I can until you stop me."

Zelimir put a hand on my shoulder. "We should actually agree if this is what we're going to do."

He swiped his thumb over my skin, and I twisted to look at him. My commander's blush grew darker. His purple gaze bore into mine, and something new sparked within. Bash chuckled. Zel shook himself and released me.

I stuck my tongue out at the dragon. "I obviously think it's a good idea."

Kay nodded, her gaze intent on the point where Zel touched me.

Shade rolled over, exposing his hardening cock. "I would like very much to be the heart on our sleeve."

Bash grunted.

I turned to Zelimir. "On the battlefield, we're yours. Off it, we're ours."

"Ours." He swallowed heavily. "I could get used to that."

THE NEXT MORNING, I ROLLED OVER, STILL NUDE, AND tumbled into a crevice between two of the cots. Only a thin band of purple force kept my ass from hitting the floor.

"Fire!"

Shade cackled. "Bash and Kay have gone to training. You may want to be careful in the bed."

I struggled back onto the mattress and glared at the necromancer. On the other side of the room, Zel sat in a chair I could swear we didn't have last night.

"Yeah, yeah, laugh at the naked guy who fell over," I grumbled.

"Wait, what the hell do you mean Bash is at training?" Along the bridges, I found Kay and Bash outside at the feet of the ChargeTech.

Zel turned, revealing a tiny desk. "Kay must have some magic even we haven't discovered yet. I don't have a meeting until after lunch, and neither of you are due to train anyone until she and Bash have finished evaluating the recruits."

"She only took Bash because the two of us 'wake up like shit.'" Shade grinned. "I don't much mind."

I sat up and ran my hand through my hair with a small smile. "Me eith—"

Pain shot through Kay's Cara, then her connection went still. I jerked my gaze onto Zelimir, then bolted upright and sprinted out the door with him at my heels. Shade took wolf form and raced ahead. I hadn't rounded the first corner before I felt her rise far above the ground and begin rocketing away from our camp—in the direction of the Academy.

Fae whistled at me as I raced past, but I didn't realize until I skidded to a stop next to Bash in the mud outside that I was naked. I didn't care. Shade shot past Bash with his nose to the ground.

I skidded to a halt beside Bash, who held a water nymph by the collar. "Water break," he panted. "I was on the other side of the She walked over to the well, and these two—" He shook the nymph.

"For Fire's sake, let him go," I growled.

Bash snarled and dropped the nymph. He scrambled backwards to where two other water nymphs stood near the well staring.

"What did you see?" I demanded.

"Um," one said. "Sir, do you know—"

"That my cock's out? You should be grateful," I snapped. "Answer me."

"A dragonkin," the other replied. "Red, maybe? And blue. He was wearing green, and I f-forgot what trainee uniforms look like. He just appeared at the well, and he talked with her. Then he took on his full dragon form and—"

I grimaced. Shade barked, and we all converged on him. He stuck his nose forward, pointing at four massive dragon prints in the mud.

"Chrysophylax," I hissed. "Taking her to the Academy. How could we have been so stupid?" I spun to face my mates. "We knew they were watching us."

Bash growled.

I ignited my fear and fury into a massive fireball and launched it at the prints with a yell. Mud splattered everywhere.

Shade howled, and Bash roared his dragon's roar.

44

KAY

I swam blearily back to consciousness. I'd called a water break, wandered over to the well and...and.... And seen Chry, standing in the shadow of the giant Tech's legs. He'd sent thoughts into my mind just like Bash. He'd begged for another chance. I'd glanced at Bash, swarmed by prospective students, and decided I would be close enough I didn't have to warn him. After that, nothing. Shit.

I swallowed down a burst of anger and betrayal. I had to figure out where Chry and his dragon family had imprisoned me. I laid on something hard. Trying to look like I was still unconscious in case anyone could see me, I moved my hands and feet just enough to assure myself they were in good working order. Wooden cuffs like the ones my mates wore when I rescued them clasped my wrists. Something tugged at the back of my neck.

My ankle scraped across a sharp edge of the surface underneath me. A creaking, splashing sound that reminded me of human mills bounced off the walls around me. The echo made the room sound large, or at least high-ceilinged, with unfinished walls. I inhaled deeply, and a moist, underground smell met my nose. As subtly as I could, I reached for my bridges. They stretched a few inches away, then faded into gritty nothingness. A wall encircled my Cara, trapping it in my gut and leaving me alone. I started to press my *energy* into the cuffs to drain them.

"This is fun, Kinnia," Elijah said, "but you can stop pretending now."

My stomach swooped, and I pulled my *energy* back. My head swam with the implications of my situation. Chry had delivered me to Elijah, instead of his dragon family? Chry worked for Elijah? How was that possible? I thought of all those times Chry had smiled at me, even flirted with me when he tried to talk me into joining his Cara and my stomach turned. I had to get out of here. Last time, I'd escaped because Elijah believed I wouldn't bother trying. Could I replicate that trick? I opened my eyes and sat up.

Most of my guesses had been right. I sat on a flat bed of light green crystal near one wall in a nook of a massive cavern. Crystals of every color, taller than Zelimir and twice as wide in some places, jutted out of the walls. What was this place? Cables hung off them in thick ropes and nets. I wore my own clothes, though without my weapons belt.

The Jalan I knew to be my maker repositioned a cable attached to one of the crystals and turned to me. A red beam swept out of his right eye just as it had on Earth and scanned me. My heart pounded in my ears, but I remained still.

The beam shut off, and he smiled to himself. "You're intact, at least."

"At least?" I asked.

He circled my bed, along the thin strip of stone floor that separated me from the cave wall. "You're also more willful than I thought possible."

I swallowed and tried to look pliant, but the way he looked at me crawled under my skin. "What did you expect?"

"Less personality, frankly. Your programming should've been incompatible with any socialization but those you made perfectly to fit alongside you."

Alex. Elaine. David. Harry. For the first time since I escaped his lab on Earth, those names stung instead of landing hollowly in my chest. My friends, my family, each of them as real as myself. I inched toward the edge of the jagged crystal bed when Elijah looked at the cables on a different spike of crystal. He should've trapped me better if he didn't want me to keep escaping.

"Nevertheless." He turned back to me. "You remain my crowning achievement, at least for next few days."

My stomach flipped. "What's going to happen in a few days?"

"That depends on you." He smiled indulgently. "I hope you find that as amusing as I do."

I forced myself to smile. "Why?"

"'Why?'" he repeated. "How human of you. With that thought, you and I surpass all of Earth science, before and after the rifts."

He adjusted the net of cables over a pink crystal, and I scooted a little farther away. My hand lay within an inch of the edge of the bed. There had to be an exit in here, probably on the far side of the room I couldn't see past the crystals. All I needed was enough of a head start.

"That seems good," I murmured.

He turned back with a wide grin. "I'm glad you're starting to come around. I hoped your look at my lab here might help you understand." He clucked his tongue. "Though if all you wanted was information, you only had to ask. I didn't know you had such...complex emotions when we last met, but I'm able to accommodate that now."

I swallowed. "What do you want from me?"

He shook his head. "I want nothing *from* you. Despite all my careful controls, you aren't something I can merely take things from." He stepped closer to my bed. "I want to work together. I want to save Earth *with* you." Elijah ran a finger along a greenish crystal. "Be honest with me. Do you actually believe these flippant little fae are suited to lead the only world? These stones are projections of the energy at the heart of this world, and they've just been keeping them in the basement of a *school*."

The Academy. Months ago, Teyr held me up as I limped to the baths and explained the only thing below us in the Academy was a cavern full of crystals that channeled Thrae's magic. I stared at the cables threaded around and across the crystals. In my mind's eye, a vision flashed before me of them turning white one by one as magic siphoned out of them.

"That's why you've been bothering with the Academy and the Councils," I said. "You needed access to these crystals to funnel the power from Thrae back to Earth."

"You are simply brilliant." Elijah's human eye shone. "Anam Caras have become too efficient. In the next ten, fifteen years, the connection between the two worlds will end because Tech won't be able to muster enough power to open rifts. Earth will die a cold, lifeless wasteland." He extended a hand to me. "Together, we can save reality."

In ten or fifteen years, Thrae would be safe. In ten or fifteen years, I could live a quiet life with my mates, if I managed to stop Elijah. Something bright and hot surged through my veins.

"Okay." I nodded. "But you said nothing could stop you from changing the world. I could've said no. What did you mean?"

"Ah." His grin faltered, and he glanced past a massive jut of blue crystal. "I'm happy to tell you everything, but that information may displease you at this early stage. You're so human, after all."

Fear shivered down my spine. The massive cavern suddenly felt smaller, and I got the sense I'd learned all I could without taking a step I could never recover from. His hand still hung in the air between us, cables threaded between his fingers. I saw my chance.

"Okay," I had to work my jaw to make the next word to come out, "Dad."

He grinned. I lunged forward, grabbing for his upper arm to pull him over and make my escape. The cables running from the cuffs tugged at the back of my neck, but I barely noticed. As I hit the edge of the crystal bed, blue-white power crackled up my arm with shocking pain. My body seized, and I toppled backward.

Elijah sighed. "I lost you for too long." He stepped back from the edge of the crystal and pointed to a few small, metal squares around the base, threaded on a single cable. "There is an electrical field around you, triggered by your particular energy signature. I hoped you could be reasoned with, but I'm not so stupid as to make the same mistakes twice." He strolled to the edge of the part of the cavern I could see. "Feel free to test the field's limits, and those of the cuffs, but I've improved on the designs of that ridiculous elf."

He put a hand on the blue crystal he'd looked at earlier. "Try not to fry yourself so badly I can't learn from your body. And think about whether that's really all you want for your life." Elijah walked away.

A moment later, a door scraped open and closed. I sat down heavily and slammed my hand down on the crystal. No reaction, other than the tugging on my neck. I snarled and pulled sluggish *energy* into my fist. I smashed my fist down again, but the crystal only shuddered.

"Shit!" My shout echoed off the walls.

"Kay?" asked Drax in a voice so weak I hardly recognized it.

I leaned as close as I dared to the electrical field, but I only glimpsed a metal wheel, spinning under the pressure of a small waterfall around the edge of my alcove walls. That explained the water sound, and the electricity in the heart of Thrae.

"Drax," I called. "I'm here. Where are you? What did they do?"

He chuckled dryly. "I didn't get the same welcome as you. I've been in a little metal cage for the last two days with only some kind of tube in my arm for conversation."

He sounded exhausted. I reached with my *energy* for the metal squares Elijah indicated around the crystal, but it rebounded with another lance of pain. I couldn't reach Drax, couldn't help him. Panic clawed up my throat.

"Take the tube out, if you can," I shouted.

"I've removed it a few times," he replied. "Every time, I wake with it reinserted. This last time, they added a small tag bearing the legend 'food.'"

When Elijah had me on Earth, he'd made a comment about my caloric intake and done something similar. I inhaled shakily. Someone didn't want Drax dead.

"How did they get you down here?" I asked. "Did anyone say anything?"

"I am not as fierce as I once was." He sighed. "Xerxes' itzal-shifter, Norrila, caught me communicating with Ar-a-mach. The old bhelrian agreed to keep the information to himself, but in a few hours' time, a group of Jalan appeared and beat me within an inch of my life." He coughed. "I've been here since, without a clue what's going on. I will admit your arrival, though pleasant, doesn't inspire confidence in the fate of the rebellion."

I couldn't damage the crystal. I couldn't touch the electrical field. My *energy* and my mates both seemed blocked by the cuffs. That left me one option. I pushed my *energy* into the wood around my wrists.

Like flipping a switch, I blacked out.

45

ZELIMIR

I locked eyes with my father, who sat at the end of the long wooden table with my sister, his three advisors, and Farquin. "Kay has been—"

Her Cara fell silent deep beneath the Academy. My mates and I held our breath until the connection swam with foggy, distant dreams. As one, we exhaled.

Had I been wrong to come here instead of riding for the Academy as I'd wanted? I hoped not. Pushing our mounts to the extreme, we could reach Kay in five days. We knew the Academy better than we would any dragon caves, but with trainee and full Caras swarming its halls, our chances of success were small.

"Kay has been taken to the Academy," I said. "We must mount an attack to rescue her immediately."

Concern flitted across Cordelia's face. Shock at my directness followed. Finally, excitement gleamed in her eyes—no doubt for what this meant to the rebellion.

"Taken?" Farquin stood. "That is Elijah's doing. We need to rescue her before—"

My father flicked a hand in his direction, and a gag of purple force covered his mouth. Farquin scowled.

"We're not ready to attack." My father gestured to the map of the Academy in the middle of the table. "We haven't planned an approach, the Upper Council saw fit to intervene in Cara movements for the first time in two centuries to keep them close, and you're the one who keeps complaining about how untrained our troops are."

Kyrios nodded. "I heard she was captured in the midst of the basic assessments, which I said were a waste of time. If it was so important that the fae be assessed, how can they fight before we know what they're capable of?"

Shade growled. "If we descend upon the Academy as a horde, even the best trained Caras will not be able to stop us."

Megare leaned forward. "There is a theory of battle that a sufficiently motivated untrained group can overcome a highly trained force by sheer unpredictability."

Kyrios shook his wrinkled head. "I will not scuttle this project on the mere hope of a theory."

Shade glared at me. *They talk and think in circles.*

You're telling me, I replied.

He sank sullenly into his wolf at my feet.

"We've been discussing approaches for weeks." Cordelia gestured at the map, covered in different colored arrows. "Kay is the beating heart of this rebellion. If we don't rescue her, the whole operation falls apart. We should attack."

My father waved his hand. "You speak with the impetuousness of youth. One person does not make or break a movement, however valuable that person is."

"Valuable?" Teyr smacked his hands on the table. "She's not valuable, she's a fucking person. If this is the sort of 'movement' that gives up on anyone it's inconvenient to rescue, you're going to find yourself with a lot less people very quickly—beginning with us."

Farquin nodded emphatically.

Theos studied my mate. "Threats will get you nowhere."

The table under Teyr's hands began to smoke. "This isn't a threat. It's a promise."

Kyrios scoffed. My father clenched his jaw. Cordelia sat back and looked from one advisor to the next. I recognized the move. Teyr had stated her stance more boldly than she could, and now she was checking the room for sympathizers.

I put my hand on Teyr's arm and winced at the heat. *They're not going to listen, but I have a plan to force their hand.*

Teyr didn't twitch. *What?*

I met my sister's gaze and said to him over the bridges, *It's still coming together, but if you trust me, storm out and gather as many rebels as you can in the hallway outside.*

Teyr threw up his hands, revealing two scorched handprints on the tabletop. "I can't talk to you people. I'll save her my goddamn self." He whirled and stormed out the metal door. The *slam* of the door behind him echoed in the quiet.

"I'm sorry." My tongue burned with the apology. "He doesn't understand how these things work."

Cordelia raised a brow.

My father nodded. "So, you concede an attack now would be reckless, regardless of the stakes. I'm glad."

Kyrios leaned forward. "In fact, I begin to wonder if an attack on the Academy would benefit us at all. Perhaps the time draws near to see if they will come to the table. We could settle this without all the... messiness."

Megare hummed thoughtfully.

A snarl tore from Bash's chest. "War is not settled at tables. Blood has been shed, your blood. Now, it's happening again. You seem weak. They will take until you have no blood left in your veins."

Cordelia gestured at him. "We started this to combat Council overreach and inattention. We cannot let them overreach into civilian conflicts while rifts run amok."

"And we will combat that overreach in due time." A note of steel entered my father's voice. "I remain the general who led our people to victory against the dragons not a hundred and fifty years ago. I know more battle than you've ever tasted, and I know when a fight isn't worth it."

Got as many as I could. Teyr's presence pressed against my bridge on the other side of the door. *They're on edge.*

Forcing their hand, I told our seething dragon. *Open the door on my count.*

I kept my gaze on my father. "Am I to understand you won't rescue Kay? That her life is not worth the fight?"

Three...two....

Bash stood and stormed to the door.

Father folded his hands and smiled. "I'm saying, son, that the loss of the woman you love is making you unreasonable."

One.

Bash swung the door open as my father said, "The rank-and-file are not ready. Kay should not be rescued at the cost of weeks and months of planning. I'm sure she'll be fine."

A murmur swept through the hall. I stepped to the side and looked at the hallway, filled to the brim with fae. Teyr grinned and saluted me. Cordelia stared, wide-eyed. A thundercloud gathered on my father's brow. He stood smoothly, whisking Farquin's gag away.

"I'm sorry," he said. "I seem to have been set up to look some kind of fool. I assure you—"

"Is Kay missing?" someone called.

Farquin launched himself forward. "Kidnapped by a madman who wants to use her power to—"

Bash grabbed the Jalan in a headlock.

"To grant the Councils even more power over our lives," I finished. "Which King Zephyr believes is not reason enough to take up arms."

Gasps and cries rippled through the crowd as they passed my words back to those in the rear. A small smile lifted the corners of Cordelia's mouth. My father glared. I'd never seen him so furious, so disappointed. I'd never cared less.

"I want to muster our forces and charge the Academy." I let a little of my manic need to reach Kay light my eyes. They needed to know I believed. "I want to come together as one and pry control from their hands. What do you think?"

A cheer went up. Shade melted back into fae form, and power gathered in his eyes. Bash released Farquin and smiled grimly.

Decent plan, Teyr said.

"And I want one more thing." I smiled. "A leader we can all believe in."

Different chants went up. I heard my name, Kay's name, my mates' names. My father gripped the table so hard it cracked. I circled the table to Cordelia's side and put my hand on her shoulder. She stared up at me with furrowed brows.

"You all know my sister, Princess Cordelia. Many of you were recruited by her. She's been vital to the rebellion since its conception, long before my eyes were opened to the corruption of the Councils. She believes we should not just fell the Councils but build a wilds that supports us all." I lifted her hand into the air. "I nominate my sister to lead Ar-a-mach!"

The titans in the room tensed. Farquin's eyes bugged out. Murmurs rippled through the crowd as the news traveled along the fae in the hallway, but I couldn't sense their tone.

I *pulsed* to be ready for a fight.

"Praise the sun, it's about fucking time," a woman shouted.

Someone whooped. A patter of applause kicked up and grew into a wall of thunder. Cheers bounced off the metal walls and rebounded, doubling and tripling the voice of the rebellion.

"What are you doing?" Cordelia tried to pull out of my grip. "This is your army."

I met her gaze. "I don't want it. I never did."

She stilled.

"Kay told me what you said about trying to pave the way for me." I shook my head. "That stops now. You're what this rebellion needs. A true leader." I smiled at Teyr. "One who listens and knows that having the right people in the right places is more important than all the training in the world."

Teyr beamed. Cordelia nodded slowly.

"I won't stand for this!" my father bellowed.

I gestured to the fae in the hall. "They've made their choice." I squeezed Cordelia's hand and released her. "You can stay as her advisor, or you can crawl back to your castle and hope she doesn't set her sights on dethroning clan royalty next."

My father, a fae I'd spent my whole life fearing and hoping to become, crumpled before my eyes. I took a deep breath and remained at my sister's side.

Megare chuckled and held her hand out to her. Cordelia smiled up at me, then shook Mother's old friend's hand. Kyrios and Theos followed suit, and Father stood alone. He scowled and shuffled to stand behind her. I'd made my sister a lot of enemies, but she excelled under pressure.

She stood and glided to the doorway like a true princess. "I am honored by your belief in me," she said. "Know that your faith in me is dwarfed only by my faith in you."

A cheer swept the halls, and I grinned.

"We march on the Academy as soon as I am certain we will not lose undue lives in our haste." She looked over her shoulder at me. "No later than tonight. We will not abandon Kay, as I would not abandon any who joined our cause."

She faced forward and inclined her head in response to the wave of cheers.

"I need the following fae to join me in my rooms as soon as possible." She rattled off a list of names, including Megare and myself. "My new generals and I must begin planning this attack."

A FEW HOURS LATER, I EMERGED FROM MY SISTER'S ROOM feeling lighter than I had in years. Bash nodded at me from across the hall. I trusted Cordelia's judgment, but we'd all been wrong before, so I'd had him read surface thoughts while we planned. No one, not even the titan she selected, bore her any ill will.

Start gathering weapons, I told him. *Get everyone something they're comfortable using.*

He took off down the hall. I headed in the opposite direction. I had a plan to implement. I passed Teyr, waving a hand-stitched flag that read "Ar-a-mach" and singing some rebellion song with a roomful of fae.

He winked at me. *Figured I'd take charge of morale.*

I grinned. *Can you lead the morale to the field below? We're going to move out as soon as possible.*

The ember nodded, and I kept walking. I found Shade on the lowest level of the ChargeTech, tracing the outline of a large, dark spot on the metal. I ran my hand through my twists. That had to be where his magic entered the machine during the Battle of Light.

"Shade," I said, "I need your help."

Shade cocked his head to one side. "Mine?"

"Yes." I smiled and sat. "We have to move several thousand fae nearly a week's ride in a couple hours. You're the only person in existence I could ask to do that."

"I can't make a portal that large." He frowned. "Not without going too deep into the magic again." He met my gaze. "I will not hurt any of you for this."

I pressed my hand to his chest. Light's bone, which he'd finally explained last night, warmed between our skin.

"No, you won't. You're a different fae than you were then. You don't need to hold back to keep us safe." I swallowed. "I never let you find your limits. I was afraid. I know you can do this safely with us at your side."

"My Kitty trusts me. You trust me." He covered my hand with his. "Light trusted me." He smiled very slightly. "It is increasingly unreasonable not to trust myself." He released me and stood without another glance at the dark spot.

I rose. "Go speak with the water nymphs at the wells. I heard something interesting about how they get water here the other day." I ruffled his hair. "Now is not the time to hold back. We need to make the impossible possible."

Shade wagged his tail and strode away. I looked at the spot on the ground. The fear I'd fought since Kay had been taken swirled in my gut. We would not lose another mate.

46

KAY

Consciousness returned to me in an instant. Someone yelped quietly. Not Drax. I opened my eyes and sat up. Odhrán straightened his robes and stared back at me, clearly trying not to look like my waking had startled him. The waterwheel noise had been replaced by some kind of mechanical grinding.

"You know, I really thought you were on my side," I said.

He stepped a bit closer. "I am. Elijah is going to bring new vitality to the wilds, allow us to step forward and join the future. You don't understand what your denial is doing to our world, our magic."

I couldn't believe it. "Are you really stupid enough to believe Elijah would do anything for Thrae?"

He waved a hand dismissively. "It doesn't matter what he thinks. We have all the power."

For a wild instant I wondered if he was right. Just because Elijah had managed to capture me, didn't mean he was actually powerful enough to pull off his insane scheme or that the Council wasn't strong enough to defeat him. Then I recalled all the infighting and the personal agendas. There was no unity amongst the Councils. They hadn't banned together with some great plan to control Elijah much less stop him.

Odhrán leaned closer, and whispered, "We will make Thrae invincible with magi-tech."

I stared. Magi-Tech? Fae hate Tech. How could he possibly think they would integrate Tech into their magic? Was that what he meant? No way the Council would allow that. Had Odhrán's obsession with Tech pushed him over the edge?

"If you work with us, we can change Thrae," he whispered.

All along I had believed the fae feared me because of my Tech. In all my wildest imaginings, I would have never guessed a fae would want to add Tech to their magic—and would want me to help.

My thoughts came to a screeching halt.

Us?

Did he mean him and Elijah or.... Fear mingled with sadness tightened my chest. Chry had delivered me here. Odhrán had partnered with Elijah. How many fae had banded together with Elijah?

I took a deep breath and channeled Zelimir's poker face. "I thought you didn't need me."

Odhrán glanced over his shoulder. "We don't...."

"But...?" I urged.

He faced me and dropped his voice. "But I have a bit more faith in a plan that includes you. If I learned one thing about you in our time together, it's that you love Thrae and your mates, no matter how often they hurt you. And, in truth, I'd simply prefer a job like this in the hands of an adult." He glanced around. "He will kill you if you don't help him. Is that not enough to convince you?"

What did he mean, "in the hands of an adult?"

A shower of sparks exploded from the part of the cavern I couldn't see. Elijah swore.

"Careful," Drax said. "You can't treat her—"

He fell silent. The mechanical hum rose again. Odhrán glanced over his shoulder but didn't seem particularly worried. I swallowed. Odhrán struck me as a lot of things, and he was definitely displaying a lot of stupidity, but he wasn't selfish to the point of ignoring another fae's pain. He had to believe Drax wasn't being irreparably harmed. Drax's voice had been rough with worry as he cried out for "her," but I sat here, unharmed.

Realization dawned with a sinking horror. Odhrán had said he didn't want this plan in the hands of a child. All those tubes, those younger versions of me I'd seen on Earth. On the other side of this cavern was a little girl with very nearly my face, and Elijah wanted to use her to end Thrae.

I sat up and swung my legs over the edge of my bed. "What do you know about her?"

Odhrán pursed his lips. "I really shouldn't be talking to you."

I had to keep from rolling my eyes. "Please," I said. "Can you turn the tube off? Stop it somehow?" I didn't know if that would kill her, but I couldn't think of anything beyond keeping her from becoming an unwitting weapon.

He frowned. "Why would I do that?"

"Because I don't have the ability to bring anything from Earth to here —and neither does she. I can't help you integrate Tech into your magic." Though, even as I said the words I wondered if I were wrong. Wasn't I an example of the merging of Tech and magic? I poured fear into my expression and spread my arms. "I do, however, have the ability take life energy, magic, and God knows what else, from Thrae. I can open and close rifts. But Earth is empty to me, a vessel waiting to be filled, and Elijah wants to fill it with Thrae." This much, I knew was true.

Odhrán frowned. "Farquin reported on your fear of Tech before he vanished. Chrysophylax as well. I thought it was a healthy fear, but it's not, is it?"

"Listen to me." I leaned forward. "You're being used. Elijah will destroy you and everything you've ever built so that he can create his paradise—on Earth. He doesn't think Thrae is real."

The mechanical hum cut off.

"Is she awake?" Elijah called.

Odhrán flinched. "Stirring. I'll be out shortly." He learned closer and whispered, "If you want my help, you'll lay down."

I laid down on the crystal slab as heavy footsteps echoed off the walls and prayed I'd gotten through to Odhrán.

"Kinnia," Elijah said from much closer.

I pulled on all my acting skills and struggled sleepily up on one elbow. "What?"

The white-coated Jalan stood next to the blue crystal, backlit by artificial light. he clutched something I couldn't quite make out. "Have you just woken?"

I faked a yawn and nodded.

He sighed. "You'd think I would learn to stop underestimating you."

Elijah wheeled on the Councilor, and the object in his hands resolved into a metal rod. He sent four blasts of bright-green laser fire into Odhrán's chest. The short elf toppled over. Blood spilled across his rainbow robes. I stared at Elijah in mute shock.

"Kay!" Drax shouted. "Kay, are you all right?"

"Yes," I answered shakily.

In the quiet, I thought I could hear his sigh of relief.

Elijah turned to me. "You told him about Earth, yes?"

I didn't respond. He shook his head.

"Fae always need such coddling." He shoved the rod into his pocket. "And I almost liked that one too. He would've followed me to the end." Elijah pressed a button on his wrist, and the crystal underneath me electrified.

My vision swam. The seconds stretched out in perfect agony. He shut the crystal off, and I collapsed onto the cool surface of my bed, panting.

"Yes," Elijah said. "You don't report to Odhrán anymore. From here on out, you work directly for me."

I peeled my head off the crystal to see him pressing a small button under his metal ear, like he had in the lab.

"He's dead." Elijah paused. "Send the satyr down, if you think he's pliable." The Jalan released the button and looked down at me, his human eye as cold as the lightbulb. "Your resistance grows irritating. I'd rather not kill you, but I will." He turned to leave.

"Wait," I gasped.

He halted, his back to me.

"I'll do it." I swallowed. "Whatever you want, I'll do it. Just don't use her."

Elijah twisted and looked at me over his shoulder, the light catching the edge of his grin. "You think I have another, hm?" The smile dropped. "How about you behave yourself, and we'll both hope I don't have to resort to that." He strode out of sight.

I curled into myself. My eyelids grew heavy, and I tumbled into an exhausted sleep, my dreams haunted by faces that weren't quite mine.

47

SHADE

Rebel fae whirled around me. The sun loomed high in the sky. I pulled sustenance from the bodies I called up and leaned on their sleeplessness. Power dripped from my eyes. My mind raced away from me with the bodies, ever deeper into the dirt. The song roared in my ears.

Still, I kept a piece of myself apart. That piece watched over the bridges as Teyr turned a group of strangers with similar beliefs into friends. It followed Bash as he tested the capabilities of fae and outfitted them as best he could. It rode with Zelimir as he settled comfortably into being his sister's chief strategist. It watched the world, so I didn't lose myself in Thrae's song.

To my left, the queen of the water nymphs, Lilly, swayed with exhaustion. At the end of a long, deep tunnel stretching away from the Tech that had been our home, one of my many pets clawed into thick, wet mud. I grinned. A droplet of water ran down my pet's forearm and dripped onto the ground. Lilly gasped.

"That's it," she murmured. "Push through."

I condensed my power into the two strongest bodies and drove them furiously at the wall of mud in the tunnel. The queen of the water nymphs, I'd learned, could teleport from one body of water she controlled to another. The bigger the body, the more people she could move. And, like the rest of the magic of Thrae, I could touch that water with my own power. The wall of mud burst, sweeping away my final two bodies as the miles of tunnel flooded.

Lilly laughed. Three blue-skinned nymphs emerged from the mouth of the tunnel as the water reached us. Four more followed, then more.

"I will return when the time is nigh." I stood. My bones cracked, and my muscles cried out from disuse. I scrubbed my hands over my arms.

Lilly narrowed her eyes, but I left without another word. My pack leader needed to know I'd completed my task. Every minute wasted was another where Elijah could do something awful to my Kitty.

I didn't get far before my pack found me. Each of them wore the cream tunic and brown pants of a full Cara.

"Is it done?" Zelimir asked.

I grinned, swaying slightly. "It is."

Bash grunted. Zelimir clapped me on the shoulder, and I stumbled.

Teyr caught me with an arm around my waist. "We're ready as well."

His excitement filled my Cara. I pressed against the barrier of awful fuzz that kept us from our Kitty, but as always, the barrier repelled me. Anger burned up my fatigue. The Councils and Elijah would regret the day they reached for our Kitty.

Zel called to a fae and sent them running for his sister with the news we were ready.

"Most of the force will go through your portal, of course." He handed me a folded Cara uniform. "But given the level of training we're dealing with, it made sense to put a strike squad, meaning us and Farquin, behind enemy lines to get to Kay faster. These clothes should give us a little plausible deniability."

Teyr frowned. "I'd rather leave the Jalan behind, but we can't risk losing Kay because of Tech we don't understand."

They led me to a spiderweb-like tent that hadn't existed when I went into my trance. Clearly, my other mates had already been briefed on this next step. I began shucking my robes as we stepped inside.

A trio of fae stared into a large portal on the floor lined with blood and glittering pink dust. A small, equally pink pixie wearing a tiny pink tube flitted over the portal. Something about her tugged at my memory. I pulled on pants I hadn't worn since I retook my fae form.

The pixie turned. "This portal will take you to the pantry."

I recognized her with a start. Gnuq's naked little assistant. "You are wearing...clothes."

"Kay made me a dress." She spun.

The pink tube had arm and head holes, but the stitches looked like the sort you'd see on a wound, and the seams were misaligned. I grinned. Definitely something my Kitty would've made.

"You look beautiful." I pulled the tunic over my head and put my finger out.

She landed on it and looked at Zelimir. "The blood is mostly pixie because they do most of the kitchen clean-up and were easiest to infiltrate. Those who donated are resting with our healers upstairs. The dust, we owe back to the—"

I drifted away from the conversation and stared through the portal. Wood shelves crowded with ingredients stared back at me. We could dive through, sneak into the depths of the Academy ourselves, rescue our Kitty before anybody noticed.

Thinking about cutting out early? Teyr asked in my mind.

I jumped.

Me, too. He sighed. *But Kay'd kick our asses if she found out we left Ar-a-mach in the lurch.*

I smiled and leaned against the ember's warm body. My Kitty wanted the best for everyone as much as she wanted it for herself. For her, I would wait.

A horn blasted through the air. The signal! I bolted for the door.

I will return, I said to any of my mates who listened.

I had to do the impossible.

I reached Lilly, where she sat by the mouth of the tunnel, what seemed like a legion of water nymphs at her back and most of the army at her front.

"Took you long enough," she huffed.

I sat on the ground beside her. Her opinions mattered little. She held out her hand, and I grasped her fingers. The song rose in my ears, haunting and slow. I pulled on the only anchor I had within Academy grounds, Light's bones. I needed to see.

Slowly, achingly, Light's skull rose to the surface of the dirt. I clutched his bone hanging around my neck with my free hand, closed my eyes, and peered through his eyes.

Afternoon light filtered down over the packed training grounds. Many of the trainee Caras and Seccas would be too busy to respond immediately. The canal that encircled the island of the main tower sparkled. I squeezed Lilly's hand once. All clear. She squeezed mine back. Time to begin.

I opened one eye and stared into the place between, where life and death reigned supreme over even space. The water glowed turquoise as Lilly opened a portal to another of her lakes.

The song thudded against the back of my skull. Here, in the space between, all magic became necromancy. I released Light's bone and reached for Lily's clean, clear portal. As I brushed the surface, the water turned dark. In my other eye, I watched the canal bubble. Lilly swayed, as if in time with music she couldn't possibly hear.

I squeezed her hand twice, and rebels began pouring into the water. They emerged on the other side of the canal, alive but stumbling into the Academy sunlight like my undead. Lilly leaned back into her people, then forward again. The water of the tunnels surged up, swallowing mouthfuls of the rebels. I shuddered with the pressure, then rolled as the song of the magic caught me.

No. I gritted my teeth and reached out with the walled off part of my mind to my mates. Teyr paced around a frowning Farquin. Bash meditated on the tent floor. Zelimir rehearsed battle plans in his head.

I exhaled. Ar-a-mach rose like a wave out of the canals. I had to control my magic by myself for a few more moments. At last, the last combatant, Zelimir's sister, slipped through the portal with a very confusing wink, and I dropped the spell. The queen and her attendants collapsed, but their life signs glowed in the space between. I leaned back, panting, and closed my other eye to watch through Light's eyes.

Cordelia's roc screeched above our camp as she stepped out of the canal at the Academy, her armor glistening with water. The army swarmed, some toward the doors, others toward the stunned trainees. Cara mates scattered to join one side or the other. Weapons clashed and magic flew. A wedge of titans sprinted toward the massive rainbow-toned doors, carrying one of the canal boats between them like a battering ram.

I didn't want to know if they were successful. I pulled my vision into myself and stood on shaky legs. I hadn't used this much magic since—since I killed Light in this very place. This time, I hadn't hurt anyone. I stumbled to the tent where my mates waited.

"Now. We must do this now," I said.

The trio of fae sat up. My mates straightened. Farquin clicked something in his blaster arm. I tumbled into the portal he'd opened in front of us with my mates on my heels.

48

KAY

I DOZED, PACED, STRETCHED, ANYTHING TO FILL THE TIME and keep me from worrying. Elijah sent a Jalan to drag Odhrán's body out after a few hours, but a dark red puddle remained, reflecting the rainbows of the crystals. The short elf had captured my mates, tortured them, and taunted me, but in the end, he was nothing more than garbage to be dragged away.

The door scraped open, and several sets of footsteps echoed off the walls. The puddle quivered. I hoped I might be something more than one body among many when Elijah finished. Past where I could see, metal clanged, and Drax bellowed. It took all my willpower not to scream.

Elijah stepped into the opening of the nook with a smile on his face. "I'm glad to see you're up."

Fists hit flesh somewhere in the darkness behind him. A red-and-blue scaled tail swept across the ground. Chry. My kidnapper. Drax's torturer. Anger tightened my gut.

Gnuq joined Elijah just as the darkness where they held Drax fell silent, and something scraped across the ground like a body being dragged. Had they finally killed Drax? I wouldn't give them the satisfaction of seeing me cry.

"So, you've been keeping her here." Gnuq licked his lips. "To think, I could've been visiting all along."

"To think," I said, "that you're so awful, and you still didn't make it past second choice for this whole stupid scheme."

He scowled.

"Kinnia." Elijah clucked his tongue. "I thought I raised you better than to talk to guests like that."

He chuckled at his joke while I took a deep breath and tried to regain myself. My compliance didn't just dictate my pain anymore. I needed to keep his attention on me to save that girl. The ground rumbled. I braced myself with a hand on my bed. A group of goblins and Jalan poured into the room and ran to the churning water wheel. They exchanged dark bricks on their blasters for ones resting on a large, black cable, then spun and ran out the way they'd come.

I smiled. "My mates are here."

"Cordelia and her army are here." Gnuq balled his fists. "Your mates have yet to show their faces."

Little did Gnuq know that not knowing where my mates were didn't bode well for him. If they could get here in time, we could save the girl and I wouldn't have to help Elijah.

Elijah stepped in front of the satyr. "It is almost time, my dear. Are you still ready to sacrifice yourself for a creature you think exists?"

"Yes." Maybe I'd been in this cave for too long, but I knew she was here. I could almost feel her.

Lir's Cara streamed into the cavern and scattered out of sight. Outside the door, Geminai's rough baritone bounced off the walls. My heart squeezed. They'd pulled a lot of heavy hitters in here. I wanted to shout at them, ask them how they could be so stupid as to not recognize how blatantly Elijah had lied to them. How could they possibly want to combine Tech and magic? Then I knew. My mates and I had demonstrated during the trials just how well Tech and magic melded. Had we fallen into Elijah and his coconspirators' trap from the beginning? Had we been nothing but one big experiment for them all along?

I forced down my fury and kept my expression neutral as Elijah stepped back and gestured to someone. A pair of Jalan dragged Drax into view. He slumped against the stone, bloody and bruised. His eyes fluttered weakly open, and he smiled at me.

He was alive. I exhaled.

Elijah pressed a blaster to the back of his head. "It seems you work better with a little motivation. Open a rift right next to me, or he dies."

I pressed a hand to my mouth. "You don't have to do this. I already agreed to help."

"You're not listening." Elijah lowered the blaster and fired.

The green laser exploded across Drax's lower back. The pink web of magic on his bare feet went out. He groaned, and pain filled his eyes.

"No!" I took a step toward them.

Elijah pressed the blaster against his head once more. "Now you're listening. Rift. Next to me."

Above his head, a shadow stretched into a long oval that glimmered with dark rainbows. The Upper Council.

The Upper Council was a part of this insanity?

Gnuq stared up at the portal. No voice issued out. No magic. Elijah gritted his teeth and pushed Drax's head into the floor with his blaster. He'd waited too long. I knew him now. Nothing would stop him except the unknown. He'd killed Odhrán on the mere suspicion I'd said something to the short elf. And for all his research, all his reams of data, I still knew my capabilities better than he ever would.

I pulled my shoulder back like I'd seen Zelimir do a hundred times. "The rift will spawn in here with me so close."

Gnuq stomped his hoof. "Liar! I've seen rifts appear hundreds of feet from you."

"Not intentionally," I said.

Elijah grinned. "Let her out."

"You can't order a Councilor around." Gnuq scowled. "You're just a Jalan, and Kinnia is an anomaly that belongs to me now."

Elijah looked at the most powerful satyr in the wilds like he was a mosquito. "I'm afraid you've misunderstood this particular partnership. Now, let her out, or I'll see if Ambrocio still has enough sanity to stand at my side."

I didn't care about the Lower Council, but I didn't want anyone else's blood on my hands if I could help it. Except Elijah. I wanted him motionless at my feet, unable to ever hurt anyone again. For that, I needed to get to him. I braced myself and plunged my hand into the electrical field around me. Pain screamed up my arm, but I didn't withdraw. The cuffs should block any fae magic in me and hinder my attempts to open a rift. I pushed my *energy* into the field. The dome around me crackled bright blue as everyone stared at me in horror. My vision began to dim. On my next inhale, I pulled. The cables on the ground crackled and sparked. My arm vibrated as the power raced into me.

I exhaled, comfortably full, and stepped off the crystal. "I can open it myself."

Gnuq faltered back a step.

David had a particular way of sidling up to adults that never made them look twice at him, and I channeled that. Elijah smiled at me. He didn't know he'd given me all the tools I needed to destroy him. I just had to put them in order. I stopped at Elijah's side and kissed his clammy cheek as I wrapped my fingers around his blaster and guided it away from Drax's skin. The old fae met my gaze with a soft smile before his eyes fluttered closed. His chest still rose and fell.

A cool vibration drew my attention, a collection of energies, the opposite of what I'd felt on Earth because I stood on the opposite side. I swallowed and plunged my hand into the patch of cool air, forcing my *energy* forward with all my rage and panic and vengeance. The ground shook under my feet. With my last push, I sent my desperate hope that my mates would reach me before I had to do something unforgiveable.

A silver tear unfolded in space slightly above me. I expected to see the sparkling white of Elijah's lab on Earth, or the planet's lifeless gray surface, but only colorless, rocky walls and a few blinking lights sat on the other side. That door in his lab built into the hill.

He rubbed the cheek I'd kissed. "Stay here and be ready to do what you do best."

I raised an eyebrow. "Don't you need me with you?"

Elijah chuckled. "If I needed us both on Earth, do you think I'd have all these idiot Thraens running around?"

Gnuq opened his to reply, but Elijah just walked through the rift.

My heart sank as he disappeared into the blackness. A few computer screens flickered on, revealing him in silhouette a few dozen feet away. All the energy I'd put into tricking him, and I stood by myself, surrounded by fae who hated me. My mates could be feet or miles away. How could I stop Elijah by myself?

In for five. Hold for five. Out for five.

Crystalline rainbows reflected off thick plastic in the corner of my eye. Slowly, I turned to face it. Her. Against one wall of the cavern stood a metal-and-plastic tube like the ones in Elijah's lab on Earth, emblazoned with K1NN15. A young girl of eight or nine with pale skin and dark hair floated within.

Maybe I wasn't alone after all.

49

TEYR

WE SLIPPED INTO THE EMPTY PANTRY. SOMEONE SCREAMED outside the door. Someone else barked an order. The ground shook. No one looked our way. Shade dropped into his wolf form, panting. Beneath the furious determination he poured into us, I could sense his exhaustion. No undead legions to bail us out this time.

Bash cracked his knuckles, then his neck. He'd admitted to me quietly before we left that he hoped we didn't run into Chrysophylax. Kay needed to come first, but he didn't know if he could resist taking his revenge on the dragonkin.

Zel amplified Shade's determination, but I caught the nostalgia in his eyes. He, Light, and I had snuck into this pantry after his first trial to steal all the liquor we could lay our hands on. We'd made it back to the suite eventually, but not before our prince took our uncultured palates on a small tour of the shelves, explaining all the delicacies we'd never heard of. I *pulsed* to him that I recognized it too, and he smiled softly.

Farquin pressed a button on the side of his neck and shimmered into near nothingness. If I looked closely, I could just discern his outline when he moved. I gritted my teeth. I didn't want the Jalan with us in the first place. If he could sneak off to the other side at any moment....

"I'm registering high levels of electricity below us," he hissed. "And one rift, newly opened."

Fire seared through my veins. Either Kay already got herself out— doubtful, with the dampened connection leading deep underground—or we had to find her against the clock.

Zel nodded. "She's too deep for the baths."

Shade shifted into his fae form and said, *The crystals.*

My fire burned hotter, fed by worry and anger. If Shade was right, Elijah took our girl to the heart of the world just long enough to let her see its beauty before he destroyed it.

We crept out of the pantry, into the silent kitchen. Outside the window, a group of trainees streaked by, magic at their fingertips.

Bash paused at the door. *Packed, but no one is paying any attention.*

I smiled. Cordelia's attack provided exactly the distraction we needed.

Shade burst through the door with the rest of us on his heels. Cara mates and a spattering of Secca officers swarmed in every direction. In the chaos, in the plain Cara uniforms Zel found for us, nobody gave us a second look. Only the occasional sharp, metallic footfall told me we hadn't lost the Jalan as we wound ever deeper into the bowels of the Academy.

Xerxes' voice crackled through the halls. "Ranged attacks to three o'clock. Melee to eight o'clock."

Bash shook his head. Shade swung through a door, and we barreled down a flight of stairs, leaving the flow of frantic fae behind. Kay's Cara grew ever closer, but the connection remained murky. I couldn't imagine traveling through the wilds like this for days, knowing we were in danger but never knowing how much.

We're coming, I thought to her. *Hold on a little longer, we're coming.* My plea bounced uselessly off the wall between us, and frustrated flames licked along my fingertips.

The halls Shade led us down grew darker, lit only by weak fifs, and less even. The smooth, dark stone of the Academy walls gave way to something craggier, and condensation slicked the ground under our feet. I'd never been this deep before. We had to be close.

Next left, Bash called.

I gathered my anger into a dense, superheated fireball. Zel nodded and ran a line of blue flame along the edge of Bash's bright-red axe as the dragon unsheathed the blade. We swung to the left and came face-to-face with a Cara in trainee green, Chrysophylax at their head. Behind them stood a round, red door.

I hurled my fireball along the ground. It smashed into Chrysophylax's knees, knocking him to the ground, and the compressed fire exploded. The blast shook the hall, raining pebbles down on our heads.

Chrysophylax is mine. Bash sprinted forward with his axe held high.

Shade hurtled past me and shifted into his wolf form as he tackled the oozekin to the ground. Zel tossed a wall of force behind us, supporting the ceiling and keeping anyone else from joining the fray.

The healer! he shouted at me.

I raced into the fray and found Leonai, Geminai's son, already on the ground, singed by my original blast but struggling to his feet with gritty magic gathering between his palms. I swept his feet with Bash's telekinesis and ignited the worry that had been pulsing in the back of my mind since we lost Kay into a constellation of tiny fireballs. One by one, I rolled them off my fingers, setting a dozen fires in his clothes. He bellowed and rolled, but I only coaxed the flames stronger.

On your left! Zel called.

I twisted to face a translucent ball of a fae flying toward me, no weapon or magic in hand. I dodged the attack I expected, but the oozekin stuck himself to my face. I tried to suck in a breath.

No air, just the faint scent of pond scum. My flames banked. My heartbeat thudded in my ears.

Zelimir reached into my magic, grabbing control of the flames and leaving me feeling like I'd just been walking in the rain. Shade leapt toward me and caught the fae on my face with one of his massive paws. His claws grazed my nose. I yelped, savoring the intake of fresh air, and stumbled back. Shade sank his muzzle into the oozing fae and tore until nothing remained but a slick puddle.

"JoJo!" Chrysophylax dodged one of Bash's swings and tried to charge Shade, but Bash dove and tackled the dragonkin to the floor.

Zel folded jagged layers of force around his fists and leapt for Chrysophylax's titanic second. I turned back to Leonai to make sure no one got up just as my fire gathered up off his clothes into a concentrated arrow hurtling at my head. I dropped a second too late, and heat seared my shoulder.

Oisin chuckled as he strode toward me, his long ponytail still perfect. "Well, traitor, I suppose you've done us a favor." He summoned a glittering yellow fireball on his fingertips. "Thank you for letting me prove all your duels were flukes at last."

I smiled. Fighting fire with fire just happened to be my specialty. He launched the fireball at me, and I threw my determination into a shield of flames between us. His attack sizzled off it.

A moment later than I "should" have, just long enough to lure him into a false sense of security, I dropped my shield and flipped out from behind it with a flame whip in hand. He faltered back a step. The line of flames snaked around his ankle with lightning speed and I yanked his feet out from beneath him. He crashed to ground, and I sprinted forward.

Right! Zel yelled.

Quin slammed a runed hammer into my side, crushing the breath out of my lungs. I toppled sideways, and he spun away to hit Shade. That old bard had me dead to rights. I may as well have waited for the fucking applause, forgetting the rest of the fight like that. I scrambled to my feet.

Oisin levered himself up on an elbow and began to summon a massive fireball too big for any fire shield to dissipate. A duel-ending move. But I didn't have to duel him. I had my mates to rely on.

Zel's magic hadn't worked for me yet, but I tried to slide my arm into the straps of one of his smaller shields, like I'd seen him do a million times. Protecting myself long enough to reach the door and reunite my Cara once more consumed my every thought. A shield, purple shot through with orange and red, appeared on my arm with a taste like dirt after rain just as Oisin launched his fireball. The flame scattered off the shield, the colors dancing merrily through the purple.

"The world is ending, and you're worried about some Emberhold crap?" I grabbed Bash's telekinesis and knocked Oisin against the wall.

The door behind them slammed open, and I straightened. If we could bolt, we wouldn't have to waste our time fighting these assholes.

A gust of air swept down the hall and pushed all of us back. I rolled to my feet and found myself nose-to-nose with Geminai. The troll grabbed my arm, and I ignited grim determination into fire in my fists.

Except Geminai didn't strike. He didn't even crush my arm in his meaty palm.

"The Upper and Lower Councils are watching as rifts are being opened in the heart of our Academy." His grip trembled. "In our home."

Oisin tried to stand, and Brettrus barreled into him. Leonai stared at his father.

Geminai shook his head. "Fix this. We will keep Chrysophylax busy."

I peered at the troll. Determination glowed in his eyes as he shoved me toward my mates. Brettrus got to his feet and helped Zel pry Bash off Chrysophylax. It had taken our old rivals a little longer, but the fiction of the Councils' authority had finally broken for them.

"Thank you," I said. "I promise, if this comes back to bite you in the ass, it'll bite all our asses." I whirled and bolted for the door behind him. Metal footsteps chased me, and I prayed they belonged to the Jalan I expected as I skidded into the room.

I'd never seen the crystals before. Trainees didn't get access, and our seventy-five of service made us a fairly young Cara. They glittered in all the rainbow hues of Thrae itself, but I couldn't look at them. I could only look at Kay, standing tall and proud in the middle of a nightmare.

She faced a rift. Gnuq and Lir's elemental Cara stood around her, but not nearly close enough to be forcing her. Drax slumped face-first on the ground, motionless but breathing. Cables netted the crystals, leading from them to a massive water wheel to...a tube. Like the one that held baby Kay in that Jalan's video in every way, including that it had an occupant. I took a faltering step forward.

Farquin sprinted toward the tube, suddenly visible once more. "Heretic!"

Kay turned. My breath caught in my throat. Cuffs like the ones she freed us from ringed her wrists. Bags drooped under her eyes, and the tips of her fingers were blackened. Farquin raised his blaster arm and took aim at the tube. She tackled him, and his blast scattered against the ceiling of the cavern. Rubble rained down. They landed in a heavy heap.

The Jalan I'd seen in the videos, Elijah, leaned out of the rift. "Ah, Farquin. I did wonder if we'd see you today."

"Heretic," he spat. "You create the uncreatable, and then you have the hubris to try again? That *thing* is an abomination."

"That thing is my insurance policy against things like that." Elijah nodded toward the door as my mates skidded to a stop next to me. "Do you have him?" Elijah asked Kay.

She nodded.

"Wonderful. I'll be done here in a few minutes." He looked to Gnuq. "Handle them, if you wouldn't mind?"

Gnuq snapped his fingers at Lir's Cara, who all turned to us. My brain whirred at top speed. Kay wasn't working with him. She couldn't be, not willingly. The cuffs could be controlling her. Elijah could have—

Teyr, your three! Zel barked.

I rolled automatically out of the way of a wave of mud. Lir's air elemental, Anan, rained blasts of wind down me. I dodged as best I could, but my best sucked. Needle-thin slivers of pain raced along my arms and shoulders.

Teyr! Zel called. *We need you on the earth elemental.*

I flung a fireball haphazardly in his direction and kept pelting forward. We couldn't win this fight without Kay. I just needed to reach her.

"Kay!" I dropped to my knees and slid the final few feet to her.

Goblins and Jalan swarmed the room. Blaster fire rained down. Shade yelped, and pain sparkled through his Cara. I pulled his magic into a translucent blue-black shield around Kay, the squirming Farquin in her arms, and me. A soft hum overlayed the noise of battle.

"Make the shield darker," she hissed without looking at me.

"What? No, I need to find how he's controlling you. Do you know? Can you answer?"

"Teyr." She met my gaze for the briefest moment. "Trust me."

I pulled magic until the shield looked like nighttime. Music whirled around me. She released Farquin and threw her arms around me. I cuddled her close. Skin still warm, breath still rising and falling in her lungs. My Kay. Our Kay.

Farquin started to sit up.

She leaned back and pinned him with a glare. "Touch her, and I'll kill you."

Farquin grimaced but nodded.

She turned back to me and cupped my face. "He made another me. He plans to wake her up and use her to destroy Thrae. I can't let him do that to Thrae—or her." Tears welled in her big blue eyes. "Do you understand? He cannot be allowed to use her. You have to stop him, just the four of you." She lifted her shackled hands. "I can't help her or you, and until he's defeated, he has to believe I'll help him."

"But you won't help him," I insisted.

She smiled gently and I knew we had to ensure that she wouldn't be forced to make that choice. I pressed a kiss to her lips. Of course. Elijah didn't need any tricks or switches. Her own soft heart, the heart she grew around the brain he built her, was more than enough to control her.

"I love you," I murmured. "We love you. We're gonna fix this."

"I know," she said, and I prayed I wasn't lying to her. With the Upper and Lower Council working against us....

I drew a breath. "Grab Farquin, then kick me in the chest on the count of three." I squeezed her shoulders, then released her.

She nodded and regathered a grumpy but willing Farquin close. I braced for the blow.

"Three...two...one!" I let the shield flicker out just as her foot connected with my sternum.

I flew backwards several feet and landed hard on my back.

How is she? Zel swept a platoon of goblins aside with his massive two-hander.

Is my Kitty herself? Shade sank his teeth into the fire elemental's flank.

Is it the cuffs? Bash pinned Anan to the ceiling with his telekinesis and wrapped a few thick strips of force over the fae to keep him in place.

I stood slowly. *She's protecting the girl in the tube. This one's on us.*

50

SHADE

I swam through the tide of battle. Snatches of Thrae's song flitted into my ears when my mates used my power, but I had no magic left. Even in my wolf, exhaustion clung to my limbs, dragging me down. I threw myself against the nearest elemental, and a frisson of color spiraled out of where I sank my teeth into his flesh. He tore at the magic of my wolf, and my teeth started to recede. I released him and skittered back.

Forget him, my pack leader said. *The goblins have no magic. Focus there.*

My hold on the wolf filtered back in as I bounded away from the elemental toward the goblins around the tube. My wolf-mind couldn't quite understand the tube and the girl inside. She looked like my Kitty, small and frail, as I'd seen her in her own mind. But my Kitty sprawled in the middle of the room, on top of the Jalan she could trust, working with the Jalan she couldn't trust.

A triangle of goblins pointed blasters at me. I lunged and caught one in my mouth, then clawed at the two behind him. Green, mossy blood coated my tongue. I spat the corpse on top of his friends, and they went down in a green-tinted pile.

Teyr said my Kitty had to betray us for the girl in the tube who was and wasn't her. I didn't understand, but I didn't need to. If my Kitty asked something of me, I would do it. The girl in the tube's eyes moved rapidly behind her lids. I pounced away from her into another cluster of goblins.

A hand wrapped around my mind. I raised my gaze to meet Gnuq's. I wanted to protect him, wanted to lay at his feet and lunge at anything that approached. My Kitty wanted that. My pack leader wanted that. I started toward the satyr.

The door to the room banged open and the grip on my mind loosened. Xerxes stormed into the room with a few Cara mates and Secca officers. Dozens of life signs crowded the hall behind him. The hand on my mind dropped away entirely, leaving an oily smugness behind.

My pack leader sent grim determination across our bond. We would die against this many enemies. I bit the head off the nearest goblin and swiped at another, then shoved myself between the goblins and the tube. Several of them fled toward the wheel to refill their hated blasters. If I had to die, I would die protecting what my Kitty chose.

"Close the rift." Xerxes didn't yell, but his voice reached my ears despite the fray.

They're on our side? Teyr asked.

I hesitated, and a blaster bolt hit my shoulder. Xerxes, on our side. Goblins, on the evil side. I swatted two away with a paw.

"I will not be tricked into fighting the wrong enemy any longer," Xerxes said.

Cara mates and Secca officers swarmed into the room and attacked Lir's Cara. Gnuq screamed and shut his eyes. I howled triumphantly. In the end, the satyr was a coward.

Gnuq's summoning reinforcements, Bash said.

I stopped howling and whirled to tear through the group of goblins returning with their refilled blasters. The taste of their blood grew dull as I shredded one after another. The frantic *pulses* to turn or to take one elemental over the other died down. When the last goblin fell beneath my maw, Xerxes' reinforcements' life signs beat an overwhelming pulse above those of Gnuq or Elijah. We would win, like my Kitty asked. I howled again and turned to my pack leader for a target.

He obliged. *Get the—*

Through a gap in the fighting, Elijah stepped out of the rift. The rest of my pack leader's words disappeared as bloodlust filled me. I would tear the metal from his bones, crunch his glowing eye between my teeth. He kicked Farquin away and held a hand out to my Kitty.

I crept through the battle, low to the ground. One pounce would take the elderly Jalan down. I could end this. *Pulses* thrummed through my Cara, and I *pulsed* back to keep fighting. I needed surprise. My Kitty accepted his hand and stood.

"It's time, my dear." He ran a metallic finger along the cuffs, then plucked out the vines in her neck. "Let's save the real world."

My Kitty swallowed. Her fear and determination poured through our bond once more. She turned slightly and I realized she intended to attack him. Something whirred in the rift, and a glint of silver sparkled in the darkness. A thick, dark cable shot through the hallway behind them. My Kitty didn't react. She couldn't hear the approaching cable. I *pulsed* a wild mixture of warnings to my pack and threw myself at the Jalan, at the cable. If I had to die, I wanted to die for something.

I wanted to die like Light.

The lump in the back of Elijah's white coat exploded outward as an array of heavily modified blasters sprang out on metal arms. A dozen green beams lanced out of their maws and one caught me in the chest.

"Shade!" My Kitty whirled on the Jalan.

Pain exploded over my skin. I seared. I burned. A scream tore from my lips. I landed in the dirt at his feet. My vision tinged gray. The cable sank into my Kitty's stomach. All her muscles locked. The gray reached out to consume me, but not before I saw her eyes turn flat white.

I died for nothing.

51

BASH

Elijah chuckled and stepped back through the rift to Earth. Dee stood, frozen. Her eyes scrolled with meaningless green numbers over a white background. Her emotions floated aimlessly, too fuzzy to understand. My dragon bellowed. Rage built in my gut until it reached that same clarity I remembered from the night I burned the church.

Teyr and I have this, my commander said. *Get him.*

I met his gaze across the chaos of battle. *I cannot take more orders after this.*

He nodded. *I know.*

I extended a hand to my dragon. He seethed forward, imbuing me with fury and power like I'd never felt before. His thoughts became mine, and mine his. My body burned. For a moment, I thought I might be able to transform after all, but short claws only burst from the tips of my fingers as my body toughened. We roared and raced for the rift. At its base, the cable in Dee's gut lay on the ground. We needed to taste Elijah's blood, but we swung on the cable first.

The axe head glanced off. We growled, backed up, and leapt for an overhanded swing. Our arms jarred, pain shooting from palm to shoulder. The cherrystone head of the axe cracked in half and tumbled to the floor.

We landed and turned to stare at the unharmed cable. Our commander had reached Dee's side. Our ember covered both their backs. Whiteness spread from her feet like a puddle, though our wolf remained dark. We couldn't help here. Our prey lay inside.

Wielding the headless axe like a club, we charged into the rift. On the other side lay a short, narrow hall of rock, beyond which we could see a dozen screens glowing in a darkened room, illuminating the Jalan we wanted. A war cry went up behind us, and more fae followed as I pounded down the hallway.

As we burst into the room where the Jalan was, a DogTech launched itself at us. We snatched it out of the air and threw the DogTech back the way it came. It crashed into another Tech, and we turned to the Jalan. The darkened room turned out to be larger than we expected, nearly as large as the cavern where the battle still raged. Only a few feet separated us from the ring of glowing screens.

We stalked forward. Nothing else mattered. Not the cables on the floor, not the doors or halls leading away, not even the small fire the Tech collision created. The Jalan chuckled but did not turn from his screens as he pressed a few buttons. A jet of smothering gas erupted over the fire, and it sputtered out. The *hiss* of many hydraulics greeted our ears.

"You were brave to come here," he said. "But you have signed your death warrant."

We roared and charged him. Before we could raise a hand to grab a limb or one of his many monitors, an arm of moving metal shreds like that of a HoldTech exploded out of the wall and lanced into our side. We staggered, pressed a hand to the flow of blood, and whirled with our other arm out.

We clenched our fist, and the shards ground to a halt on the arm. Momentum built behind our hold, and we released. The shards exploded away from each other, piercing the Jalan and his monitors. He hissed in pain. We barely noticed the small cuts on our own skin. Something hummed in our Cara.

That arm had given our prey the moment he needed. Tech poured into the chamber. Fae flooded past us to engage the metal monstrosities on all sides. The chamber lit with rainbow magic and the sounds of pain.

A DogTech double, maybe triple, the size of any we'd ever seen before scraped the ceiling as it barreled toward us. We wrenched our commander's force forward and jammed wedges into its jointed knees. It stumbled, and we vaulted onto its jagged back.

The spikes there rivaled Rocky's talons. We merely sank our mind into the attachments and ripped. The spikes screeched off, clattering to the floor as the DogTech stood to crush us against cable-wreathed stalactites.

We flattened. On the ground, trainees scooped up the spikes to use as lances against monsters we couldn't name. Our prey's glowing red eye remained in place, surrounded by dancing screens. We braced to jump.

Farquin rushed in, firing his blaster haphazardly into the crowd. Tech sparked and crumpled. Fae screamed.

"I will die before I let you desecrate her!" he yelled.

Our prey laughed a horrible, grating laugh. "I do think you're correct in that."

Farquin shot at the screens, the cable, Elijah himself. Every blast bounced off a clear shield and scattered throughout the cavern. Elijah had shielded his whole array of monitors. Elijah's blasters swung around to face Farquin.

"It's unfortunate." Elijah crossed his arms. "I'd hoped to leave you on Thrae to monitor everything left behind. You always showed promise."

The blasters fired as one. A thick, green beam exploded forward, frying Farquin along with any Tech or fae behind him. Screams echoed off the walls.

Our connection to Dee vibrated in our veins. We yanked the power forward and sank it into the top of the Jalan's shield. It wedged open the barest gap for us to grab onto. The searing pain rocked us, but we pulled. The top of the shield didn't tear away, but it disintegrated in our hand like nothing more than static.

Elijah smiled, and we leapt toward him. Our feet skidded against metal coated in cables, but we caught ourselves with a few bursts of telekinesis. A monitor popped with a burst of sparks. We hefted the bare handle of the axe and approached.

"Kill me if you want." Our prey spread his arms wide. "There's no stopping this now. Earth will live again."

On the monitors, a gray metal sign became red, though vibrant dirt and mold obscured its white message. We roared and swung. The handle connected with his shoulder, and he grunted. His jacket and skin spit, exposing metal plates and cables. He caught himself on a slim bar below the monitors and smiled.

The thing in front of us was more metal than man. We could bludgeon against him all we liked, but only his human brain remained vulnerable.

We met his human gaze. His thoughts and memories poured into us. Images of Earth in its former glory, his desperate need to rule what had once been. Madness tinged the edges. Like every door, every shield, we reached for his thoughts and pulled. He screamed and dropped to the ground, cradling his skull.

We released the pressure. "Release her."

He gasped for breath. "I can't control her. Otherwise, the simulation wouldn't be worth running." He spit blood and chuckled. "She has no off switch."

We laid our palm against his skull and tore at his memories once more. Metal grated in his throat as he screamed. He tugged at our grip weakly, and we ripped his hand off.

"Let her go." We lessened the pressure.

He swung the array of blasters on his back toward us and unleashed with a cry. We threw our arms up in front of us, and a shield of Shade's blue-black power blocked most of the blast. Our shoulders seared outside the narrow beam of our focus, and we roared in fury.

Between Elijah's legs, the thick cable holding our girl in place met the bank of monitors. We needed the Jalan dead. We needed the cable destroyed.

We hacked at his mind with half our attention, forcing him to crumple once more, then kicked him out of the way and ducked beneath the panel on a bed of Zelimir's force. With Teyr's fire, we burned around the place where the thick cable connected to the computer to see the insides more clearly. The thick, black coating melted to reveal a mess of smaller, woven strips of plastic. A brief tug told us the cable would not give way in this state. Inside Dee, the covered cables had been strong, and the uncovered ones, weak.

The battle raged wildly around our head in screams and blasts and the ring of metal on metal. Elijah coughed wetly next to us. We wanted him dead, wanted it so badly our hands burned with the effort of not taking him by the throat and squeezing until the life left his eye. But Dee deserved that pleasure.

Rage and determination tore through us, narrowing our attention even more. We wound a thread of telekinesis, delicate but strong, and reached for the cable.

52

ZELIMIR

I KNELT NEXT TO TEYR ON THE NEWLY WHITE STONE AT KAY'S feet under a purple shield he held in place. To our left, a trainee healer in red leaned over Shade while trying to patch together the massive hole in his chest. Every time I looked at him, my breath caught. Only his ragged heartbeat in his Cara told me he remained alive.

Teyr's arms faltered, and the purple shield flickered out of existence. A blast of some magic I couldn't identify slammed into the ground next to me. The next caught me in the side of the head. My vision went white as my ears rang.

Sorry. Teyr dragged the shield back up.

I shook my head to clear the ringing, then returned my attention to the cable. With one hand, I pulled away a bit of cut tunic to see where the cable bit into Kay's skin. No closure, no fastening. Just slick black plastic meeting my mate's soft flesh as though it always belonged there. A thin line of blood ran down into her pants. I wiped it away uselessly.

With every second, more white spread across the dark stone of the cavern floor as Kay's Tech drained it of all magic. Thankfully, Teyr, Shade, me, and even the healer all stood within our bubble without any issue. For now, anyway.

The trainee healer sat back on his knees. "I've done all I can. He's not going to die, but he's in bad shape. I wouldn't expect much more than limping out of here."

A crystal exploded as the white spreading from Kay's feet reached its base. The shards scattered against the shield, and the healer flinched.

"Go," I told him. "You've done more than enough. Spread the word, get people out."

He nodded and leapt across the floor onto a section that hadn't yet turned white, then sprinted toward the door. Behind us, the fourth Cara to try to draw the runes to close the rift failed. The ancient magic always stuck at the top of the rift and the clear barrier around the cable batted it away at the bottom. Silvery magic crackled above me. Someone yelped. I craned my head upward. Through the purple of the shield, I could just make out Councilor Ambrocio, who hovered midair in front of the Upper Council's shimmering portal.

"The Upper Council," he shouted, "wishes this whitening stopped."

I turned back to the cable. Very little mattered less to me than the edicts of fae who could've stopped Elijah long before now. I reached out to touch the cable and hit the barrier an inch off its surface. The barrier didn't hurt me if I didn't attack.

"The Upper Council wishes the rift closed!" Ambrocio shouted.

"Then shut it!" Teyr hollered.

I stood and cupped Kay's face. Numbers scrolled across the surface of her eyes as she stared blankly forward. Her emotions, though dimmed, floated peacefully. If she could recognize us enough to keep us safe, could I reach her?

"Kay," I murmured. "Dee, Kitty, love. I need you to listen to me. I need you to fight this."

She didn't respond. Fae fled the cavern. Geminai raced past, carrying Drax's slumped form.

"No!" Ambrocio screamed.

I jerked my attention onto him. He scrambled as though trying to climb an invisible rope, but he sank inexorably down toward the cavern floor.

"Help me!" he shrieked.

The old Councilor's right foot touched the white floor. Spindly white veins of nothingness crawled up his leg, then his other leg and torso. He screamed and clawed at that invisible rope. The veins consumed his arms, his neck. His screaming cut off. Finally, the white veins spread across his face, and he collapsed.

I stared at the dark, rainbowed portal in nauseous horror. It rippled, and a tall fae in hooded robes the same color as the portal stepped out with his hands folded in front of him.

"You will stop this." The Upper Councilor's voice vibrated. "You all will."

The chains of compulsion closed around my neck. Teyr dropped the shield. Shade struggled onto wobbly feet.

"Fuck...you...." Teyr hissed through gritted teeth.

The Upper Councilor melted back into the portal without another word, but the portal itself remained. I turned in a slow circle. The cavern around us lay nearly completely white. All the crystals had been reduced to shards, but a few points of color remained, along with us and the Upper Councilors' portal. The metal water wheel, cables, and other instruments I guessed had been brought here by Elijah and the tube, where a much younger Kay floated also retained their own color. I swallowed. Kay didn't want the girl used as a weapon, but maybe she could help us save the world.

I lifted my foot to cross the floor to her and froze in place. My chains tightened. The problem was right here. I should stay right here to fix it. I thought intently about how much I believed this girl could help us fix everything and managed to take a step.

Get Bash's attention, I told Teyr. *I think we're going to need him for whatever comes next.*

The ember gritted his teeth and, after a similar struggle to move, he leapt through the rift. Shade melted into his fae form and pillowed his head on Kay's feet. "I may have enough magic to help."

I nodded as I reached the tube.

This close, the differences between the girl and Kay were more obvious. She had rounder cheeks, narrower shoulders, thinner lips. But the coloring and the build were nearly the same, and she had a matching cable in her gut. I put a hand to the plastic of the tube. No button presented itself, nor any latch.

I took a deep breath. I didn't have time. I pulled off my tunic and threw it over my shoulder. Then, I palmed the handle of a sharp-edged hammer of force and swung on the thick plastic at the bottom of the tube. It cracked, and a little of the fluid leaked out.

The fluid lost color as it touched the ground. I grimaced and swung again. The plastic cracked a bit more. I stuffed wedges of force into the widening gap and swung. The plastic shattered, the fluid washed out, and I dropped my hammer to catch the girl in my arms.

She coughed, and her eyes fluttered open. "What?" Her voice sounded strange, like she'd never used it before.

"I'm sorry." I wrapped her in my tunic. "I can't explain, but I need you to trust me."

I picked my way back across the cavern.

Teyr appeared in the mouth of the rift. *Bash won't leave, but I got him to pay attention.*

The girl squirmed to get free. "Put me down! I don't know you!"

"You will die if I put you down." I held her tighter. "I'll explain everything soon. For now, look at that woman there."

The cable connecting her to the tube tugged, and she grimaced. I took a step back. A handful of feet separated us from Kay and Shade. Nearly as much as separated them from Teyr, and, I hoped, Teyr from Bash.

The girl in my arms twisted. "That's the back of some lady. I don't get it."

Kay, I said. *If you can hear me, I need you to turn around.*

No response.

I pressed my essence to the very edge of the bridge and stopped bothering to speak to her alone. *Kay, please.*

Shade wobbled his essence forward enough that I could feel it. *My Kitty, I know you are there. I know the pressure of staying still, but you have to wake, to move.*

Teyr joined us. *Love, I believe in you. I will always believe in you. Just turn around.*

Bash surged forward, more dragon than I'd ever felt him. *You are supposed to live. Turn and face the best chance you have of living.*

The fogginess didn't clear, but Kay turned on slow feet.

The girl in my arms gasped. "That's me. But she's Tech!"

"She put herself there so you wouldn't have to." I swallowed. "Now, she needs you to get her out."

The girl's lower lip wobbled. "For me?"

I nodded. "She loves you. She's never even met you, and she loves you."

Tears filled the young girl's eyes, a shade lighter than Kay's. She crossed her arms and scowled. "Whatever you need."

All of us now, I said to my mates. *At once. Just think of how much you love her.*

I opened myself fully, pouring love into Kay's body. My emotions mixed and mingled with my mates' love, then surged into something greater still.

Kay stumbled forward.

53

KAY

Power flowed around me in a silent storm. I didn't need to think, to move, merely to let the power flow. I sank myself into it and relaxed. Years passed in that ease. Something pressed against the edges of my awareness. I twitched but remained submerged. That something pressed harder and harder.

Tastes filled a mouth I'd forgotten having. Neatly tilled and tended fields in the wake of a flash flood that brought the hydration they needed. An underground river, revealing gemstones and ore with centuries of work. A light-dappled forest full of hidden life. The underside of a decayed log covered in a strange but thriving ecosystem. Love. *Love*, I thought. *Love*.

Pain sank into my gut, and I stumbled forward. Someone caught me with reedy arms. Something hot seared Bash's back—a blaster shot, a burn I knew too well, as I knew Bash and the necromancer belonging to the arms around me.

I had to stop Elijah.

I gasped in a lungful of dry air. Shade crushed me to his chest, and I sank against him. The flow of power coursed dimly through the back of my mind, unforgettable but possible to think around.

"I'm sorry," I mumbled. "I'm sorry, I'm so sorry."

He stroked my hair. "We will fix it yet, my Kitty."

We almost have this end exposed, Bash said. *We cannot get the cable out, but it will no longer contain its own blast.*

The sounds of battle reached me from within the rift. At least a dozen combatants, if not more.

Clear the chamber, I said. *I'll get everyone out when this is done.*

Teyr stroked my shoulder with one superheated hand. "Zel has one more thing you may want to consider."

He and Shade helped me stand and took the weight of the massive cable in my belly as we turned. Zelimir, shirtless and covered in blood and dust, adjusted the young girl in his arms until she could sit up. She clutched his tunic around her. A much smaller cable peeked out of her stomach and led to the shattered tube behind them both.

I pressed a hand to my mouth. "Are you...?"

She pushed her shoulder-length hair back and stared at me with such fierce determination I almost giggled. "I'm the girl who's gonna save you." She pursed her lips. "I just need someone to tell me how."

I looked at Zelimir. *That cable isn't keeping her alive. You can cut it.*

He slid his fingers into a set of force shears and snipped the cable a few feet from her body. She shivered but otherwise seemed fine.

"Do you have something we can call you?" I asked.

"Kinnis," she replied.

Tears welled in my eyes. I held out my arms. Zelimir brought her forward but didn't offer her to me.

"Well, Kinnis," I said in a choked voice, "I think we're going to save everything by heading through there"—I pointed at the rift—"and doing some pretty dangerous stuff. My friends and I think you can help, but we can keep you safe here if you prefer."

She scowled. "I'm gonna help. Once I put on this shirt properly and get off the floor that's gonna kill me, you couldn't stop me from helping."

I laughed wetly. "I bet I couldn't."

Zelimir met my gaze. "Are you sure that's a good idea?"

"I don't know if we have enough shields for the kind of blast you're talking about." Teyr pushed a slightly shaggy curl of hair back from my forehead.

Shade kissed my shoulder. "We certainly cannot stay here. The siphon will continue as long as we do."

I nodded. "Then help me in."

Teyr and Shade took the cable like some kind of fucked-up train while Zel helped Kinnis into his tunic. Together, we wobbled through the rift to Earth. The flow of power in the back of my mind stuttered and started to dry up. I might still siphon some while the rift remained open, but magic no longer raced through me like a rushing river.

Kinnis wiggled from Zel's hold and stood. "Now what?"

I didn't know how many lives had been lost to the siphon, much less in the battle, but I would fall to pieces if I thought of that now.

"Now," I stared at the monitors in the distance, "we see how close we have to get before this blows."

The sounds of battle died down, turning into nothing more than the constant hiss of hydraulics as we achingly trudged the scant feet to the cavern ahead.

It is bare, Bash said. *Though we will need to return to Earth to rescue the fae who fought.*

Come to us when you can, I replied.

Kinnis kept racing ahead and circling back. I held out my hand to her, too terrified of some trap we missed or loose Tech to let her run ahead. She rolled her eyes but took my hand. The power flow in the back of my mind turned sharp and hot. I stumbled and pressed my hand to the cable. Kinnis gasped.

Zelimir caught me. "Kay?"

"I'm okay," I lied.

I kept my hold on Kinnis' hand. We might only be able to blow this thing together.

She met my gaze and raised an eyebrow. She wanted to know if this was the dangerous thing she decided to help us with. I nodded. She squeezed my hand and turned resolutely ahead.

Pain bloomed along Bash's side, and he yelled. I sprinted forward, heedless of the ache in my gut or how Teyr and Shade ran close behind me, the cable in hand, or how Kinnis struggled to keep up. We burst into the cavern. Magic and blaster fire marked every surface. Blood dripped into puddles of oil. Fallen Tech surrounded the monitors in the middle, and not a single living soul remained outside that circle. Bash and Elijah lay within it. My maker pulled a shard of Tech out of Bash's side. Gray blood pooled, and Elijah rose.

"Ha!" he said. "Try crushing my mind now."

I took two steps forward and my stomach heaved again. The power flowing through me swelled, pressing against the seams of my body.

Elijah whirled. "What are you doing here?"

I crumpled to my knees and vomited. Kinnis danced out of the way but didn't release of my hand.

"You can't—the loop—and how did you—?" Elijah began hitting buttons furiously. "You can't do this to me!"

I grinned up at him through vomit-stained teeth. "I am always more than you anticipated." I squeezed Kinnis' hand. "We are."

Bash lunged forward and threw his arms around Elijah's knees. The Jalan toppled. Pain raced through Bash's Cara, but he gritted his teeth, hoisted the bladeless handle of his axe, and smashed Elijah over the head once. My maker went still.

"Not dead." Bash coughed. "We're saving him for you."

I smiled weakly. "You all should go."

My skin prickled. The flow in the back of my head became a cycle. Too much power. Too much power with nowhere to go but into me and into her, over and over and over again.

Please, run, I said across all my bridges. *I can die. I'm not even technically alive, and neither is she. We get to die heroes, which is better than we ever could've hoped for.*

Teyr laughed long and loud. "You think at the end of all of this we're just gonna run away and let you blow up?"

"Yep." Kinnis sat cross-legged next to me. "I'm gonna stay here with my sister or older twin or me from the future, and we're gonna save each other ourselves. That's how this works."

Tears filled my eyes. She couldn't be more than eight or nine. I'd gotten kicked out of my last foster family at twelve, but I knew the bitter determination in her face too well. No one had been on her side in so long. She needed me, like I'd needed someone then.

I squeezed her hand. "No, Kinnis, he's right. We don't have to save ourselves."

She frowned. I extended a hand for one of my mates to take. Bash settled heavily at my side and accepted it. He opened his Cara and the power flowed through all three of us, lessening a little of the tension.

Teyr sat and took Bash's hand. "Exactly."

"We would never leave your side, my Kitty." Shade took Teyr's hand.

Zelimir took the final spot and offered his hand to Kinnis.

She stared at it, then up at me. "They're all gonna die, aren't they?"

I swallowed back tears. "I don't know. But I know there's a better chance of none of us dying if we work together."

She sighed and took Zelimir's hand.

The power ebbed and redoubled, gaining speed as it raced the new loop. I grimaced.

"When I say so"—I panted—"put everything you have into shields."

My mates nodded. The power circled faster and faster, pressing out, desperate for somewhere to go. My gut seared.

"If we survive this," Kinnis whispered, "do I have to go back home?"

I smiled through the pain. "Never again."

The power reached its crest.

Now.

My mates' multicolored magic swirled around us. A high whine reached my ears. The cable superheated in my gut, and the world went black.

EPILOGUE
KAY

I LEANED BACK ON A LAVENDER STONE AND LET THE SUN warm my leather-clad chest as I stared out over the Academy from the mountains at the edge of the valley. The first time I'd seen this view, I'd been Declan, a mercenary trying to fit into a world where I didn't belonged. Today, four months after the battle under the Academy, the view had changed and so had I. Except for the very top level, the central tower had been bleached completely white. Even fingers of whiteness stretched out into the training yards beyond. The siphon had taken seventeen lives.

It could have been much worse, but I would never forget those seventeen. We'd engraved one white stone with their names and laid it at the edge of the bleached area, memorializing everyone we lost. I tried every day to blame Elijah for what happened. I carried a smaller piece of that stone in a new necklace, engraved with the names of my family. My mates each had a matching one. They were as real as Kinnis or I, and I wanted them remembered.

Kinnis bounced up to me, seemingly no worse for wear for having been exploded a few months ago. She'd decided, unlike me, that her name coming from her serial number didn't bother her. She only knew Elijah as that guy who stabbed Bash and died, and she'd left the simulation after a couple months on the street, so she was more pleased to learn her life hadn't been real than anything else. Or at least, she was satisfied when I promised her that her time in a simulation didn't make her any less real than the rest of us.

"You're so slow!" She grabbed my hand, and the matching, rainbow-toned burn scars on our hands lined up.

All six of us had the same burns. Kinnis and I kept waiting for ours to disappear, but something about the nature of the explosion seemed to have actually gotten through our healing abilities.

I laughed and stood. "All right, all right. I was just taking a moment."

My mates, Drax, Cordelia, and Xerxes waited for us next to five very loaded packs.

"Get lost?" Teyr asked as we approached.

I rolled my eyes. "Can't a girl get a moment to herself?"

Kinnis released me, sprinted over to Drax, and threw herself into the hovering chair he used to navigate now. Despite all the restorations of the past few months, Elijah still left his mark. Drax hadn't regained feeling below his waist, but he smiled at Kinnia indulgently.

When my mates, Kinnis, and I had survived, and I realized she needed somewhere to live, the old Councilor had been the obvious choice. She kept his spirits high.

Cordelia frowned as I joined my mates. "Are you sure this is what you want?"

She'd spent the last few months putting the Academy back together. The Upper Council disappeared after the explosion, and only Gnuq, Drax, and Xerxes remained of the Lower. Nobody could find Farquin's body, so Cordelia had complete control of the place. She'd thrown Gnuq in prison and taken Drax and Xerxes on as advisors, but the Academy was only a starting point for her. She'd begun building a new seat of power where new crystals had emerged and worked on bringing the whole of the wilds together under Ar-a-mach. Last time I checked, her audience chamber had been packed to bursting with fae ready to share their opinions and have a hand in building the wilds what they wanted.

Zelimir wrapped his arms around my waist and pressed a kiss to my cheek as I nodded.

"Thrae and Earth are connected," I said. "After the siphon, we can't expect that'll change anytime soon. We need someone on that side to keep an eye on things. Energy doesn't disappear, and we don't know what changed."

Bash tugged me into his arms and helped himself to a handful of my ass. "And we need a little distance."

Xerxes nodded. "But you will make regular reports at the assigned point."

Teyr frowned. "We'll make the reports we deem necessary as we can. We're not your little spies."

Xerxes stepped back. "Old habits."

The spymaster had apologized profusely for his role in the events leading up to the battle, but everyone was still a little touchy. According to him, Elijah managed to completely obscure his work from Xerxes' networks, and Xeres distrusted a rebellion led by King Zephyr. Cordelia liked him for his outside perspective.

Cordelia raised an eyebrow at me. "But you will check in, right? Even if there's nothing to report, I need to know you're all alive."

I grinned. "And we'll come back for every other holiday."

She laughed. "Perfect!"

I wriggled out of Bash's arms and hurried over to my friend. She wrapped her arms around me.

"You're going to be amazing," I whispered. "Just keep listening and keep good people around you."

"I wish I could keep you, but I understand." She chuckled. "I'll send an army after you if you don't check in regularly."

I released her and stepped back. "Don't threaten me with a good time."

She laughed. Xerxes stepped to the side, whispering. Another contact from an informant.

I crossed to Drax and Kinnis.

"Be safe," Drax said. "I look forward to hearing of your travels."

"Be cool!" Kinnis cried. "Do all the badass stuff you can come up with and send home the heads of the best Tech you kill."

I wrapped both of them in a massive hug while Zel exchanged a private goodbye with his sister.

Wind swept over the mountain, rattling green and yellow lava flowers. Tears welled in my eyes as I looked over the people that loved me. As much as I carried my family in my necklace, as much as my mates were my family, I had to leave behind even more. Declan came here with nothing. Kay left with everything she could have imagined and more.

"I love you all," I said.

My mates shouldered their packs, and I led them toward a cool vibration that would let me open a rift.

Teyr bumped my hip. "Sap."

I bumped his back. "Shithead."

He bumped me harder, and I stumbled into Shade's arms. Without hesitation, the necromancer pressed a heated kiss to my lips. Bash crushed in on my other side and cupped my breast through my armor.

My cock will fall off if we have any more sex, Teyr said.

Shade leaned back. "I would be okay with that. Your tongue pleasures her most, and to make you scream—"

I pressed my hands to my flaming cheeks. "Shade! We might not be out of earshot."

Teyr smirked and kissed one of my cheeks. "We'll have all the privacy you want before long."

"Nope." I squirmed out of their hold. "I don't want anybody's cock falling off. Let's get going."

Zelimir laced his fingers through mine and smiled. We rounded a final bend to where a small cherrystone plinth had been built for our reports with a constant spell to keep a collection of energies available for me whenever we needed it.

I took a final deep breath of the rich air of Thrae and looked at my mates. "Ready?"

ANAM CARA

A Flash of Silver
Behind Stone Walls
The Crystalline Heart